RER

A Wartime Weddi

Betty Firth grew up in rural West Yorkshire in the UK, right in the heart of Brontë country... and she's still there. After graduating from Durham University with a degree in English Literature, she dallied with living in cities including London, Nottingham and Cambridge, but eventually came back with her own romantic hero in tow to her beloved Dales.

Also by Betty Firth

Made in Yorkshire

A New Home in the Dales
War Comes to the Dales
A Wartime Christmas in the Dales
A Wartime Wedding in the Dales

Betty Firth

A Wartime Wedding *in the* Dales

hera

DK | Penguin Random House

First published in the United Kingdom in 2025 by

Hera Books, an imprint of
Canelo Digital Publishing Limited,
20 Vauxhall Bridge Road,
London SW1V 2SA
United Kingdom

A Penguin Random House Company

The authorised representative in the EEA is Dorling Kindersley Verlag GmbH.
Arnulfstr. 124, 80636 Munich, Germany

A CIP catalogue record for this book is available from the British Library.

Print ISBN 978 1 80436 973 9
Ebook ISBN 978 1 80436 972 2

Cover design by Diane Meacham

Cover images © Shutterstock and Colin Thomas

Printed and bound in Great Britain by Clays Ltd, Elcograf S.p.A.

Look for more great books at
www.herabooks.com
www.dk.com

For my editor, Keshini Naidoo, for all her support both practical and emotional over the eight books we've now worked on together

Chapter 1

January 1942

In the Yorkshire Dales village of Silverdale, the day always began at cock-crow – or at least, it began when one might have expected the cock to crow. Fowl of any kind were scarce in these days of wartime shortages, especially right after Christmas. But Bobby Bancroft found her trusty alarm clock to be a perfectly adequate substitute when it woke her that morning at five a.m.

It was the Monday following her Christmas holiday, and just as miserable as the first day back at work always felt. As much as Bobby loved her job as a country reporter for *The Tyke* magazine, the return to the daily grind felt like such a depressing contrast to the gaiety of the Christmas and New Year festivities. The tree had been returned to the garden, the visitors gone, the coloured streamers confined to the cellar for another year, and on the chill winter nights, the blackout felt longer and deeper than ever before. With the weather, too, cold and dismal, it seemed as though all the colour and warmth had been stripped from the world.

Nevertheless, Bobby pushed herself out of bed and wrapped her dressing gown around her as she prepared to fetch water from the old iron pump that served Cow House Cottage, where she lived with her father. She had a chore to do in the village before work and had risen an hour earlier than usual, which meant that her dad was still snoring in his bed.

A recent fall of snow had turned into slush, which had frozen solid overnight, and Bobby gripped the wall of the cow house as she slid her way over the ice to the pump. It wouldn't be safe to ride her old bike with its failing brakes in these conditions. She would have to walk to the village to drop off her parcels.

Her hands were numb and her arms aching from the stiff pump by the time she returned to the house with her bucket of water. There were shards of ice in it, and the shock of splashing it on her face soon woke her fully.

While she brushed her hair, Bobby smiled at the picture that now occupied pride of place on her bedside table. It had been her Christmas present from her fiancé Charlie: a photograph he'd had taken after getting his wings, looking proud and handsome in his RAF uniform. He had given an identical picture to his brother and sister-in-law, Reg and Mary, which was now on the mantelpiece across the way at Moorside Farm. Since the farmhouse parlour was also the office for *The Tyke*, that meant Bobby could now gaze at him while she worked. She wondered that Reg had ever given his consent for such a distracting photograph to be displayed.

It had been a joyful Christmas, with Charlie home on leave for perhaps the last time in a long time, Bobby's twin sister Lilian back for an unexpected but welcome visit, and Florence and Jess Parry – the two little evacuees Reg and Mary were hosting – infusing the season with joy the way only children can. With her loved ones around her, Bobby had almost been able to shut out thoughts of the frightening things they would all have to face in 1942.

Almost… but not quite. The future had been there all the time, hovering on the edges of her consciousness like the proverbial ghost at the feast. She hadn't been entirely able to silence her worry about Charlie's imminent posting to a new base where he would be joining the fight for real, or unmarried Lilian's as yet unannounced pregnancy.

And there was the war – always the war. After more than two years of fighting, there still seemed to be no end in sight. No decisive battle that would allow them to at least begin to hope for an Allied victory. Would 1942 be the year the tide would turn? And if it did, in whose favour would it go? As grim as the first day back at work after Christmas always felt, Bobby was grateful to at least have something to take her mind off things now Charlie and Lilian had returned to their respective posts with the Air Force and Navy.

'Don't be sad, darling,' Charlie had murmured when she clung to him as he said goodbye, dampening his RAF tunic with tears.

'But it could be so long until you're next home on leave,' she whispered. 'I'll miss you to pieces, Charlie.'

'Ah, but when I am next home, it'll be for our wedding.' He pressed a kiss on top of her hair. 'Having that to look forward to ought to make being apart easier to bear, don't you think?'

Bobby hadn't answered. She had just let out a deep sigh and held him tighter, wishing she could keep him with her. This goodbye hadn't felt like any of the others. This time, she had known she was really waving him off into danger.

After dressing, Bobby scribbled a note to her dad to remind him she had an errand to run before work and would see him for breakfast at Moorside Farm, or at supper if they missed one another. Then she stepped out into the cold, her pixie hood fastened tight around her ears and a pile of parcels in her shopping basket.

She had spent much of the Christmas holiday helping Mary make up parcels of food for the Red Cross to send out to servicemen who were prisoners overseas. She had enjoyed feeling as though a little of her time off work was being used to help the war effort, and had reflected pleasurably on how the men who received each parcel would feel. It must be a comfort to have a taste of home, and know you hadn't been forgotten.

The villagers had generously donated what they could spare. Each parcel contained an assortment of tins and packets – cheese, biscuits, pilchards, condensed milk, cocoa, chocolate, honey, cigarettes – and sometimes a paperback book too. These were the last four packages, which Bobby had promised Mary she would drop off at the church that morning for members of the Women's Voluntary Service to collect and take to an official Red Cross centre.

It was a treacherous walk into the village. Bobby looked like she was attempting the Palais Glide as she slid over the old packhorse bridge and stepped gingerly in the direction of Silverdale, with only the thin light of her blackout torch to light the way. The usually pretty village looked the very soul of January that morning as a watery sun started to rise: grey and bleak, with puddles of dirty slush bleeding on to the roads. A raw, sleet-dappled wind blew down from the high fells that surrounded the village.

St Peter's Church had been kept unlocked so that parcels could be left there. As precious as rationed foods were these days, the villagers were honest folk and patriotic in their quiet, pragmatic way, so there was no worry that anything would be taken. Even Silverdale's local poacher and rogue-of-all-trades, Pete Dixon, wouldn't have stooped so low as to steal food from a church.

Bobby left her parcels with the others, said a brief prayer to wish them Godspeed and hurried back towards home, conscious there was now only half an hour until she was expected to start work. Charlie's brother Reg, editor of *The Tyke*, would no doubt be very sarcastic if she was late after such a long holiday – even though it was for a noble cause.

She was cautiously crossing the packhorse bridge once more when she heard hurrying footsteps. She turned to find little flame-haired Gil Capstick, Silverdale's sub-postmaster, not far behind her.

'I've chased you halfway from t' village, Miss,' he panted. 'I've your post here. Did you not hear me calling?'

'Sorry, Gil. I didn't, otherwise I'd have waited,' Bobby said. 'I don't suppose I'd have heard much with my hat tied on tight enough to stop the blood flowing.'

She smiled, but there was no answering smile from Gil. The lad's freckled, honest face, almost always split by a wide grin, was creased with worry. Bobby wondered what was troubling him.

'Anyhow, you've no need to go all the way down to the farm,' she went on. 'I can take our post back with me.'

'It's only for you, Miss. No one else has got owt this morning.'

Bobby frowned at his tone. He sounded as anxious as he looked.

'Gil, what is it?' she asked.

'I'd not have come down with it so early, to be honest – not while it were icy. But when I noticed… well, see for yourself.'

He took two letters from his bag and handed them to her. Bobby stared at what was printed on the uppermost envelope.

'On His Majesty's Service,' she murmured.

'Aye. Thought you'd want it right away, since it's official.'

A chill passed through her that had nothing to do with the weather as she stared at those dreaded words.

Her first thought was for Charlie, preparing to leave his training post to join the fight. Then for her brothers, Raymond and Jake, both soldiers: one on active service in North Africa, the other learning to dismantle bombs with the Royal Engineers. But when Bobby tore open the envelope, she discovered it wasn't any of the men she loved that His Majesty was writing to her about.

It was her.

Gil was still hanging around, looking worried. 'Hope it's nowt bad, Miss Bancroft?'

'Um, not… really,' Bobby said vaguely. The words were swimming before her eyes, and she felt suddenly dizzy.

'You're white as a ghost. Do you want me to walk back with you?'

'No.' Bobby tried to pull herself together. 'No, thanks all the same. It was kind of you to bring it down. I'm all right.'

'Well, if you're sure,' Gil said, still looking doubtful.

Bobby forced a smile. 'I am, I promise. You ought to get yourself somewhere warm. Goodbye, Gil.'

After hesitating a moment, Gil strode off in the direction of the village, leaving Bobby to wander back to Moorside Farm in a somewhat dazed state.

When she reached the house, she drifted in by the side door, entered the parlour and took a seat at her desk there, the letter still gripped in her hand.

Reg, who was correcting proofs at his own desk, started speaking to her. However, just like the letters on the page, the words he spoke became muddled somewhere between her ears and her brain.

'Summat up this morning, lass?' he asked as she sat silent. 'Can't seem to get a word out of you.'

'It's… this letter. It came for me in today's post.'

He frowned at the official-looking envelope. 'What is it then? Bad news?'

'No. Yes. I mean, it's…' She took a deep breath. 'Reg, I've been called up.'

Chapter 2

Reg looked almost as shocked by this news as Bobby was.

'Don't waste any time, do they?' he growled, his brow setting in a scowl. He raised his voice to call to his wife. 'Mary! Better get that teapot in here. It's an emergency.'

Bobby tried to collect herself as Reg hobbled from his desk, leaning heavily on the stick he used to support his lame left leg, and took the letter from her. The numbness within her had started to subside, giving way to a fist of icy dread.

'Well, it's not a sure thing,' Reg said when he'd scanned the text. 'You've not rightly got your call-up yet, have you? You're to report for your medical in two days, that's all.'

'What's the difference? It means I'll have to go, Reg. In weeks, I'll have to leave here and… I'll have to go.'

'Not necessarily. Happen you'll fail.'

'I won't fail.' She laughed. 'I'm too damned healthy. I don't even wear reading glasses. I'll have to leave you and Mary, the girls, my dad… oh Lord, my dad.' Bobby pushed her fingers into her hair. 'He can't live alone. Not again.'

'Told him, have you?'

'Not yet. Gil only just gave me the letter.' She swallowed a sob. 'Reg, I don't know what to do,' she whispered.

'Now, now. None of that.' Reg gave her shoulder a clumsy pat. 'It'll be reet.'

She gave a small smile as Mary came bustling in with the tray of tea things held out before her like the cure for all ills. Bobby could almost believe Reg's statement that things would be all right in his wife's calm, motherly presence. War was a force to be reckoned with, but so was Mary Atherton.

'Now then, what's to do?' Mary said, putting the tray down on Bobby's desk. She frowned when she caught sight of the OHMS envelope. 'Oh,' she said in a gentler tone. 'You've not had bad news, love?'

'You might say so.' Bobby nodded to the letter in Reg's hand.

Wordlessly, Reg handed it to her. Wordlessly, Mary read it and handed it back. Then she started pouring the tea with an air of businesslike efficiency.

'Well?' Bobby said.

'Well what?'

'What do you think?'

Mary stirred some tinned milk into the teas and handed Bobby a cup.

'You knew it was a possibility, didn't you?' she said. 'A lot of girls will be opening a letter like this since that new National Service Act has gone through.'

'I knew it could happen, but I didn't think it would happen quite so soon.' Bobby stared into her teacup, hoping to find answers in the thinly brewed liquid. 'What I can't understand is why I'm to go to a recruiting centre for this medical. That means the forces.'

'Is that not what you said you wanted when you'd to go register?' Reg asked.

Bobby massaged her temples as she thought back to that day in the summer when she, along with a lot of other women her age, had been summoned to Bradford Employment Exchange to register for war work if it ever became a necessity. So much had happened since then, she'd half-forgotten it.

'I told the clerk my preference was Land Army,' she said. 'I thought that if it did happen – conscription of women – then I might be able to get a place on one of the local farms. Then the Soviets came into the war, and the Americans, all those men joining the fight, and I started to hope...' She gave a soft laugh. '...started to hope maybe they wouldn't need us girls after all.'

Mary's gaze fell on Bobby's reporter's notebook, lying on her desk covered in shorthand. 'Did you tell them all you could do?'

'Well, yes, I…' Bobby pressed her fingers into her eyes, suddenly unutterably weary. She was so very, very tired of this damned war. 'They asked about qualifications and work experience. I told them I was a reporter and I'd been a typist before that, and I'd learned secretarial skills at Pitman's College. I didn't think it would make much difference.'

'Seems it must do.'

Another sob bubbled up. Reg gave an awkward little cough. Bobby had learned over the past fourteen months that a kind heart lay under her employer's gruff exterior. Still, he was a man – a Yorkshireman at that – and he was naturally embarrassed by any display of emotion from the womenfolk.

She dashed the tear away. It was pathetic, she knew. People were being called up every day. Some of them – many of the men and even some of the women – would be sent to face horrors Bobby couldn't begin to picture. Some might never come home. But they had to go, because the consequences of losing this war were too horrific to even imagine.

Yet here she was crying because, what – she'd be home-sick? Miss her job, her friends, her family? Men and women made greater sacrifices all the time. Her own Charlie had left a comfortable job in a reserved occupation to do his duty as a bomber pilot, risking death daily for a higher cause. And here was Bobby Bancroft, sobbing because she was being asked to do a bit of typing for the war effort.

But it wasn't only that she'd miss her home and job. It was her father. The thought of letting him live by himself after what had happened the last time. That dreadful night she had rushed home to Bradford, not knowing if he was dead or alive. And then there was her sister Lilian, pregnant and unmarried, needing her…

Her gaze drifted to Reg's lame left leg, damaged beyond repair in the last war.

'I'm sorry,' she whispered. 'I suppose I must seem like a scrimshank or something, when the two of you have given so much.'

'Now don't talk daft,' Mary said. 'Them sort of propaganda words is all well and good for the pictures, but that's not real life. We're women, Bobby, not soldiers, and there's more to that than keeping only our husbands and bairns – others who depend on us, when they've no one else to depend on. A woman makes a house a home.'

'I can't help feeling guilty though.'

'Well, you've no need. Now have a mouthful of tea then come into the kitchen, the pair of ye, and we'll talk it over while young Bobby has a bite of breakfast. You can't deal with a shock on an empty stomach. The bairns have gone off to school, so it's just we three.'

Bobby sipped her tea obediently, finding the tone of command a balm to the helplessness she was feeling. Mary was right: she did feel a little stronger after swallowing it. She followed Mary to the kitchen, Reg bringing up the rear holding the letter.

A homely scene met them. One of Mary's hens was ensconced in a cotton wool-lined vegetable crate by the fire, her feathers fluffed contentedly. Ace the border collie, who belonged to the two evacuees, sat diligently to attention beside her as if he were the hen's personal bodyguard.

'Daft hound thinks yon Hetty's a sheep,' Mary said as she guided Bobby into a chair at the kitchen table and started filling a plate with bacon and toast.

'Why is she in the kitchen?'

'Jessie brought her in this morning coughing away, poor old biddy. Whisky and quinine's the best thing for a hen that's taken cold, but she should be so lucky nowadays. A warm spoonful of Reg's brown ale is the best I can do for her. Lord knows what flavour our boiled eggs will be next week.'

Despite her worries, Bobby couldn't help laughing.

'You're worried about your father, I suppose,' Mary said as she put a plate of food in front of her.

Bobby nodded. 'He needs someone to keep house for him. He couldn't do for himself. He isn't used to it, and the cow house is hardly replete with modern conveniences.'

'You've no need to worry about that. Plenty of old girls round here missing sons and husbands who'd snap up a man to mother, and you needn't fear I'd let any family of mine go wanting.'

Bobby smiled to hear Mary refer to them as family. She knew that had nothing to do with her impending marriage to Charlie. It was just what they'd become, somehow. A little patchwork family: Reg and Mary, Charlie, her and her father, and the two Parry girls from London. Funny how the war had pushed them all together.

And now, perhaps, the war was about to pull them all apart. She would have to leave her family and the Dales, for who knew how long. And there was Lilian, and the baby, and her dad...

'It isn't only about my dad getting his tea on the table,' Bobby told Mary, choosing her words carefully. 'He... he might be lonely.'

'He knows he's always welcome here.' Mary refilled Bobby's teacup from the pot. 'We won't let him sit on his own by an unlit fire, dwelling on the dark times.'

'You don't understand. When he lived alone in Bradford, he...'

Bobby hesitated, not knowing how to get out what she wanted to say. Reg and Mary knew something of her father's demons – his struggles with shell shock and liquor – but neither knew what had really happened that night nearly a year ago. About the suicide attempt that had left her dad in hospital and almost cost him his life. Bobby had vowed, then, that she would never again leave her father to battle his devils alone, no matter what she decided to do with her life.

But now King and Country had come to call, and it seemed the course of her life was no longer hers to decide.

'When he lived alone, he really struggled,' she finished lamely, poking at her bacon for Mary's benefit, although she hardly felt as though she could eat. 'He had a lot of nightmares. He was drinking too much. I know you'd look after him for my sake, but it needs to be family.'

'Aye, I know what you mean. There's some things as only kin ought to see.' Reg, who had been poring over the letter, put it down beside her and pointed to a paragraph near the bottom. 'But there's provision made for that, look. Hardship cases.'

Mary bent to read it too. 'You're right, Reg. Clever old stick to spot it. Bobby, see what it says: after your medical you can tell the clerk you want to apply for a postponement certificate on the grounds of exceptional hardship and she'll give you a form.'

Bobby frowned. 'What does that mean though – exceptional hardship?'

'Any situation where you've others relying on you, I suppose.'

'But if it's talking about money… my dad relies on me to keep house for him and, you know, for company, but he doesn't need my wages. Topsy pays him a decent salary as gamekeeper – double what I earn.'

'His house is courtesy of your job with me,' Reg said. 'Not that we'd throw the old man into the streets, but I'm happy to tell them we would. I don't mind being the baddie if it'll help you get out of it.'

'Besides, you and our Charlie will be wed before long,' Mary said. 'It's only unmarried women eligible for the call-up. Tell them you've got a wedding arranged and they'll surely let you off.'

'We're hoping we can do it soon, but it isn't arranged yet, Mary,' Bobby reminded her. 'Charlie will need official permission from his commanding officer at RAF Binbrook once he's posted. He's just had a week's home leave for Christmas so they'd be entitled to tell him he has to wait while some of the other lads take their turn.'

'Still. You've a ring on your finger, haven't you? I'd have thought that'd be good enough.'

'I doubt that would make a difference, now wheels are in motion. Marriage wouldn't bring any change to my domestic responsibilities, with no children and Charlie away. It seems the war effort needs every man and woman it can get nowadays.'

'Huh,' Reg muttered. 'They'll have called up the whole ruddy country by the time we get to the end of this thing. They'll even have my old bones hobbling out to face the Hun.'

Bobby was silent, passing stringy pieces of bacon rind to Ace under the table.

It was so much to take in. Only an hour ago, she had been just a country reporter: writing articles on their little rural affairs, keeping house for her dad, doing her small bit for the war effort by making up Red Cross parcels and acting as one of Silverdale's air-raid wardens. She had known call-up was a possibility, yet she hadn't thought it would happen so quickly. She had hoped it wouldn't need to happen at all. But now the war had come for her, she couldn't just hide under the bedclothes and wait for it to go away.

Her dad needed her, Lilian needed her, but so, apparently, did her country. Did she have any right to shirk, now the summons had come to join the fight? If Charlie and her brothers were out there risking their lives, why should she stay cocooned in the Dales, where war had never felt truly real? Britain needed every man, which meant it needed every woman. That was how men were to be freed up so they could win this thing.

But then Bobby thought of her father as he had been a year ago: white and feeble in a hospital bed, his will to live sapped. Of poor Lilian: unmarried with a baby coming, needing her sister more than ever.

Never had the conflict between her duty to her family and her duty to her country been laid out more starkly before her.

Chapter 3

By the time Bobby had finished breakfast, the numb dread she had been feeling had transformed into something else: a sort of strained, feverish excitement that played perpetually on the edges of her jangling nerves.

Her brain had refused to settle to any writing that day. After filling the inkwells, tidying her desk and rearranging the shelves of reference books behind Reg, she had spent the rest of the afternoon staring at a blank sheet of paper.

Reg clicked his tongue as he scanned his books for a volume he needed.

'Can't find a ruddy thing up here,' he grunted.

'Hmm?'

'Don't know why you had to mess about with 'em.'

'Oh,' Bobby said vaguely. 'Sorry. I thought they ought to be alphabetical by author.'

He turned sharply as she drummed her fingers on the desk. 'And can you give over that racket?'

Bobby stopped at once. She hadn't even noticed she'd been doing it.

'Sorry,' she said again.

Reg sat back down with his book. 'Look, lass, you might as well go home,' he said in a softer voice. 'You're getting nowhere fast sitting there fretting. Get your old man's tea ready and have a think about how you'll break your news.'

Bobby sighed. 'Yes. I do need to tell him, don't I?'

'Don't see how you can get round it when you've only two days while your medical. Mind, be sure he knows it's not a sure thing. I reckon this hardship committee's bound to see it your way when you explain that he's… not always himself.'

'Do you really think so?'

'They're folk like any others, aren't they? They'll not be harsh for the sake of it.' He met her eye. 'And be sure you tell them everything when you fill in your form. I can see why you'd want to be sparing with what concerns your dad, but they need to know the true state of affairs.'

'I don't know, Reg. The war comes first – that's what they'll be thinking. People are making so many sacrifices. Saying goodbye to loved ones – perhaps even forever. What right do I have to plead I'm a special case?' She rubbed her face. 'I'm not even sure applying for postponement is the right thing to do.'

'Well, that's for you to decide.'

She looked up at him. 'You fought in a war. Do you think I'm shirking?'

'I did fight in a war, same as your old man. And when I hear him screaming of a night, I know full well why any bairn of his would rather owt than leave him trapped there in his head,' Reg said firmly. 'Seems to me Rob did his duty enough for the pair of you.'

Bobby coloured, dropping eye contact. She knew her father's nightmares were common knowledge for the folk at the neighbouring farmhouse – there was only so much privacy you could expect when the residences were practically door to door – but it was uncomfortable to hear them talked of. He'd be so humiliated if he knew.

'Oh, don't worry,' Reg said gently, reading the feeling in her face. 'He'll never hear it from us. Now get yoursen home, and try not to worry, eh?' He summoned a smile. 'Icy out there. If you're lucky, happen you might break summat before your medical.'

Bobby gave a wan smile in return. Reg didn't joke often, and it was kind of him to try to lift her spirits, but she didn't quite have a laugh in her that afternoon.

15

'Thanks, Reg,' she said. 'I'll be better tomorrow, and write that piece on the Swaledale silver mines. It was a shock, that's all.'

'Mind you are, and be here all the earlier for your half hour off. Bad enough I've to spare you a day for this medical.'

Bobby stepped over the grey, hairy mass of Barney and Winnie – Reg's aged wolfhounds, who were snoozing on the carpet – and went to the parlour door. Something made her stop and turn back, however. Reg was already bent over his work again.

'Reg?'

'Mmm?'

'If I did have to go… what would happen here?'

'Oh, we'd muddle along as best we could,' he said vaguely, his blue pencil skittering over a page of copy. 'Mary'd miss your help in the kitchen, no doubt, and the bairns would sob fit to burst. Happen I might even be sorry to say goodbye to you missen. Still, I'm sure we'd bear up. War won't last forever, and you and our Charlie will be back.'

Something about this speech made Bobby smile. For so long, Reg had seen her as just his townie girl reporter. Now, he barely seemed to question that she belonged here. Of course she'd be coming back, his tone seemed to say. Where else would she go?

'That wasn't what I meant,' she said. 'I mean, what would happen to my job?'

Reg looked up, frowning, as if this was the first time it had occurred to him that he was losing not only Bobby herself but his top – indeed, his only – staff reporter.

'You told me you were going to take on a junior reporter instead of relying on freelancers,' she reminded him. 'You said…' She flushed slightly. '…you said there'd be a deputy editor role for me once they started work.'

'Aye, well, that'll need another think if I'm having to train someone from scratch. Still, I'll have to advertise for a lad. Can't do it all on my tod.' He paused. 'Or a lass. I reckon you've taught me that, at least — I'm not the stuffy old fuddy-duddy I was before you and the girls showed up to turn my life topsy-turvy.'

'But after the war. What then?'

'Never mind what then. It's what now you ought to be worrying about.' He tapped his forehead. 'You just be thinking about how you can win round these hardship people. Then it's academic.'

'But if I can't, and I have to go. You'd have me back, wouldn't you?'

Bobby could hear the note of pleading in her voice. She couldn't help it. After her concerns about what would happen to her father and sister if she had to go, the permanent loss of her job was her biggest worry. If her place on the magazine was filled by someone else, would that mean the end of all her hopes for her career?

'You'll always have a home at Moorside,' Reg said, turning back to his work.

He didn't meet her eye. Bobby knew what he was saying. As a close friend of the family, his brother's future wife, she would always be welcome at the farmhouse. As for her job, he couldn't or wouldn't guarantee it would be waiting for her when England dumped her unceremoniously back on Civvy Street.

'Right,' she said, her shoulders slumping. 'Thank you.'

—

Moorside Farm had proper plumbing, with indoor taps and an outhouse with a flush lavatory that they shared with the folk at Cow House Cottage. The ancient barn Bobby lived in with her dad, however, only had its old pump. When she visited it that afternoon to fill her bucket, she found it was frozen solid and had to make a trip back to the farmhouse to beg some water from Mary's kitchen taps.

When she got home, she put the kettle on and set about building the fire in the parlour.

It was 'fair nithering' in the draughty stone barn, as if there were ice crystals hovering in the air itself. Bobby's fingers, numb and purple, fumbled as she stacked the last of their supply of coke in the grate. She found tears falling and dashed them away with sooty fingers, but they soon fell so thick and fast that it was useless to try to keep them at bay.

She did so much for her father – she was sure he had no idea how much. Men never did realise how many things the women in their lives did to ensure their comfort. How every day she made her arm ache filling the bucket at the stiff, freezing pump to make his tea; lit the fire; turned, aired and made his bed; washed his clothes; drew and heated the water for his weekly bath; bought his food; cooked his meals; cleaned his home, and still managed to fit in a full-time job and her shifts at the ARP shelter.

And the one thing no stranger could do: soothing him after one of the all-too-frequent nightmares about his time in the trenches, and carefully controlling his access to the spirits he used to chase them away – and which he was apt to abuse if left to himself. When the low moods came, when he felt burdensome and useless, that was where the danger lay. Then the drinks became more frequent, the periods of depression deeper and longer, the memories harder to escape from. Until eventually, when life seemed too painful to be borne…

Another tear fell, putting out the wax taper Bobby was using to light the fire, and she struck a match to light it again.

She didn't feel she could talk to Mary about what her dad had tried to do, or even to Reg, although he had seen horrors enough of his own in the last war. Suicide was viewed as such a shameful thing. A sinful thing. Her father would be hurt beyond belief if he knew Bobby had been discussing it with others. Only Charlie, her good friend Don Sykes and her sister Lilian knew what had happened that night. How Bobby wished she could talk to Charlie, or any of them, if only for a moment! Her mind was so full she didn't know what to make of it all.

But her nearest and dearest weren't here to give her counsel, and besides, they had worries of their own. Don had written just after Christmas to say he'd had an important letter himself demanding his urgent presence in khaki at an army barracks very soon, and so he was preparing to leave his wife, young daughter and newborn child. Charlie would be moving on from his training post ten miles away any day now, and could soon be in the air over Europe. And Lilian... Bobby sighed. God knew what state her twin's mind was in, with no husband and a baby on the way.

That reminded her: the other letter, which she had stuffed forgotten into her pocket after opening that all-important summons from King and Country. She thought it had been addressed in her sister's familiar cramped, neat hand. Bobby took it out to read while she waited for the fire to start giving out some warmth.

She frowned as she examined the envelope. It was her sister's handwriting, but there was no military censor's stamp; no service number on the back.

Had something happened? The last time she had spoken to Lilian had been three days after Christmas, as Lil prepared to return to her post in Greenwich. Bobby had said goodbye at the bus stop by the Black Bull pub, Lilian in her navy-blue Wren's uniform – perhaps very slightly snugger around the waist than it had been months earlier, but with little evidence otherwise of the predicament she was in. Lil had written to Tony Scott, the baby's father, the day after Boxing Day and told Bobby she would wait to hear from him before she made any decisions about the future.

'You'll come home though, won't you?' Bobby had said as she'd hugged her sister tight. 'After you leave the Wrens, I mean. Here, to me and Dad.'

Lilian had smiled sadly. 'If I'm still welcome once Dad finds out what I've done.'

'He'll come round.'

Lilian sighed. 'I don't know, Bob. He'll be so disappointed in me.'

'At first, perhaps, but he loves you, Lil.'

'Well, I'm not going to rush to resign my place – not until I've heard from Tony. There's still a couple of weeks before I'll really start to show. More, if I keep my corsets laced tight. I'm going to need all the money I can get.'

That had been less than a week ago. Yet the letter Bobby was holding looked like a civilian letter, and the postmark on it was Leeds. Was Lil not still at her billet in Greenwich?

Bobby tore it open, hoping she wouldn't find yet more worrying news inside. What she read there... she didn't know whether to call it good news or not. But it was certainly news.

> *Dear Bobby,*
>
> *I suppose the envelope this letter comes in must have given you a clue that things have taken a rather different path to the one I had envisaged. I know nothing gets past my clever little sister. I hope you have a cup of tea in your hand, or something stronger from Dad's supplies, for you're likely to need it when you read what I have to tell you.*
>
> *Please don't worry, however – I have good news. At least, it's the best I could have hoped for, given the pickle I've managed to get myself into. But I'll stop beating about the bush and put you out of your misery. It's simply this: that Tony and I are to be married.*
>
> *Are you still reading? Have you swooned with shock? I know you must think him a poor match. I confess I wish... but it doesn't matter. The consequences of my actions have turned up to bite me on my bottom, and jolly well serve me right.*

Bobby stared at the words on the page, if not quite swooning with shock then certainly knocked for six. Lilian, engaged to

Tony Scott! Whatever news she had expected on opening her sister's letter, it hadn't been that.

Tony, Bobby's former colleague from her days working for the *Bradford Courier*, had always been feckless, lazy and with an eye for a pretty girl. The surprise Bobby had felt on learning he was to blame for her sister's condition had been due to Lilian alone: that she could have been so foolish as to fall for Tony's lines. It had come as no shock to Bobby that her old friend would have been irresponsible enough to father her sister's child. But learning he was not only prepared to support the baby but actually to legitimise his child through marriage – now that was a shock. Bobby knew she ought to feel relief, for Lilian's sake and the baby's, but all she felt as she read on was worry.

> *You'll be dying for the full story, I imagine, so here it is. You know I wrote to T with the news of what he'd done – or what we'd done, I ought to say, for I'm no less guilty. I hadn't expected much. All I asked was if he would be willing to advance me money to pay for a private nursing home where I could deliver the baby and give it away for adoption without anyone being the wiser. Knowing he was out of work, even that seemed a forlorn hope. The very day I got back to my digs, I found a letter waiting for me with an offer of marriage!*
>
> *We spoke on the telephone that evening. He told me it isn't only for the baby's sake. That he had long admired me, which I know to be true, and that he had fallen in love with me, which I know to be untrue but am willing to accept as a pleasant fiction to help me go through with this thing. I know T is shiftless but I can't believe he is truly bad. He says he is going to try, really try, to be a better, more dependable man. You know him better than me, for all that I'm carrying his child, so you will know how likely this resolution is to come true. Still, it is the best outcome – I had so wanted to keep the baby, and*

*for it to grow up happy and respectable with me as its
mother. Tony is offering me all of that, which I suppose
is rather noble for a man of his habits. But oh, Bobby! I
had so many dreams.*

There was an illegible line here, the ink blotted where tears had
fallen.

*I'm sorry. I shouldn't give in to emotion, when really
it's all worked out rather well. I suppose it's the baby –
I certainly seem to cry at the drop of a hat these days.
Perhaps I can learn to love Tony, in time. But I had
wanted my life to turn out differently, Bob. Sometimes I
daydream about how things could be if I broke it off with
Tony and you and I went somewhere together, found
a little cottage and raised the baby just we two... but
I'm rambling, and you're probably long ready for this
bittersweet letter to be over.*

*In short, I spoke at once to the senior Wren officer
to tell her I was to be married and wished to resign my
place. I was frank about why the wedding was a matter
of urgency and she was a sport about it. I'm not the first,
I suppose, and surely won't be the last. She issued me
with a Para II and I found myself back on Civvy Street
before you could say knife.*

*I'm now on my way home. I've scribbled this nonsense
on the train, to drop into the postbox when I change
at Leeds. I suppose by the time you read it, I'll be
back in Bradford. I've arranged to lodge with Clara for
a fortnight, and Tony and I are intending to arrange a
quick wedding at the registry. Tony has the licence ready.
Hardly Rhett and Scarlett, is it? But hey-ho and serve
me right.*

*One of the Greenwich girls has a neat little parlour
trick she used to bring out on beano nights. She's able
to tell fortunes by laying out cards, just like the gypsy*

woman I dragged you to see once in Blackpool. Before Christmas she told me I was to expect great joy in 1942, but also great sadness. Do you think there can be anything in it? Or have I gone quite barmy?

As soon as I'm legally Mrs Scott, I'll be dragging Tony to Silverdale to introduce him to Dad. Tin hat at the ready, young Bobby! I'll see you very soon, and please, don't fret.

All my best love,
Lilian

Chapter 4

Bobby knelt motionless by the fire, her sister's letter in her hand. A spark jumped out and set light to the corner, bringing her back to life. She blew it out before the whole thing went up in flames.

She could hardly believe it! Her brain, so full of her own worries moments before, was whirling now with thoughts of her sister.

Her pretty, lively, fun-loving sister, courted by every lad she'd ever met, engaged to Tony! Tony Scott, who wouldn't recognise a hard day's work if it were painted blue and dancing a hornpipe. Tony Scott, who oiled his way round the pubs of Bradford like a dog on heat. He was so very far from everything Bobby knew her romance-loving twin had dreamed of.

But what could be done? In less than six months a baby would be coming, and Tony was that baby's father. Lilian was right: this was the best outcome. It was the only outcome that would allow her to keep both her baby and her reputation.

Not that that made Bobby feel any jollier about it. Could Tony really make her sister happy? Could he provide for her and the baby?

Then again, he'd always been keen on the idea of matrimony, despite his flirtatious ways. It certainly sounded as though he'd jumped on the opportunity to snag himself a wife. How Bobby wished she could talk to the man! There was a lot she intended to say to her old friend when she finally got her hands on him.

Could they be married already? Surely not so soon as that. Bobby was tempted to jump on a train to Bradford that very evening and try to talk her sister out of it – except she knew in her heart that there really wasn't anything else to be done.

Her eyes flickered to the passage of Lilian's letter where she talked about her daydream of the two of them raising the baby together, somewhere far away. If only that was possible…

Bobby started when she heard snow being knocked off boots outside. Her dad was home. Hastily she stuffed Lilian's letter into her pocket.

'Dad.' She summoned a smile as he came in, and stood to give him a kiss of greeting. 'How was work? I'm sure Topsy would have granted you a day's holiday with the weather as bad as it is.'

'Nay, I'll not beg holidays from Her Ladyship for a little ice and snow. Never let it be said I'm not earning my keep in them woods, our Bobby. I've been salting paths since dawn.' He frowned when he took in her appearance. 'What's up, lass?'

Bobby took out her handkerchief and wiped away the sooty tears that clung to her cheeks. 'Oh, nothing to worry about. I was being foolish.'

'No bad news? You've not heard from one o' t' lads?'

'Nothing to do with Jake or Ray, or Charlie either.' She went to their Bakelite wireless set to tune it to Radio Éireann, the Irish station, which usually played light music at this time. It gave her an excuse to keep her face averted while she broke her news.

There was no need to tell her dad about Lilian's engagement. Not yet. If he found out what Tony had done, he'd have beaten the man to a bloody pulp before Lil had a chance to get him to the register office. He'd never approved of Bobby's friendship with 'that nowt', as he always called Tony. And if he ever found out that the situation was, in some ways, because of him – that Lilian and Tony had only begun walking out because Lil felt obliged to pay Tony back for suppressing a newspaper piece about her dad's black market activities – it could send his mental state spiralling. Besides, Bobby was determined to speak to her sister before she went through with the wedding.

But her medical was in two days' time, and her dad needed to be made aware.

Bobby tried to keep her tone light as she twiddled the knob on the wireless.

'It isn't bad news,' she said. 'But I am going to have to disappear on Wednesday – just for the day. I had a letter this morning summoning me to Bradford for a medical examination.'

Her dad had been about to sit in his chair by the fire. He stopped, frowning.

'Medical examination?' He sounded suddenly afraid. Bobby knew he was thinking of her mother, and the cancer that had taken her from them nine years earlier. 'You badly wi' summat then?'

'I feel as well as I ever did. But... well, see for yourself.'

She passed him the crumpled War Office letter. Her father's blank look told her he still didn't understand.

'It's the forces, Dad.' She went to take his coat and guided him into his chair, trying to keep her voice reassuring. 'Women's conscription – do you remember? They passed a new bill before Christmas. But it's nothing to worry about. Reg found a loophole.'

'Loophole?' her dad said, looking dazed.

'Yes, for hardship cases. You have to have someone to keep house for you, don't you? If I tell them you're a widower and I'm the only family left at home, they're bound to see it my way.'

Her dad didn't answer. He looked rather helpless, and smaller suddenly, hunched in his chair. His eyes darted around the room, into the shadows that filled the old barn, as if contemplating the terror of having to occupy the place alone.

Bobby approached his chair from behind. She removed his cloth cap and bent to kiss his bald crown.

'Don't worry, Dad,' she said softly. 'I'm sure they wouldn't make me go. Even if they did, you've Reg and Mary just across the way, and your friends in the village, and your work for Topsy to occupy you. Mary would make sure you had everything you needed. You'd hardly even miss me.'

'But you'll not go? You'll tell them you're needed at home?' His voice shook, and he looked up into her eyes. 'I don't know how I'd get on without you, our Bobby.'

The pleading note cut her right to the heart. She knew what he meant. The temptation to drink, without the steadying influence of a daughter who looked up to him, would perhaps be too great to resist.

'I'll do everything I can,' she said. But something made her add, 'Everything I think is right.'

—

Bobby rose earlier than usual again the next day. Her alarm clock rang once more at five a.m., although she might as well not have bothered setting it, as she had barely slept the night before. An uneasy rest had been interrupted by the racking sobs of her father, crying in his sleep. Once she had brought him back from the dark place and quieted the ghosts in his head with a measure of the potato-peel spirit her friend Don Sykes got for her, Bobby had been unable to get back to the land of dreams. Her brain had been too full of her predicament, and her sister's.

Her gaze fell on Charlie's photograph. How she wished she could speak to him, just for a moment! Letters were so dry, and it was hard to pour her heart out as she would if she had him with her. She longed to be held, comforted, told everything was going to be all right.

There were still patches of treacherous ice about, but the thaw had set in, and Bobby was able to ride her bicycle into Silverdale without much danger. She found Gil Capstick opening up the post office.

'Morning, Miss,' he called out jovially. 'You're out and about early again. More of them Red Cross parcels to drop off?'

'No, this is for me,' Bobby said, panting slightly — she had pedalled like the blazes to reach the village so she wouldn't be late for work. 'I've a couple of wires to send. I'll pay the extra shilling for priority. Can you take them down for me, Gil?'

'Well, we're not rightly open for quarter of an hour, but since it's you. Come on in where it's warmer.'

She did so, although if anything, the old stone post office felt even colder than the winter air outside. Bobby shivered as she waited for Gil to dig out his pencil and pad.

'Now then, who're we wiring?' he asked.

'Charlie first, please. RAF Ryland Moor.'

'Still there, is he? I heard they were sending him to Lincolnshire somewhere.'

'They are, soon, but he hasn't gone yet.'

'All right, what's the message?'

Bobby hesitated. 'Just say... "LLP tonight? Need to see you. Urgent."'

'That military jargon, is it?'

'He'll know what it means. It stands for Late Leave Pass.'

Gil frowned as he jotted the rest down. '"Ur...gent." There you go. Nowt wrong, I hope, Miss?'

'Just a bit of a family crisis.'

Bobby bit her tongue as soon as the words were out of her mouth, realising how they might be misconstrued. Gil was a lovely lad but he could gossip for England. The last thing she wanted was it being all over the village that 'that Miss Bancroft from t' paper is in the family way'.

'My family, I mean — my sister,' she clarified hastily. 'I need Charlie's advice.'

'To do with your letter yesterday, is it?'

'One of them, yes.' Bobby changed the subject swiftly before he probed further. 'Is that good to go, Gil?'

'Unless you've owt else to add. You can have another two words for your ninepence.'

'There's nothing else I need to say.' She coloured a little. 'Actually, better add "love". A few kisses as well.'

He smiled. 'I should hope so. And the other?'

Bobby was glad Lilian had told her where she was staying so she knew where to direct the telegram. Clara Soames kept a boarding house on Southampton Street in Bradford, near their old home. Bobby gave Gil the address, praying her sister wasn't married already. She had no idea what she was going to do, but she knew she needed to speak to Lilian before she committed her life to a man she didn't love.

'What's the message?' Gil asked when he'd taken down the name and address.

'Just this. "In Bradford tomorrow: 7th. Do nothing till I come. Please."'

'Sure you want the "please"? It's another penny.'

'Yes, it's worth the extra.'

'All right, then with the priority that'll be two and seven.'

The bell over the door jangled as Bobby handed over the coins. Her friend Topsy Sumner-Walsh came in, a worried look on her attractive, girlish face.

'Oh, Birdy, you're here,' she said, coming forward to embrace her. 'I was going to come to you afterwards if there was any news. Is there, Gil?'

He shook his head sorrowfully. 'Sorry, Your Ladyship. Nowt from t' airbase.'

Bobby frowned. As usual her friend seemed to think that whatever she knew was common knowledge, but several days of bad weather had kept the folk at Moorside closeted from any village gossip. Why would Topsy be expecting anything from an airbase, and why did she look so worried? As far as Bobby knew, she had no family with the RAF since her cousin Archie had been invalided out.

'Topsy, what's happened?' she asked.

'Oh my darling, didn't you hear?' Topsy blinked wide eyes at her. 'It's Ernie.'

Bobby felt her stomach plummet.

'No,' she whispered. 'He isn't…'

'Dead? No. That is to say, I don't know. Nobody does.'

'That's right, Miss,' Gil said soberly. 'Them Canadian fellers billeted with Louisa were expecting their mate back from a sortie three day ago, but he never turned up. There's been so much of this bad weather about, blizzards and whatnot, you can't help fearing the worst.'

There was a Canadian aerodrome just over the border in Lancashire, and a number of the airmen based had been billeted in nearby villages. Three of them – Chip, Ernie and Sandy – had arrived in Silverdale back in the autumn, to stay with postmistress Louisa Clough and her husband Wilf. However, Bobby hadn't seen Ernie since before New Year.

She turned to Topsy. 'Surely the base would tell Chip and Sandy if anything had happened to Ernie, wouldn't they?'

'Chip's waiting for news. I've his permission to check if I come in.' Topsy sighed. 'My poor boy is worried sick. Teddy and Ernie had started to become ever so pally.'

'I do hope it isn't bad news,' Bobby said fervently. The handsome, grinning face of Flying Officer Ernie King, so young and full of life, had appeared in her mind's eye. 'I couldn't take a bit more bad news about someone I love.'

Topsy frowned. 'Did something happen, Birdy?'

Bobby rubbed her forehead. 'Oh, nothing. At least, nothing compared to this. He has to be safe, doesn't he? Otherwise it would be so… unfair.'

'I don't think this stinking war cares a whole lot about fair and unfair,' Topsy said bitterly. 'But for Ernie's sake, I hope you're right.'

Chapter 5

A telegram arrived for Bobby a few hours later, as she typed out a piece about some old Roman silver mines in Swaledale. She saw Gil arrive on his bike, and heard him speaking to Mary. She held her breath, hoping it would be the news she was waiting for.

A moment later there was a tap at the parlour door, and Mary came in.

'Sorry to interrupt,' she said, holding out the telegram. 'It's one of these blasted things, for Bobby. Hope all's well.'

It was no wonder that these days, telegrams were seen as something to be feared rather than welcomed. The news they contained was so often devastating. Every family with a man in the forces dreaded opening one to find those terrifying words: *Deeply regret to inform you…*

But here was one that was very welcome indeed, as Bobby discovered when she read it.

> *2 hours. 7 p.m., Skipton Memorial. Going tomorrow.*
> *Love C xxx*

'Yes, it's all right,' she said, her face breaking into a smile. 'It's from Charlie. He's got a pass out tonight and wants me to meet him in Skipton. Only for two hours though.' She frowned. 'Oh, but he's being posted tomorrow.'

Reg sighed. 'Well, we knew it was coming. He would join up, the young fool.'

'I feel like I'll not sleep a minute until we get him back safe.' Mary arched an eyebrow at Bobby. 'Your last bit of time together before he really goes to war then. You'll want to make the most of it, won't you?'

Bobby smiled. 'We certainly will.'

—

With an effort, Bobby pulled her lips from Charlie's as they cuddled on a bench in Skipton churchyard that evening. It was more than quarter of an hour since they had met, and she still hadn't had a chance to talk about what had been worrying her. Her lips had quickly been requisitioned for other purposes.

'Charlie, when I said I needed to see you urgently, this wasn't what I meant,' she said, laughing breathlessly.

'It wasn't? Are you sure?'

She smiled as she allowed him to kiss her again, and he drew her body close. She had never craved his touch so badly, but this wasn't helping with the dilemma she was facing.

'Mmm... no,' she said, extricating her lips again. 'I wish we could do this all night but we haven't got long.'

'Can't we do this all night?' His hands burrowed under the folds of the RAF greatcoat he had put on her earlier, his fingers closing around her waist. 'It's the last chance we'll get for a while – until the wedding night, probably. I had to beg on my knees for this pass out and I'd very much like to make the most of it.'

'Please, Charlie. It's important.'

He sighed. 'Give me a minute then.'

Charlie closed his eyes for a moment.

'All right, I've had a stern word with myself and I think I can manage to cool my ardour for ten minutes.' He proved it with a chaste kiss on her forehead. 'What's the matter, darling?'

She smiled. 'Thank you.'

'Is something wrong at home?'

'Not yet, but I'm so terribly afraid there's going to be.' She snuggled against him. 'I'm to be called up, Charlie.'

She felt his body stiffen around hers. 'You're what?'

'I got the letter yesterday. I've to report for my medical tomorrow. That means the forces. There's a form I can request to make a case for hardship, but if they don't accept then I'll have to go.'

'I thought you told them your preference was Land Army.'

'They must believe I'll be more use elsewhere. Mary thinks it's because of my secretarial training. The armed forces must be desperate for typists or something.' She looked up at him. 'I don't want to shirk my duty, but I'm so worried about everything at home. My dad, and my sister...'

'Lilian? Is she not in Greenwich?'

'Not any more. She's in Bradford.'

'What, more leave? She just went back.'

'No.' Bobby pressed her fingers to her temples. She felt strangely feverish. 'Just... kiss me again. Then I'll tell you all about it.'

He smiled. 'Do I have permission? I thought kissing was banned.'

'Clearly I can't resist you,' she said, smiling too. 'Just a little one though, or we'll get carried away and I'll never tell you everything.'

He pressed his mouth to hers, and Bobby felt that sensation of freedom and release she only experienced in her lover's embrace. If only she could stay there, safe, protected, knowing Charlie was safe likewise. But for both of them, tomorrow had to come. War had to come.

Charlie's lips, gentle at first, became harder and hungrier as passion took hold, and Bobby felt an answering fire stirring within her. How easy it would be to get lost in that fire, and let it consume you! Something her poor sister had found out to her cost. Summoning her willpower, she drew away again.

'You're far too good at that,' she said breathlessly.

He pressed one finger to her mouth. 'Back atcha, hot lips.'

She laughed. 'Charlie, you spend too much time at the pictures. You're starting to talk like a cowboy.'

'I could fancy a life out in the Wild West, my best gal by my side. The hat'd suit me.' He leaned over to nibble her ear. 'How about you mosey over and sit on my lap, little lady? Then I can kiss your neck while you tell me what's worrying you.'

'Hmm. Sounds a dangerous plan to me.'

'Sounds like having our cake and eating it to me.'

'I don't know, Charlie. We are in a churchyard.'

'The ghosts won't mind. It'll liven up their afterlife.'

'Someone might see though. Supposing they tell tales to the vicar and he comes out to throw a bucket of holy water over us?'

'Best thing about the blackout is that no one sees anything. Courting couples have never had such luck.' He nudged her. 'Come on, Bob, it's our last chance. Besides, are we not practically man and wife? Surely that entitles us to a kiss and cuddle on holy ground.'

She smiled. 'Well, all right, but behave yourself. Hands where I can see them.'

Bobby shuffled over to sit on his knee. Charlie wrapped his arms tight around her, his hands slipping once again under the voluminous greatcoat. She tried to ignore the soft, teasing tickle of his lips brushing the nape of her neck while she spoke.

'This is between us, OK?' she said. 'Mary and your brother don't know, or my dad – especially not my dad.'

'Intriguing,' he murmured as he moved on from her neck to kiss her right earlobe.

'Charlie, are you listening?' she demanded in her best schoolmarm tone.

'Yes, Miss.'

'Promise? This is important.'

'I promise. Go on.'

She sighed. 'Our Lilian's going to be married.'

'You mean that naval lieutenant she was so crazy about realised he'd made a mistake?' he said, lifting his lips from her skin. 'Sounds like good news.'

'Not to Lieutenant Cartwright. It's...' She pressed her eyes closed. 'It's Tony. Tony Scott. You remember me telling you about him?'

'I remember. One of your old pals from the *Courier*. He helped you build a portfolio as a writer, didn't he?'

She snorted. 'That's one way of looking at it. Another is that he got me to write reams of his copy without a byline while he bunked off work to take out girls. If you look up "feckless" in a dictionary, you'll find a picture of Tony.'

Charlie's lips moved on from her right ear to give her left its share of attention. Bobby felt like she ought to ask him to stop when she had such weighty things to discuss, but his closeness was both comforting and exciting in a way she found hard to resist.

'Doesn't waste time, your sister, does she?' Charlie said, his voice deep and breathy against her ear. 'She only just finished with the last fiancé.'

'Yes, it was a fast engagement. It'll be an even faster wedding. Next week, probably.'

'As soon as that! Why?'

She looked over her shoulder. 'Come on, Charlie.'

It was a second or two before the penny dropped.

'Oh,' he said. 'I see.'

'It wasn't her fault.'

'I didn't say it was. Is this friend of yours definitely the one responsible?'

'Of course he is, if Lil says so,' Bobby said, shooting him an indignant look. 'My sister isn't some pick-up girl. It was one mistake.'

'Yes, all right. I didn't mean to suggest anything.'

She twisted round so she could look into his face, or what she could see of it in the gloom. Only the thin pinprick of light from a blackout-dimmed streetlamp over the wall prevented them from being in complete darkness. 'Are you shocked?'

'Of course not. I'm a man of the world – a bit of the world anyhow.' He sighed. 'Poor lass. That's some bad luck.'

'I'm so worried about her,' Bobby whispered. 'I know the wedding has to happen, but... to a man like that.'

Charlie reached up to caress her cheek, and she pressed her hand against his.

'You think he'd mistreat her?' he asked softly. 'Knock her about?'

'I don't think he'd do anything like that. It's not that Tony's bad, exactly, but he's a million miles away from the sort of man I'd have wanted for her. He's irresponsible, flirtatious, out of work since Don let him go, spends money twice as fast as he earns it, and he's far too fond of a good time.'

'I remember you once accusing me of similar besetting sins.'

'Tony isn't like you. He so rarely thinks of anyone besides himself. I can't see how he'd ever be able to provide for Lil, or love her as she deserves.' Bobby swallowed a sob. 'She's my sister, Charlie. I know she made a mistake, but should half an hour of foolishness really mean she has to sign her whole life away?' A degree of bitterness crept into her tone. 'It's so easy for men.'

'Huh,' Charlie muttered. 'You think so? Tell that to the hundreds being shot down every day.'

His tone had altered suddenly. Bobby tried to make out his expression, but it was too dark to see.

He could be such a puzzle these days. Before he had gone to war, she thought she'd known Charlie Atherton inside out and back to front. Now she didn't know how to interpret his moods.

'I don't mean in general,' she said. 'I mean when it comes to love and... and the things that go along with love, or with desire anyhow. The world lets your sex do as they like about it. If they want to walk away from the consequences of their actions, they can. While a woman has one moment of weakness and every choice she's presented with seems terrible.'

'You're right, it is easy for us to walk away. Which means that if this Scott fellow has stepped up for Lilian, he can't be all bad. Maybe you're wrong about him just like you were wrong about me.'

'Even if that's true, she doesn't love him.' Bobby paused. 'And yet it's still the best outcome. She did so want the baby. I wish I could stay at home, and do what I can to help when the little one comes. Between worrying about her and worrying about my dad, my brain's aching.'

'You said there was a hardship loophole.'

'There is, but…' She nestled her face into the collar of his RAF tunic and dampened it with tears. 'Even if I did apply, do I have that right?' she whispered. 'Others have to go. *You* have to go. That's why I needed to see you tonight.'

Charlie turned away to look out over the faint silhouettes of the headstones.

'I see,' he said, his voice flat. 'You needed me to tell you it was all right. That it was allowed.'

'I suppose… yes. At least, I wanted your advice. I feel like I've never been needed more at home, but if I try to get out of it, I'll be haunted by the thought that I cried off while others did their duty.'

Charlie was silent for what seemed like the longest time. He no longer kissed her neck, and his arms circled her waist loosely, as if he'd forgotten they were there. Bobby tried to shuffle off his knee.

Charlie roused himself, and his arms tightened around her waist.

'Don't go,' he said softly. 'You're keeping me nice and warm.'

Bobby felt her cheeks heat, despite the chill in the air. 'I thought perhaps you didn't want me here any more.'

'Why would I ever not want you here?'

She smiled, relieved, and pressed his hand. 'You went so quiet I thought you must be angry. You want me to go, don't you? Join the forces, I mean.'

'I don't want you to go. I want you to stay right where you are, with Reggie and Mary, and stay exactly *as* you are. I want

37

everything at Moorside to stay just as it was when I left, not even a picture moved in the parlour, so when I'm in the thick of it I can remember there's a home worth going back to. I want you to stay out of it, so at least one of us hasn't been tainted by this filthy war.' He paused. 'I mean, if I was being completely selfish then that's what I'd want. But...'

'But you think it's my duty to go.'

He sighed. 'Honestly, Bobby, I don't know what to tell you. There are so many people risking their lives to win this thing, it feels like if we aren't all in it together then it's as good as giving Hitler and the rest of those evil buggers a free pass.'

'Mary says women aren't soldiers,' Bobby said vaguely. 'That our first duty is to our homes, and the people who need us to care for them.'

'Says that same redoubtable Valkyrie who once marched me up a mountain to rescue injured men from a burning plane. I've never seen anyone who looked more like a general at the head of their troops than you did that night, Bobby.'

'Be serious, please.'

'I am being serious,' Charlie said quietly, and it was true that there was no mirth in his tone. 'When there are men fighting with not much to keep them going other than the thought of making the world safe for the girls they love, it seems hard that those same girls won't answer the call when it comes. No one's asking them to fly to Berlin.'

Bobby's face burned with shame, although he was only articulating what she had been thinking herself. Again she moved to get up from his lap, and again he held her tight.

'Please stay,' he murmured. 'I'm sorry. I don't want to say things that will hurt you, but I have to tell you what's in my heart.'

He was trembling – not, she felt sure, from the cold.

'Charlie, what's wrong?'

'I'm afraid, Bob,' he whispered. 'I've never been more afraid in my life. Every day I think about those men we found on the mountain.'

'I know, love. They're on my mind a lot too.'

'I find myself shaking from thinking about it. Sometimes it's hard to breathe, and my heart beats like it might burst out of my chest. What do you think that makes me?'

'I don't know. A human being, I suppose.'

'You don't think I'm a coward?'

'For being afraid, and doing your duty in spite of it? Don't be daft. I'm ever so proud of you.' She sought one of the hands at her waist and linked her fingers with his. 'I want to do what's right too, Charlie. I'm not afraid of sacrifice, where it purely concerns me. If it was only leaving my home, or my job...'

'I didn't mean to make you feel guilty,' he said, and she felt the welcome pressure of his lips against her neck once more. 'I do understand about your dad. Surely now he's got his job things are better though? You said he'd all but stopped drinking.'

'Apart from the odd pint in the Hart, and a glass of spirits when he wakes in the night.' She lifted the hand she was holding and peeled back his glove to press the skin to her lips. 'But I never know when something might send him spiralling. I told you what happened when he lived alone.'

'You did.'

'What would you do? If you were me?'

Charlie thought about this.

'I don't know about being you, but if I were me... I'd have to go,' he murmured. 'If you realised how sticky things were out there, Bobby, the things we hear are happening in Europe...'

She frowned. 'What sort of things?'

'Nothing I'd ever want you to know about,' Charlie muttered darkly. 'Still, things are going to come to light before long that will open a lot of eyes. Perhaps I didn't always think as I do now about it all, but I'm a long way from playing soldiers. Now I know what I know, there's very little I wouldn't sacrifice to win this thing.'

Bobby twisted round to look into his eyes. She was filled with such admiration for him, this man who loved her. But it frightened her, too, to hear him sound so unlike his old self.

'You talk so differently these days,' she whispered. 'Sometimes you're the same old you, and other times you're so unlike yourself that I barely know you.'

'I'm sorry,' he said, a faraway tone creeping into his voice. 'I can't help it. One side of me just wants to soothe and hold you, and tell you everything you want to hear. But there's another part of me that made a promise to fight this thing till the end, and that part of me has to tell the truth. I respect you too much to lie to you, Bobby.'

For a long time they didn't speak, listening to the plaintive mew of a cat as it begged to be let in from the cold.

'Poor creature,' Bobby murmured.

'Me or the cat?' Charlie said, and she could tell from his tone that he was smiling once more. She found these fleeting but increasingly frequent dark moods so hard to understand. They seemed to pass as quickly as shadows on the face of the moon.

She leant back to rest her head against his shoulder, and Charlie stole the opportunity to plant a kiss on her lips.

'Ernie's missing,' Bobby told him quietly.

Charlie frowned. 'Canadian Ernie, from your pantomime?'

'Yes. He didn't arrive back at his billet after an op. His friends are waiting for news, but it's hard not to fear the worst.'

'Well, I'm sorry. I hope it's nothing.' He reached up to stroke her hair. 'Do you still have my picture?'

She smiled. 'Of course. By my bed, so that whenever I go to sleep it's the last thing I see.'

'And then you'll dream of me.'

'That's the idea. Although last night I dreamt Mary's hen Hetty had grown to the size of a house and was pecking at the chimney pots, so it doesn't always work.'

Charlie laughed, and Bobby experienced a thrill as she felt that deep chuckle vibrate through her. Her fiancé was so often solemn now, it gladdened her to hear him laugh as of old. The carefree boy she had first fallen in love with was gone for good, she supposed, but it lifted her spirits to be reminded that the man he had become could still be merry.

'And you'll be ready?' he whispered, burying his face in her neck. 'As soon as I've got the Binbrook CO's permission to marry and I can beg twenty-four hours' leave, I expect you to be waiting for me in a white dress, pink lipstick and satin undies. I don't care if I have to kidnap a vicar on my way home to do it.'

'I'll be ready.' She turned to look at him. 'You are sure, Charlie, that it's still what you want? Because if you'd rather wait…'

He took her hand and rubbed her glove where the hump of the sapphire engagement ring he'd given her stood out. 'I've never been more sure of anything. So don't think you can wriggle out of it that easily, Roberta Bancroft.' He met her eyes. 'You haven't changed your mind, have you?'

'Of course I haven't. I want you to be certain, that's all.'

'I am certain. There's nothing I want more than to be able to say that you're mine at last.' He stroked her cheek. 'And on a more practical note, I want to know you'll be provided for if the worst does happen. Get your widow's pension.'

Bobby shivered. 'Oh, please don't say that. It's tempting fate.'

'We have to think about it, Bob,' Charlie said gently. 'I wish we didn't, but men are dying up there every day. I can't presume I'll be one of the lucky ones.'

'I don't want to rush into marriage for that. Not for something so grim.'

'It isn't only for that. We love one another, don't we? What's to wait for?'

'It's just such an odd thing to be married when there's a war going on,' she said with a sigh. 'You can't set up home, have a honeymoon or do any of the things married people did before all this. I know wartime brides who say that when their husbands come home on leave, they've seen so little of them they feel like strangers. And…' She flushed. 'Well, war changes people so. Suppose your squadron was to be posted overseas, and it was years before we saw one another again? I would understand, if you said you'd rather wait until it was all over.'

'What I want is to come home on leave and do this, legally, without any of those blighted sensible voices in my head telling me I have to stop. And I fully intend to do so before the summer comes around again.'

He grabbed her collar and pulled her on to his lips. The kiss was so sudden and so intense that it took Bobby's breath away. Charlie had never kissed her that way before. He was passionate, yes, but there was always control. Always a holding back. This kiss wasn't holding back. It was the sort of kiss that was equal parts tender and fierce, bruising the lips and setting every nerve on fire – a kiss filled with vitality and need. Bobby was glad they were in public and not alone together somewhere.

Or was she?

When Charlie drew back, panting heavily, Bobby was speechless. All she could do was let out a gasp. Charlie gave a breathless laugh.

'What's up, Bob?' he asked, grinning. 'Kiss got your tongue?'

'Huh.'

'That's all you've got to say about it?'

'That was… some kiss,' she managed to pant as her breath returned. 'But you've no need to look quite so pleased with yourself.'

'I've every right to be pleased with myself, and a more gracious kissee than you would be entirely on my side.'

'Who taught you to kiss like that? I'm sure it couldn't have been me.'

He shrugged. 'I saw it in a film.'

'Liar. They'd never get a kiss like that past the censors.'

'Well, let's say you were the inspiration if not the tutor,' he said, smiling. 'I'm saving the rest of it for the day I carry you over the threshold as Mrs Atherton. And it had better be soon, Bobby, because I'm just about done waiting.'

Chapter 6

Charlie's short period of leave soon passed. He returned to camp to complete preparations for his departure the following day, and Bobby found herself on the dark bus back towards Silverdale. It was too late for Bert the coalman to be out and about, ferrying folk from the bus stop to the village, which meant a two-mile walk home at the other end. Bobby wasn't much looking forward to that in the blackout, invisible patches of ice making the road treacherous, but she wouldn't have missed seeing Charlie tonight for the world.

Not that she felt any more settled for it. She had been hoping he would be able to make everything right for her, somehow. Settle the qualms of conscience and give her a clear path out of her dilemma. But if anything, she felt more ill at ease than when she had left Silverdale.

When she thought of what Charlie had said about duty, the way forward seemed clear. She would have to go. She owed it to her country, and to Charlie too – to all those who were fighting. But then memories always arose of her father, as he was at his worst. Half-dead in a hospital bed. Wild-eyed and helpless after another nightmare. Confused and far away as his brain sought refuge in the past, forgetting even who she was. Bloated, shamefaced and hopeless the morning after a drinking spree. Did she not have a duty to him as well? It was easy for others to tell her to look at the bigger picture, when it wasn't their loved one who suffered. A war had done that too. Now she had to live with the consequences, as it was so often the lot of women to do.

Thinking of her father made Bobby shiver. War had changed him so utterly and terribly, in a way she had never fully comprehended while her mother had been alive to shield her from it. After her mam's death, it had been she and Lilian who had had to deal with the consequences of his wartime experiences. Too many times, Bobby had looked into eyes made mad with remembered horrors and thought how very far they were from the twinkling-eyed boy in the only photo she had of her father in uniform, before he had served in the trenches. Would Charlie, too, return to her so beaten and broken? Already his moods were taking him to dark places where it was impossible for her to follow, just as her father's nightmares so often did.

Suppose she did decide it was her duty to go. Might she, too, be changed irrevocably by this war? Women didn't fight but that didn't mean they didn't see horrors of their own while serving. Men they befriended – even loved – being lost to them over and over. Pain and grief and fear. War was war, however you were called on to face it.

But then, suppose she chose her duty to her family over her duty to her country and fought tooth and nail against her call-up? Where would that leave her and Charlie? He clearly felt strongly that every man and woman ought to do whatever was asked of them to win this thing. Would it drive a wedge between them after they were married? Would he always hold anger in his heart, and resent her for what he saw as a failure to do her duty at a time when he had been risking his life?

The snatched time they were able to spend together these days so often felt bittersweet. In many ways, her fiancé was the same old Charlie Atherton. He still teased and joked, although sometimes Bobby felt that it seemed forced – she had noticed it more and more when he had been on leave over Christmas. He seemed to love her as much as he always had, however, and was eager for their wedding.

But then there were the shadow times. Sometimes he only seemed irritable or nervy, but the worst times were when he fell quiet, or spoke in that strange, flat, un-Charlie-like tone. She felt so far away from him, then. Every night when she looked at his photograph before turning out the light, Bobby fought to suppress a fear that, one way or another, the war might rip the man she had fallen in love with away from her for good.

The bus was nearing her stop now. She stood to get off.

'Slacks?' A Canadian accent cut through glum thoughts, and a heavy hand materialised on her shoulder. 'Hey, is that you? It's so darn dark I never saw you.'

She blinked. 'Ernie?'

Bobby turned around, and there he was: Ernie King, as large as life in his RCAF uniform. One greatcoat sleeve hung empty, suggesting his arm was in a sling, and he was badly in need of a shave, but otherwise he was no different than when she had seen him last.

Bobby couldn't help laughing, she was so relieved to see him safe, and scandalised an older lady sitting nearby when she threw herself at her friend for a hug.

'Whoa.' He laughed as he wrapped his good arm around her. 'Mind the war wounds, OK? Injured hero here.'

'Oh, you… Ernie, I could kiss you! Or slap you. We've all been worried sick.'

He laughed again: a deep, unrestrained, joyful sound. 'The reports of my death are greatly exaggerated, as a great man once said. I'm right as rain, Slacks.'

'Where on earth have you been?'

'Field hospital, with the rest of my crew. Our Wimpey had a spot of trouble and I had to bring her down on the coast. You might say it was a bumpy landing.' He nodded to the door as the bus started to slow. 'This is us. Come on, kid, you can walk me home.'

Bobby noticed as she followed him off that her friend grimaced when he descended.

'You're hurting,' she said as the bus pulled away. 'What was injured, Ernie?'

'Dislocated shoulder, arm broken in two places and a chunk of shrapnel got into my gut. The quacks fixed me up, but it'll take me a while to heal fully, they tell me. Here, take a look.'

Bobby switched on her blackout torch as Ernie unfastened his greatcoat, fumbling one-handed with the buttons. He shrugged the coat off to reveal the sling that cradled his left arm, then unbuttoned part of his tunic so she could see the bandages wrapped thickly around his stomach.

'Impressed?' he asked, grinning.

Bobby smiled. 'I'm not sure that's quite the word I'd choose, but I'm glad to hear there'll be no permanent damage.'

'Put this on.' He passed her the greatcoat. 'No arguments. You might as well take it or I'll be all night doing up the buttons one-handed.'

Bobby did as she was told, knowing it was useless to argue with Ernie King's stubbornly chivalrous streak. She couldn't help feeling a little guilty, though, as she fastened the heavy woollen coat. It had been not more than an hour ago that she'd been wrapped in Charlie's RAF greatcoat, and in his arms. Ernie was only being a gentleman, but something about wrapping herself in a coat still warm from the heat of his body felt… intimate. As silly as she knew it was, it felt like a tiny betrayal.

'You're sure you can walk?' she asked, putting aside the foolish feeling. 'There's a telephone in the pub. I could ring Topsy and ask if her car could make it over this ice.'

'Don't you dare. I'll not be made an invalid of.' He glanced at her. 'Besides, when I've got a pretty girl to walk with in the blackout, a ride home is the last thing I want.'

'Now don't start,' she said, laughing. 'I've no patience with that sort of teasing. Save it for——' She stopped.

'For what?'

'For Topsy, I was going to say.' She was quiet a moment. 'It's so strange that she's to be married in a few months. Of course I'm thrilled for her and Teddy, but…' She sighed. 'It does feel like everything's changing.'

He frowned. 'You OK, Slacks? You don't sound yourself.'

'I'm just feeling a little wistful tonight. Older than I ever have before.' She summoned a smile. 'Sorry. It's been a funny couple of days.'

'Here, give me your arm while we get across the street.'

He took hold of her elbow. Ice puddles glittered silver under the faint light of Bobby's torch, while the stars that shone on the fells from a clear black sky made the frosty landscape twinkle. There was no moon that night, which she was grateful for. These days, a clear night and a full moon nearly always meant trouble for some poor town.

'So how was your date?' Ernie asked.

She blinked. 'How did you know I had a date?'

'Because you smell of cheap smokes and aftershave lotion. Your lipstick's smudged, and so's your mascara.' He glanced sideways at her. 'And you've got that look on your face.'

'What look?'

'Half sad, half besotted. Every time I saw you during your Christmas vacation, you were wearing it. Had a falling out with your dream boy, have you?'

She yelped as she slipped on a patch of ice, and Ernie grabbed her hand to stop her going over.

'Here,' he said, tucking it into the crook of his good arm. 'Any more of that and we'll both be going home with our arms in slings. So what was the bust-up about?'

'There was no bust-up. Not exactly.' She sighed. 'Charlie can just seem so distant these days. Not all the time. But when he talks about the war and how he feels about it, it seems a world away from his life with me. I'm worried we'll start to drift apart now he's being posted.'

'Sorry to hear that. Hope it works out.' He turned to look at her. 'I'm glad I saw you tonight. I've actually come back to say goodbye.'

She frowned. 'You're not going home to Canada?'

'No such luck. I've been grounded for four months. Not safe to fly ops until I'm all healed, apparently. I've got a week's

47

leave, then they're sending me to teach schoolgirls how to bake soufflés until I'm allowed back in my own cockpit.'

'I'm sorry?'

'I'm being given an instructor post with your boys – the RAF, I mean, showing sprog pilots how to handle their bombers.' He grinned at her. 'Will you miss me?'

Bobby chose not to answer that.

'How do you feel about it?' she asked.

He shrugged. 'I'll miss the boys in my squadron, but to tell the truth I'll be glad to get out of it for a while. Catch up on some sleep, enjoy knowing my life's my own. If I'm lucky, maybe your boyfriend will have won the war by the time I'm due to fly again.'

'I'm to go too,' she said soberly.

'Yeah? Where?'

'I don't know yet, but into one of the auxiliary services. My medical's tomorrow, then I guess it'll be a matter of weeks until I'm drafted. Unless I make a case for hardship.'

'Are you a hardship case?'

'Perhaps. If I go, there's no one to keep house for my dad.' She looked up at him. 'I suppose you think that's dreadfully wrong.'

He shrugged. 'No. Why would I?'

'Well, because it's my duty. What right do I have to shirk it? Given your recent brush with death, I'd have thought you'd feel pretty strongly about it.'

'I do, but not the way you think,' he said quietly. 'Wars and armies are no place for dames. Makes them hard. Makes them forget what it means to be women.'

'I don't believe that.'

'You should see some of the girls at our camp. If they joined up to do their patriotic duty, you could've fooled me. All I see is them rouged up like sidewalk strollers, acting loose with a lot of different fellers. All they want is to get drunk and have a good time with guys they pick up.'

'The way men do, you mean,' Bobby said, but the irony in her tone was lost on Ernie.

'Exactly. Wouldn't like to see any girl of mine in uniform. Hell!'

This time it was Ernie who lost his footing on the ice. He flailed for the drystone wall as he went down, but it was no good. A second later he was flat on his back, and Bobby, her hand still under his arm, was pulled down on top of him. Her torch dropped beside her.

'Oh gosh,' she said, laughing breathlessly. 'That was a tumble. Is your injured arm OK?'

'Don't worry. Luckily you missed the tender spots when you decided to dive on top of me.'

'You pulled me down! Is anything else hurt?'

'Just a bruised ego and a bruised – well, never mind what else is bruised,' Ernie said, laughing. 'Are you all right?'

'Yes, but – my foot. It's caught up in a bramble or something,' Bobby said as she wriggled to extricate it.

'Take your time. I'm in no hurry.' Ernie put his mobile arm behind his head, for all the world as if he were sunbathing. 'I guess you think I did that on purpose.'

'I'm sure you're far too much of a gentleman,' she answered automatically, still wrestling with the troublesome bramble that held her captive.

'You think so, do you?'

Ernie's voice sounded different suddenly. Lower, huskier, the teasing merriment all gone. He met Bobby's eyes with a look she hadn't seen there before: a look of pure fire, which brought the colour rushing to her cheeks. She gave her foot a final hard tug, cursing as she felt her last decent stockings tear, then hastened to grab her torch and scramble back to her feet.

'Going to need a hand here, Slacks,' Ernie said, holding out his good arm. Reluctantly she helped him up. Ernie tried once again to tuck her hand under his arm, but this time Bobby pulled it away, opting to support herself using the wall alongside the road. Ernie raised an eyebrow, but he didn't say anything.

'So. I guess your fiancé feels differently than I do about this broads-in-battledress business,' he said, picking up the threads of their conversation.

'Yes. I could tell he was disappointed with me when I told him I was thinking of making a case for hardship. He says we all have to be in this together if we expect to win.'

'That's Brits for you,' Ernie said. 'You guys always go big on that honour and duty stuff. If you ask me, the primary duty of a woman in wartime — if she's a woman who loves a man out there fighting — is to try her hardest not to change a whit. Her man wants to think about her keeping herself pretty and soft for him, and feathering a nice nest for him to come home to. Not living it up with other men, swearing and drinking and forgetting how to be feminine. Hearth and Home should always come before King and Country for the fairer sex.'

She smiled at him. 'Anyone ever tell you you're kind of an old stuffed shirt, Ernie?'

'Yeah, you,' he said, smiling back. 'Nothing wrong with being a little old-fashioned, is there?'

'But women don't exist only to be what their men want them to be. They might not be called on to fly fighters or sail ships or fire a gun, but they've got lives to lead all the same. We're people, not an ideal.'

'I think you girls should be looked after is all. You're better than us — always have been. Some of us want to see you stay that way.'

'Not me though.'

'Oh, no, not you,' he agreed solemnly. 'You're the absolute pits, Slacks.'

She laughed, feeling the awkwardness of that moment on the ice ebb away as he teased her. 'So you think I should make a case for hardship?'

'Sure I do, and fight for it. Your place is here, looking after your old man. Have a word with Topsy. There's sure to be some pal of her father's can get you out of it.' They had reached the old packhorse bridge that led from the village to Moorside Farm, with the squat silhouette of Cow House Cottage visible ahead. 'The parting of the ways. I guess this is goodbye.'

'Not forever though,' she said as she returned his greatcoat to him.

He put it over his shoulders. 'Depends what the RCAF decides to do with me once I'm fighting fit again.'

'You'll at least be back for the wedding?'

'For Topsy's, as long as they let me out for it. Not for yours, so you can spare yourself the invite.' He put out his hand to her. 'Put it there then, Bobby Bancroft. I won't forget you.'

Bobby smiled as she shook it. 'I swear I'll never understand you if we stay friends a hundred years. Are all Canadian men like you?'

'Oh, no. Not nearly so good-looking.' He bent towards her, and before she could object he'd planted a kiss on her forehead. 'You're a swell kid, for all your odd ideas. Hope to see you again.'

He strode off into the darkness, leaving her staring after him. In his own way, he was as much of a puzzle to her as Charlie.

She would miss him when he left Silverdale. Ernie King had brought something into her life, these last few months they'd been getting to know one another. Something exciting and fun and carefree. But as Bobby watched that tall, broad figure walk away and thought back to how he had looked at her, lying under her on the ice… perhaps she had imagined it, but still, she felt strangely relieved that he was going to be out of her life for a while.

Chapter 7

The next morning, Bobby prepared to make the journey to Bradford for her medical. Reg had given her the day off – he hadn't had any choice, of course – with her lost wages and travel expenses to be reimbursed by the War Office.

Her medical wasn't until four, but she wanted to leave early. She had told Reg this was to avoid being late if there were delays on the railway, as there so often were these days due to air-raid warnings, troop movements and bomb damage on the line. In reality, she was determined to see her sister as soon as she could.

Mary had instructed her to call in for breakfast before setting off, so once she was dressed, Bobby headed to the farmhouse.

She frowned when she entered the kitchen. Mary was alone – at least, alone apart from Hetty the hen, who was once again cough-clucking away at the fireside. Mary was at the hob boiling eggs for their breakfast, but her shoulders were shaking with soft sobs.

'Mary! What on earth is wrong?' Bobby went to embrace her.

Mary gave a damp laugh, taking out a lavender-scented hanky to dab her eyes. 'I'm a silly old fool, that's all that's wrong. Now you mustn't say a word to the bairns. Florrie's so happy, I'd hate her to think I was miserable for my own selfish sake.'

'What do you mean?'

They were interrupted by Florrie herself, who came bouncing into the kitchen in a somewhat dishevelled state. She had only one sock on, and her pinafore frock hung unbuttoned over one shoulder. Jessie followed more sedately and went quietly to the fire to sit by Hetty.

Florrie beamed when she saw Bobby and rocked gleefully on her heels.

'I knew I heard you,' she said. 'Did Mary tell you our news, Bobby?'

Bobby cast a puzzled look at Mary, who had turned away while she composed herself.

'I don't think so,' she said, bending to button the child's dress for her. 'What news should Mary have told me?'

'It's Dad! He's to be... oh, I can't remember the word. Dematerialised, that's it. Mary got a letter this morning.'

Bobby blinked, thoughts of little green men with ray guns popping into her head. 'Dematerialised? Like in that Flash Gordon serial I took you to?'

Mary turned around, smiling like her usual self again, although her eyes remained rather red. 'I think she means demobilised, the daft apeth,' she said, coming forward to kiss the top of Florrie's ginger curls. 'And I hope that when your father returns, Florence Parry, he comes back to hair that's been better brushed than this mop top. Now go finish getting ready for school, the pair of ye.'

Jessie, who looked a little pale, blinked at her from the fireside where she had taken the poorly Hetty on to her lap. 'Mary, are you sad?'

'Don't be foolish, child. Why on earth should I be sad?'

'Your eyes look like after crying.'

Mary mopped up an escaped tear with her handkerchief. 'Oh, pay that no mind. I've been chopping leeks for dinner, that's all. They're as bad as onions for bringing on the water-works.'

'I'm going to get Dad's room ready,' Florrie announced. 'It ain't half so big as the one he had in our old house but we can soon make it nice, can't we, Jess?'

'I think so,' Jessie said uncertainly.

'You're going to do no such thing.' Mary tapped Florrie's head with a wooden spoon. 'You're going to make yourself smart for school. You pair, me and Reg will have a little talk later about arrangements for when your dad gets home. He won't be leaving the Army until April at the earliest.'

'All right. But I'm going to draw him a picture if there's wet playtime, and we can put it on the wall for when he gets here. Jess, come on.'

Florrie ran out of the room again, a little ginger whirlwind, and her sister followed more soberly in her wake. Mary gave the smaller child's shoulder an affectionate press as she went by.

'Poor love,' she said quietly to Bobby. 'Florrie's all excited, but Jess has seen so little of her dad these past few years that he must seem more like a fond uncle than a father – someone who shows up every once in a while to give her a hug and press a florin into her hand before disappearing. She looked so worried when I said she was to live with him again, bless her heart. But the captain's a fine man, and she'll soon remember how to love him.'

'I had no idea he might be getting his ticket.' Bobby put an arm around Mary's waist. 'That must have been a shock.'

'Yes, right out of the blue. It's that wound in his shoulder. It gives him so much pain that he applied for medical discharge. Never said a word about it in case it should be refused, so it came as a big surprise when I opened his letter this morning.' She swallowed a sob. 'I knew they were never really mine to keep,' she said in a choked whisper. 'But I had hoped God would grant us a while longer.'

'Oh, Mary. I am sorry.' Bobby gave her a hug.

'I'm a soft old baggage,' Mary murmured. Bobby patted the older woman's shoulder while she got a fresh batch of tears out of her system.

'Florrie seems convinced the captain's going to live here with you,' she said.

Mary gave a damp laugh. 'Aye, the foolish child. I'll set her right gently this evening. It doesn't occur to her for a minute that this isn't their real home, but only temporary for the war.'

'Why would it? They've been made so welcome, and been so loved. When you and Reg told them they'd always have a home here, I suppose it seemed only natural in the minds of children that that extended to their father as well.'

'I'd offer, if we'd only the space – at least until they got on their feet with a home of their own. But we've only Charlie's little box room, and George isn't going to want to live under another man's roof for long, I suppose.' Mary let out another sob as she took his letter from her pocket. 'He says... says that now the blitzes are less frequent, he's aiming to take them back to London.'

Bobby took the letter from her.

'Well, perhaps not,' she said, skimming it. 'He only says maybe. I'm sure he'd talk to the girls first. Once he knows how strongly they feel this is their home now, he'll surely reconsider. He was a tailor as a civilian, wasn't he? There must be as much work here in textile country as there is down in London – more, even.'

'Perhaps. But he's relatives there, and friends – folk who can help him get on his feet. George Parry is a proud man. He'll not want to be dependent on the charity of a pair of strangers.'

'You and Reg aren't strangers. Not to the girls. You're family.'

She sighed. 'But will he see it that way? He barely knows us from Adam, for all that the childer have grown fond of us. Besides, he won't like the idea that anyone else has been filling his place in their lives.'

'He surely wouldn't be so petty. I'm certain he'll just be glad his girls have been well cared for while he's been gone.'

'I don't know, Bobby. It's natural to get a little jealous when it comes to those we love. Already Jessie feels afraid of going back to a life she only half remembers. It's three year since she last lived with her dad; that's a long time in the life of an eight-year-old. How would you feel, if she were yours and you came

55

home to find her clinging to strangers instead of running to her mam?'

'The captain's an upright man. He'll do the right thing.'

'I'm being daft, I suppose. Crying my silly old eyes out when Florrie's thrilled to pieces, and quite right she should be. Too many bairns don't have daddies to come home to them at all these days.' Mary wiped her eyes and summoned a smile. 'I'm all right now. Sit down while I bring your egg, and tell me all the news of that young scapegrace Charlie.'

Bobby sat down and poured herself a cup of tea from the pot on the trivet.

'He isn't the same scapegrace we used to know, Mary,' she said quietly. 'He isn't so young any more either. At least, his mind seems far older, even if his body is still twenty-seven.'

Mary frowned. 'This is funny talk. The two of you haven't had a falling out?'

'Nothing like that.' Bobby stirred her tea thoughtfully, watching the thick evaporated milk they were forced to rely on when fresh was in short supply curl through the weak brown liquid. 'I love him,' she said simply. 'He loves me. It feels like he loves me more than he ever has, when he holds on so tightly it almost feels like pain for him to let me go again. And I've never admired him more than I do now. But… he isn't our Charlie.'

'How so?'

Bobby smiled wistfully. 'When I met him, it felt like Charlie Atherton was everything I wasn't – carefree, fun, full of jokes and laughter. Exactly what I needed to help me find the joy in life instead of working all the time. He was good for me, and I felt I was good for him. Things are different now.'

'He's still the same old Charlie, isn't he?' Mary asked. 'A little sober sometimes perhaps, as you'd expect given the work he'll be doing shortly, but he was all games and merriment over Christmas.'

'In company, maybe, and when he'd the bairns to entertain. But it feels less real than it used to. As if he's putting on a mask for us all.' She sighed. 'If you could hear the way he was talking last night, Mary. Feel how he trembled...'

'Trembled? Our Charlie?' Mary came over with Bobby's egg and sat in the chair beside her, looking worried. 'Is he sickening for something?'

'Not anything medicine could cure. It's his nerves.' Bobby cracked the shell on her egg absently. 'I used to worry Charlie would never take life seriously. That no matter how much he loved me, our marriage would be a constant battle to get him to accept adult responsibilities. He seemed such a Jack the Lad, always gadding. These days...' She bowed her head. 'I love him so much,' she whispered. 'When I look into his eyes and see that brave, frightened, noble soul looking out at me, I feel like it's physical pain how much I love him; that I can hardly bear it. But I don't *know* him – not like I used to. And it scares me to death to think that by the time this war ends, I might find myself married to a stranger.'

'Oh, Bobby.' Now it was Mary's turn to embrace her while Bobby shed tears. 'I had no idea things had got that way.'

Bobby frowned at something in her tone. 'You know, don't you?'

Mary smiled sadly. 'Aye, I know. Reg and Charlie aren't so different as they like to think, for all that there's twenty years separating them. My Reg was never quite as frivolous as his little brother, but he laughed a lot, once. He wasn't the man you know now. The war did that to him – that and losing our little Nancy.'

'Was it hard for you?'

'Oh aye, very hard for a time. I felt much as you do. I loved him, still. Respected him with my whole heart, after what he'd been through. But he felt half a stranger when he came back to me, like you say. It'll surprise you how many war wives will tell the same story.'

'How did you get through it?' Bobby asked wonderingly. Reg and Mary were such a devoted couple, it was hard to

57

imagine a time when there hadn't been perfect understanding between them.

'I'm not rightly sure,' Mary said. 'There was a long time, after we lost Nancy, when I worried I wouldn't. That we'd spend our lives sharing a home and never saying a word to each other.' She smiled. 'But Reg found his way back to me. I just kept still and quiet, kept on loving him and kept on showing him I loved him the best way I could, and eventually we grew closer for it than we ever had been as giddy young newlyweds. It'll be the same for you and Charlie.'

'Do you think it's the right thing to do, going ahead with the wedding? Last night I asked Charlie if he wanted to wait, he was talking so strangely, but he's still determined to do it as soon as we can.'

'I do,' Mary said firmly. 'Atherton men don't love by halves, Bobby, and no amount of war's going to change that. Charlie will always be our own Charlie in his heart, never you fear.'

'I do hope you're right,' Bobby whispered.

'Of course I'm right. I generally am, you know.' Mary tapped Bobby's egg in businesslike fashion. 'Now eat up. You'll need your strength for this medical. And for Pete's sake, don't forget that form.'

Chapter 8

Bobby was rather relieved, as she sat on the train from Skipton to Bradford, that there was indeed a delay due to problems on the line – although it was the weather rather than the war that held them up. It made her feel better about the fib she had told Reg so she could get away early and see her sister. Even with the delay, she should still have an hour or two before she was due at the recruiting centre.

When she stepped off the train, she reflected on how different winter looked in the city than the countryside. Never had the sooty, smog-filled streets of Bradford looked as dreary as they did that January morning, with puddles of dirty yellow slush filling every pothole. Still, something about being back in her home town cheered Bobby in spite of that.

This wasn't the Bradford she remembered, however. As she proceeded towards Southampton Street, she took in her surroundings.

The whole town seemed to have been repainted in khaki, blue and green. It felt like every other person she passed was in some sort of uniform: soldiers, ATS girls, Home Guard, ARP wardens, the firemen and women of the NFS. There was nothing gay or bright to be seen – the people felt as if they matched the soot-blackened buildings in their sombre attire.

The uniformed folk made her think of Charlie. He was leaving today for his new post. Did he tremble as he travelled, poor frightened boy, as he had in Bobby's arms last night? Did his heart beat like something wild trapped in his chest? And oh, when would he be in the air? Bobby hated to think of him flying ops, never knowing if the next telegram she received would be the one every wife and sweetheart dreaded. But in some ways that strange, blank look she had seen in his eyes frightened her even more, because it felt like there was something at work inside him that was changing him as a man. She wanted to comfort him so badly, and feared she no longer knew how.

Bobby walked in the road to avoid the harried Bradford housewives jostling each other in queues the length of streets, hoping they would be lucky enough to get whatever off-the-ration treat might be at the end before it ran out. There seemed to be little of the camaraderie she remembered, with women joking and laughing as they waited. Now everyone had a hungry look, and they eyed one another in silent suspicion.

It wasn't on her way, but for some reason Bobby found herself wandering towards Hustlergate, where the offices of the *Bradford Courier* were located. She stopped outside the familiar black door with its brass plaque.

The scrim tape that criss-crossed the windows of her old workplace, designed to stop the glass shattering in the event of an explosion, was yellowed and peeling from neglect: a reminder of the bombs that had been expected to fall on Bradford but – with the exception of one terrible night in the summer of 1940 – had never come. Bobby could only imagine the horror of living in Birmingham, Liverpool or London: wheezing and cowering in cold, damp shelters every night while explosions rang out around you.

Nostalgia flooded her brain as she looked at the old building. She had been happy here. Not in her work particularly, which had been unchallenging other than the few pieces of copy Tony had given her to write, but she had loved being part of a team. The way Don had mentored her as a writer. Tony's jokes, and his endless battles with Don over what programme to tune the wireless to. Young Jem, the seventeen-year-old cub, and his deep blushes whenever Tony teased him about girls. The weekly darts match against the Home Guard men at the pub, and Bobby's acceptance as one of the lads.

She could understand what Charlie meant when he talked about wanting his home to stay just as it had been when he left – something reassuring to cling to in a world that was going mad. In many ways, Bobby had felt the same about the *Courier*.

Home had never really felt like a haven to her – at least, not since her mam had died. Her dad had been too troubled after that for it to be anything other than a place of hardship and care. But even after moving to the Dales, Bobby had liked to think of the boys at the *Courier* sitting at their desks the same as always. She could still conjure up the smell of the office – Don's Tom Long tobacco mingling with the smell of over-brewed tea and the ancient parchment of the archives, with perhaps the vinegary tang of some chips and scraps Tony had managed to cadge from the local chip hole. It was telling, she supposed, that the first thing she had thought to do after the harrowing night she had climbed Great Bowside to rescue the injured airmen was to telephone Don and ask to see him at work. It seemed impossible that his reassuring, big-brotherly presence wouldn't be behind his desk waiting to welcome her whenever she chose to drop in.

She smiled as she thought back to the day she had left for her new job in the Dales: Don, Tony and Jem surprising her on the railway platform with a sign they had made bearing the message 'We'll Meet Again', and the farewell gift of an onion that had cost a whole guinea between them in a charity auction.

Yet now they were all gone. Poor Jem, only barely a man, Bobby never had met again. He had been called up shortly after and killed in action the previous spring. Tony, unable to be conscripted on account of his asthma, had been out of work ever since Don had let him go from the paper. And now even Don himself, the one person who had always made the *Courier* feel like the *Courier*, was gone, preparing to leave for the Army. Their old boss Pete Clarke was back at the helm, Don had told Bobby in his last letter, coming out of retirement to keep things running until the war was over and men could be found to fill the jobs.

Bobby stared at the door a while longer before she carried on.

She would drop in on Don later. Time had been too short to write and let him know she was coming, and Lord knew she couldn't afford to be sending telegrams all over the place at ninepence a time, but she did want to say goodbye.

She wondered how he was feeling about being called up. At thirty-nine, Don had been almost at the maximum call-up age and probably hoped he'd get away with it – until the age had been extended to fifty over Christmas. It would be a wrench to leave his wife Joan and daughter Sal at home with a new baby. Their little lad Robert, Bobby's namesake and godson, was barely six weeks old.

Of course, Bobby reflected as she turned on to Southampton Street, as much as she valued Don as a friend and mentor, in some ways it would have been better if she had never gone to work for the *Courier*. She couldn't help feeling guilty that it was through her that Lilian had first become acquainted with Tony Scott. And like a fool, she hadn't bothered to warn her sister away, thinking the man essentially harmless even if he did enjoy a flirt.

But it wasn't her fault, was it? It was Tony's fault, and it was for damn sure she wouldn't be leaving Bradford without giving him a piece of her mind.

Bobby didn't have long to wait. She found Tony at Clara's lodging house, sitting beside her sister in the public lounge.

It was a strange scene. Tony had his arm around Lilian, but he didn't look much like a lover. It lay limply over her shoulders, like an understuffed draught excluder. The pair sat in silence while Tony smoked one of the pungent Egyptian cigarettes he'd favoured since Capstans had become scarce. He appeared wan and worried, and Lil, too, was pale. But she smiled when she saw Bobby, and stood to embrace her.

'Oh, Lil, I'm so glad to see you,' Bobby whispered, squeezing her sister tight. 'Is it done?'

'Not yet. It's to be Monday.' Lilian held her back. 'It's all right, Bobby, I promise. You really had no need to come.'

The expression in her eyes was resigned and somewhat wistful, but not unhappy. She sounded like the same old Lil, even if the bright note in her voice was rather forced. But there were other people in the room, and Bobby couldn't speak freely to ask her sister how she was really feeling. She did, however, turn a glare on Tony, who looked a million miles away as he smoked his cigarette.

'So,' she said, folding her arms. 'It's you, is it?'

'Heyup, Bob.' He made an effort to summon the old Tony grin, although it looked ill at ease on his tired, drawn face. 'Here for the wedding? You're early.'

'I'm here to—' She stopped, glancing around at the handful of people reading their newspapers or listening to the wireless. 'What are you doing here anyway?'

'Spending some time with my future wife. That's allowed, I suppose?'

'You'd be better off getting down the Labour Exchange and trying to find a job.'

Lilian put a hand on her arm. 'Bobby, it's fine. It's our business. Anyhow, Tony was just leaving. We can go up to my room and talk.'

Tony stood up. 'Actually, Bobby, could I have a word in private? Want to ask a favour.'

'A favour? You'll be bloody lucky,' Bobby muttered, still looking daggers at her old friend. 'But I'll talk to you in private. I've got a few things to say that I don't want to turn the air in here blue with.'

Lilian looked worried. 'What is it, Tony?'

'Nothing to do with… nothing that need worry you,' he said. 'Something Bobby can help me with, that's all. If it works out, I'll tell you.'

'Tell me now. If you think I'm going to be one of those wives who let themselves be kept in the dark about what their husbands are up to, you're very wrong.'

63

'Look, let me handle it, all right? I don't want to get your hopes up if it comes to nothing.' He hesitated, then planted an awkward kiss on her cheek. Lilian flinched slightly. 'I'll see you soon. Um, dear.'

He headed for the door. Bobby cast a look at Lilian, who shrugged, before following him.

'You're a piece of work, aren't you?' she said when they were on the empty street outside. 'My sister, Tony!'

He sighed, with no trace of his usual cockiness or swagger. He looked so weary, she might almost feel sorry for him in other circumstances – almost.

'All right, I know,' he said. 'I never meant… but it doesn't matter now. Go on, fly at me and scratch my eyes out or whatever it is you're going to do. Call me all the names you like. Let's get it out of the way.'

'You're just lucky it's me here and not my dad.' She glared at him. 'Well? What have you got to say for yourself?'

'It was an accident, OK? I thought we could have a bit of fun. She's a laugh, your sister. I never meant for this to happen, did I?'

'That's the thing about actions, Tony. They so often come with consequences – something you've never quite managed to grasp, have you?'

'It was an accident,' he repeated helplessly, as if he was a naughty boy who'd broken his mother's favourite ornament.

'Couldn't you have…' Bobby lowered her voice. 'You know, used something? You know what I mean.'

'What, and have her think I make a habit of it?'

'She'd better be the first,' Bobby said. 'Or is there already an army of little Tonys running around the city? Don told me about your tricks, using the paper to blackmail women into dates.'

'I didn't blackmail them. It was a way to meet girls, that's all.' He met her eyes, and she had to give him credit for at least looking like he meant it when he said, 'Those days are over, Bob. I swear it.'

64

Bobby laughed, turning away from him. 'You know, the worst thing is that it was me who introduced you. Actually thought that despite what you might be capable of with other girls, our Lil was safe. Because whatever else I knew you to be, I did genuinely believe you were my friend.'

Tony had the decency to look shamefaced. 'All right, I deserve that. But I'm not a complete swine, I promise. I mean, I did like her. I love her.'

'Don't be absurd. You barely know one another.'

'Well, I love what I do know and I'm working on finding out the rest.'

Bobby thought about how she had found the two of them, sitting in silence, just going through the motions of being lovers, and a small sigh escaped.

Tony put a hand on her arm. 'I fouled up, Bobby. Happy to admit that like a man. But I'm doing the right thing now, aren't I?'

'The right thing was not to do it in the first place.'

'I can't change that. But I do want to be a good husband, and a good dad to the baby.' He rubbed his head. 'Which is pretty bloody difficult when no one in this town will so much as spit on me, let alone give me a job.'

'You're struggling that much? I thought employers were desperate for men. The fact you can't be called up ought to be a qualification in itself.'

He let out a mirthless laugh. 'You might say my reputation precedes me when it comes to getting work in this city. Don point-blank refused to write me a reference as well.'

'How are you keeping yourself then?'

'With difficulty. Odd jobs here and there, that's all.'

'Well, what are you going to do? Lil's relying on you, Tony.'

'Lilian will move in with me at my mam's for now,' he said. 'There isn't much room, but it doesn't cost. Then I guess we'll start again somewhere – maybe Liverpool. Mate of mine says there's all the work you want in the shipyards. Not much money but plenty of hours.'

Bobby frowned. 'Liverpool?'

'What's wrong with Liverpool?'

'Nothing, just… there's been so much bombing there. They've had it nearly as bad as London.'

'Seems to be easing up now Jerry's busy with Uncle Joe.'

'Easing up isn't stopping. Just last week there was another blitz on the place.'

'What choice do I have?' Tony asked. 'A man's got to work.'

Bobby smiled dryly. 'You really have turned over a new leaf. I just hope it lasts.'

'It will,' he said, with at least the impression of determination.

'Still, Tony, Lil ought to stay close to her family. She'll need support when the baby comes. I'd hate to think of her so far from everyone she knows, with a newborn to care for and the bombs falling.'

He put a hand on her shoulder. 'Then you can do your new brother-in-law a favour and talk to Don for me. That was what I wanted to ask you.'

She frowned. 'Talk to Don?'

'That's right.' Tony took out one of his smelly cigarettes and lit it clumsily, his ungloved fingers stiff from the cold. 'You were always his pet. Tell him I've turned over a new leaf – he won't believe it coming from me but he listens to you. Tell him about the baby if you think it'll help. If he gives me my old job back, I promise he won't regret it. Must admit, I have missed the old place since he hoofed me out.'

'What, didn't you hear? Don's not there. He got his call-up right before Christmas. He's going this week.'

Tony frowned. 'Then who's in charge?'

'Clarky. The trustees got him out of retirement for the duration.'

Tony groaned. 'Oh Lord. I'll never get back in if Clarky's editor. He always did think I was a waste of space.'

Bobby raised an eyebrow. 'And whose fault is that?'

'All right, all right, enough with the Sunday School homilies. I said I was going to do better, didn't I?' He exhaled a thoughtful stream of blue smoke, making Bobby cough. 'Clarky might listen to Don though. If he were to put in a good word for me.'

'So you want me to talk to Don to ask him to talk to Clarky about taking you back?' Bobby said. 'I don't fancy your odds much.'

'It's the best I've got. No one else in this town wants to hire me. You might at least see if Don would write me a reference.'

Bobby sighed. 'All right, I'll ask. But for Lilian's sake, not yours. If it wasn't that my sister needed you, you'd be lucky to get me to spit on you if you were on fire. And when my dad finds out about all this…'

Tony looked worried. 'Old soldier, isn't he?'

'Very much so. And he's also a gamekeeper, which means he always keeps a loaded shotgun in the house. Thanks to his time in the trenches, he's a crack shot.'

Bobby enjoyed watching Tony squirm, but eventually she took pity on him.

'Oh, don't worry,' she said. 'He isn't going to shoot you. Don't think he won't thump you though. Honestly, when Lil told me what you'd done I almost jumped on the train so I could thump you myself.'

'How long are you going to be like this about it? We'll be family next week.'

'I can still be angry with you once we're related. Expect at least another thirty years' worth.' She hugged herself, shivering. 'I'm going back inside.'

'You won't forget though? About asking Don?'

'I won't forget. I'm going round to see him later. I'll have a word then — not that you deserve it.'

Bobby turned to go back into the guest house, but Tony put a hand on her shoulder.

'Hey,' he said. 'I really am sorry, Bob.'

Bobby pushed away the hand and marched inside without looking back.

Chapter 9

Bobby sought out her sister in the public lounge, still seething. Lilian smiled when she saw the black look on her twin's face.

'Did you give him a going over then?' she asked, taking Bobby's elbow to lead her upstairs. 'He's been worried sick about meeting Dad, but I told him it was you he should be scared of. I hope he isn't going to have two black eyes on our wedding photograph.'

'How can you joke about it? Honestly, I could kill the sod!'

'He's trying to make it right. That's as much as we can expect of him,' she said as she ushered Bobby into her bedroom.

'What I expected of him was not to do it in the first place.'

'I keep telling you. It takes two to make a baby, Bobby, and I'm as much to blame as he is.'

'You are not. He's had a reputation for years, oiling his way around the pubs looking for women to pick up.'

'Was my reputation so very spotless?'

'You liked to have fun, but you weren't irresponsible.'

'And yet here we are,' Lil said, resting a hand on her stomach.

Bobby sighed as she sat down on the bed. 'Perhaps it is anger making me see it that way. I never thought Tony was a real danger, until… well, until he proved he was.'

Lilian sat down beside her and gave her a hug.

'You really mustn't worry about us,' she whispered. 'What's done is done. I think we can be content, once we get to know one another better. We'll have the baby to unite us soon.'

'Is that going to be enough?' Bobby held her back. 'I saw how you were when I came in. Not speaking, looking so miserable.'

'We weren't really miserable. It's all happened so suddenly that it's left us both a little shell-shocked. Tony's still learning how to behave like a husband, and I'm... I suppose I've been letting myself brood too much on what might have been instead of resigning myself to what is. It'll come right.'

'Do you truly believe that?'

'I have to,' she said quietly. 'What was the favour Tony wanted to ask?'

'He wants me to talk to Don on his behalf,' Bobby said. 'See if he can put a word in with Pete Clarke at the *Courier* that'll help him get his old job back.'

'Oh, I do hope he can! Liverpool feels so far away, and so frightening. I know Tony needs to work, but it feels sinful to take a baby right to where the bombs are falling.'

'You could come to us in Silverdale. Evacuate to the countryside for the duration.'

'Hmm. I'm not sure leaving Tony alone in a big city is the best idea, are you?' Lilian said with a dry smile. 'For all that he says he's turned over a new leaf, I think he's better for being under someone's watchful eye. Besides, I don't really want to be apart so early in the marriage. We're starting off on such shaky ground, we need to make sure we're putting down firm foundations.'

'It would be far better if you could both stay here,' Bobby said. 'I will talk to Don but I can't guarantee anything, Lil. Tony's burnt a lot of bridges in this town. He's got a reputation for laziness and shirking that too many people are aware of, and Clarky's seen it first-hand.' She gave her sister a squeeze. 'But for you, I'll do what I can.'

'I suppose I ought to fly indignantly to his defence when I hear people running him down as feckless,' Lilian said with a sigh. 'He is about to be my husband. That'll come, I guess, once he's proved himself to me.'

'He says he loves you,' Bobby said quietly.

Lilian smiled. 'He'd like to believe he does, but that's just talk to ease a guilty conscience. He does have a guilty conscience though, and that's something. Plenty of men would turn their backs.'

'He's not entirely hopeless,' Bobby agreed. She rubbed her sister's shoulder. 'But however real or otherwise his feelings might be, you don't love him, Lil.'

'I'm carrying his baby. And for love of that little unhatched life, I'm prepared to throw in my lot with Tony Scott.' She sighed again. 'But I did have such dreams about the man I'd marry.'

'I remember,' Bobby said, smiling. 'You had your wedding day all planned out when we couldn't have been more than seven.'

'Your toff friend has got a big wedding planned, I suppose,' Lilian said wistfully.

'As far as anyone can with a war on. Topsy's well-off family and friends have chipped in with money and clothing coupons to help it go off with a bang.'

'When is it to be?'

'It was supposed to be at the end of this month, but Teddy petitioned to move it to April so they could do it when the days are longer. It's arranged for the fourth.'

'I always imagined what a joyful thing it would be to marry someone I loved,' Lilian said. 'Dad giving me away, looking so proud. You my maid of honour. I never dreamed of something like this. Something shameful to be got out of the way as soon as possible, that I'd rather everyone I cared about stayed away from.'

Suddenly she burst into tears – silent, racking sobs that convulsed her whole body. Bobby put her arms around her sister and held her tightly until she was calm again.

'Lil, I'm so sorry,' she whispered.

Lil drew back from the hug to blow her nose. 'I'm all right, honestly. It's only the baby making a mess of my emotions. I really should be grateful I've had as much good luck as I have.'

Bobby raised an eyebrow. '*Good* luck? I'd say you've had about the worst luck there is.'

'Not compared to some girls. Did I ever tell you about Meg Woods, who I shared a billet with when I was training?'

'I don't think so.'

'She was only twenty: good-natured, very pretty. She was married to a lad who was with the BEF at Dunkirk – not one of those lucky enough to get back, but still, lucky enough to be among the captured rather than the killed. He's been in a POW camp since June 1940.' Lilian laughed softly. 'So there was no way out for Meg when she found herself in a delicate condition over a year later.'

'She was expecting a baby?'

Lilian nodded. 'Poor kid. She truly loved her husband, but she was lonely – lonely and afraid for the future. And now what's her poor husband got to come home to? It feels like a sin to be crying for my own selfish sake, when I'm lucky enough to have a father for my little one.' She winced, and then smiled. 'Here. Feel this.'

She took Bobby's hand and placed it on her lightly swollen stomach. Bobby experienced a thrill when she felt something jerk almost imperceptibly under her palm.

'Oh!' She flashed her sister a look of delight. 'He kicked me!'

'Yes, he just started moving yesterday. He's an early kicker, the doctor said when I saw him this morning, which is a good sign all is as it should be. Seems he's going to be a fighter, just like his mother.'

Bobby kept her hand there, feeling the tiny twitches as Lilian's baby shifted inside her. It hadn't seemed quite real until she had felt that. It triggered something in her – a sort of visceral joy at the indomitable nature of life, and excitement for the arrival of this little person who would soon belong to them.

The feeling faded, however, as she looked up at her sister's drawn features and tear-stained cheeks.

'You didn't have to come all this way just to see me,' Lil said. 'What were you going to do, try to talk me out of it? You know it has to happen.'

'I don't know. I just wanted to see you before you went ahead with it.' Bobby withdrew her hand from her sister's stomach. The baby was still now, sleeping perhaps, oblivious to the storm his little presence had created in the world outside. 'Besides, I didn't come only to see you. I've to be at a recruiting centre in an hour for a medical.'

Lilian frowned. 'You didn't join up? I thought nothing could drag you away from that little magazine.'

'I was called up – that is, I will be, once they've satisfied themselves I'm healthy. I don't know where I'm to be sent.'

'Oh.'

Lilian was silent, frowning down at the tatty olive carpet.

'What's wrong?' Bobby asked.

'Nothing, just…' She sighed. 'I guess I was still clinging to that daydream, that if I couldn't make things work with Tony there'd be my little sister, waiting with open arms. I know it's foolish. You've got your hands full with Dad, and besides, you'll be married yourself soon enough. But as long as I knew I could run to you if I ever had need of an escape, it felt like I wasn't completely alone, you know? That I'd always have somewhere I could call home.'

Bobby remembered how she had stood at the door of the *Courier*, thinking about how everyone needed a haven: something unchanging and stable in a chaotic world.

'Yes,' she said. 'I know.'

Lilian smiled. 'I'm a selfish mare, I suppose. It never occurred to me you might be somewhere I couldn't get at you.'

'Oh, love.' Bobby put an arm around her. 'I will always be there for you. If Tony doesn't shape up, you write to me and I'll… I don't know. I'll work something out. I don't want you to feel you're going into this alone.'

'What about Dad?'

Bobby sighed. 'Yes, that's the other worry. He's doing well at the moment, but you know as well as I do that can change pretty quickly if something happens to derail him. Mary's said she'll keep a close eye on him, but it's not the same as having one of us there. She doesn't know what it's like in the really dark times.'

'I wish I could be there,' Lil said quietly. 'Not that he'd want me now, I suppose. Do you have to go?'

'I can apply for postponement, but I can't decide if I ought to. When I think about Dad, and that you might need me, I feel like it's my duty to fight call-up any way I can. But then I watch the newsreels, see all these terrible things occurring, and I feel selfish for caring only about what's happening on my own hearth.' She sighed. 'Charlie thinks I ought to go. It's hard to argue when he's putting his life on the line to win this thing.'

'I see what you mean.' Lilian patted Bobby's knee. 'Well, don't worry about me,' she said, with sudden brightness. 'Tony will look after me – he's sworn he will. You do what you have to, our Bobby.'

Bobby took her sister's hand to give it a squeeze. 'Lil, you don't have to go through with this. There are other ways.'

'Like what?'

'You could live away somewhere. Tell people you've been evacuated, or that your husband's overseas, or he was killed. Any lie you want. I'd send what money I could and Tony would pay to support the baby, or a court can make him if he refuses. You can take in laundry to earn a little extra, or... or get a job in a factory maybe, once the baby's weaned. A lot of the munitions places have a WVS creche now to look after the little ones while their mams work.'

Lilian smiled, her eyes filled with a strange sort of peace – or at least with resignation. 'No, Bobby. I made my bed and now the time's come to lie in it.'

'At least consider it, Lil. I can't bear to think of you trapped in a marriage that's going to make you unhappy.'

74

'I feel like as long as I can keep my baby, I'll be a type of happy. And you never know, perhaps Tony will surprise us when it comes to the sort of husband he'll make. Do you remember Mam telling us that it was the wildest colts would grow to make the steadiest mounts?'

Bobby smiled. 'I remember. I asked if she was talking about Dad, and she went very pink. I wish she was here.'

'Oh!' Lilian laughed. 'Here he goes again. I think he's longing to be out, and to hell with the next five months.'

Lilian once again placed Bobby's hand on her belly. The baby seemed to be giving her insides a particularly vigorous battering. Bobby let her head sink on to her sister's shoulder as she felt her future nephew – or niece, she supposed, although Lil was convinced the baby would be a boy – make his presence in their lives felt. One thing was for certain: once he arrived, life for Lilian would never be the same again.

Chapter 10

Bobby's time with her sister felt all too short, and there were many tears as they parted.

There had been no real resolution to their conversation. Bobby wasn't sure what she had wanted, except to make her sister understand that she had options other than marriage to Tony, but no matter what she said, Lilian seemed determined to go through with it. She had promised to send a telegram as soon as she was wed, so Bobby would know it was done.

It felt so strange that the next time Bobby saw her sister, Lil would be a married woman. She wished she could at least be there for the ceremony, but Lilian had said she didn't want anyone from the family, since it was hardly going to be an occasion for celebration. Tony's mother and younger brother would be witnesses, with no one else in attendance, and Lilian would move straight in with the Scotts afterwards. There would be no reception, no honeymoon, no gifts to help the couple set up home together – everything would be done as quickly and quietly as possible.

Lord knew how poor Lil was going to cope once she was ensconced in what was to be her first marital home, Bobby thought as she hopped on a tram. The Scotts weren't wealthy. Their house was one of the many cramped two-up-two-down terraces that crowded the Bradford streets, where the newly-weds would have to share a bedroom with Tony's brother Oliver. Bobby could only imagine how crowded the place would feel if they were still there once the baby arrived.

She also wondered how Lil would get along with Tony's parents. She had met them on a couple of occasions. Tony's father was a quiet, pallid man with a toothbrush moustache and a dirty neck who blended into the background so well that you soon stopped noticing him, but Bobby hadn't much liked Mrs Scott's looks. She had a vinegary expression that suggested she didn't suffer fools gladly, or anyone else for that matter.

Bobby tried to put worries about her sister to one side as the tram slowed to let her off. The women's forces recruiting centre, which was in the old Mechanics' Institute not far from the *Courier* offices, was just a short walk away.

When she entered, Bobby found an ATS girl manning the front desk. The woman, who had been filing her nails, looked up to give her an uninterested look.

'Name?' she asked.

'Roberta Bancroft.'

'WAAF or ATS?'

'Um, I'm not sure.' Bobby handed over the letter she had received and her registration certificate. 'I was just told to report for a medical.'

The girl glanced at the registration number and matched it to one on a list in front of her. 'Yes, I see. You've an appointment with the RAF doctor at four. Down the corridor, second room on the left. The doc will call you when it's your turn.'

Bobby blinked. 'I'm being assessed for the WAAF?'

The woman smiled. 'Let me guess. Blue isn't your colour.'

'No. I just... I'm surprised, that's all.'

'Second room on the left,' the woman repeated, nodding to a queue that was developing behind Bobby. 'We've got a lot of you to get through.'

'Right.'

They wanted her for the Air Force? Bobby hadn't put much thought into which service she might be assigned but she had assumed it would most likely be the Army, since that was where most of those called up were sent. If she did have to go, it would be something to be in the same service as Charlie. Perhaps sharing a routine would bring them closer.

Bobby entered the second room on the left as directed. Several other women were there waiting, most of them young – few looked much beyond twenty. She took a seat by the only one who looked to be around her age.

The woman wore a pair of small, round spectacles, but managed to avoid looking studious in spite of that. In fact she looked every inch the fashion plate, with her face heavily made-up and her hair in Betty Grable rolls. She gave Bobby a friendly grin, exposing a smudge of cherry lipstick that had stuck to her slightly protruding front teeth.

'All right?' she said, in a broad Bradford accent.

'Um, hello,' Bobby said, wondering whether it would be perceived as a favour or rudeness to point out the lipstick on the woman's teeth. She decided against it.

The woman laughed. 'Blimey, love, you're white as chalk. Don't worry, eh? They don't make you drop your knickers or owt. Our Trish had hers a few month ago. She says they just check your heart and breathing, make you read a bit off a chart then tick you A1 and send you home to wait for your enrolment.'

Bobby smiled a little more warmly, appreciating this new acquaintance's attempts to reassure her.

'I'm not really worried,' she said. 'At least, not about that.'

The girl took out a packet of cork-tipped cigarettes and lit one.

'Oh, sorry,' she said, taking it out of her mouth. 'Do you mind? Probably not supposed to right before they examine you. Does things to your heart or summat. The doc'll give me a rollicking, but it calms my nerves.'

'No, don't mind me.' Bobby put out a hand. 'Bobby Bancroft.'

'Carol Boyes. Middle name Can't-get-enough-of-the, our mam always jokes.' Carol shook Bobby's hand vigorously before taking another drag on her cigarette. 'What trade are you hoping for, Bobby?'

'I hadn't really thought about it. How about you?'

'Oh, anything that keeps me close to the lads,' Carol said cheerfully. 'I'm twenty-five this year. If I don't come out of this war with a ring on my finger, I might as well give up. Never been so many chances for a girl to nab a husband. My sister had bagged herself a man two weeks in, and she's no looker. That was when I made up my mind to join up.' She turned to examine Bobby more closely. 'How about you?'

'Oh. I'm engaged already. Um, to a pilot.'

Carol laughed. 'All right, no need to be smug. I meant did you volunteer, or did they make you come?'

'I was told to come,' Bobby said.

'You don't look right happy about it. Would you rather not be called up then?'

'I'm just worried about leaving home. My dad's a widower and I look after him, you see.'

'Ah well, I'll tell you what to do about that,' Carol said, lowering her voice so the other women couldn't hear. 'Just nip into the little girls' room and run on the spot for a bit, get yourself good and out of breath. Then when the doc checks your heart rate and breathing, he'll think you're no good and let you off.'

Bobby laughed. 'Oh no, I couldn't cheat. Besides, I'm sure they must know all the tricks by now. But I'll take a postponement form away.'

'If you've got a feller, best way to do it is get yourself in the family way,' Carol, who seemed a worldly-wise sort of person, told her matter-of-factly. 'Don't bother waiting for the wedding, you can sort that out after. Soon as you've skipped a monthly, your senior officer will send you home.'

'That seems a bit extreme,' Bobby said, blinking.

Carol shrugged. 'It's the surest way to get out of it.'

Bobby hadn't thought there was much possibility of failing her medical, but Carol's advice did kindle something like hope.

Supposing the doctor did find something wrong with her? Nothing too awful, but just bad enough that the WAAF would decide they didn't want her after all – a rare blood group, perhaps, or mild asthma like Tony Scott. Then she could stay at home with her dad, and Charlie would have to understand.

She was destined for disappointment, however. The doctor called her in shortly afterwards. Her heart and lungs were soon pronounced in fine working order, and Bobby couldn't bring herself to be dishonest when she was asked to read a table of letters in increasingly tinier typefaces. She read right to the bottom line.

She was weighed and measured, her tonsils and ear canals inspected, then she was asked about childhood illnesses. The stiff-looking RAF doctor seemed thrilled to learn she had never been troubled with TB or rheumatic fever, or indeed anything more serious than the usual mumps and measles.

The only question that gave Bobby pause was when she was asked if there was any history of mental weakness in the family. Again she thought of her father, softly sobbing in his sleep as he dreamed of horrors from days long gone.

'Um, no,' she said after a moment's hesitation. 'No, there's nothing like that.'

'Well in that case, missy, you're quite the model recruit,' the doctor said as he scribbled her answer down. 'I think we can safely say you're A1 – practically strong enough for the front lines. Now if you'll go into the room next door, Squadron Officer Mulligan will interview you about the type of role you might be suitable for. Give this to her when you go.'

He tore off the form he had been filling in and handed it to her. Dazedly, Bobby went into the corridor and knocked on the room next door.

The letter she had received had said nothing about an interview, or even about the service she would be assigned to. It felt like everything was extremely rushed, and there was no time for explanations. Bobby supposed places like this must be processing hundreds of women a day, and she was just one face out of many to be shunted around like a draughts piece.

A clipped 'Come!' answered her knock, and Bobby went in. The interviewer, Squadron Officer Mulligan – a stern-looking woman in middle age – was glancing at some notes on a clipboard. Next to her, a young WAAF corporal sat ready to take notes.

'Good morning,' Bobby said.

Squadron Officer Mulligan didn't answer. She just gestured to a seat without looking up. Bobby sat down.

There was silence. Bobby wondered what she was supposed to do.

'The doctor said I was to give this to you,' she said, remembering the form in her hand.

Again, there was no answer. Squadron Officer Mulligan waved vaguely to the WAAF at her side, who seemed to be fluent in this type of communication. She took the form from Bobby, glanced at it, then scribbled something in shorthand. Bobby tried to make out the squiggles upside down. *Roberta Bancroft. A1, passed for immediate enrolment*, it said.

'You can read this?'

Bobby jumped. Squadron Officer Mulligan had finally deigned to pay attention to her and had clearly caught her studying what was presumably supposed to be confidential.

'Um, yes,' Bobby said. 'Sorry. I didn't mean to be nosy, it just... caught my eye.'

'Roberta Bancroft,' the officer read from her clipboard. 'Studied at Pitman's. What shorthand speed?'

Bobby felt even dizzier than she had when she entered. The military seemed to operate without time to waste, or even to draw breath.

'A hundred and fifty words per minute,' she said, not without a trace of pride. The NCO making notes looked up to give her an impressed nod.

'Typing?'

'Eighty words per minute.'

'Shorthand typing as well?'

'Yes, although it's been a little while since I was called on to do any.'

'And do you play an instrument?'

Bobby blinked. 'As in, a musical instrument?'

'Yes. A cornet or euphonium, ideally.'

Bobby had no idea what the significance of this was, or if it was something all WAAFs were expected to do, but it had been such a bizarre afternoon that she no longer had the capacity to feel surprise.

'Um, no,' she said.

'Pity,' the officer murmured as she struck through something on her clipboard. 'They're desperate for cornets in the WAAF band at Debden. Still, we can certainly use you in administration. You can expect to be summoned back here for enrolment within the next week, then it's likely you'll be placed on deferred service until we can find a spot for you at a training school – perhaps for several months. There aren't nearly enough places to accommodate every new WAAF. I don't think there's a bed left at West Drayton or Wilmslow, and Harrogate's bursting at the seams.' She clicked her tongue. 'This is what happens when you have a government filled with men – no thought for the practicalities. They expect all these girls they're conscripting to sleep dangling from the rafters like bats, I suppose.'

Bobby's head was fair spinning now. Everyone in this place seemed to take it as read that she understood military procedure, and knew what would happen at each step of the call-up process. She was almost embarrassed to admit just how much of a clueless civilian she was.

Mulligan was ignoring her again. Bobby didn't know if this meant she was dismissed or not, but she wasn't going without some information.

'Excuse me?'

Squadron Officer Mulligan looked up. 'Yes?'

'The letter I was sent said I could claim for travel and lost earnings.'

'Oh, yes, yes,' Mulligan said with a dismissive motion, as if such petty concerns were beneath her. 'The girl on the door will give you a form.'

Her attention drifted back to her clipboard, but Bobby wasn't finished.

'Can I request to be close to home when I'm posted?' she asked.

'You can request it,' the officer said vaguely. 'Whether you'll get it is another matter. Priority goes to married women. But we can note it here as a preference.'

'Yes, please. And, um... I'm sorry, but the letter did say something about a postponement form?'

Mulligan looked up sharply. 'Postponement form?'

Bobby felt her cheeks heat. The officer's look was suddenly none too friendly.

'Yes.'

'Employer making trouble, is he? If he wants to make a case that your work's vital to his business, he can write requesting a postponement himself.' Squadron Officer Mulligan's gaze drifted to something on her clipboard. 'Huh. Journalist. Well, I wish him luck with that.'

'It isn't him.' Bobby's face turned an even deeper shade of crimson. 'It's me. I thought I might... that is to say, there was something about exceptional hardship.'

'You're unmarried with no children, it says here.'

'I am, although I'm to be married shortly, but that hasn't anything to do with it. My fiancé's in the forces too. It's my father.'

Mulligan raised an eyebrow. 'Elderly?'

'Well, no. He's fifty-one next month. But he... suffers.'

'Suffers?'

'Yes, because of the war – the last war, I mean.'

'Has he got a handicap that prevents him from working?'

'No, physically he's fit. He's a gamekeeper.'

'Decent wages?'

'Enough to live on. But he… he has bad dreams.'

The expression on Mulligan's face told Bobby this sounded just as feeble to the officer as it had coming out of her mouth. It was so hard to explain to strangers just what she had to fear from leaving her father alone.

'And he's a widower,' Bobby said, realising she was starting to sound desperate. 'I'm the only one left to take care of him.'

'There's no one else who could come in to cook and clean? No woman relation, or a home help he could hire?'

'There's Mary – my fiancé's sister-in-law. But she has her own home to keep, and besides… well, he really ought to have someone living with him.'

'Right. Because of his "bad dreams".'

Bobby tried to ignore the sneer in the woman's voice. 'Yes. Do you think they'd consider my case?'

'Oh, no doubt they'd let you off,' Mulligan said, her tone conveying exactly what she thought of this state of affairs. 'These committees still occupy that rose-tinted past where it was believed a woman existed to make a home first and foremost. That having a hot dinner on the table and a fire in the grate for some man was more important than work that could save lives. Thank goodness not all of us are living in cloud cuckoo land.'

'So, um, what should I do then?' Bobby mumbled.

Squadron Officer Mulligan scribbled something on her clipboard. 'Speak to the girl on the front desk and ask her for an NS13 – that's the form you need. But I hope I don't need to tell you, young lady, that a lot of people are giving their all to win this war. We'd be in a fine mess if everyone tried to weasel out of it.'

'I know that, but—'

'We've got a lot of others to see. You're dismissed, Miss Bancroft.'

Mulligan again ignored her. After hesitating a moment, Bobby left the room, humiliation burning her cheeks.

She wasn't sure what she had been hoping for. That the officer would see her point, she supposed, and give her blessing to a postponement application. Anything that might help her feel better about it. But Mulligan's disapproval had been palpable, and Bobby was once again left with nothing but her own conscience to guide her.

Chapter 11

It had started snowing when Bobby stepped into the street. The stuff fell in huge wet blobs, quickly absorbed by the yellow slush that already filled the gutters and slunk into the cracks in the pavement.

She had filled in the form to reclaim her travel expenses and lost earnings, but the more important form – the NS13, which would allow her to apply for a postponement – was tucked into her handbag. She had just four working days to return it to the address on the bottom, which meant she had little time to weigh the matter up. The form would have to be in the post no later than Friday, the day after tomorrow.

It was a question of where she was needed most. Could her humble, unimportant presence really help win the war? It seemed such a far-fetched idea, but if this war had taught people anything, it was that little things could make a big difference. All the previously unthought-of household rubbish collected for salvage; the rows of beans and peas that occupied her friend Topsy's former flowerbeds; the frequent reminders about the danger of one misplaced 'careless talk' whisper. If Bobby was freeing up a man to join the fight, perhaps she really would be making a bigger difference than the mundane work of typing and filing might make it seem.

But even so – what would be the cost to her family?

Mary and Reg had been adamant she ought to apply for postponement, and her father had looked so forlorn and helpless when she had told him she might have to go. But then Bobby thought of Charlie. What if she did get out of it, and he could never forgive her? What if it created a rift between them that would poison their marriage before it had even begun? And if anything were to happen to him in action – if he were injured, or, God forbid, killed – would she ever be able to forgive herself?

Bobby's brain was spinning, and it point-blank refused to give her any answers to the question that preoccupied her. She put it to one side as she walked to the tram stop that would take her to Great Horton, where Don and his family lived. Perhaps her friend's ever-reassuring presence would help her find the calm she needed to think it through.

Don's wife Joan answered the door. She looked red-cheeked and flustered, in a floury pinny with her sleeves rolled up and her hair escaping from under a headscarf. Baby Robert was sleeping over one shoulder, limp as a rag doll.

'Oh! Bobby,' Joan said, trying to tame her escaping hair. 'Come in out of the cold, love. We hadn't expected you. Does Don know you're in town? He's just sitting down to tea.'

'Um, no,' Bobby said as she stepped into the hall. 'Sorry, I would have telephoned, but it was rather short notice. I was summoned for a medical at the WAAF–ATS recruiting centre. I wanted to call in and say goodbye before Don left.'

Joan smiled. 'So they got you as well, did they?'

'Afraid so,' Bobby said, smiling too. 'Are you all right, Joan? You seem all at sixes and sevens.'

'I'm all over the place thanks to his nibs here,' Joan said, nodding to the sleeping baby. 'You'd think butter wouldn't melt, kipping there so peacefully, but this is the first time he's shut his eyes all day – and his gob. What with trying to keep him happy, get Don's things ready for when he leaves on Tuesday and finish this batch of tarts for the WVS cake sale tomorrow, I've scarce had time to draw breath. It's young folks' work, this mothering malarkey.'

'Can I help with anything? I expect you want your tea too. I'm happy to mind my little godson while you eat.'

'Oh, you're a blessing sent from God,' Joan said gratefully, gathering up the little bundle of baby and handing it over. 'As soon as Sal's finished her food, she can take him upstairs. Then if you really want to do me a favour, you can take that husband of mine out for a drink while I finish baking. I wish the paper could have kept him on until it was time for him to go. There's nothing worse than husbands for getting under your feet when you're busy – you'll learn that soon enough when you've one of your own.'

'Yes, of course. I mostly came to say farewell, but there is something I'd like to talk to him about if he can spare me an hour.'

'Come this way.' Joan ushered her into the living room, where a fire was burning. 'Pull up a chair. I'll send Sal in for Robbie in ten minutes.'

Bobby took a seat at the hearth and settled little Robert in her lap. He was sleeping soundly, swaddled in a knitted blanket with eyes scrunched up tight against the electric light, but he instinctively gripped Bobby's finger when she placed it on the palm of his hand.

'Ow,' she whispered, smiling. 'That's some grip you have, young Master Sykes.'

The baby screwed up his face as if in agreement, letting out a little raspberry through pursed lips, and Bobby laughed.

He was so tiny still, with just six short weeks of life in which to have experienced the world. So very, very delicate and precious. How must the world look to those fresh and wondering eyes?

It made Bobby think of Lilian, and the little bundle she would soon be nursing. Poor Joan had looked so tired as she struggled to manage her home and a demanding baby, and she had both her daughter Sal and a part-time home help to spread the load. Lil would have nobody – nobody except Tony, jobless at home, and as Joan had rightly pointed out, even the best husbands were a burden when they were stuck in the house all day.

How Bobby wanted to stay at home, and be there for her sister! If Lil was in Bradford, Bobby could come at weekends to give her sister badly needed respite from domestic cares. But if Lilian ended up in Liverpool as Tony was threatening, and Bobby was drafted Lord knew where with the Air Force, the sisters might not see one another for months on end.

She ran a thumb tip over the baby's tender, downy cheek, stroking his cottongrass-soft black hair with her other hand. Don and Joan's little wartime blessing. Lilian's baby would be just such another. It made Bobby's heart swell to watch his tiny chest rise and fall: the soft, rhythmic breathing and cheeks rosy with a healthful glow.

This was what it was all for, wasn't it? The war. The lives being lost, and the men and women sacrificing everything to keep the enemy at bay. Men who bled and shed blood, who fought and killed and died. It was all to make a better world for little ones such as this. When Bobby looked into the sleeping features of her godson and felt the instinctive lightness of heart that his chubby fist around her finger produced, she felt that she, too, would sacrifice anything if it only meant a world at peace for these tiny ones to grow up in.

She was pulled from her reverie by the arrival of Don and Sal.

Sal, who was still in her school uniform, waved enthusiastically at her. 'Hullo, Miss Bancroft. Mam said you'd come. D'you remember me?'

Bobby smiled to see the girl so jolly and confident. She had been wondering if Don's imminent mobilisation might be upsetting for his sensitive little daughter, but Sal looked full of health and happiness.

Sal Sykes wasn't so little any more either, a growth spurt meaning the nearly twelve-year-old girl was now up to Bobby's shoulder. Her dark hair, which had been in two plaits the last time Bobby had seen her, was now styled in the same side-swept waves as the young Princess Margaret Rose wore. When

Bobby remembered the pale, anxious little waif who had almost been made ill through bullying when she had been evacuated to a boarding school in the Dales, she felt she wouldn't have recognised the girl.

'Of course I remember you, Sal,' she said. 'You look ever so grown up since I saw you last.'

'Huh. Growing up too fast, I reckon.' Don lowered his voice and told Bobby in a stage whisper, 'Our Sal's courting.'

Sal blushed. 'Dad, stop. I am not.'

'Tell that to the baker's boy. Half an hour you were hanging over the fence chelping at him yesterday, and in the cold an' all. The bread were half-frozen by the time your mam got her hands on it. I've a good mind to come out next time and ask him what his intentions are.'

The girl's cheeks looked like tomatoes now. 'Oh my word, Dad, please don't! Jimmy'll never talk to me again.'

Bobby laughed. 'Don, don't tease her. You know you'll do no such thing.'

'Aye, well, happen not. Sal, take your little brother upstairs and settle him in his cot. Your mam needs a rest.'

Sal approached to take the baby. Bobby felt the little fist slip from her finger as she reluctantly handed him over, and Sal tucked him expertly into the crook of her arm. She gave Bobby a wave before heading upstairs.

Don sighed. 'She'll be courting in earnest before long, and me halfway across the country not able to keep an eye on her. We've broken the back of this thing now, I hope, but still, it don't look like there's much chance of it ending any time soon. Scares me to death, Bobby, I don't mind telling you.'

Bobby stood up. 'Do you really believe that?'

'What?'

'That we've broken the back of the war.'

'Why, don't you?'

'I don't know. You keep hearing people say it'll all be over by summer or winter or next spring, but nothing seems to change.

Boys are still dying, food's still short. Chamberlain told us to prepare for a three-year war, didn't he? Well, it'll be three years come September and there's still no end in sight.'

'Ah, but now we've got the Yanks.'

'Yes, and Hitler's got Europe. All those resources, as much slave labour as he needs. Anyhow, Churchill certainly doesn't think it's over. He was forecasting another invasion attempt in the spring.' She pressed her palms to her eyes. 'It's the sheer on and on-ness that frays the nerves. It feels like it'll carry on this way forever, Don.'

Don sighed. 'Maybe you're right and I'm kidding myself. Can't face the thought of being gone for years; of coming home to find a daughter almost grown and a little boy who don't remember me. It feels like Sal's at that age where she changes every day. By the time they let me come home for good, happen she'll be a young woman and I'll have missed the last precious bit of her childhood.' He sighed again before summoning a smile. 'Same for dads the country over, I suppose. Anyhow, I wasn't expecting to see you today.'

He shook her hand in a frank, manly fashion that made Bobby laugh.

'I wasn't expecting to have to come,' she said. 'Still, I'm glad to have the chance to say goodbye.'

'Been for a medical, have you? They'll have the whole bloody country in the forces before long.'

'Joan says I've to take you for a pint and get you out from under her feet.'

'That, young Bobby, is just what I need,' Don said, clapping her on the shoulder. 'It's been driving me dotty hanging around this place all day. I'm not a man idleness sits well on, but that's all I can be in this weather. Can't even do a bit o' gardening.'

'Let's go to the Swan.'

'The Swan? That's nearly a half-hour's walk. There's the Brewer's not fifty yards away.'

'I know, but... I feel that I'd like to go to the Swan. For old times' sake.'

He smiled. 'Feeling nostalgic, are we? I know what you mean. All right, button up and let's go.'

Chapter 12

Bobby tied her pixie hood over her ears and pulled her coat tight around her as they set off walking towards the pub near their old offices. In her days at the *Courier*, they had visited every Tuesday for a game of darts after putting that week's paper to bed.

'Everything's changing, Don,' she said with a sigh.

'Aye.'

'Are you afraid?'

'Of the Army?' He shrugged. 'At my age it's bound to be Pioneer Corps they pack me off to. Not much danger there – just me and a load of other broken-down old buggers doing a bit of navvying. I'm more worried Clarky'll get a taste for being a newspaperman again and I won't have a job to come back to when I'm demobbed.'

'I know how you feel.'

Don glanced at her. 'The war going to put you out of a job too, is it?'

'All I know is that Reg refused to guarantee he'd still have a place for me. He never liked the idea of keeping me on after marriage, and now this has happened, I wouldn't be surprised if he decided replacing me was for my own good. Once the WAAF's finished with me, he'll expect me to settle down to being a housewife like a good little woman should.'

'The WAAF? That's where you're going?'

'Unless I get a postponement. I could try claiming hardship – you know, for my dad's sake. I've got the form in my bag.'

'Huh. I tried that as well. Said I had a new babby and a wife who weren't as young as she used to be, and I was needed at home. No good, I've still got to go. You might have better luck, being a lass.'

'The WAAF officer who interviewed me seemed to think they'd let me out of it if I applied,' Bobby said. 'She didn't approve though. I felt two inches high the way she was looking down her nose at me.'

'Better than peeling potatoes in the ATS, at any rate. Your young man's RAF too, isn't he? Maybe you can get a posting on the same base.'

'Maybe, but that doesn't help my dad.'

'Hmm. Suppose not.'

They fell into a thoughtful silence as they walked. It was dark now, and Bobby took out her little torch to light their way. One thing about Bradford compared to the countryside was that there were at least streetlamps on the main roads, even if they were only the blackout-approved 'starlighting' type with their thin, sickly glow. It glinted wanly off the ice crystals in the gutters.

Bobby smiled when they entered the pub. That, at least, had remained the same. There was even a group of Home Guard men playing darts, as of old.

'Home sweet home, eh?' Don said, kicking the slush off his boots. 'I'll get the drinks. You can claim the table.'

Bobby sat down at what had once been their usual table while Don visited the bar for a pint and a half of mild. He shook his head as he put her half in front of her.

'Never thought I'd see the day I was paying over a shilling a pint for beer that's half water,' he said. 'This cost of living's getting daft. God knows how I'm going to manage on a private's salary with a family to support. I just hope they promote me quickly.'

'I wonder when we'll be able to do this again,' Bobby said.

'Not for a long while, I reckon.'

'No.' She sighed. 'I suppose not.'

Don started stuffing his pipe. 'Well then, what are they going to give you to do in the Air Force? Will you be flying Hurricanes or Spitfires?'

Bobby smiled. 'Administration, the officer who interviewed me said. They seem to be desperate for shorthand typists. Well, that and euphonium players.'

'Shorthand typing all the livelong day? You'll be bored rigid, Bobby.'

'I know, but if that's what's needed to free up men then I guess that's what I have to do.'

'Just remember you're a writer. Don't let that journalist's nose of yours get permanently stuffed up.'

'I'll try.' She stared into her beer. 'It's so strange, the way nowadays you can just be summoned to a whole new life. I haven't been told a damn thing about what to expect. I don't know where I'll be sent, who I'll be sharing quarters with, what I'm to wear or how my day will look. I know it's the same for everyone, time of national emergency and so on, but... it makes me feel so helpless. Like a child who has all her decisions made for her with never a word of explanation.'

Don lit his pipe. 'I know how you feel.'

Bobby inhaled the smoke from his pipe deeply, relishing the familiar, comforting smell. This seemed to tickle Don.

'Going to start smoking one of your own, Aircraftwoman Bancroft?' he asked, laughing.

'It reminds me of the *Courier*, that's all. I do miss it.'

'That's your fault, isn't it? I've offered you a job every time I've seen you since you left. No good deciding you miss it now that it's too late for me to offer you another.'

'I don't mean I miss the work.' She glanced around the familiar old local. 'Just... us. The way we all used to be. They were happy times when it was you, me, Tony and Jem.'

Don sighed. 'That poor kid.'

'I know. I often think about him.'

'Well, let's try to stay off morbid subjects, eh? I miss them days myself, I must say.'

Talk of the *Courier* reminded Bobby of her conversation with Tony, and the promise she had made.

She nodded to her friend's pint. 'Have a drink, why don't you?'

'What for?'

'Because it'll put you in a good mood and I'm about to ask you for a favour.'

He raised an eyebrow as he took a sip of beer. 'Another one? What do you need this time?'

'It's not for me, it's for... someone else. And before you say no, just let me finish, all right?'

'Huh. I can guess what this is about.' Don planted his pipe back in the corner of his mouth, and it wobbled as he spoke. 'You're going to ask me to help out that work-shy loafer Scott. I wouldn't waste your breath, Bobby. Tony Scott's a dead-end kid and it's long past time both of us washed our hands of him.'

'How did you know that's what I wanted to ask?'

'I know Tony. He's begged me twice for a reference, and I could've guessed his next stop would be you. Well he's had more lives than a cat and he's spent them all, so the answer's no. I'll not be persuaded to tell lies that'll help him make a mug out of the next poor sod.'

'You don't understand. I'm not asking only for Tony's sake. There's a little more to it.'

He frowned. 'Oh?'

'Tony's engaged, Don.'

He gave a hoarse laugh. 'What, and for the sake of whatever deluded mare's said she'll marry him, you think I'll do him a favour? If she's a girlfriend of yours, Bobby, best thing you can do for her is warn her off before she's signed her life away. She'll get nowt from marriage to Tony but misery.'

'Oh, please don't say that,' Bobby said quietly.

'You know it as well as I do.'

'You see, it's no good.' Bobby broke eye contact to watch the swirling bubbles in her barely touched beer. 'This girl, the one Tony is to marry... she has to go through with it. I mean, she's got no choice, Don. Do you understand?'

Don was silent for a long time, watching her. Bobby felt her cheeks getting redder and redder under his gaze.

'You bloody idiot, Bobby,' he said quietly.

'What, you think...' She laughed aloud, the idea was so absurd. 'Oh Lord. No, it's not me.'

Don let out a whistle of relief. 'Thank God for that. I didn't think you could be that stupid, but I did wonder when he'd be winking at you in the pub if he might've had his eye on you.'

'He had an eye on everyone female-shaped when he'd had a few. That didn't mean anything. But it is someone I care about, very deeply.' She lowered her voice. 'It's Lilian.'

He frowned. 'What, your Lilian?'

'It wasn't her fault. He tricked her into going on dates with him – took advantage. She says he didn't, but I know what he's like.'

Don didn't speak, but puffed on his pipe. He didn't look shocked, or surprised, or anything much other than thoughtful.

'Don?' Bobby said after a moment had passed.

He roused himself. 'Sorry. Was just thinking about our Sal.'

'It wasn't Lil's fault,' she said again.

'No. I know that.' He sighed. 'It's a man's world, all right. How's she bearing up, your sister?'

'She says it's for the best – the wedding, I mean. She was so worried she'd have to give the baby away, but now Tony's stepped up she can do everything respectably. But I know she wanted so much more, Don. She was crying her eyes out today. Tried to convince me it was the pregnancy making her emotional, but she must be so terribly afraid for the future.'

'And has he truly stepped up? This is Tony Scott we're talking about.'

Bobby shrugged. 'As much as I wanted to wallop him when she told me what he'd done, I have to give him his due – he came straight back with a proposal when he found out our Lil was in trouble. Never questioned if the baby was his or anything, the way some men would to get out of it.'

'You talked to him, did you?'

'Yes, today. He was adamant he'd turned over a new leaf.'

'And you believe him?'

'I think he believes himself, at least. Whether it lasts is another matter.'

'Hmm. He'd turn over a new leaf every few weeks on the paper, I recall. One week he was going to give up smoking, another he was determined to prove himself with some big story. A fortnight of sucking on barley sugar sticks or working more than an hour a day and he was soon back to the old habits.'

'I know, but he can't easily turn his back on a wife and child, can he? Anyhow, for Lilian's sake, I have to hold on to that hope.' Bobby took a sip of her neglected beer. 'He wants to move the family out to Liverpool.'

Don raised his eyebrows. 'Liverpool?'

'Apparently they're desperate for men in the shipyards. Tony says if he can't get work in Bradford, he'll take Lilian and the baby down there.'

'Lot of bombing in Liverpool.'

'I know.' Bobby reached out to press his wrist. 'Please, Don. I'm not asking for Tony, or even for Lilian really. I'm asking for me. I want my sister and her baby to be safe, and close to friends and family in case Tony lets them down. It would mean a lot to me if they could stay in Bradford.'

'I wish I could help, Bobby. I mean, I'll write the man a damn reference – one he doesn't deserve, full of the biggest fibs I can bring myself to tell about him, since there's a babby to consider. But too many folk in this town know him by reputation. I can't in all honesty say it'll help.'

'He wanted me to ask if you'd talk to Clarky about getting him back on the paper.'

'Clarky won't listen to me.'

'Why not? He respects you.'

'Perhaps, but I had to plead enough times for Tony's job when he was still working for us. Clarky would've let him go long ago if it hadn't been for me making excuses for him.' He laughed quietly. 'God knows why I did it. Suppose I couldn't help liking the man in spite of my better judgement – until he spent his last chance.'

'But you could try, couldn't you? Tell Clarky that Tony's changed?'

He drained the last of his beer.

'I'll give it a go,' he said. 'But if you ask me, you'd be better talking to your boss.'

Bobby frowned. 'You mean Reg?'

'Aye. Don't forget him and Clarky were in the trenches together. I doubt he'll listen to me now I'm on the outside but he might do a favour for an army pal. Those old soldiers stick together.'

Yes, that was right, wasn't it? Reg and Clarky had served together in the last war. The very first time Bobby had met Reg, he had dropped into the *Courier* offices to ask his old friend for a favour – it seemed so long ago now, she had half forgotten.

'I don't think I ought to tell Reg about the baby though,' she said. 'He can be old-fashioned about some things. I don't want to be shouting about my sister's condition all over the place.'

'No need. Just tell him she's to be married, the prospective husband's out of work and you'd be grateful if he put in a good word.'

'I don't know. We haven't told Dad about the engagement yet, or the baby. I'd have to ask Reg to keep it quiet until we do.'

Don shrugged. 'That's your business. But like I said, Clarky'll listen to Reg Atherton before he listens to me.'

Chapter 13

It was late when Bobby returned home. Travelling back in the blackout, the night chill freezing the slush into hard ice, she half wished she had arranged to stay the night in Bradford. The government would only cover one day's lost earnings, however, so she could ill afford to do so.

She hadn't thought much about the money situation if she were to go, but it was a point to consider. The daily wage for WAAFs during basic training was pretty poor, but if Bobby got into a trade with good promotion prospects, she might find she was quickly on better money than she earned on the mag. She wouldn't have food and clothing to pay for either. She could afford to send part of her wages home, which meant that financially, at least, her dad would be better off – as long as he could manage to remain in work himself. They had been lean days when Bobby had been the only one at home earning.

She would send her contribution directly to Mary for house-keeping though. The last thing her dad needed when he was by himself was the temptation a pocketful of brass would bring. That meant more money to chuck into the till at the Golden Hart – or into the pockets of his spiv pal Pete Dixon, who was always happy to sell him bottles of the strong foreign spirit he dealt in.

Her dad was in bed when Bobby arrived back at the cow house, for which she was grateful. She felt far too exhausted to try to hide her feelings, and was worried everything would come pouring out with the slightest provocation. Lilian, Tony, her guilt over whether to apply for a call-up postponement – everything.

–

By the time Bobby awoke the next morning, however, she felt sufficiently refreshed to put on a brave face. The postponement form was next to her bed, under Charlie's picture. She had filled in all the essential information the night before – her name, registration number and so on – with the exception of the final box, where she was invited to make her case for hardship. Her intention was to fill it in that evening, then she could take it to the post office tomorrow with the other office correspondence. That was if she decided to send it.

As for the Lilian/Tony situation, she felt the best time to discuss that with her dad would be after the wedding had taken place. However angry he might be about the baby, once his daughter had been legally bound to Tony Scott, he would understand there was no going back. Bobby hoped he would have calmed down and accepted the situation, however reluctantly, by the time the couple arrived to pay their marital visit.

By the time her dad got up, Bobby had just completed her morning chores. She had visited the pump, given the partially carpeted stone flags of the cottage a sweep and scrub, raked out the grate, prepared a packet of sandwiches for her father's lunch, darned a hole in his favourite work jumper, and finally got herself ready to begin her own day's work. As she rubbed her aching arm, which she was sure must be developing muscles the size of a circus strongman's from pumping the water every day, Bobby reflected that life in the Air Force might seem a relaxing change of pace compared to the rigours of keeping the cow house.

'Morning,' she said when her dad emerged, dressed for another day of work in the woodland around Topsy's hunting lodge.

'Aye, morning,' he said wearily. He looked as though he might have passed a bad night, although, exhausted from her journey, Bobby hadn't heard any sound from his room to wake her. 'How was Bradford then?'

'Good.' Bobby turned away to hide the twitch in her features. She had no intention of telling him that Lilian was anywhere other than Greenwich – not yet. 'I dropped in to see Don and the baby. That's why I was so late back.'

Rob smiled at the mention of the baby. As the child's other godparent, he always took a lively interest in the sections of Don's letters that concerned the little lad.

'How is he?' he asked.

'Oh, a real strapper,' Bobby said with a laugh. 'He nearly cut off my blood flow when he grabbed my finger. I think Joan's feeling the strain though. She and Sal will miss Don when he goes to the Army.'

'He'll miss them, I reckon.'

'Very much. He's always been a family man. Are you coming over for breakfast?'

'Give me quarter of an hour. I need to clean out my gun. Had to unload it on a family of mink yesterday.'

'All right, have a good day if I don't see you at the table. Sandwiches are in the pantry.'

As soon as Bobby opened the door to Moorside, she was confronted by the children's border collie Ace, who came sniffing his way along the corridor. When he reached her, he jumped up and snuffled with his cold, wet nose under her cardigan.

Bobby grimaced. 'Thanks, Ace.' She pushed him down again. 'What's the matter with you, you strange dog?'

But Ace was already snuffling his way back down the hall, like a bloodhound on the trail of an escaped convict. He stopped to explore a small table with a vase of flowers on top, knocking it down in the process, then very suddenly bounded off up the stairs.

Tutting, Bobby set the table right. It was lucky the vase was filled only with artificial flowers at this time of year, or Mary's precious carpet would be soaking wet.

Mary herself appeared now, Reg leaning on his stick at her side. She shook her head when she saw the flowers strewn across the hall carpet.

'Now what's all this mess?'

'I swear it wasn't me,' Bobby said with a smile, stuffing the flowers back into their vase.

'Aye, I know who it was. That daft hound Ace.'

'What on earth is up with him? He was acting very oddly when he came to greet me just now. Like he'd lost something.'

Mary sighed. 'It's old Hetty. Her cold took a turn for the worse yesterday. We lost her in the night, dear little chuck.'

'Oh, I am sorry, Mary,' Bobby said, glancing up. 'After you tried so hard to get her well again.'

'The pup's behaving like he's lost one of his flock. He's been turning the house upside down, convinced we've hidden her away.'

Bobby set the vase, once again replete with flowers, back on the table. 'How's Jessie?'

'Sobbing fit to burst in the attic, poor soul,' Mary said. 'You know what store she sets by them hens – loves them like they're her own bairns, I'm sure. She says she couldn't manage a bite of breakfast.' She turned to her husband. 'Could we not write a note saying she's too badly for school, Reg? I'm sure she barely slept for worrying about Hetty.'

'She'd be better for summat to take her mind off it, I reckon,' Reg said. 'She'll only sit brooding if we let her stay here.'

'She can help me in the kitchen. Once she's baking bread she'll cheer up a mite. She loves kneading the dough.'

'You know that as soon as you say she can stay off, you'll have her sister suddenly in paroxysms of grief and demanding equal treatment. Then we've to explain to their father that we let them miss a day's learning on account of a ruddy hen.'

Mary looked solemn. 'Oh. Yes. I suppose we would have to let the captain know.'

'Well, it's up to you. But Jessie would be better off laiking with her schoolmates than thinking on at home is my opinion.' Reg gave his wife's arm a fond squeeze and hobbled towards the parlour. 'I'll be at my desk if anyone wants me.'

'I keep forgetting it's not for us to make decisions about their schooling,' Mary said to Bobby when Reg had gone, her tone rather chastened. 'We're not their mam and dad. Reg is right to remind me.'

'Jessie isn't only upset on Hetty's account, is she?' Bobby said quietly.

'I don't think so, although she don't say much. I'm sure she's still brooding over the changes that have to happen when her dad gets home.' Mary sighed. 'She's not the only one. I try to put a bright face on for the girls, but Jess is a clever little thing and senses what I'm really feeling, I'm sure.'

Bobby came to slip an arm around her. 'Do you want me to talk to her?'

Mary smiled gratefully. 'Would you, love? I feel on the edge of a crying fit half the time myself since we learned they were to leave us, and I'm sure I'm as likely to make things worse as better.'

'I'll go now and see if I can get her to come down for some food.' Bobby planted a kiss on her cheek. 'I'm sorry, Mary. I know what you must be feeling. I hope everything works out.'

'Aye, pet, me too. Me too.'

Bobby climbed the stairs to the attic. She could hear Jessie's soft sobs drifting down as she mounted the second flight. She found the little girl sitting on the bed, being comforted by her sister. Ace lay on the blankets behind them, looking almost as miserable as Jessie about the loss of their charge.

'Don't cry, Jess,' Florrie was saying as she patted her sister's head. 'I know it's really sad about Hetty, but now she'll be in heaven with Ma, won't she? I bet that's loads better than living in a cold old henhouse. There's probably all her favourite things to eat, sherbet lemons and stuff, and no stupid war on that says she can't have them.'

She paused, watching her sister hopefully, but Jessie just snuffled into her shoulder.

'And soon Dad'll be home,' Florrie continued, not to be deterred in her mission to cheer her sister up. 'I bet then we'll never be sad again. It'll be just like before the war when we were all so happy.' She turned a look of appeal on the grown-up arrival. 'Won't it, Bobby?'

'I'm sure it will,' Bobby said, smiling.

This time there was a definite effect. Jessie's sobs redoubled, and she struggled to catch her breath. Florrie gave her a puzzled look.

'You are excited about Dad coming home, aren't you, Jess?' Florrie asked.

Jessie was unable to speak through her gasps, which spared her the necessity of answering.

'Florrie, why don't you go get your breakfast?' Bobby said. 'It'll be school soon. I'll look after Jessie.'

'All right, but she's really sad,' Florrie said solemnly as she stood up. 'She ain't stopped crying since Mary told her about Hetty.'

'That's all right. Go on, downstairs you go.'

The little girl ran off down the steps, her irrepressible light-ness of heart buoying her up as ever. Ace jumped off the bed to follow, not so troubled by grief as to lose his appetite, or his optimism that a share of his mistress's breakfast might be coming his way. Meanwhile, Bobby sat down next to the more serious younger child and gathered her up in her arms.

Jessie snuggled against her, sobbing as if her heart might break. Bobby didn't say anything. She just held her until she felt the little body cease to tremble, and the shuddering sobs slowed to a gentle weeping.

'I am sorry about Hetty, sweetheart,' Bobby said softly. 'I know how much you loved her.'

'Fank 'oo,' came a muffled voice from her chest.

'We'll have a funeral for her, shall we, and bury her near the henhouse where her friends are?'

'OK,' Jessie mumbled.

'The other hens will miss her a lot. You'll have to give them extra attention while they're sad and sing them some of your jolly songs. Do you know that I can always tell by how my egg tastes when you've been singing to them?'

Jessie drew back, her wide, wet eyes looking up at Bobby. 'Really truly?'

'Really truly.' Bobby took out a clean handkerchief and handed it to the child so she could blow her nose. 'When you've been singing, they have these lovely rich golden yolks. It would be interesting, don't you think, to make an experiment of it and see if different songs make for different types of eggs? You and I could keep an egg diary.'

Enthusiasm kindled in the girl's eye. She had an enquiring mind and a love of all things scientific, as young as she was. The word 'experiment' was as good as milk chocolate to her. But her face quickly fell again.

'But we won't be able to do the experiment though, Bobby,' she said in a funereal tone. ' 'Cause you'll be going away to the war, just like Uncle Charlie. Mary said you would.'

Bobby wanted to smile, although she suppressed it for Jessie's sake. It was nice to be reminded that the girls were fond of her. Of course it was Mary who really loomed large in their lives, standing in the stead of a mother to them, and 'Uncle' Charlie who was ever their favourite playmate. If they regarded Bobby in any sort of familial light, she supposed it was as a sort of big sister. But they did care for her, and would miss her if she had to go. It rather bucked her up to be reminded that she, too, occupied a little place in their hearts.

'Well, it isn't certain yet,' she told the little girl. 'The war people might decide I ought to stay and take care of my dad.'

'You will though. The stupid war takes everyone away from us, same as it took our house. And then Daddy'll make us go away to London, where we won't have Ace or Boxer or Winnie or Barney or Henrietta or Harriet or Hannah or the cats or Reg or Mary or Mr Bancroft—' she stopped to take a breath '—or you or Uncle Charlie or our friends at school, or the beck to play in when it's hot or a garden to make snowmen or a hill to toboggan on or owt that's good. An'… an'…'

The little girl burst into tears again, and Bobby held her until she was calmer.

'Perhaps not,' she said. 'Your dad only said he *might* go back to London. If the idea upsets you, my love, then speak to him. Write him a letter – I can help you with your spellings if you don't want to tell Florrie about it. I'm sure he'd want to know if the idea was distressing you.'

'He might be cross though.'

Bobby frowned. 'Was your father often cross with you for telling him how you felt when you lived together?'

'Don't know. Don't remember,' she mumbled, taking up the little rag doll Bobby had made for her at Christmastime so she could cradle it. 'I was a baby then.'

Bobby smiled. 'It wasn't so long ago as all that, was it? You were five when he went to the Army.'

'Five's as good as a baby though,' said the mature young lady of eight. 'I don't remember him being cross much, although I think he was sometimes sad. Maybe because he missed our ma after she died.'

'Tell me what you do remember,' Bobby said softly.

'Only little bits, like when we'd all sit by the fire after our baths, and we'd have cocoa and he'd read stories out of this big old book. It had all the fairy tales you could ever think of, Bobby.' Jessie's eyes sparkled at the memory before her face fell again. 'But it got burnt up when the bomb dropped on our house, like all our books and playthings.'

'That sounds a happy memory though.'

Jessie rubbed her fists in her eyes. 'I think so. I could remember more things, when an' I was littler. But now I only remember that one thing, and some stuff from after Daddy went to the war when we lived with Aunt Sadie. We weren't very happy then. Every night in my prayers I used to ask God to send Daddy back to live with us again. But then our house got ruined and we come to Moorside, and now I just want to stay here.' She sobbed again. 'With Mary and Reg and you.'

'I know,' Bobby said gently, planting a kiss on her ginger curls. 'But your father loves you very much too, Jess. I think he'd be quite sad if he thought you didn't want to live with him any more. You do forget some of your early memories when you're a little person growing up, because your brain is still small and it has to push them out to make room for the new ones. But your dad will remember every happy time the three of you had together.'

'Florrie remembers too, don't she? She's never stopped talking about Daddy coming home since he wrote.'

'Well, there's a lot of difference between a brain that's only had eight years to grow and one that's had a whole eleven.'

Jessie sniffed. 'You really think Daddy would be sad if he knew I wanted to stay living here? I don't want him to be sad.'

'He'll be sad because he loves you, and he'll think that perhaps while he's been away, his little girl has forgotten how to love him.'

'I do. I do love him, really,' Jess declared with more determination than fondness, looking guilty. 'I just don't remember very well, that's all. Because of my brain got filled with new memories like you said.' She rubbed at her nose with the hanky, scrunching up her eyes in a way that might be comical under other circumstances. 'I wish Daddy could live somewhere near, like with you and Mr Bancroft, while I got used to him being here again. Or if we have to live with him, then maybe Reg and Mary could live with you in the cow house and we can live here with Daddy. Then Mary can come to make us our food and read us stories at bedtime.'

Bobby couldn't help smiling at this efficient and ruthless redistribution of Reg's property.

'And where would your Uncle Charlie live when he came home from the war?' she asked.

Jessie frowned, as if this point hadn't occurred to her.

'I guess he can live here with us and Daddy,' she said after pondering a moment. 'That'll be best, because we'll need him here for games anyway.'

'Yes, but don't forget that he and I are to be married soon. We had thought we might quite like to live together afterwards.'

'Oh well, then that's easy,' Jess said, waving a magnanimous hand. 'Uncle Charlie can stay with you and your dad and Reg and Mary. We won't mind, as long as he still comes over to play with us. But then there won't be much room, so all the dogs will have to stay with us. That's OK though. We like having them here and we know how to look after 'em.'

Bobby laughed at the notion of five full-grown adults squeezing into the cow house's two tiny bedrooms. Of course in a child's view of the world, everything was simple – and naturally it revolved around them.

'I don't think Reg and Mary would be too pleased about being thrown out of their house to live in a cold barn,' she said. 'It would hurt Reg's bad leg, you know, and make Mary's rheumatism worse. I think they had better stay here.'

'Oh.' The girl's face fell. 'I didn't think about that.'

'But I wonder if the captain has thought about living some-where nearby. I think he might be surprised at how many opportunities there are for work here, for a man with his skills.' Bobby was talking half to herself now. 'I've a mind to write to him. I know Mary would feel too awkward to do so, and perhaps I ought not to stick my nose in, but I'm sure he'd want to know how things stand for his daughters.'

Jess wiped her eyes and looked at her hopefully. 'Would you really, Bobby?'

'Hmm?' Bobby collected herself. She had drifted into thinking out loud, or she wouldn't have said so much. It didn't do to get the child's hopes up.

'Will you write to Daddy?' Jess asked, blinking up at her. 'And ask him about if he wants to live with you and your dad in the cow house?'

Bobby smiled. 'I won't ask him that. I'm sure the last thing your father's bad shoulder needs is a bed in our draughty old shippon. It never was meant to be a house, you know. But… well, would you like me to write to him and tell him how you're feeling?'

'Oh, yes!' Jessie said, clapping her hands. 'You can write it ever so much gooder than I could. Reg said he thinks you're the bestest writer he ever worked with.'

Bobby pulled herself up straighter. 'Did he really?'

'Yeh, I heard him tell Mary,' the girl went on happily. 'And will you tell Daddy he's not to take us back to London, but to let us live here with Mary and Reg forever?'

'I can't tell him anything, chicken. He has to make up his own mind and do what's best for your family. Don't forget he needs to find a job – that might be harder than it was before the war, with his injury. But if you'd like me to write on your behalf, I will.' Bobby planted another kiss on the girl's head. 'Now will you come down to breakfast, and then we can finish getting you ready for school?'

Jessie jumped up, all smiles now. 'Thank you, thank you, thank you! I know it'll be all right if *you* write to him. And you won't go to the war, will you, Bobby? Then if Uncle Charlie comes home, we can all be as happy as happy.'

'I can't promise that, my love. I have to be where I'm needed most. But I'll do what I can.'

Jessie beamed. She threw herself impetuously at Bobby for a hug before running off downstairs.

Chapter 14

Where I'm needed most. The words whirled around Bobby's head all that day.

She didn't have an ARP shift that evening, and had been hoping to keep it free to give some thought to the predicament she was in. It wasn't to be, however, as one of the village lads appeared at the door that afternoon with a note for her. Mary brought it into the parlour with a cuppa each for Bobby and Reg.

'Looks like young Topsy's writing,' she observed. 'Happen she's got some wedding jobs for you, Bobby.'

Bobby unfolded the note.

'You're right,' she said. 'She wants me to go over this evening to help her and Mrs Hobbes with their sewing. Don't knock, just come right in, she says. I never realised society weddings involved quite such a huge amount of sewing, did you?'

Mary raised an eyebrow. 'More sewing? I'm sure I've sewn myself silly for that girl since she announced the engagement.'

'I know, I was hemming tablecloths for hours in the ARP hut last week. I thought every last scrap of linen in the Dales had been used for our pantomime, but Topsy's friends have been donating material and clothing coupons in swathes.'

'Topsy Sumner-Walsh never could do things by halves,' Mary said, smiling. 'Will you go?'

'I don't suppose I can say no, since I was the matchmaker for the thing,' Bobby said with a laugh. 'I won't stay late though. I've things to do at home.'

Reg, who had been contributing only the odd muttered 'humph' while this female nonsense ate into the working day, glanced up.

'Filled that form in yet?' he asked Bobby.

'No. That was the other thing I needed to do tonight.'

'Well, don't leave it too long. You can't depend on the post these days. Pop it in the box soon as you can.'

Mary said goodbye and left the room with her ever-present teapot. Bobby didn't start work again immediately, however. She blew on her tea thoughtfully. For once it was a rich conker brown – made with real milk, not the evaporated stuff or powdered Household Milk, and brewed with fresh leaves.

An idea had been evolving since her conversation with Don. It had come back to her that morning, as Jessie had casually divided Reg's property between their three families.

She had to agree with Don. Tony's chances of getting back on the *Courier* staff now Clarky was in the editor's chair again were slim to none, no matter who put in a good word. He only had himself to blame for that. But Bobby had a better idea – one that, if everything worked out, could solve two of the problems that had been worrying her in one go. It wasn't ideal, but it was better than any of the alternatives.

'Reg?' she said.

'Hmm?'

'You know you said that if I had to go – I mean, if they don't accept I count as a hardship case – you were going to advertise for someone to take my place?'

'Aye, what of it?'

'Don't advertise. I know a chap who could be just what you're looking for.'

Reg looked up. 'Got a good nose for it, has he?'

'When he applies himself,' Bobby said, thinking about the meat-raffling story Tony had uncovered that had ended up getting poor Lilian into this mess. It had been a good bit of journalism, despite the consequences. 'He's got experience too.'

'Hmm. It's not much money. Does he know that?'

'He's not in a position to be choosy. He's to be married soon and needs to find work to support himself and his wife.'

Reg frowned. 'What age is this lad?'

'Thirty.'

'Thirty!' Reg gave a hoarse laugh. 'A man that age'll not work for a quid a week, lass. Besides, the Army will have him soon enough if they haven't already.'

'He can't be called up. Asthma. And he really does need the work, even at that salary. If it included accommodation, that would make a big difference to him.'

'Well it don't – not any more,' Reg said, going back to his work. 'Not unless I kick your old man out, which for his sake and yours I've no intention of doing.'

'That's just what I mean.' Bobby flushed. 'This man. The woman he's engaged to is… is my sister.' She met his eyes. 'Please don't say anything to my dad though, Reg. She hasn't broken the news yet.'

Reg frowned. 'Your sister? I thought she were engaged to some naval sort.'

'That didn't work out.'

'Well who is he then, this young man?'

Bobby hid her face behind her tea for a moment. This was the difficult part.

'Tony,' she said quietly. 'Tony Scott, from the *Courier*. I mean, formerly from the *Courier*.'

Reg laughed. 'What, him?'

'Well, why not? He might not've been crafting deathless prose on the paper but when it comes to writing up a story, he knows what he's doing. Don Sykes has given him a glowing reference.'

'Huh. Scott slip him a oncer for it, did he? I remember Nobby Clarke telling me about that one. Wouldn't know a hard day's work if it bit him on the ar— on the backside.'

'He's changed now,' Bobby said, realising even as the words fell from her lips how unlikely this sounded. 'Tony's really settled down since he and Lil started walking out.'

Reg watched her for a moment, one eye narrowed.

'There isn't any more to this, is there?'

'In a way.' Bobby forced her voice to remain even. 'You know I've been worried about leaving my dad. If Tony was able to find work here, then he and Lilian could move into the cow house. I know there's not much room but Lil knows how to take care of our dad when he… well, you know. And she'd have friends and family nearby to support her once she—' She stopped. 'I mean, if she and Tony were to start a family.'

'I see.' Reg went back to his work.

Bobby waited, but Reg didn't say anything else. It seemed as if, to all intents and purposes, the subject was now closed.

'Um, Reg?'

'What?'

'Are you going to… If I asked Tony to send you a letter of application, would he be wasting his time?'

'No need, is there? If you send that form off.'

'And what if I don't?'

He looked up sharply. 'That's what you've decided, is it?'

'I haven't fully decided anything, but I can't help thinking about it. That I really ought to do my duty and go.'

'Listen, Bobby, I already waved off a brother who for reasons best known to himself developed a sudden case of chronic patriotism.' His brown eyes, like his brother's in everything except their sternness, met hers. 'You stay here, where you're best off. If you want to serve the war effort, do it by giving folk summat to smile about on the pages of the magazine. As a writer you're worth ten Tony Scotts.'

'This isn't about the magazine, Reg,' Bobby said impatiently. 'Don't you get it? There are things happening out there – big things that are going to change the whole world, for a long time after they're over. Things that matter more than you and me, and the damn magazine. Charlie understands that. Perhaps it's time I started getting my priorities in the right order too.'

He blinked. 'All right. What's brought this on?'

She sighed. 'I'm sorry. I didn't mean to go off at you. Just... Charlie said some things when he had that bit of leave the other night. It got me thinking that I really didn't have any right to make a claim for hardship. I'd hate him to resent me for trying to duck out of doing my bit while he's up there with his hide on the line.'

Reg laughed. 'What, because you didn't give your all short-hand typing for the war effort? They're hardly asking you to go to the front lines.'

'But it isn't about that, is it? I'd be typing to free up a man from somewhere else. I might not be on the front lines, but he could be. Because of me.'

'Huh. Then I'd think you might stay for that poor sod's sake.'

'If everybody thought that way, we'd lose the war.'

'Aye, all right. It were only a joke.' Reg sighed. 'Well, do what you think you have to. Mind, I can't promise I'll be able to take you back once you go.'

Bobby bowed her head. 'I know.'

'God knows if the mag'll even make it through the war, the way they're rationing paper. A few more years of it'll finish us.'

'And... Tony?'

'He can apply, but I'm not promising owt.'

Bobby smiled. 'Thank you. That was all I wanted.'

Chapter 15

After work, Bobby had a hasty bite of tea before mounting her bicycle to ride to Sumner House. It was time she could ill afford to spare, but as she was to be the maid of honour at the forthcoming wedding, it didn't feel right to refuse her share of the work.

As instructed, Bobby didn't knock when she reached the cottage in the grounds that Topsy and her former nanny, Mrs Hobbes, were occupying since Topsy's manor house had been requisitioned for use as an RAF hospital.

She found a cosy scene inside. Mrs Hobbes was sewing in her rocking chair by the fireside, her tame goose Norman curled in her lap like a huge feathered cat. Topsy, meanwhile, sat at the feet of her fiancé Teddy, who was on the other side of the fire in his wheelchair. She sat between her lover's knees with her head resting on his thigh and one of his hands held in hers.

Topsy had a pile of napkins and her sewing box by her feet, which lay neglected as she opted instead to trace the lines that crossed Teddy's palm. Bobby had never seen her Polish friend, who was often depressed since the crash that had cost him the use of his legs, look so content.

Bobby crept in quietly, not wanting to disturb the reigning serenity, and lingered by the door.

'Do you see my future in this hand, Topsy?' Teddy asked softly, stroking her hair back from her face.

'I do, darling. Your lines show you are to have a long and happy life filled with love.' Topsy grinned up at him. 'But you're to give a lot of trouble as a husband. Of course, I don't need to examine your palm to know *that*.'

Teddy chuckled while Mrs Hobbes tutted at them.

'You know I don't approve of these heathenish fairground tricks, Topsy,' she said sternly. 'They're not for well-brought-up young ladies.'

'Oh, Maimie, it's only fun. You act as if I'd made a pact with the Old Gentleman. I don't know a thing I'm talking about, you know.'

Norman woke up and let out a resentful honk in Bobby's direction. Topsy glanced up.

'Birdy, you're here at last,' she said, beckoning her forward. 'I was worried you wouldn't make it in time. Join us, do.'

Bobby noticed a glint in Topsy's eye that she had come to know well over the past year. It usually meant she was plotting something. The last time her friend had got that look in her eye, Bobby had found herself playing Cinderella in a Christmas pantomime. What could Topsy be planning to recruit her for this time?

'A good thing someone's come who won't shy away from hard work,' Mrs Hobbes said, pursing her lips at Topsy. 'Madam here thinks her share of the sewing is to be done by the fairies while we sleep, I'm sure. She hasn't lifted her needle in an hour.'

'Maimie is ever so cross tonight,' Topsy whispered as Bobby drew a chair over to the fire. 'It's all Jemima's doing.'

Bobby raised an eyebrow. 'Norman's wife Jemima?'

'Oh, her marriage vows mean nothing to her, the brazen hussy. Maimie caught her canoodling on the lake with another gander. At least, Jemmie allowed him to give her a bread crust as a gift. I said there was probably nothing in it, but Maimie is furious on Norman's behalf.'

'These geese ought to be in a moving picture, do you not think, Bobby?' Teddy said, laughing. 'What colourful lives they lead! We are all quite dull beside them.'

Mrs Hobbes smiled. 'Such nonsense you young people talk. Topsy, hand over some of those napkins for Bobby or we'll never be done.'

'Here you are, Birdy,' Topsy said, passing them to her. 'They're to be hemmed with gold thread so they're all matching, like these finished ones. Maimie had some thread saved from before the war. It all feels rather extravagant, doesn't it? But I'm only going to do this once, I suppose.'

'And so you ought to suppose,' Teddy said, bending to kiss her head. 'I do not intend to let you go once you're lawfully mine, Topsy.'

Bobby threaded her needle, smiling. 'I thought it was to be a quiet wedding.'

'Oh, it is,' Topsy said. 'At least, the ceremony will be quiet. That will just be us and those we love best at St Peter's. Still, we must put on a good do afterwards. It's a shame it has to be in the church hall instead of at Sumner House as it ought to be, but there is a war on.'

Teddy sighed. 'I confess, I would much prefer something small and quiet, with just our few friends. But I want Topsy to be happy, and it is the bride who must have her way on her wedding day.'

'It isn't for my sake, darling,' Topsy said, looking up at him. 'It's for yours.' She looked determined suddenly, and rather fierce. 'I won't have Aunt Constance and all those toffee-nosed friends of my father's thinking I want to hide you away. If I was marrying a sultan, there couldn't be a grander reception – you know, wartime allowing.'

'I wish you would not, Topsy. I don't need the acceptance of your father's friends, or of anyone.' He took her hand. 'Only the love of my wife.'

'You'll always have that,' she said, pressing his hand to her lips. 'Still, I want them to know just how proud I am of you. I want everyone in the wide world to know.'

'Your high-born friends will think you mad, to be proud of one who is poor, and foreign, and a cripple.'

'Oh, they can think me mad all they like. I'm sure they always did. But they'll never think I'm ashamed.'

Mrs Hobbes smiled, glancing around the cluttered room. 'I should say there's little chance of that, Topsy.'

Bobby followed her gaze to the piles of embroidered linen that filled the room. A table heaved with tinned food, sweetmeats and bottles of wine, all donated to the happy couple by Topsy's relatives and society friends. It looked like a feast to make Bacchus weep. Topsy was refusing to let anyone but Mrs Hobbes see her wedding gown, which had been refashioned from a family heirloom, but Bobby felt sure that it, too, would be fit for a princess.

Certainly, wartime weddings were very different when you belonged to Topsy's class. Just before Christmas, Bobby had made a telephone call to her old schoolfriend Bess Jenkins – Bess Slater as was – to congratulate her on her own recent marriage. Bess had described the difficulties of arranging a wedding when there was a war on: how her soldier husband had only been able to get forty-eight hours leave in which to rush home, marry his fiancée, enjoy a short wedding night and hurry back to his barracks. How her wedding dress had been a simple cotton frock, the best she could buy with her clothing coupons; her bouquet a handful of Michaelmas daisies plucked from the back garden; the wedding cake a small, un-iced malt loaf, and the gifts from family and friends merely vegetables gleaned from allotments or contributions from their precious rations – technically against the law, since rations could only be transferred within a household, but everyone did it.

Yet it had been a joyous event, humble though it was. Bobby could hear Bess's love for her new husband suffusing every word she spoke. That, at least, she and Topsy had in common. While Topsy might feel she needed gold thread and iced fruitcake to prove to the world she was proud of the man she was marrying, it was Teddy himself – and the presence of all those who truly valued the bride and groom – that would make the event a happy one.

Bobby couldn't help but think of her sister. She was counting down the days until Monday: the day set aside for Lilian and Tony's wedding. Just four days until it was all over. What a different event that would be! No gifts, no cake, no dress, no feasting – no celebration of any kind.

Not that any of those things mattered, if there was love between the bride and groom. Dresses and gifts weren't what was important. What counted was that the couple were able to share the joy of being united as man and wife with those who cared for them.

But when there wasn't that love, it all felt so bleak and empty. There would be no festivities for Mr and Mrs Scott on their wedding day. Only the bittersweet satisfaction of an unpleasant but necessary task completed.

Topsy tapped Bobby's arm, interrupting this sombre train of thought.

'I say, isn't it ripping about Ernie?' she said. 'I haven't seen him myself, but Maimie bumped into Chip in the pub and he says it's no worse than a broken arm.'

Bobby found a blush rising as she thought about Ernie King. Worrying about her call-up and her sister's situation had put the awkward moment when she had fallen on him on the ice out of her mind, but it recurred vividly now. The scent and warmth of him; his broad chest against her body; the fire in his eyes when he had looked up at her; the change in his voice, which had sounded so soft and husky suddenly.

She wondered if she ought to confess the incident to Charlie in her next letter. Nothing had really been wrong – it had been an accident, that was all – but the look Ernie had given her had unsettled her. Bobby was sure she hadn't imagined it, and could no longer feel quite comfortable about Ernie's jokey flirting.

Yes, she knew he was the same way with all the women in the village, even those old enough to be his grandmother – it was part of that old-fashioned chivalry in his nature to pay women compliments. He never got fresh with anyone, although there were plenty of the younger women who would welcome it. Still, after what had happened, Bobby couldn't help but feel guilty that she had never rebuffed him. Perhaps she had actually encouraged him, if she had been misunderstanding his intentions all this time.

Bobby knew Ernie liked and respected her, despite his oft-stated disapproval of her dress, ideas and independent habits, but she had never believed he had an interest in her beyond ordinary friendship. He knew she was engaged, and besides, it had been Topsy he had always given the glad eye to – at least, until he realised her heart belonged to Teddy. Topsy was rich, titled, beautiful and vivacious, and she captivated men without trying. Bobby was none of those things.

Not to mention that Ernie surely received too much attention from pretty girls fascinated by this handsome, exotic foreigner to take any notice of Bobby Bancroft, with her mud-splattered trousers and her frazzled hair. He hadn't tried to hold her that night, and had kept his free arm respectably behind his head while she had extricated herself from the bramble. Perhaps the look he had given her had meant something other than what she had felt it to mean. There had only been the dim light of her blackout torch in which to make it out, after all.

And yet it preyed on her mind. She wished Charlie was here, so she could throw herself into his arms and confess everything; soothe the jealousy that would naturally arise, be reassured of his feelings, and kiss away the worry. But the more Bobby thought about it, the more it didn't feel right to put it in a letter. Charlie might worry, and he had enough to occupy his mind when he was about to start flying ops. It wasn't fair to add to that over an incident that really amounted to nothing.

Besides, Ernie would be gone soon. She would miss him, but nevertheless Bobby couldn't help feeling relieved at the idea of some distance being placed between them.

'You did know he was back, didn't you?' Topsy said as Bobby remained silent.

Bobby stirred herself. 'Sorry. Yes, I bumped into him on the bus. His injuries are a little worse than a broken arm – there was some shrapnel in his belly too, and a dislocated shoulder – but he's expected to make a full recovery.'

'It sounds as though he has been lucky,' Teddy said somewhat wistfully, glancing down at his legs.

'Did you know he was leaving the village?' Bobby asked. 'He's been grounded for four months while he heals, so he's being sent to take up an instructor post.'

Topsy's eyes widened. 'Leaving? But what about the wedding?'

Teddy laughed. 'I am afraid the war machine does not stop even for something as important as our wedding day, my Topsy.'

'Oh, but it must! He was to be part of the guard of honour. The Canadian boys, Piotr and some of the men from the hospital would insist on having one for us, since Teddy was a flyer too. We'll be beastly uneven without Ernie.'

'He did say he was going to try to get some leave,' Bobby said. 'I don't suppose it's something he can guarantee though. You know how things are.'

'I do hope he can come.'

Bobby looked down at her sewing. She had been dreading breaking this news. Topsy was so excited about the wedding, around which everything in her world currently revolved, and she hated to cause her friend upset. Still, it wasn't to be helped.

'I'm afraid I have bad news as well,' she said. 'I'm so sorry, but I can't guarantee I'll be here for the wedding either.'

'But that would be even worse! We couldn't do without you at all, Birdy. I'd rather postpone the whole thing than not have you.'

'I'll certainly try to be there, but… well, there's a chance I could get my call-up soon.'

Topsy frowned. 'The government can't call you up just like that, can they?'

'They can and they will, unless I can persuade the WAAF I have to stay and keep house for my dad. I was in Bradford yesterday for a medical, which I'm almost sorry to say I passed with flying colours.'

'Oh well, if you don't want to go then that's just fine,' Topsy said breezily. 'If it's the Air Force I can easily get you out of it. I'll speak with Uncle Geoffrey tomorrow and tell him you mustn't be made to go.'

Bobby was accustomed to hearing of Topsy's assorted 'uncles'. They were mostly old public school chums of her late father's, and seemed to be in privileged positions all over the country. Uncle Geoffrey, Bobby assumed, must have some power within the Air Ministry. But while she might still be undecided on making a hardship application, she'd be damned if she was going to cheat her way out of doing her duty.

Teddy seemed to read the sentiment in her face.

'Your friend would not wish this, I think, Topsy,' he said quietly. 'Our Miss Bancroft does not like an easy way out.'

Bobby nodded. 'Teddy's right. Sorry, Topsy, but I have to go through the proper channels.'

Topsy fixed her with a puzzled frown. 'But why make it difficult for yourself, when this is the easiest way? It isn't wrong to want to stay with your father. They might turn you down if you ask, but Uncle Geoffrey can make sure of it for you.'

'Because it's a privilege others don't have,' Bobby said, with a degree of impatience. As much as she cared for her friend, she did find it exasperating that Topsy seemed unable to pierce the bubble in which she'd been raised and see the world as it was for other people. 'I haven't decided yet whether I ought to apply for a postponement, but if I am granted one, I want it to be because the powers that be feel I'm entitled to one – not because I'm lucky enough to have a friend with influential connections who can "get me out of it". I don't want to dodge my duty through unfair means. Do you understand?'

'Well, I suppose so,' Topsy said, somewhat doubtfully. 'But it will be a tragedy if you have to miss the wedding. I almost feel being maid of honour isn't good enough for you, and it ought to be you who marries us instead of the vicar. We'd never have found one another but for you, Birdy.'

Bobby smiled, appeased once more. It was hard to stay cross in the face of Topsy's irrepressible good nature. 'I sincerely hope I'll be there, whether or not I apply for postponement. The officer who interviewed me did say a lot of women are being put on deferred service after enrolment while they find places for them, so I might not have to go immediately. If I do get posted, I'll speak to whoever's in charge about whether it would be possible to have a day's leave. If I can be here, I swear nothing's going to keep me away.'

Chapter 16

They were interrupted by the telephone ringing out in the hall, and Bobby once again noticed the sly glint that so often meant trouble appear in Topsy's eye.

'I wonder who that could be,' Topsy said, with a rather affected nonchalance. 'Birdy, would you be an angel and answer it? I'm far too comfortable to move.'

Bobby narrowed one eye. 'What are you up to, Topsy?'

'Nothing, I swear!' Topsy said, her eyes wide with performative guilelessness. 'Please, before it rings off.'

Teddy was grinning too, and even stern Mrs Hobbes seemed to have a smirk at one corner of her mouth. Casting them a suspicious look, Bobby went out to answer the telephone.

'Hello?'

'Is that the future Mrs Atherton?' a familiar voice said.

Bobby clapped a hand to her mouth. 'Oh my goodness! Charlie!'

'I'd know that voice anywhere. The most beautiful girl in the world.'

Bobby laughed. 'I'm sorry, sir, but you must have the wrong number.'

Topsy appeared in the hall now, looking exceptionally pleased with herself.

'Isn't it a lovely surprise?' she said. 'Charlie said in his last letter that he was being posted on the 7th and I knew you'd be ever so worried about him, so I wired to tell him that if he was able to get to a telephone, he could reach you here at seven p.m. The sewing was only an excuse.'

Bobby beamed at her. 'Thank you, Topsy.'

It was such a rare treat to be able to speak to one another. Telephone calls for personal reasons were discouraged in wartime, and it wasn't easy for either one of them to get to a phone under ordinary circumstances. Even the work phone at Moorside, which Reg could occasionally and very reluctantly be persuaded to allow Bobby to use for a personal call, had now been disconnected for cost reasons. Just hearing Charlie's voice immediately cheered her spirits.

'I haven't got long,' he said. 'Bob, tell Topsy to make herself scarce and let me have you to myself.'

Topsy understood this without being told, however. She had already disappeared, closing the door behind her so they could have some privacy.

'Oh, it's so wonderful to hear your voice,' Bobby said. 'I've been thinking about you every minute, Charlie. How's Binbrook?'

'Pretty good so far. Getting used to the new routine. And I've a pal here already.'

'Who is it?'

'Young Bram. We're in the same unit. Perhaps we might even be assigned to the same crew.'

'I am glad.' Knowing the young friend Charlie had made at Ryland Moor was with him didn't make the danger any less, of course, but she at least knew he wasn't alone among all those new faces.

'Did you speak to your commanding officer yet?' she asked.

Charlie laughed. 'I hadn't been here an hour before I was hounding our poor Wingco, determined to thrust my official written request into his hand personally. Once I've got his letter of approval, I just have to wait until they can spare me some marriage leave and I'll be back to Silverdale before you can blink.'

'Are you sure you wouldn't prefer to wait, sweetheart?' Bobby asked, somewhat hesitantly. 'Things seem to be changing so quickly for us at the moment. In our lives, I mean.'

'All the more reason to do it as soon as possible. Something to hold on to while we can't be together.'

'Yes, I suppose so.'

'This isn't the enthusiastic bride I was hoping for, I have to say.' Charlie's words were light but Bobby could sense the worry underpinning them. 'Nothing's changed, has it? You can tell me if it has.'

'I do want to,' she said, in as reassuring a tone as she could muster. 'I just don't want it to be done all in a hurry, and have you go away right after. Everything lately feels like I'm on a speeding train, never knowing where I'm going or what the stops are. Do you know what I mean?'

'Sounds familiar.'

'I really don't want my wedding day to be that way. It would be nice to have a little room to breathe and get used to being married people together, don't you think? You know, a honeymoon – even if it was only a few days at Moorside.'

'I want that too, but I don't intend to wait any longer than I have to. The honeymoon can always come later.'

'Don't you worry, Charlie? Don't you ever think, what if there is no tomorrow?'

'Every time I get in the cockpit,' he said quietly. 'That's exactly why we ought to relish being alive and loving one another in the today. I need this, Bobby.'

He sounded so earnest, she didn't have the heart to press the matter.

'All right,' she said soothingly. 'But do try to get at least a few days' leave, won't you?'

'If I can,' Charlie said. 'Oh, I wanted to ask. Did you have any news about your Canadian friend?'

Bobby started. 'News about Ernie?'

'You said he was missing.'

'Oh. Yes,' she said, relieved. For a moment, she had worried some gossip about the two of them might have reached his ears. 'It was all right, thank God. He was injured and spent a few days in a field hospital, but the doctors say there won't be permanent damage.'

'I'm glad to hear it.'

Bobby paused, that moment on the ice once again recurring in her mind – with all its associated guilt.

'Charlie?'

'Yes?'

The sound of raucous laughter reminded her that other men were present, probably waiting for their turn to use the telephone, and the time she and Charlie had to speak was limited. The catharsis of confession would have to wait for another day.

'Never mind. I'll tell you when I see you.' She lowered her voice. 'Any other news?'

Bobby knew they needed to be careful about what they said. The call would be monitored to make sure no sensitive military information was being passed between airmen and civilians. But it didn't matter; Charlie understood her well enough. She wanted to know when he would start operational flying.

'It'll be soon,' he told her soberly.

'I thought there was to be four weeks' operational training before you were assigned front-line duties.'

'Could be half that or less, since I was flying Wellingtons during service training. There's a desperate shortage of pilots here.'

'Oh, Charlie.'

'I wish I could tell you not to worry, darling,' he said. 'I'm worried half to death myself, so I know I can't expect it to be any different for you. But even so...'

He fell silent. Bobby knew they hadn't been cut off. She could hear his breathing, slightly ragged, down the line. She waited until he was ready to speak again.

'Even so,' he said after a while, 'I feel... I feel *ready*, Bobby, you know? It's such a strange feeling, like there are two different Charlie Athertons. One is scared out of his wits that he'll make some dreadful mistake. Naturally I'm afraid to die – I'm sure any man who says differently is a liar – but if I were to cause the deaths of people I was responsible for, if I had to live with that… I think that's my biggest fear. But the other part of me… it's hard to describe, but I feel almost euphoric.' He sounded feverish, speaking low and fast. 'I mean it's strange, you know, to be so scared and yet have this feeling like I'm a kid at Christmas who can't wait to open his gifts. When I think about what I'm doing and how much it matters, I feel so proud to be part of it all – proud to think I'm doing it for you and Reggie and Mary, and those two little girls. Like I'm going out there to…' He laughed quietly. 'To save the world.'

'And so you are.'

Charlie laughed again. 'Oh Lord, I've been gibbering like a madman, haven't I? You could stop me, you know.'

'I don't want to stop you,' Bobby said softly. 'I'm incredibly proud of you, Charlie, and I love you so very much. Don't ever forget that.'

'Don't let me forget it. I want two letters a week minimum, Bob, and I want to know absolutely everything. Don't miss out a thing, d'you hear? I'll cry if you don't tell me what you had for breakfast every day, what colour knickers you're wearing and how much sugar you put in every cup of tea.'

Bobby smiled. 'Daft lad.'

'But you love me.'

'More than I ever did.'

A voice behind Charlie called out that his time on the telephone was up.

'Sorry, I have to go. There's a queue of lads behind me waiting for their turn,' Charlie said. 'I wish we had longer. Did you decide what to do, darling? About your call-up?'

Bobby was silent for a moment.

'Yes,' she said at last. 'Yes, I think I did.'

When she arrived home, Bobby went straight to her room and took up the postponement form that lay under Charlie's photograph. She tore it into two halves and put it in the dustbin.

Chapter 17

There was much to do, now Bobby had made up her mind where her duty lay. She spoke with Reg and Mary the next day to tell them what she had decided. Reg was disappointed, of course, but he accepted it as graciously as someone of his temperament was able to. Which was to say, he grumbled rather a lot but didn't try to change her mind.

'I distinctly remember you saying when you convinced me to give you this job – much against my better judgement – that one advantage to having a lass on my staff was that she couldn't be called up,' he muttered when Bobby broke the news.

'I'm sorry. I didn't know this would happen, did I? But now it has, I have to do what my conscience tells me is right.'

'Huh,' was the only answer she got.

Mary only looked rather wistful.

'Things are going to be so quiet without you, Charlie and the bairns,' she said. 'It won't feel like a home at all with no young folk around. Do come back whenever you can, Bobby. You'll be missed more than you know.'

Bobby pressed her hand. 'Whenever I can get leave, I'll be here.'

'What made up your mind in the end?'

'It was last night, when I spoke to Charlie on the telephone. He was talking in that strange new way he has, telling me how he felt about flying ops. How afraid he was, but how proud to do his duty.' She smiled. 'He said he felt like he was going out there to save the world.'

'Delusions of grandeur,' Reg muttered. 'The lad was always prone to them.' All the same, he looked proud.

'That was when I knew going was the right thing to do. Because Charlie's right, isn't he?' Bobby said. 'This is about saving the world. I am still worried about leaving my father. God knows I don't want to go away from the Dales, or leave my job, or both of you. But none of those things will matter if we don't win this thing, and I have to do my bit in spite of what I want. I know it's only admin, but that's a part of saving the world too.'

'Have you told your old man yet?' Reg asked.

'No. I'm going to wait until after the weekend. I doubt I'll be summoned for enrolment until at least Tuesday, and... well, there's something else I need to tell him that has to wait until Monday.' She looked up at him. 'You won't forget what I asked, will you, Reg? You'll hold off advertising for a new reporter until I've spoken to my friend?'

'Aye, I'll hold off. Just remember—'

'You can't make any promises. I know.'

—

In fact, it was Monday morning when Bobby received the official letter summoning her to enrol at the recruiting centre in Bradford in one week's time. She found it on the mat when she got home from Moorside.

She had known it was coming, but it still felt like a shock to see it there in black and white with the official RAF letterhead at the top.

> In accordance with the National Service (No. 2) Act, 1941, you are called upon to enrol in the Women's Auxiliary Air Force on Monday the 19th of January, 1942...

This was it, then. There could be no going back. In one week's time she would be enrolled officially as an airwoman, and her days as a civilian would be numbered. She would be leaving her home and her life in the Dales and going off to a new life serving her country. It hadn't felt quite real until she had seen it written down.

Bobby felt a shiver pass through her – someone walking over her grave, as her mam used to say. What was it? She certainly felt anxious about this strange new future, and worried for her father, but there was pride mixed in with the other emotions. For the first time, she understood what Charlie had meant when he had said he felt like he was going out there to save the world.

There was one other letter for her, but it wasn't in her sister's writing. Bobby had been thinking about Lilian all day, wondering if it was done yet. Lil had promised to send a telegram as soon as she was officially Mrs Scott.

A hope that really had no right to exist swelled in Bobby's chest: a foolish, futile hope, but one that pushed up within her, demanding to be heard. Could Lil have thought better of it? Perhaps she was even now on her way here, a single woman still. Bobby knew it was wrong to hope for such a thing when there was a baby coming, but she simply couldn't help it.

Once she had lit the fire and put a pan of lentil soup on to heat, she sat as close to the flames as she could and took out the letter that had arrived along with her enrolment notice. It was military, with the Army censor's stamp, but the service number didn't belong to either of her brothers. It couldn't be Don, who would still be in Bradford until tomorrow. Who else did she know in the Army?

That question was answered when Bobby tore open the envelope and skimmed to the signature: Captain George Parry. She had written to the girls' father the day after speaking to Jessie, following a rather solemn funeral for Hetty the hen in the garden at Moorside. The little girl had cried bitter tears for that poor old bird, Ace had whimpered his goodbye, and like a true housewife, Mary had looked more than a little wistful at the waste of the meat. It couldn't be helped though. Jessie would never eat chicken from her beloved pets, and besides, it might not be safe if the disease that had killed poor Hetty was still present. So the family had said goodbye and sat down to a post-funeral tea of brown bread and dripping before Bobby had gone home to write her letter to the captain.

In it, she had tried to explain as kindly as possible how his little daughter was feeling. It had been something to take her mind off her own worries, and made her feel she was helping in the only way she could: with words.

Choosing the right ones had been a challenge though. She didn't want to risk angering the man, who might well feel she was interfering. Nor did she want him to be hurt by what must seem like his daughter's alienation, even though Bobby had endeavoured to reassure him that both his children loved him very much and it was only the sudden change in her way of living that was distressing poor Jessie.

The captain must have written back to her almost immediately. Bobby read what he had written with some trepidation. Would he be angry? Resentful? Might she, in trying to help, actually have made things worse?

> Dear Miss Bancroft,
>
> I would like to thank you for taking the time to write, and to let me know how my little Jessie is bearing up. I can't tell you what my feelings were on reading about her sufferings. At first I felt pained that she should so dread a homecoming I had believed would be heartily welcomed. This was soon replaced by guilt, knowing my absence from her life these past few years had caused her to forget the love she once felt for her father.

Bobby found herself flinching. She had tried to soften the nature of Jessie's feelings to avoid giving too much pain, but clearly even this had been enough to wound. The captain was naturally formal in expressing himself, and it gave Bobby a pang to know that his carefully chosen words must mask more pain than he was able to fully give voice to.

She returned to the letter.

> *I confess I did feel aggrieved that a stranger should write to tell me she enjoyed the confidence of my children while I did not, and knew their feelings better than I ever could. But this was only the impetuous response of the moment. Once I had thought through what you told me, I saw that there was much sense in what you said. Jess has had a very little taste of life, and it is natural that what is recent should be uppermost in her thoughts and affections. When I had subdued my feelings, I found myself grateful that though their early life may have contained much tragedy, the last nine months have been joyful ones for my two little girls thanks to the kindness of their hosts and the healthy nature of their environment.*
>
> *To be entirely truthful, I confess that while of course I do not wish to tear the girls from the place they have come to see as home, I am afraid. When other feelings inspired by your letter had been overcome, that fear remained: that in the new life they have found, my little ones may no longer feel there is room for me. Were I a selfish man, this alone would have persuaded me to take them far away. Your faith in what you call my 'honourable nature' reminded me it is my daughters I must think of first, however, and so I am persuaded to seek a compromise.*
>
> *I must here ask for help. I have a little put aside with which to rent a small property – enough to live on for a few months while I seek civilian employment. If either you or Mr and Mrs Atherton were able to recommend an affordable cottage where my children and I could—*

Here Bobby was interrupted by the arrival of her father, home from his day's work. He was later than usual, which probably meant he had paid a visit to the Hart.

'Evening,' he grunted affably, evincing the good mood that a pint or two usually inspired. He nodded to the letter in her hand. 'Who's writing to thee this time? I swear you get more letters than Father Christmas, our Bobby. There's whispers in the village that Gil Capstick must be sweet on you, he's seen heading down here so often.'

'It's the captain,' Bobby told him with a smile. 'Captain Parry, I mean. Jess asked if I'd write to him for her. She's a little befuddled by the idea of living with her dad again once he's been discharged, poor soul. I really think she thought evacuation was going to be forever.'

Her father laughed. 'So you've been sticking your oar in, have you?'

'What is a journalist if not a professional oar-sticker-inner?'

'What's he say then?'

'He's planning to move here to Silverdale, at least until he's seen whether he'll be able to find work,' Bobby said, skimming the rest of the letter. 'I hope the family can stay nearby. Mary would be devastated if the children had to go back to London. So would Reg, although he'd never admit it.'

Her dad raised an eyebrow. 'Moving here, is he? That must've been a good letter you wrote.'

She smiled. 'No need to sound so surprised.'

'Oh. Here.' He fished in his coat pocket for an envelope. 'Speaking of young Gil, I bumped into t' lad on my way to the pub, getting ready to head down with this for you. Told him not to bother, I'd bring it back wi' me.'

Bobby looked at the telegram he handed her, and felt her spirits sink. It had to be from Lilian.

She tore it open, still with the tiny flame of hope that something might have happened to prevent her sister's marriage, but that quickly died when she saw the message.

It's done. Tell Dad. There Wednesday week. Lilian xxx

'What is it?' her dad asked.

'It's from our Lil,' Bobby said, endeavouring to keep any tremor from her voice. 'She's coming to visit next week.'

'Again? She's not long gone back. Happen the forces can't need lasses as badly as all that if they're giving them home leave every other week.' He sank into his easy chair by the fire and started unlacing his boots. 'Still, be good to see her, eh?'

'It will.' Bobby forced a smile. 'You get warm while I serve up this soup. Your slippers are on the fender. Then I need to talk to you.'

He frowned. 'What's up wi' thee? You sound off.'

'Have your soup first. I know you must be frozen. Afterwards we'll have a chat.'

Bobby took her time serving the soup. By the time she had sliced and buttered some bread, her dad was in a half-doze. She didn't summon him to the small dining table, but served the meal on a tray so he could eat it at the fireside. It was too cold to move far from the flames that evening.

'Dad?' she whispered, pressing his shoulder.

'Hmm?' He roused himself. 'Just resting my eyes.'

'Here. Eat this up, it'll warm you.'

'You not having any?' he asked as she took a seat opposite.

'I've a shift at the shelter later. I'll take mine in a Thermos.'

She watched as the spoon moved back and forth to his lips. His hand shook, as it always did – part of the legacy of his time in the trenches.

Bobby had made her choice and she was sure it was the right one, but still, she felt a worry verging on dread about how everything would work out at home. Reg had said he couldn't guarantee he would take Tony on, and even if he did, it was such a low wage. For a man of Tony's age – a man who would soon be the head of a family – accepting a salary of twenty shillings a week would be beyond humiliating. Yet Bobby knew Reg couldn't afford to pay more, when he was himself living on the subscription postal orders as they came in.

It was true that the job came with accommodation, but the draughty barn Bobby lived in with her father was hardly ideal for a young family. It could feel crowded even for two, the thin walls making it feel as though there was very little privacy, and it was so very cold in the autumn and winter months – even in the summer there was a perpetual chill in the air. When it was wet the roof leaked, and they were forever tripping over the pots and pans dotted around the place. When the wind blew, which it invariably did, each icy blast howled down the chimney and crept into aching bones. There was no plumbing, and the electric was unreliable. Too often during periods of bad weather, they had to sit in the dark for days until a man could get to them from Skipton to fix it.

And then there was Tony. Her dad had long despised the man, whose reputation as a ladykiller had been well-known in the pubs of their home town, and Tony Scott with his ever-fragile *amour propre* was not the sort of person who would relish sharing another man's home. Both men would likely resent having to share the title of head of the household. Supposing Tony decided his family would be better off in Liverpool, where higher wages were to be had, in spite of the bombings? Lilian would be so isolated there, and so afraid for her little one.

Still, the idea of her dad being left alone frightened Bobby more than any of the alternatives. No housekeeper could under-stand him the way his daughters did – not even Mary could do that. Bobby knew he would feel humiliated at the idea of anyone outside the family knowing how he passed his nights – the tears and the screams – or how he struggled to resist the temptations of the bottle. Feelings of humiliation and worth-lessness had always been where the most danger lay.

Bobby had seen for herself the consequences of leaving her dad to dwell in the dark places in his head. Her father needed someone who knew how to help him, Lilian and her baby needed a home where they'd be safe from danger, and Tony needed a job. As imperfect as it was, this was the only solution that would give everyone what they required.

Chapter 18

When her father had finished eating, Bobby took his bowl to the sink and sat back down again.

'Did you see anyone you knew at the pub?' she asked, as a way of opening the conversation.

'Ran into Pete.'

'Pete Dixon?'

Her dad's friendship with that local ne'er-do-well had largely petered out since he had started working for Topsy, but Bobby always worried Pete would try to drag her father into some fresh trouble.

'Aye. Gave him an earful about them rabbit traps I found up by t' lake last week.'

'What did he say?'

Rob shrugged. 'Just laughed and bought us a pint. Hard to be angry wi' t' man for long. Still, he knows full well I'll smash 'em up soon as he puts 'em down. Don't know why he wastes his time poaching on my patch.'

'Don't let him talk you into anything, will you? I know what he's like.'

'I know which side my bread's buttered, don't worry. I'll not chuck a good job away for Pete Dixon's benefit.'

'Glad to hear it.'

Bobby hesitated, wondering how to broach the tricky topic of her sister and Tony.

'It'll be nice to see our Lil, won't it?' she said after a moment.

'Aye, always nice to have the pair of you at home,' her dad said with a vague smile.

The wireless was on in the background. Bobby went to turn it off. The swing music it was playing didn't feel appropriate to what she was about to say.

'Dad... Lil wanted me to tell you that, um, she won't be alone when she visits,' she said when she had taken her seat again.

He frowned. 'Who's she bringing? One of her girlfriends from down south?'

'No. An old friend from Bradford.'

'She put all that in a telegram? That must've cost her a few bob.'

'Actually she told me before. I was just waiting to pass it on until some things had been sorted out.' Bobby took out the telegram and smoothed it on her knee. 'It's... Tony Scott. You remember him, from when I worked at the *Courier*?'

Her dad stared at her. 'Scott? What on earth would she want to bring him here for?'

'Look, I know you won't like this but stay calm, please.'

His brow knit. 'What's to stay calm about, Bobby?'

'It's just that Tony and Lil, they've sort of been... walking out,' she murmured. 'That was why it ended between Lil and Lieutenant Cartwright.'

Rob looked too dazed to be angry.

'Walking out?' he repeated.

'It began last year, when Lil had some home leave. I don't think they meant it to be serious, but she and Tony quickly found themselves getting fond of each other.'

He laughed in disbelief. 'Fond? Of that idle bugger?'

The news seemed to be sinking in now as the initial shock wore off. Rob stood up and started pacing the floor. Bobby winced, knowing there was worse to come.

'You're telling me that worthless bastard has got the bloody... *presumption* to go after my daughter?' he demanded. 'With his reputation? If I was still in town he'd never have dared.'

'This isn't some trivial fling, Dad. He's been courting her – seriously courting.'

'Are you joking? Men like him don't court, whatever promises they might make. There's only one thing they go after a lass for. I can't believe your sister's as green as that at her age.'

He took off his cloth cap and tossed it away. Bobby retrieved it and quietly hung it over the mantelpiece. Perhaps it was best to let him get all this out of his system before she broke the next lot of bad news.

'Honestly, I really think he's changed,' Bobby said, resting a hand on her dad's shoulder. He shook it off impatiently.

'He won't change. Not that one. No doubt he's "seriously courting" four or five other lasses an' all.' He stopped pacing and turned to her. 'Here, bring us a pen and a bit of paper.'

'To do what?'

'I'm going to write to her, aren't I? If you've not bothered to tell her the sort of man this worthless friend of yours is, it's down to me. I am still her father, for all that she's over twenty-one.'

'What would you say?'

'For a start, I'll tell her it's over my dead body she brings that nowt across my threshold. She can damn well understand it's him or me.'

'Dad. Sit down, please,' Bobby said soothingly. 'Look, you can't… well, there's more.'

He refused to be guided back to his chair. 'More? What else?'

'Won't you sit down?'

'Say what you've got to say, Bobby.' His expression had darkened, as if he had guessed what she was about to tell him. 'You're not going to… He didn't…'

'They're married,' Bobby said simply. 'Today, at the registry. That was what the telegram was for. Lil's Mrs Scott now.'

He just stood staring at her. Then he sank back into his seat.

'Mrs Scott!' he repeated, as if he could hardly believe the words.

'I'm sorry. I know you ought to have been told, but she is over twenty-one, and, well…' Bobby flushed. 'The wedding had to happen. I think you've guessed why. But Tony does love her, he says, and he's promised to take care of her and… and anyone else who makes an appearance. He wouldn't have been my first choice either, but that's up to Lil, isn't it? He really isn't half the rogue you think he is.'

Her dad just stared with glazed eyes. Judging it best to give him a moment to absorb the news, Bobby stood up and filled the kettle to heat water for the washing-up. She spotted her dad's shotgun propped by the door and went to put it away.

'Leave it,' her dad murmured.

'I was going to put it in the surgery out of the way.'

'I said leave it.' He turned his gaze on her, his face livid now – whether with fear, anger or a combination of the two, she couldn't tell. 'This is your doing, Bobby.'

She blinked. 'Me?'

'He was your mate, wasn't he? You introduced the pair of them. A man like that, you should've done everything you could to keep your sister away from him. Instead you're encouraging him with one hand and keeping the whole thing behind my back with the other.' He stood up and turned away from her. 'Your own sister.'

Bobby stared at him. 'You're seriously going to blame me for this?'

'Without your mam around, I'd have thought you girls would take better care of each other, that's all.'

With a sudden movement he punched the back of his chair, making Bobby flinch.

Her dad had never been violent within the family. Not even to punish her brothers, who as children had been given their spankings by their mam. But her dad's black tempers, rare but unsoothable, were almost as frightening as any threat of physical violence.

'Tony bloody Scott!' he said, in a voice strangled with grief and rage. 'She's to be kept on a newspaperman's salary, is she, with a bairn to feed and clothe?' He laughed, pressing his head between his hands. 'Scott'll have spent his wage on other women before she gets a penny out of him in housekeeping. That's if he hangs around. Marriage don't mean much to men like that.'

Bobby flushed. 'Actually, Tony's not working for the paper any more.'

Her dad turned to glare at her. 'Not on the paper? What's he doing then?'

'Nothing. He's looking for a job.'

'Bloody hell, Bobby!' He spun away from her, his whole body shaking. 'I'll not have that man coming here – nor her either. You write and tell her. Neither one of them is welcome in my house.'

Bobby laughed. '*Your* house? Don't I live here too?'

'I'm head of it, aren't I?'

'But it's me that makes it a home.' She glared at him. 'You've got no idea, have you, Dad? No idea how much time I spend scrubbing and boiling before work while you're still in bed, to make this place habitable for you. No idea how often Lil and I gave up our meat and butter rations when we were all living in Bradford so you and Jake could have extra. How many hours we spent queueing to get you what was going short, on top of working so we could bring money into the house – money that went straight down your throat.'

Rob flushed deeply. 'You'd no cause to bring that up.'

'You need to know. It's about bloody time you did.'

'Watch your damn language.'

'I will not. I've spent enough of my life watching what I say.' She shook her head. 'Men always are too blind to see all that women do for them. Without us, you'd have no homes to be the heads of. And you'd really deny our Lilian this house, after everything she's done for you?' Bobby turned away from him, her cheeks on fire with anger and hurt. 'Well if it's your house then you can bar the door to me too, because I won't set foot in any home where my sister isn't welcome.'

'You knew,' her dad persisted, although there was a quaver in his voice now, as if he was close to tears. 'Knew all this time, and did nowt to stop it. How could you have let this happen, Bobby?'

'It's nothing to do with me! Lilian's an adult, isn't she?'

'You could have told me.' His glance rested briefly on the shotgun. 'I'd have put a stop to it quick enough.'

'You could've put a stop to it before it happened, if you'd only thought about how your actions might affect other people,' Bobby snapped, the words falling out of her mouth before she could stop them.

He frowned. 'What's that supposed to mean?'

'It was because of you, Dad! The meat raffling, with Pete Dixon. Tony found out about it and was going to run a story, but he pulled it when he found out you were involved. For Lil's sake.'

'You what?'

'That was why Lil started walking out with him – sort of a thank you. And then one thing led to another, and now…' Her voice sank to a whisper. 'Now this.'

Rob stood for a long time in dumbfounded silence, different emotions flickering over his face. His eyes fell once more on the shotgun in the corner, and Bobby went to take it up. He didn't stop her this time. She took it to the adjoining room – the one that had been Charlie's veterinary surgery in civilian life – and locked it away in the cupboard, in case he should get any ideas.

She stopped in the room for a moment, resting her elbows on Charlie's examination table and propping her head on her palms. The fight had gone out of her now, and she felt defeated and inexpressibly weary. Sobs shook her, but no tears went with them. Her grief fell from her in dry gasps.

Why had she said that? She had never meant to. Over and over she had reminded herself that Lilian's situation wasn't her father's fault; that he could never have foreseen this outcome. But there had still been that little flame of anger, buried deep inside. When he had accused her, said it was all her fault, it had burst from her in a sudden explosion.

And had guilt, too, eased its way? Because Bobby did feel responsible. For all her reminders to herself that Lilian was an adult who could make her own choices, the natural urge to protect her sister couldn't help but make her feel that she had betrayed Lil in some way when she had allowed her to get close to Tony Scott.

Oh God. What had she done?

When Bobby had got herself under control, she went back into the parlour. Her dad was once more sitting in his chair, his expression blank. He didn't even look up when she entered the room. He looked like he often did when he'd drunk too much: far away in the past, unable to engage with the world around him.

'Dad, I'm sorry,' she whispered. 'I shouldn't have told you that. None of this is your fault. You couldn't have seen it coming.'

He didn't answer her.

'Dad?'

Rob rubbed his head, and forced his vacant gaze to focus on her. 'Well. Happen I said a few things I shouldn't have an' all.'

'I'm so sorry. Please let me take it back.' She approached to take his hand, which rested limply in hers. 'I love you. So does Lil – that's why she went out with Tony. But it was her choice, and I do believe she and Tony are fond of each other despite how things started. At the very least, he seems determined to put things right as best he can. We shouldn't grieve for her.'

'There's a bairn coming then?'

Bobby allowed herself a small smile. 'Yes. You're to be a grandfather again.'

She had hoped this might elicit some sort of positive response, but he only looked blank. Bobby sank back into her seat.

'I have to go,' she said quietly. 'To the WAAF. I'm sorry, Dad.'

'Aye, well.' His voice was flat; devoid of emotion. 'Don't suppose it matters much now.'

'Please don't talk like that.' She leant forward to take his hands. 'You didn't mean it, did you? About denying Lil the house?'

'I… No. I reckon not.' He blinked hard, as if to force himself to remain present. 'You were always good girls. It's him. That Scott.'

'But like it or not, Tony is Lil's husband. And she's lucky, in a lot of ways. You wouldn't want her to have to give the baby away, would you?'

He sighed. 'No. I'd never want that.'

'Dad, if I was able to arrange things so that Lil could stay here with you – I mean, with Tony, and the baby when it comes – how would you feel about that?'

'Don't seem to be able to feel owt right this minute.' Rob rubbed his face. 'Fetch us a drink, will you, our Bobby?'

She bowed her head. 'I thought you might ask.'

'Special occasion, isn't it?' He laughed harshly. 'Wetting the baby's head. Have one yourself, why don't you?'

'Tonight, I think I will.'

She went to unlock the surgery cupboard where she kept the potato peel spirit she administered to chase away his nightmares, poured them both a generous measure and took them back to the parlour. They drank in silence, not meeting each other's eyes.

Chapter 19

Over the days that followed, Bobby tried to be at home as much as possible. She exchanged shifts with the two other Silverdale air-raid wardens, pleading a cold – not exactly a fib, since conditions in the cow house at this time of year invariably meant she was harbouring sniffles.

She was so afraid that her outburst the day she had told her dad the real reason Lil had become involved with Tony Scott would send him straight to the bottom of a bottle. She didn't dare to take her eyes off him, knowing that when he was craving spirits, he would find a way to get them.

Bobby made sure she was at the cow house every day when her father arrived home, and watched carefully to see if there were any telltale humps under his coat that suggested he had been buying the liquorice-scented spirit he got from Pete Dixon. She checked the outhouse for concealed bottles, and made sure there was no sign of tampering with the locked cupboard in Charlie's surgery where she kept the stuff she bought for him from Don.

There was no evidence her dad had tried to get access to strong alcohol behind her back, however, which was some relief. He did ask for a drink in the evening more often than usual – ever since he had started working again, the only time he had seemed to need one had been after a nightmare, but now he frequently had two or even three generous measures before bed. But he submitted tamely when Bobby took the bottle away, and didn't ask for more. At his worst, he would have drunk many times that amount – as much as it took to send him into a stupor black enough for no bad memories to permeate.

Nevertheless, the atmosphere in the cottage was heavy with words said that couldn't be taken back. Bobby was grateful her dad had his job to occupy him during the day, when the temptation to drink alone might have been too strong to resist, and made sure she was always there in the evenings. Still, many was the time as she sat opposite her father while he ate the food she had prepared for him in silence, avoiding her eye, that she longed for the warmth of the farmhouse across the way, or a cosy evening sewing beside Topsy. Even a shift in the freezing ARP hut would have been welcome if it spared her the oppressive atmosphere of home.

'I'm so sick of walking on eggshells around him,' she grumbled to Mary a week later, in the kitchen at Moorside as she helped with the washing-up.

It was the 19th of January, the day Bobby had been summoned to go back to Bradford for enrolment in the WAAF. Her appointment was relatively early, so she had promised Reg she would be back as soon as she could to fit in at least a few hours' work – although she was planning to pay a short visit to Lilian at the Scotts' home too. In fact it was her new brother-in-law she needed to speak to, but she was keen to see how the newlyweds were getting on in their married life before they visited here in two days' time.

Mary had ordered her to drop in to Moorside for breakfast before leaving, and Reg had offered to take her to the bus stop in Charlie's horse-drawn trap. Their pony Boxer needed the exercise, Reg said, after weeks of being trapped in his stable by the weather, but Bobby could sense Reg was anxious to do her a favour.

Mary laughed. 'Walking on eggshells, is it? I know it well. Good practice for marriage, Bobby.'

'Oh Lord, I hope not. I'd like to think Charlie was a different sort, but who knows what his nerves will be like when we come out of this? I couldn't bear to live my whole life that way.'

'If they ever realised how we put ourselves to one side to keep them happy, happen our menfolk would stop acting like beneficent emperors when they dole out our little bit of housekeeping,' Mary observed. 'We've ourselves to blame, I suppose, for trying to keep all we do for them invisible. I'm sure they think their home comforts are conjured by the pixies.'

'My dad's no different from Reg in that respect. I suppose they're both men of their time.'

'Is your father often this way?'

'He can be distant when his spirits are depressed,' Bobby said. 'I can't get through to him at all at the moment. The only time he opens his mouth, it's to ask me to bring him his tea or a— or for something else he wants. No conversation about work or the wireless, or any of the things we'd normally talk about.'

'Hmm. Sulking, is he?' Mary said, pursing her lips. 'I've always said a man is just another bairn in the house.'

'I don't think it's that. He isn't angry with me — at least, I don't think so. He's just gone off somewhere in his head. I always worry when he gets like that.' Bobby sighed. 'And it's my fault. I said something I shouldn't have — told him a home truth he was better off for not knowing. Now I feel like I'm perpetually tiptoeing around him, trying not to make his mood any worse. I know he hates feeling like I'm watching him, but I have to when he's like this.'

Mary handed her the pan she'd just washed to dry. 'What was it you told him?'

'Nothing he'd like me to share, I'm certain. But I oughtn't to have said it. I was cross and it slipped out.'

'There's only so far we can bottle things up for the comfort of men before it all comes fizzing out like shaken lemonade,' Mary said. 'It's not good for the nerves, trying to keep too much in. We need to know when to coddle and when to stand up to them, and sometimes our weary bodies make that decision for us regardless of what our brain thinks we ought to do.'

'I suppose that's true.' Bobby bent to put the pan away in the cupboard. 'I have been living on increasingly frayed nerves since Christmas.'

'Are there big objections to this lad of your sister's then?'

'Not *big* objections,' Bobby said slowly. 'Tony's always been wayward, and not overly fond of hard work. Has an eye for a pretty girl. But he isn't vicious or violent.'

Mary smiled. 'Sounds like what they used to say about Charlie. The love of a good woman soon settled him. Lads will go through that wild-oat phase.'

'Mmm. Tony's turned thirty so I'd say it was high time his wild oats were all sown.'

'Heard from him, have you? Our Charlie, I mean.'

Bobby smiled wanly. 'Yes, this morning.'

'I'm assuming from your expression it wasn't good news.'

'There was some good news. His CO has approved his application to marry, although he's unlikely to get leave to do it until spring. Once I know when and where I'll be posted, we might finally be able to set a date.'

'Then why the sad little smile?'

Bobby sighed. 'I think sad little smiles are all I'm going to have in me until I get used to the idea of him flying ops. Every minute, I have to think about him up there. I feel so nervy and restless, like I can't concentrate on anything knowing he's in danger. Do you think it'll ever get easier?'

'I wish I knew, my love,' Mary said, giving her arm a squeeze. 'I've been worried to bits myself, so I'm afraid I don't have many words of comfort. Did he mention his missions? He never says a word about them to me.'

'There's not much he's allowed to say, but he did tell me his squadron lost some men recently. He sounded cut up about it.'

'He'd do better not to tell you about things like that. You'll be worrying enough as it is.'

'No, I want to know,' Bobby said quietly as she ran her tea towel over the plate Mary handed her. 'I'd hate him to feel he had to keep things from me. It would only push us apart if he couldn't talk to me about what was happening out there when it's such a big part of his life.'

'Your sister ought to count herself lucky,' Mary observed. 'Few enough young wives these days get to hang on to their husbands. Has he not been called up, this lad she's married?'

'He can't be. Asthma.'

Mary glanced at her. 'And what's your opinion of him as a husband?'

'I do think he isn't entirely hopeless,' Bobby said. 'My dad had him marked down as a wolf bent on the seduction of innocent girls a long time ago though. It's going to be hard work persuading him differently. I hope it doesn't end in a row when Tony and my sister come on Wednesday.'

Mary arched an eyebrow. 'They must've got wed quick. It wasn't so long ago you told me she had another man's ring on her finger.'

Bobby didn't look at her. 'Yes.'

'Ah well, it's nowt new,' Mary said gently. 'It's nature, that's all, and many a young girl has to find that out the hard way. I can't say how it is in the city, but out here, folk are always generous when it comes to doing their sums on behalf of newlyweds.'

Bobby summoned a smile. 'Thanks, Mary.'

Reg's voice called to them from the hall.

'You coming then, lass? Bus is in half an hour. Sooner you go, sooner you can be back at your desk.'

Mary laughed. 'Always it's that ruddy magazine with him.' She wiped damp hands on her pinny so she could give Bobby a hug. 'Well, off you go. And for what it's worth, I do think you're right to do what you're doing – you and Charlie both. I'm right proud of the pair of you.'

–

A couple of hours later, Bobby was once more at the recruiting centre in Bradford for her enrolment. The whole thing took a little under two hours, most of which she spent sitting on her bottom with a lot of other women waiting to be called into various rooms. While they waited, an NCO filled in forms with details such as hat and shoe sizes, waist measurement and next of kin.

It all felt rather unremarkable as the starting point for a new life, with the exception of the oath they had to take on being sworn in. Only when swearing loyalty to her country did Bobby feel a touch of the sentiments Charlie had expressed. It didn't feel quite like saving the world just yet, but it meant she now belonged to the armed forces. Miss Bancroft the reporter had to be wrapped in cotton wool and put to one side – not, she hoped, forever, but at least for the time being – to make way for Aircraftwoman Bancroft the WAAF. It was a title that was going to take some getting used to.

Bobby looked around the other women to see if she could spot the person she had met the day of her medical, Carol Boyes. There was no sign of her, however. Bobby hadn't been able to decide whether she and Carol were destined to be friends if they found themselves together again, but the woman's down-to-earth presence had been reassuring. She would have liked to have seen her once more.

After being sworn in, Bobby was summoned to another room.

'You're to be placed on deferred service for eleven weeks until a place becomes vacant,' the WAAF corporal told her when all the required paperwork had been signed. 'You'll be expected at your station on Monday the 6th of April. Here's your certificate of enrolment.'

Bobby stared at the document she was handed, which bore her new rank of ACW/2 – Aircraftwoman Second Class. It felt so odd to see her name sitting beside it.

'Any questions, make them quick,' the corporal said. 'We've a lot more to get through.'

They ought to put that on the door outside, Bobby thought dryly. She must have heard that phrase a dozen times in the hours she'd spent at this place.

'Do you know where I'm to be sent?' she asked. The enrolment certificate bore the date she would be required to report for training, but nothing about where she would be going.

The woman glanced at the paperwork in front of her. 'Says in your notes you wanted to stay close to home.'

Bobby felt hope burgeon within her. 'Why, is there a place for me near home?'

'Yes, you're lucky. There's accommodation for WAAF recruits being installed at Ryland Moor, to be attached to the RAF training school there. You'll be sent further details when you're summoned to report for service.'

'Ryland Moor!'

The corporal looked up. 'Is that a problem?'

'No. Sorry. That's where my fiancé did his service flight training, that's all. I didn't realise they offered training to WAAFs too.'

The woman flashed her a wry smile. 'Neither did they, until they were told to be ready to receive an initial cohort of forty by the end of March. We're having a devil of a job finding places for everyone. You might find conditions are spartan, but it does mean you'll be able to have the odd bit of home leave during your six-week basic training period.' The corporal placed Bobby's papers in a folder. 'If you have any further questions they'll have to wait, I'm afraid. I have to move on or we'll never get through everyone.'

'Yes. Thank you.' Bobby flashed the young corporal a grateful smile. In all her dealings with the military, this was the first time anyone had spared her the time to actually answer some of her questions. She pocketed her certificate of enrolment and the travel warrant she had been given and left.

Chapter 20

After she left the recruiting centre, Bobby jumped on a tram to East Bowling, where the Scotts lived – if not quite with a song in her heart then at least with a lightness of spirits she hadn't been able to feel since the day she had learned she was to be called up.

It was the best she could hope for. For her training period, at least, she would be within easy distance of Silverdale. That meant she could spend all her leave there, even if she only had a pass out for a few hours.

And she could stay in the Dales. Bobby hadn't realised how much the thought of leaving the stark and magnificent fells, and the terse but generous-natured folk who lived among them, had been weighing on her heart. The fells felt like a bridge, somehow, between this unasked-for new life and the old one she was leaving so reluctantly behind.

She would feel closer to Charlie too. Ryland Moor had been where he trained and now she could see it from the inside. Knowing something of his routine, having mutual acquaintances not only in the civilian world of Silverdale but in the Air Force, would go a long way to closing that distance Bobby was always afraid might grow between them.

She would be at home for Topsy's wedding as well. Bobby would have hated to miss seeing Topsy and Teddy finally tie the knot after everything she had done to help them reach their happy ending.

When the tram halted, she almost skipped off it.

Bobby walked to the Scotts' grimy terraced house and rapped the door knocker. Mrs Scott – or Mrs Scott Senior, as Bobby supposed she ought to call her now – answered a moment later. She was wearing the bottle-green uniform of the Women's Voluntary Service, hat on and coat over her shoulders as if preparing to go out. She was unsmiling as ever while she smoked a cigarette.

'You're the other one,' she said, on looking Bobby up and down. She didn't remove her cigarette, which perched precariously at one side of her mouth.

Bobby hadn't exactly expected her sister's new mother-in-law to roll out the welcome mat, but a 'good afternoon' might have been nice.

'Um, yes,' she said. 'Hello again.'

'Come up from t' country, have you?'

'That's right. Is my sister at home?'

'In the kitchen,' Mrs Scott said, jerking her head in that direction as she buttoned up her coat. 'Mind you take your shoes off. I'll noan have mud and cow muck smeared all over my clean carpets.'

Without another word she marched out of the house, brushing Bobby aside as she did so.

Bobby assumed this was as much of an invitation to come in as she could expect and entered the dark little house, closing the door behind.

The carpets didn't look particularly clean to her. They were faded and threadbare, yellow in places from decades of tobacco smoke. Still, not wishing to arouse Mrs Scott's ire, Bobby removed her shoes as instructed.

It was less than a fortnight since she had last seen Lilian, but when she sought out her sister in the kitchen, Bobby was shocked to see the change in her. Lil looked harassed and ill-kempt, her normally carefully styled hair shoved untidily under a headscarf. She had no make-up on, which emphasised her pallor and the dark circles under her eyes. When Bobby came in, she was on her knees sweeping out the fire grate.

'Should you be doing that in your condition?' Bobby asked.

'Bobby.' Lilian put one hand against the small of her back, wincing as she knelt upright. 'I thought I was dreaming when I heard you talking to the Wicked Witch of the West. Isn't my new mama a delight?'

Bobby smiled, pleased to hear that her sister's sense of humour hadn't been quashed by this spartan new life. 'Don't ask me. I'm only a humble country peasant girl covered in cow muck, apparently, and hardly worthy of an opinion.'

'I see you've been given the traditional warm Scott welcome.' With an effort, Lilian got to her feet. 'I won't hug you, since I'm covered in cinders. Has she gone?'

'Yes, she went out as I came in.'

'Thank the Lord. Then I can have a rest.'

Lilian went to a cupboard and took out a bottle of Wincarnis. After pouring a generous glass of the syrupy, slightly meaty-smelling tonic wine, she threw herself into a nearby chair.

'Honestly, I think the only reason she agreed Tony and I could live here was slave labour,' she told Bobby, drinking her tonic wine down in one gulp. 'At first she was absolutely raging about the baby, Tony says. Determined I'd done it on purpose to trap her precious boy into marriage.'

Bobby smiled dryly. 'Right. Because he's such a catch.'

'Oh, please don't say that,' Lilian murmured, rubbing her temples.

'Sorry.' Bobby went to crouch by her sister. 'It was supposed to be a joke. Perhaps it was in rather poor taste.'

'Well, Mother Scott soon changed her tune when she realised me being here meant she never needed to lift a finger.' Lilian flopped back in her chair. 'I don't think I've stopped scrubbing since we signed the marriage register, except for the hour a day she spends at the WVS centre, gossiping when she's supposed to be rolling bandages.'

'How's married life, Lil?'

'Goodness knows. I'd hardly call skivvying for the evil mother-in-law while sharing a camp bed in Tony's brother's room a taste of married life.'

Lilian swallowed a sob, and Bobby took her hand.

'There has to be more to it than this, Bob,' she whispered. 'Three days in and I'm exhausted, and the baby's not even here yet.'

'Things will get better.'

'They have to.' She dabbed at her damp cheeks with a duster. 'I feel like we've skipped over the courtship and landed straight in domestic hell. The few dates we had weren't enough to really get to know one another. But I do so want it to work, for the baby's sake.'

'It's only been a few days.'

'I know,' Lil said with a sigh. 'I suppose it's been rather a rude awakening. Perhaps I could fall in love with Tony, if we only had a little time for us. But there isn't a moment in the day where it's just me and him.'

'Couldn't you go out dancing, or to the pictures?' Bobby asked. 'Just because the courtship didn't happen before you were married doesn't mean it needs to be dispensed with completely. You're still two young people, and you really ought to be making the most of the time you've got together before the baby comes.'

'I'm too exhausted for dance halls after scrubbing all day,' Lil said with a sigh. 'Dancing was all very well when I was a single, fun-loving young Wren, but it isn't for expectant housewives. Besides, we really ought to be saving our money while Tony's out of a job.'

'I'm sure Tony can spare a few bob to take you out to a film. If he can afford fags and beer, he can afford a couple of ninepenny seats at the Majestic.'

'Perhaps. But his mam would humph so about it, while we're living here rent-free.'

Bobby glanced at the bucket of cinders her sister had raked out of the fireplace. 'Looks like you're more than paying your rent in labour.'

'Mmm. She doesn't think so. Still, she hasn't realised I've been helping myself to a salary out of her precious Wincarnis yet.' Lilian sat up straight. 'What are you here for anyhow? You didn't forget we're coming to you the day after tomorrow?'

'Government summons again,' Bobby said with a shrug. 'I got called to enrol in the WAAF. I'm to be placed on deferred service and drafted the 6th of April.'

'You made up your mind against applying for postponement then?'

Bobby sighed. 'I'm sorry, Lil. I had to.'

Lilian slid down in the chair and rested a hand on her swelling stomach, clearly visible under her housecoat today in the absence of corsets.

'I knew you would,' she said with a wistful smile. 'I know how that nagging conscience of yours works, Bobby.'

'I'll be close to home, for my training at least.' Bobby gave her sister's hand a reassuring press. 'Only ten miles from Dad in Silverdale, and a train ride from Skipton to you. We'll be closer to each other than we are now – for as long as you're in Bradford anyway.'

'You always do the right thing, don't you?' Lilian said dreamily. 'You'd think, being twins, I'd be more like you.' She glanced down at her stomach. 'I wish I was, for my own sake.'

'I don't always do the right thing.' Bobby lowered her gaze. 'I didn't do the right thing the other day. Did you get any letter from Dad?'

Lil sat up straighter. 'No. Have you told him?'

'I told him more than I meant to. I got cross when he said some things and I…' She swallowed. 'I've been such an idiot, Lil.'

'What did you tell him?'

'I told him that you and Tony had been walking out. I told him you were married. He worked out for himself why. And I told him… why you'd started walking out in the first place.'

'Oh Bobby, you didn't!'

'I'm so sorry. He was angry, and he said some things that hurt me. Said it was all my fault for letting you get close to Tony, and keeping it a secret from him. I was so upset that it slipped out before I could stop it.'

'How did he take it?'

'I think I can safely say, not well,' Bobby muttered. 'He was in a blind rage when I told him about you and Tony walking out, and by the time I broke the news of the marriage and the baby, I was getting seriously worried about the way he kept looking at his shotgun. Then when I said it was for his sake you'd started seeing Tony, he just went sort of… numb. He's been like that ever since.'

'Has he…'

'Sometimes, in the evenings. No more than three. But he hasn't tried to get any more, or drunk himself into a stupor.'

'Then perhaps he's not too bad.'

'I don't know. He's not drinking heavily – yet – but I can tell he's far from settled in his mind.'

'Is he very angry with me?' Lilian whispered.

'I think he's mostly angry with himself, after what I told him. With Tony a close second.'

'Whatever are we going to do about him when you have to go? Mary can't watch him constantly. She's got her hands full in her own home. Besides, he isn't her responsibility, kind as I know she is.' Lilian rubbed her head. 'I don't suppose he'd agree to us hiring a housekeeper, even if we could afford it. He wouldn't live with a stranger.'

'I did have one idea.' Bobby stood up so she could rest a hand on her sister's shoulder. 'Supposing I could help Tony into a job near Dad? You two could live with him in the cow house.'

Lil blinked. 'The cow house?'

'Yes. I know it's cold and small and a far cry from perfect as a family home, but it has to be better than this place,' Bobby said, glancing around the cramped, dingy little kitchen. 'Or Liverpool, with bombing raids every other night. Don't you think so?'

'Well, I suppose so, but—'

'And once the baby's older, you might be able to earn a bit on the side too,' Bobby went on, warming to her theme. 'I'm sure Mary would mind the baby if you needed to go out to work a few hours a day. I don't like to presume too much on favours from her and Reg, but she adores little ones.'

'What is there for women to do out there? Charring?' Lil said, curling her lip.

Bobby shrugged. 'Better to get paid for it than stay here doing it for nowt, isn't it? If you could only bring in a little extra then it might be enough to rent a more comfortable cottage, as long as Dad's still able to work and Tony can hang on to a job. I'll help out too.'

Lilian placed a palm on her forehead. 'We're getting ahead of ourselves, Bobby. I can't keep a family on a few bob a week charring, and it'll be a year or more until I can leave the baby. What's Tony going to do? He's the one who'll have to support us.'

'Isn't it obvious? He'll do my job, over at *The Tyke*.'

Lilian blinked at her. 'Your job? Aren't you doing it?'

'I'll be off in April, won't I? For who knows how long – years perhaps. Reg was going to advertise for a boy, but I asked if he'd hold off until I'd spoken to Tony.'

'A quid a week though, Bobby. It's no wage for the head of a family.'

'Yes, but that includes the cottage,' Bobby reminded her. 'Mary will be around to help with the baby, and you'll be there for Dad and him for you. I know it isn't perfect, but I do think it's the best answer.'

Lilian still looked dazed.

'Reg has really said he'll give this job to Tony?' she asked. 'Does he know him?'

'Well, he knows of him,' Bobby admitted. 'But I spoke up in Tony's favour, and Don's written him a glowing reference. Reg said he couldn't promise anything, but he's soft-hearted. I do think if Tony applies, he's got a good chance.'

A glimmer of light appeared in Lilian's eyes as she caught a little of Bobby's enthusiasm.

'It isn't a bad plan,' she admitted. 'Tony thinks he can earn forty or fifty bob a week in the shipyards, but rent isn't cheap in Liverpool, and we might need to hire help while the baby's small. We could be not much worse off at the end of the day.'

'Where is Tony?' Bobby asked. 'I'd like to talk to him before the pair of you come on Wednesday, and persuade him he ought to apply. He can speak to Reg while he's there.'

Lilian rolled her eyes. 'He's out "job-hunting". Which means he's at the pub around the corner, sobbing over the Situations Vacant page.'

'Right. I'll go find him.'

'Be gentle, OK?' Lilian said, standing up. 'If he thinks you're trying to do him a favour offering him a quid-a-week job – one a woman's been doing as well – he'll go all stuffy and refuse to consider it.'

'Oh, don't worry. I've known Tony Scott a long time. He'll always go for a distressed damsel act,' Bobby said as she fastened her coat. 'Leave him to me.'

Chapter 21

Bobby found Tony in the George pub, just as Lilian had said. He was sitting glumly in the public bar, head resting on his palms. In front of him was an almost-finished pint, a newspaper and an overflowing ashtray that suggested he had been there some time.

Bobby approached and nodded to the paper. 'Is that the *Telegraph*? You'll never get back on the *Courier* if Clarky hears you've been seen around town with the competition.'

'More jobs in here. Not that I can do any of the buggers.' Tony finished his cigarette, added it to the pile of butts in the ashtray and glanced up at her listlessly. 'What're you doing here? Have you really come to thump me this time?'

'I'm sorry I threatened to thump you,' Bobby said. 'Well, no I'm not, you deserved it. But right now, I've come to buy you a pint.'

Tony blinked. 'Have you? What for?'

'Call it a wedding present. Bitter?'

'Mild. Ta.'

Bobby went to the bar. The pub was a disreputable-looking place in spite of its kingly name, and the landlord eyed her with silent suspicion as he poured the drinks. This evidently wasn't the sort of place women frequented, and Bobby attracted further looks of disapproval from the old men standing around smoking as she took a seat opposite Tony. Probably they thought she was a lady of dubious morals looking for a pick-up.

But none of that mattered. She only needed half an hour.

'Here you are.' She slid Tony's pint to him.

'Why're you being nice to me?' he asked, taking a mouthful. 'Did you see the missus?'

'I did. She told me you'd be in here.'

'She tell you to be nice to me?'

'She asked me to check up on you.' Bobby gestured to his paper. 'No joy?'

'No.' He lit another cigarette. 'It's going to have to be Liverpool. Sorry, Bob, but it's time I faced facts. Clarky won't have me back, even with the reference I got off Don, and there's nowt else for me round here.'

'I was afraid you were going to say that,' she said with a sigh.

'The bombing's eased up, at any rate. Maybe it won't be so bad.'

'It only takes one big shock for a woman to miscarry, Tony. You'd be putting Lil and the baby in danger. Is that what you want?'

'Course it's not. But I can't feed the pair of them on air, can I?' He tapped the ash from his cigarette rather violently.

Bobby watched him. He didn't look like the Tony Scott she remembered: perpetually grinning, always ready with a quip or an off-colour joke. He looked tired, and angry, and frustrated.

'Tony, can I ask you something?' she asked quietly.

He shrugged, which she took to be a yes.

'Why did you marry my sister?'

'What do you mean, why? There's a baby coming.'

'So? Plenty of men walk away from that.'

'Aye, I know what you're thinking,' he said, glaring at the newspaper. 'Plenty of men like me. That's what everyone thinks, isn't it? Tony Scott, who never worked a day in his life, who can't be trusted with other lads' girls, who doesn't give a damn about anyone but himself.'

'Are you saying that's not fair?'

His hand shook as he took a sip of his pint. 'Maybe it was, but not any more. Your sister was in a spot thanks to me and I wasn't going to leave her high and dry. Hard as it is to believe, Bobby, I'm not a complete bastard.'

Bobby regarded him with one eye narrowed.

'All right,' she said at last.

'Believe me, do you?'

'You've successfully exorcised any lingering desire to thump you, at least. But do you have to move your family down to Liverpool? It's so far away.'

'A few hours on the train isn't too bad. I mean, if you wanted to come help out when the baby gets here.'

All right. Now was the time for Operation Damsel-in-Distress. Bobby lowered her gaze.

'I will if I can get the leave,' she said solemnly.

Tony blinked. 'Leave? From that magazine?'

'No, from the WAAF. Didn't Lil say? I'm to be drafted in a few months. I don't mind telling you, Tony, I'm worried sick about it.'

Bobby sighed again, making sure it sounded good and heart-felt. In his own way, Tony was a bit of a romantic. At least, he had a soft spot for a woman in need, despite his roving ways. If he thought he was doing Bobby a favour rather than the other way around, she could avoid wounding his oh-so-fragile male pride.

'What're you worried about?' Tony asked. 'They're not going to send you up in a Spit, you know.'

'Can I have one of your cigarettes?'

'If you want.' He tapped one out of the packet and struck a match to light it for her. 'Didn't know you smoked.'

Bobby took a drag and coughed.

'I don't,' she gasped. 'Bloody Nora, Tony. Are they those Egyptian ones?'

'Yes, why?'

'Your throat must be like sandpaper.' She coughed again, then for appearance's sake took another drag, trying not to inhale. 'I thought it might help settle my nerves. I honestly don't know what I'm going to do.'

She wondered if now would be a good time to turn on the waterworks, but decided that would be a bit much. Tony had known her too long to fall for fake hysterics. Instead, she worked on making her eyes wide and helpless. Men liked that.

'About what?' Tony asked.

'My dad. The cottage we live in is a sort of grace-and-favour arrangement courtesy of my job. Once I go, he'll be homeless.' She swallowed hard to suggest tears might be just around the corner. 'He earns forty shillings a week as a gamekeeper, which isn't too bad considering he's new to the work, but it wouldn't be enough to rent a decent cottage and hire a housekeeper to look after it.'

'Hmm. Guess it wouldn't.'

'And Lord knows how Reg is going to find someone for the magazine,' Bobby went on. 'He needs someone who can write and who's nimble enough to get around the Dales, and there are so few young people left now the War Office seems intent on conscripting the world and his wife. Me leaving is putting everyone in a proper pickle. I feel ever so guilty about it – and that's on top of worrying about Lilian.'

'Lilian's all right. I'm looking after her,' Tony said, putting out his cigarette and immediately lighting another. Deciding that the one he'd given her had served its purpose as a prop, Bobby stubbed it out and tried to wash away the acrid taste with a mouthful of beer.

'You're not though, are you?' she said. 'You're in the pub, Tony.'

'Aye, looking for a job.'

'And failing to find one,' Bobby pointed out, tapping his newspaper. 'What with worrying about Lil, my dad, the magazine and the damn war, I'm finding it hard to sleep.' She let out another deep sigh. 'It's all such a mess.'

Tony didn't say anything. He just drew thoughtfully on his cigarette. Bobby drank her beer in silence, waiting for his brain to make the connection she'd pointed it so firmly towards.

'Not much money on that mag, I suppose,' he said at last.

'No. Only twenty bob a week.'

He snorted. 'You manage on that?'

Bobby shrugged. 'I know it doesn't sound much, but it comes with the cottage, and some of our meals are shared with the folk at the farmhouse, which cuts costs. It's better than a private in the Army gets.'

'Small, is it, your cottage?'

'It's not really a cottage at all. It's a converted barn – very snug. Still, there are two bedrooms, and a kitchen,' Bobby said, trying not to give away that she knew what he was getting at. 'No indoor plumbing but there's a flush privy in the outhouse and a pump outside for water. Electric too. It's perfect for just me and my dad.'

'Hmm.'

'The cold is probably the worst thing, but when the fire's blazing it's a cosy little home,' Bobby continued. 'I felt like I'd really fallen on my feet when we moved in, with my work at *The Tyke*, the cottage, good fresh air and all that splendid countryside. Plus I was able to make a home for my dad away from this smoky, disease-ridden town, and help him find a healthy job he loves.' This time, a tear arose naturally at the thought of all she would be saying goodbye to. 'Now I'm going to lose it all, thanks to the bloody war,' she said in a choked voice.

Tony gave her hand a clumsy pat.

'There, there,' he said, looking rather out of his depth. Still, Bobby could tell he was sympathetic. And what was better: there was a certain calculating sparkle in his eye that meant he was well on the way to where she wanted him to be.

She dabbed at her eyes with a hanky and summoned a grateful smile.

'Thanks for listening, Tony,' she said. 'I don't know why I'm telling you all this. I needed to unburden, I suppose, and I didn't want to give our Lilian anything else to think about. She'd worry herself sick about Dad if she knew he was about to become homeless, and that wouldn't be good for the baby.'

'No.'

'Can I get you another?' she asked, nodding to his nearly empty pint. She needed to be getting back to Silverdale, as she had promised Reg, but she wasn't prepared to leave until her work here was done.

'Best not,' he said, rather to her surprise – she'd never known Tony to refuse a beer when someone else was paying. 'Your Lil'll have my guts for garters if I go home reeking.'

Bobby laughed. 'Spoken like a true married man.'

Tony looked pensive while he finished his cigarette.

'Is your boss wanting a young lad for this job then?' he said after a bit.

'I suppose he'd prefer someone older with a bit of experience, but a quid a week isn't likely to tempt anyone when there are well-paid jobs going begging for men not in the forces. He'll have to take what he can get.'

'Would he consider me, do you reckon?'

Bobby had never been so grateful for the acting experience she had gained when Topsy had recruited her for the village pantomime. She made her eyes wide with feigned surprise.

'You?' she said, blinking.

Tony shrugged. 'Why not? I've got experience.'

'You wouldn't want a job at that wage, would you?'

'The wage isn't so bad if it comes with a house. Like you said, I'd be no better off in the Army, and I'd rather be at a nice warm desk than getting my brains shot out in Africa or lugging sacks around in Liverpool.' He stubbed out his cigarette. 'Anyhow, owt's better than being crammed in at my mam's listening to our Oliver snoring. It's hard to enjoy your conjugal rights when you and your wife can't even have your own room.'

'I hadn't thought of it like that,' Bobby said. 'I suppose there are a lot of advantages, when you look at it that way.'

'Your sister would like it too, I reckon. Being with her old man, away from the bombs.' He met her eyes. 'Don't you think she would? You know her better than me.'

Bobby couldn't help reflecting on the irony of this: that a man should know so little of the woman he had married.

'She'd appreciate being near Dad,' she said. 'I'm sure Mary would help with the baby too – Reg's wife. She loves children. Do you think you'll apply?'

Tony still looked hesitant. 'Your dad might not be keen. He knows now, does he?'

'He knows.'

'Everything? The baby too?'

'Everything. Including how you held back that story to get Lil to go on dates with you.'

'It wasn't like that. Pulling the story was a favour – to you as well as Lil.'

'Mmm. But it wasn't me you wanted a date from, was it? Anyhow, I can tell you now that my dad doesn't see it that way.' Bobby met his gaze. 'But you're right – if he can be talked round, it could be the best arrangement for everyone.'

'Reckon he can be? Talked round, that is?'

'I think so. Just leave it to me and Lil, and be as charming as possible when you visit on Wednesday, all right? I can arrange for you to talk to Reg too.' Bobby stood up. 'I need to get back. If I were you, I'd go home and start drafting a letter of application.'

'Right. I'll do it in the morning when I'm sober.'

She started to leave, then turned back. 'Tony?'

'Mm?'

'Did you mean it?'

'Mean what?'

'When you said you were determined to do right by Lil. That this time you really were going to change.'

He shrugged. 'If a wife and bairn don't straighten me out, nowt's going to.'

Bobby watched him for a moment.

'Here,' she said at last, fishing out a few coins from her purse. 'There's half a crown there. You can use it to take our Lil out tonight. See if *Rebecca*'s showing anywhere, that's her favourite.'

Tony blinked at the money. 'You're giving me cash?'

'Yes, and you can tell your mam that's where you got it if she gives you grief. Have a night out with your wife, eh? Lil looks exhausted, and you don't look much better. Some time alone together is just what you need.'

For the first time, Tony managed to summon his old schoolboy grin. 'Cheers, Bobby, you're a gent.'

'And mind, I'll be telling Lil you've got it,' Bobby told him sternly. 'If I hear it went straight behind the bar, then that's the last time I'll do you a favour.' She nodded to him. 'Look after my sister. I'll see you both soon.'

Chapter 22

'Oh Birdy, you're an angel,' Topsy said the following Wednesday, when Bobby unhooked a bag of hemmed table-cloths from her bicycle handlebars and put it into Topsy's arms. 'Will you come in? Maimie, Teddy and I were about to have some tea.'

Bobby grimaced. 'I can't. My sister and her new husband are paying their wedding visit tonight.'

'You're pulling faces about it,' Topsy observed. 'Do you not like this new husband?'

'It's more that my dad doesn't like him. I just hope there isn't a row.'

'I don't remember you telling me your sister had married. Did you?'

'Oh, I'm sure I did,' Bobby said vaguely, knowing full well she hadn't. 'It was only a quiet do at the register office. Lil didn't want any fuss.'

'Well, give her my congratulations, won't you? From one bride to another – or at least, I will be a bride soon.' Topsy hugged herself, beaming at the prospect. 'I can't wait to sign myself Mrs Nowak.'

'Is that how it works?' Bobby asked. 'I thought there were rules about titled people marrying commoners. Doesn't the husband have to take his wife's name or something?'

Topsy laughed. 'You read too many novels, darling.'

'So you'll just be a plain Mrs after you get married?'

'If I choose to be. Mine is a courtesy title – that is to say, I'm only Lady Sumner-Walsh thanks to Father. Although it ought to be Lady Honoria really. The surname should only be used by itself if one is the wife of a knight or baronet, but I couldn't bear to have people calling me by my ghastly first name.' Topsy pulled a face at the idea. 'Thankfully, no one in Silverdale knows any better.'

'I had no idea it was so complicated.'

'Isn't it foolishness?' Topsy said, laughing. 'So dreadfully out of date, but there are still enough people who care about this nonsense to fill the pages of Debrett's. Personally, I'm rather looking forward to turning my back on the business and becoming just an ordinary pilot's wife – or former pilot, I ought to say.'

An ordinary pilot's wife who owned her own country estate and had more money in the bank than Bobby could imagine, she couldn't help reflecting, but she smiled at her friend's enthusiasm.

'It'll be a happy occasion for us all,' she said. 'I'll see you soon, Topsy.'

'Goodbye, darling. Do remember me to your sister.'

Bobby mounted her bicycle and pedalled off as fast as she dared. She was expecting to have to work on soothing her dad's temper before the arrival of their guests, who were coming on the five p.m. train from Bradford to spend the night. Mary's help had been enlisted too, as had the Parry girls. All three were now at the cow house, making sure all was spruce before the newlyweds showed up. Bobby was particularly grateful for the presence of the children, whose innocent chatter usually managed to make her dad smile in spite of his mood.

At home, she found the fire lit and her dad in his chair by it, wearing his slippers. Florence was with him, prattling about some object on his knee, while Jessie helped Mary with the dusting. Rob looked a little dazed at the incessant flow of chatter from Florrie, but he was smiling. Bobby smiled too, pleased to see him looking happy for the first time since the day she had broken her sister's terrible news.

'Well this is very cosy,' she said, bending to unlace her boots. 'I'm sorry I took so long. It's so dark in the evenings, I don't dare ride too quickly no matter how urgently Topsy needs her precious tablecloths.'

'It'll soon be spring. Longer days are coming, Bobby.' Mary nodded to a vase of snowdrops that had been placed on the table by her dad's chair. 'See what our Jessie picked to bring you. A little reminder of new life to come.'

Bobby went to give Jessie a kiss. 'Thank you, sweetheart. They brighten up the room perfectly.'

'Bobby, guess what?' the child demanded immediately.

'I can't guess without a clue, Jess.'

'All right, then the clue is... Daddy.'

'Your dad? Has he written a letter?'

'Better'n just a letter,' Florrie said. She scooped up whatever it was she had been showing Rob and skipped with it to Bobby. 'Dad sent us this from the war. He said his friend who's been in Africa brought it back. Louis Butcher offered to swap me and Jess two bob and a go each on his airgun for it, but I said no. It's wizard, ain't it?'

Bobby looked at the small, squat green thing that Florence held out to her. It looked like a large seed, although Lord knew what plant it had come from.

'What is it, Florrie?' she asked.

Rob came to join them.

'What, lass, so long since you've seen one you've forgotten what they look like?' he said, smiling. 'It's a banana, that.'

Bobby blinked at the squat little shrub.

'They're not quite as I remember them,' she said. 'I'm sure they used to be bigger. And yellower.'

'Happen they look a little different when they're plucked right off the plant.'

'Now don't either of you be tempted to eat that,' Mary told the little girls sternly. 'I've never seen a fruit so calculated to bring on a belly ache.'

'Oh, no,' Florrie said, looking horrified. 'We'd never *eat* it. Not when it's worth two bob and a go on an airgun. We'll keep it for show.'

'And guess what else Daddy says?' Jessie asked Bobby.

'Has he been given a date for his discharge?'

Florrie nodded vigorously. 'In May. And you'll never guess what else.'

Bobby laughed. 'Sorry, Florrie, I'm all guessed out. You'll have to tell me.'

'He's found somewhere we can live,' the little girl said glee-fully. 'And the best thing of all is it's not in London or anywhere far away. It's across the bridge, where Mr Horsely lived before he died. It's a bit frightening to live somewhere a dead person was, but I suppose old places all have had some dead people in so I'm going to not think about it.'

'That's wonderful news.' Bobby crouched to talk to Jessie. 'How do you feel about it, my love?'

'Welllll, it's scary still to live somewhere else,' Jess said, cocking her head. 'But we can walk here every day to visit. Mary says we can come to breakfast before school if Daddy says it's all right, and I'm still to take care of my hens, and feed Boxer. Reg said our room would be left just as it is, and we can sleep over if Daddy needs to go away anywhere. So I think it will be OK.'

Bobby gave her a hug. 'I think so too.'

Florrie pointed to the tinny old piano in the corner, only used when Charlie – the sole piano player in the family – was home on leave. 'Mr Bancroft, may I try that, please?'

Rob laughed. 'Happen we'll need cotton wool in our ears first. Aye, go on.'

A moment later she was tinkling away tunelessly, having the time of her life finding out what sound each key made.

'Oh my word,' Mary said, laughing as she put her fingers in her ears. 'What a din, Florence Parry! I don't think we'll be booking the Albert Hall for you just yet. Now get coats and

172

shoes on, and we'll leave Bobby and Mr Bancroft alone. Their guests will be here soon.'

'Aww.' Florrie poked out her lip. 'But I was just getting the hang of it.'

'My ears beg to differ,' Bobby said, smiling. 'Perhaps you can have a lesson with Uncle Charlie next time he's on leave, and learn some proper tunes. You had better go now, girls, and have your supper and cocoa. We'll be packed in like sardines if you're still here when my sister and her husband arrive.'

'How come your sister's got a husband now, Bobby?' Jessie asked as Mary buttoned her coat up for her. 'She never had one when she come at Christmas.'

'Well, ladies do tend to get husbands once they reach a certain age, you know, Jess. Even you might have one someday.'

Jessie poked out her tongue. 'Urgh. No thank you.'

Bobby laughed. 'We'll see. Goodnight, girls.'

When they'd gone, her dad slumped back in his chair, looking windswept.

'Why do I always feel like I've been tossed about in a hurricane after a visit from them two?'

Bobby smiled. 'It does feel rather that way, doesn't it?'

Her dad smiled too, a little sadly. 'I remember I had a pair of my own like that, once. Little whirlwinds. All the time it were "Daddy, look at this" and "Daddy, you must take me to see that".' He sighed. 'Long time ago.'

Bobby crouched down and rested a hand on his arm.

'But we're still those same girls, even if we are grown up. Your girls,' she said softly. 'It was nice to see you smiling tonight, Dad.'

'Aye, well. Hard not to with little ones around.'

'And soon there'll be a little one of our own arriving. One who'll need their grandad very much after the difficult start they had in life.'

Rob sighed again, but he didn't speak.

'Dad, I'm really so sorry,' Bobby whispered. 'I never meant to say what I said, that night. You're right, it was my fault. I didn't see the danger until it was too late. Still, you have to believe that Tony isn't the scoundrel you think he is.'

'Huh.'

'For the sake of one of those little whirlwinds who always loved you, you will be polite, won't you? No matter what happened in the past, Tony's trying to do what's right. He deserves to be given a chance.'

Rob didn't answer. He just sat in silence, staring into the fire. Realising nothing would be achieved by saying more, Bobby went out to the pump to get water and set the kettle to boil ready for the visitors.

It was just over half an hour later that a tentative knock sounded. Bobby glanced at her dad, who stood up.

'This is it,' she whispered. 'Please, Dad. For Lil.'

He didn't say anything. Bobby went to answer the door.

Both her sister and Tony were in Sunday clothes: Tony in a grey suit that was just beginning to grow shabby, and Lilian in her best sky-blue dress. The finery looked a little out of place in the cow house, but Bobby was pleased to see they had made an effort to impress her father. Tony looked rather nervous, as well he might, and was clutching a small brown paper parcel.

Lilian's dress was decidedly snug, now her pregnancy had passed twenty weeks. Bobby saw how her dad winced when he noticed. However, he didn't immediately run into the surgery and try to break into the cupboard where she had locked his shotgun away, which was something. Not that she really believed he'd use it on any living thing other than mink and foxes, but she felt better knowing it was out of his reach.

Tony was looking at Lil, waiting for her to make introductions.

'Um, good evening,' Lilian said, uncharacteristically bashful. 'Sorry we're late. There were delays on the railway.' She gave an awkward laugh. 'When aren't there these days?'

'I can't remember the last time I caught a train that arrived when it was supposed to,' Bobby said, forcing a laugh too.

She went forward to embrace her sister, and felt some of the tension leave Lilian's body.

'Don't worry,' she whispered. 'It'll be all right. I'm here.'

'Thanks, Bob,' Lilian whispered back.

Bobby took her sister's hand to lead her to their father, who still stood by his chair with an inscrutable expression on his face.

'Dad, here's our Lil.' She summoned a smile. 'Now you've got both your little whirlwinds at home again. Do you think you can stand it?'

Rob remained silent for a moment.

'Aye,' he said at last. 'Aye, I reckon I can put up with the pair of you a spell.' His eyes flickered to his daughter's stomach, and Bobby noticed him flinch. 'Come over to the fire, eh? You don't want to catch a chill.'

Lilian beamed, and threw herself at him for a hug. 'I missed you, Dad.'

'All right. No need to make a fuss,' he said, a smile flickering on his lips. 'Good to see you, love.'

Lilian drew back, turning to Tony. 'I, er, brought someone to meet you.'

Tony was still lingering by the door, looking uncertain what to do. Bobby gave him a nod of encouragement, hoping he'd remember her advice to turn on the charm when he came face to face with her dad.

He took the hint, and strode forward to shake his new father-in-law by the hand.

'It's a pleasure to meet you properly, sir,' he said. 'These are two fine girls you've raised.'

'I know it.' Rob regarded the younger man icily. 'Found yoursen a job yet?'

'Not yet, but soon, I hope.' Tony suddenly remembered the parcel in his hand, and held it out. 'I got these off a mate. Wills' Whiffs – Lil said you enjoyed the occasional cigar. I thought after we'd had tea, we could leave the girls to chat and go to the pub for a smoke and a pint.'

Bobby smiled approvingly. He was really trying. Her dad still looked icy but he had taken the gift of cigars, and she was sure a slight thaw had crept in.

'I'm buying,' Tony said when Rob remained silent.

'Huh. Wonder you can afford it, with a wife and a—' He glanced again at Lilian's stomach, and again Bobby noticed the obvious flinch. 'With a wife to support and no money coming in.'

Tony's shoulders sagged, and Bobby leapt to his rescue.

'Oh, I don't think Tony's as destitute as all that,' she said, as brightly as she could. 'Go on, Dad, you'll enjoy it. Besides, I want Lil to myself to help make up the bed in my room for her and Tony. I didn't have time earlier.'

'Hmm.' Rob glanced at the cigars in his hand. 'Well, happen a beer or two wouldn't go amiss, since the womenfolk are determined to evict us.'

Bobby and Lilian both beamed at him. Tony, meanwhile, looked a combination of relieved and terrified. It was clear that while he welcomed the thaw in his father-in-law's attitude, an evening at the pub tête-à-tête was far from his idea of a good time. The edge seemed to have been taken off the atmosphere, however, and Tony took a seat opposite Rob by the fire. Lilian went to whisper something to him before following Bobby to the kitchen.

'How's your little godson: Don's boy?' they heard Tony ask. 'I saw him and his dad last week. He's a fine chap.'

'Aye, he is that,' Rob said, with a very small smile.

Bobby nudged Lilian. 'Good choice of conversation topic,' she whispered.

'I was trying to remember what Bradford friends they had in common, and I remembered you saying Dad couldn't get enough of hearing about Don's baby,' Lilian whispered back.

'That went as well as we could have hoped, don't you think?'

Lilian put an arm round her sister's waist. 'Thanks to you acting as our fifth column here. I'm sure without you speaking up for us, Dad would have barred the door and never let Tony over the threshold – or me.'

Bobby put a pan of stew she'd prepared the day before on the hob while Lilian took over tea-making duties. 'He wouldn't really do that, whatever he might threaten when he's in a rage. He loves you, Lil.'

'I know.' She sighed. 'But he can't bear to look at me now I'm showing, or mention the baby.'

'You know he's always bashful about those things. He blushed fit for a beacon when I told him about little Robert Sykes being born, even though I barely mentioned any details of Joan's labour.'

'I hope he and Tony don't get into any trouble at the pub,' Lilian said. 'Where are you sleeping if we're in your room?'

'In the box room at Moorside.'

'And did you arrange for Tony to see Reg? He's got some samples of his work in his overnight bag.'

'Yes, Reg is going to talk to him over breakfast tomorrow morning.'

Bobby turned to look through the door at her dad and Tony by the fire, talking if not exactly animatedly, then at least with mutual forbearance and respect. The cow house looked at its cosiest tonight, with the fire blazing, the chill in the air banished and the little vase of snowdrops giving a feel of spring. As she watched the two men and felt the reassuring presence of her sister at her side, Bobby felt a warmth spread through her. It felt, for the first time in a long time, as if perhaps everything would be all right.

Chapter 23

Bobby slept badly that night, over in the box room at Moorside Farm.

It had been her room when she had first worked for Reg, before her dad had come out to the Dales to live with her, but afterwards it had been occupied by Charlie, and it was still reserved for him whenever he came home on leave. Many years before, it had been the nursery for Reg and Mary's one deeply mourned child, Nancy, who had died at just two years old. The wallpaper still bore the faded print of what had once been colourful merry-go-round horses.

It smelled of Charlie. That was the problem. He seemed to have got into the walls and furnishings somehow, in spite of Mary's rigorous housekeeping. Whichever way Bobby turned her head, she could smell the tobacco he smoked and the aftershave lotion he used. On the bedside table was her photograph of him, which she had brought from the cow house, and hanging on the wall was Mary's painting of a stag, with those eyes that so reminded her of Charlie's: deep brown and soulful. It felt like he was all around her.

At first, Bobby found the ghost-like presence of her fiancé comforting, but her thoughts soon cycled to worry. Whenever she shifted on her pillow and caught the scent of his tobacco, she felt a wave of warmth, as if Charlie was there with her. But this was quickly followed by a sharp, gut-wrenching pain when she remembered that he wasn't – that he could be anywhere in Europe at that moment.

Was he on a raid tonight? It was a clear night, which meant he might well be. Where would he be? Germany? France? Could he be in the midst of one of those 'sticky' moments he had hinted at in his letters, with a German fighter on his tail? Would he be coming back?

Bobby buried her face in the pillow, endeavouring to shut out the presence of Charlie all around her, and dampened it with her tears.

Oh God, she couldn't bear it. She didn't know how any woman could. Every time one of Charlie's letters didn't arrive when it was expected she fretted herself into knots, fearing the arrival of a telegram to say he'd never be coming home. Dread like a lead weight settled in her belly every morning when she awoke and remembered he was out there. Every moment, she wondered if he was safe; alive. She wondered how many men he had killed so far, and how many cities he had helped destroy. Every time a letter arrived, the sweet relief of knowing he was safe was made bitter through the knowledge that somewhere the wife or sweetheart of a German airman was opening a telegram telling her he wouldn't be coming home.

After waking from an uneasy sleep filled with horrifying visions of the man she loved in a flaming cockpit, Bobby turned on the light.

The clock showed it was half past five – she would need to get up for work in an hour. Giving up on further sleep, Bobby sat up and took Charlie's most recent letter from her handbag. She always kept his latest one with her. Perhaps seeing his words would help settle her worried mind.

It was quite a long letter for a change. Charlie's letters had been getting shorter since his move to Binbrook – there was so little he was allowed to tell her, now he was engaged in operational flying. But long or short, they were more affectionate than they had been before – more like love letters. Bobby had welcomed this at first, but now even that worried her. In her fiancé's earnest expressions of love, she saw only his fear that this might be the last time he would have the opportunity to tell her.

My dearest Bobby,

It seems like a thousand years ago that we were together in Skipton. I certainly feel a thousand years older. Was it really only three weeks ago? I hadn't realised it was possible to miss someone this much. I feel so far away from you here — physically far away, I mean. You're in my heart as much as ever. How are you bearing up, sweetheart?

You asked in your last letter how I found my new comrades-in-arms. Well, the boys in my squadron are a good bunch, although rather raucous compared with the recruits at Ryland Moor. Flying ops certainly seems to have given them a lust for life — beer and girls are very much the order of the day. They seem like such experienced old lads, smiling indulgently at us new boys while they tell us tales of their feats in the sky, and yet they're all younger than me. Some are barely twenty. It feels like they've become old men in boys' bodies, trying to cram a lifetime of sensation into every day in case they never see another.

Anyhow, I soon learnt my lesson about trying to match my geriatric old bones with them drink for drink when they dragged me to the NAAFI to 'baptise' me, as they call it when they have a new chap to bring into the fold. I almost ended up on a fizzer when I could hardly open my poor bloodshot eyes at parade the next morning.

You needn't worry that I'm drifting back into old habits though. You wouldn't recognise this new, abstemious Charlie, who never has more than three pints of an evening and averts his eyes like a monk whenever he passes the dorm noticeboard, which the lads use to show off their favourite pin-ups. I'd rather read quietly in my bunk with my photograph of you beside me and think about the next time we'll see one another – our wedding day, I sincerely hope.

The Wingco has approved me to marry but he was being very coy about my chances of getting some leave to actually do the deed. However, I've finally pinned him down to forty-eight hours on the 2nd and 3rd of May. Three months feels like so long to wait, but only fair, I suppose, when some of the lads here have been waiting yonks for home leave. I hope your commanding officer is equally sympathetic, and we can synchronise our watches soon. I'll arrange the licence if you put one of the village holy men on reserve, then everything is ready for the 2nd. The more organised we are, the less your CO is likely to refuse.

We lost six men last week. A whole crew. They were shot down over the Channel and are now at the bottom of the drink, I suppose. Never even reached their target. Another crew was more fortunate, and went down over Germany with no casualties. They're in a POW camp now, where they can sit out the war listening to the wireless and drinking cocoa from their Red Cross parcels. Lucky devils.

I can't stop thinking about those men who went down – men I'd shared smokes and drunk and joked with. They were so alive – so real. One of them was to be married shortly. Another was excited about going home to see the baby girl he'd never met. I can see the photograph of his pretty young wife and their two little daughters next to his old bunk as I write. It seems so horribly unfair, doesn't it?

As I'm writing, my hand keeps pausing, wondering if I ought to share such bleak news. I know what your worries will be when you read it. Still, something tells me the Bobby I know would want to hear about everything I'm feeling, and not have me pretend for her sake.

Even so, I don't dare say too much about my own experiences in the sky. The censor and my heart would never allow it. Suffice to say, I crawled into my bunk after the four raids I've been on so far feeling that I'd looked on Armageddon.

I often think about you, you know, and where you'll be. I look at my wristwatch and think, 'It's eight o'clock in the morning. Bobby will be at Moorside, having breakfast in the kitchen with Reggie, Mary, Rob and the girls, feeding scraps to the dogs'. Or 'It's seven o'clock in the evening. Bobby will be sitting with her father by the fire, or knitting in the ARP hut'. I wish that wherever you are now, I was there with you.

Please write soon, and tell me all the news from home. Don't leave out a single detail, no matter how trivial. Do you know yet when you're to be drafted, and where to? What news of Captain Parry's discharge? Is your sister married? How do Topsy and Teddy's wedding plans go? Has my brother found a new reporter? How are Norman and Jemima getting along in married life? What of the dogs, and Boxer? I want to know everything that's happening, whether human, horse, dog or goose, and feel closer to you all there. It can feel like my old life in Silverdale was all a dream sometimes, until your letters arrive to make it real for me again.

I suppose I had better sign off, before this letter becomes as long as a novel. I know such frivolous waste of paper would make Reggie cry. I love you very much, darling. Don't forget me.

All my best love,
Charlie x

It was such a different sort of letter from the buoyant, teasing ones he had once sent her. Bobby smiled as she read, and yet tears slid down her cheeks. The story of the crew lost over the Channel made her stomach churn with familiar dread.

Six young men, wiped out just like that. All with people who loved them, and with hopes and plans for the future. Somewhere a girl who had been excited for her wedding day was sobbing over her broken dreams. A baby would grow up never knowing her father. It all seemed so futile. Such a waste.

And it could be Charlie. Every time Bobby read a death notice or heard of someone being killed in action, that was the first thought in her mind: *It could be Charlie.* He had only been flying ops for a couple of weeks, but already her nerves were frayed to breaking point. How did other women cope? It was hell.

And soon she, too, would be a part of it. The war machine. The death machine. Before, Bobby had thought only about duty – how important it was that good triumphed over evil, at the last – but now she thought of the lives lost. In freeing up men to join the fight, some of the death being doled out to Allies and Axis alike would be on her hands. Casualties might be necessary for the war to be won, but knowing that didn't banish the images of children without fathers and women grieving for the men they had loved, did it? When you were raised as a girl it was with the understanding that your ultimate role would be to give life – to nurture it. The idea she could be responsible for taking it went against every value that had ever been instilled in her. Bobby wondered if she would ever be able to have a settled night's sleep again.

–

Bobby's eyes were dry and sore when she sat down in front of the mirror to get ready for work, and her skin an unhealthy shade of grey from the restless night she had passed. She did what she could with rouge and powder, but still, she knew she looked a fright.

Mary noticed this right away, of course. Rob and Lilian were in the midst of eating breakfast when Bobby entered the kitchen, while Florence and Jessie had just finished.

'You all right, love?' Mary asked, frowning. 'You look like you might be coming down with something.'

Bobby summoned a smile. 'Just a bad night's sleep. Sorry, Mary, I ought to have come down sooner to help with the breakfast. Everything seems to be an effort today.'

'Don't worry. I've had the other Miss Bancroft helping me – or Mrs Scott, I should say, shouldn't I?' Mary smiled at Lilian, who, in contrast with her sister, had a healthful glow about her this morning. A night spent away from the snores of Tony's brother in a room to themselves had clearly done her good.

'Oh gosh, that sounds strange,' Lilian said, laughing. 'It's going to take time to get used to a new name.'

'Florrie, Jess, upstairs and get ready for school,' Mary ordered. 'Make some space at the table.'

'Oh, but may we show Lilian our banana first?' Florrie asked.

'School clothes on and hair brushed before you do that. Then you may show it.'

Lilian raised an eyebrow at Bobby as the girls ran out. 'A banana?'

Bobby laughed. 'I wouldn't get too excited. It's the least appetising-looking thing I've ever seen, although quite the novelty in the playground, apparently. I don't suppose their schoolmates will remember ever having seen one before.' She took a seat, sniffing the air, which carried the delicious scent of frying fish. 'What's for breakfast, Mary?'

'We've a treat this morning,' Mary said, putting a plate down in front of her. 'I saved up our points to get two tins of kippers. Make the most of it.'

Bobby was hungry after being awake most of the night, and tucked in with relish.

'Where's Tony?' she asked her sister between mouthfuls.

Lilian jerked her head towards the parlour. 'With Reg at his desk.'

'An interview? I didn't realise it was to be anything so formal.'

'I presume so. They both seemed keen to get it done as soon as they'd wolfed down their kippers.'

'I hope you didn't keep him out too late at the pub, Dad,' Bobby said to her father.

'Nay,' Rob said. 'Two pints each and a smoke, that's all.'

'How did it go?'

Rob shrugged. 'All right. Got chatting to Pete. Reckons he'll have some off-ration offal to flog next week – oxtail and sheep's brain. Legal, not black market.'

'We'd get a good stew out of that,' Mary said. 'Although I'd never give much credence to owt that old crook says about it not being fiddled. Still, bring us some back if you can, Rob. I'll do mash and dock pudding with it.'

'I meant, how did it go with Tony?' Bobby asked her dad. 'Did you have a nice chat?'

'Not bad.'

Bobby gave up, realising this was all she was going to get out of him. Instead she turned to Lilian, who nodded slightly to let her know that all had been well when the two men had come in. It didn't sound as though they were exactly bosom pals, but nor did it sound as if there had been a row of any kind, which was reassuring.

Bobby wondered how her dad was feeling about the idea of sharing a home with his daughter and her husband now. She had tentatively raised the topic a couple of times, but had struggled to get him to engage. Nevertheless, she had endeavoured to make him understand that while it might not have been his first choice, the alternatives would be even less preferable – he never could stand to live with a stranger, and leaving him alone wasn't an option. Was the idea more palatable, now he and Tony had called a shaky truce over their peace-making pints?

As soon as Bobby heard Tony emerge from the parlour, she swallowed the last mouthful of her breakfast and jumped up.

Mary blinked. 'You're keen to start work this morning.'

'Sorry. Things to get finished.'

Bobby darted out into the hall. She was too late to catch Tony, however, who had left by the side door, so she went into the parlour and sat down at her desk.

'Morning,' she said to Reg.

'Aye, morning,' he muttered, not looking up. Bobby tried to guess from his tone whether her new brother-in-law had found favour in the editor's eyes, but as usual Reg was giving nothing away.

Bobby took her time arranging the notes she had made for a story on wild flowers. She made a show of scribbling down a few facts from a reference book before nonchalantly observing to Reg, 'I hear you had Tony in.'

'Best to get it out the way.'

'What did you think of his portfolio?'

'His writing could be a lot sparer, but he's learnt a bit about what makes a good story. Knows how to train up a newspaperman, does Don Sykes.' He looked up at her sharply. 'None of that was yours, was it? I know you wrote under his byline when you worked on the paper.'

'I doubt it. The only bits he ever asked me to write were about cake sales and things.'

'Huh. The stuff he showed me was wall-to-wall murders.'

'That'll be Tony. He likes the juicy pieces.'

'Not much juicy around here,' Reg said absently, skimming a document in his hand. Bobby wondered if it was Tony's letter of application. 'Nobbut old traditions, flowers and wildlife. He'll be bored to tears in a week.'

'He *will* be?' Bobby sat up straighter. 'You mean you're going to give him the job?'

He looked up at her. 'Your sister in the family way, is she?'

Reg was bluff in most matters but not generally about those that concerned women, and Bobby was caught off-guard by the directness of the question.

'Um, that really isn't for me to say.'

'Don't matter. I've got my own eyes to see.' Reg glanced at the letter in his hand. 'Where's he planning to take her if he can't get work?'

'Liverpool,' Bobby said quietly. 'He thinks one of the shipyards would take him on. He'd be dragging her right to where the heaviest bombing is.'

Reg stared at the letter for a while longer, then sighed.

'Well, I'll give him a chance,' he said. 'Same terms as I gave you: a quid a week, residence at the cow house and a month's trial to convince me he can do the job. I hope he don't make me regret it.'

Bobby beamed. 'Oh, thank you! Reg, you're an absolute saint. Really. I can't tell you how grateful I am.'

Reg flushed at this fulsome praise. 'All right, let's not get carried away. Go tell your sister, eh? Don't take too long, mind. I want plenty more pieces out of you before you leave, so I've got summat to work with if Scott's no good.'

Chapter 24

The weeks passed in a flurry of activity, now arrangements could be made for Bobby's departure. She tried to make the time stretch, to savour every precious moment with the little family she had built in Silverdale, but there was so much to be done that the days seemed to fly by with scarcely time to draw breath. Before she knew it, it was the 3rd of April – the day before Topsy's wedding, and Bobby's last Friday as a civilian. It was also to be her final day in the job she loved.

She had resigned as an ARP warden at the end of February, handing over her whistle to Gil Capstick, who had volunteered in her place. Bobby was sorry to say goodbye to the cold tin hut, but she was glad to call her evenings her own again. What with preparing for Topsy's wedding, getting ready for her own imminent departure and making sure the cow house was ready for its two – well, two and a half – new occupants, there seemed to be an unending list of chores to be done.

Lilian and Tony would be arriving with their few belongings that evening. Bobby would then move into the box room at Moorside for her last two evenings as a civilian, before departing for her new life as a WAAF on Monday.

'What're you up to at this hour?' her dad asked, emerging from his bedroom in the morning to find her standing on a chair, covered in plaster dust. 'You look like the Ghost o' Christmas Past, our Bobby.'

Bobby sneezed. 'Ugh. This stuff gets everywhere. I'm sure I'll be sneezing it out for weeks.' She got down from the chair.

'I'm plugging up some of the gaps to keep out the draught a little better.'

'It's man's work, that. Leave me do it, or young Scott.'

'I just want to know it's done before I leave,' she said, dusting herself down. 'I'd hate Lil to get ill from sleeping in a draughty house now she needs her strength.'

Her dad winced, as he always did when anyone mentioned Lilian's condition.

He hadn't even been able to look at the little cradle the Athertons had given them to put in the Scotts' room ready for the baby – Nancy's old one, which Reg had kindly sanded and painted fresh. It looked very sweet at the foot of the bed: the wood now a fresh grass-green with little daisies painted on the sides.

'What do you think?' Bobby had asked her dad when she had brought it home from Moorside.

'Bad luck, that. Bringing a crib over the threshold before t' bairn's arrived,' was his gruff answer. Bobby couldn't get him to look at it, or make any further comment.

While he seemed to have come to terms with the fact his daughter was married – and to the even more unpalatable truth that he now had Tony Scott for a son-in-law – Lilian's pregnancy seemed to be taking her dad longer to accept. Bobby hoped this would wear off when he grew accustomed to seeing Lil every day. At nearly seven months pregnant, she would be a fair size by now.

While their father had the natural male squeamishness of his generation when it came to pregnancy and birth, the fact of it was hardly new to him. He had been at his wife's side through multiple pregnancies – four babies who had lived, and one who had died before ever seeing the world. He was exceptionally fond of his two granddaughters – Rose and Susie, Raymond's children – and of children generally. Bobby did so want him to have a good relationship with the new baby.

'How are you feeling, Dad?' she asked gently. 'Things are going to be different after today, aren't they?'

He sighed. 'It'll be a new life, all right.'

'You'll soon settle to a new routine. I hope I will too.' Bobby glanced wistfully around the old barn. 'I'll miss this place. Funny to think last night was my final sleep under this leaky old roof.'

'Wish you didn't have to go.'

'So do I. But I do.' She summoned a smile. 'Anyhow, we've got something joyful to celebrate before you wave me off. It's the wedding tomorrow.'

Her dad smiled too. 'You ought to get a move on and sort out one of your own, lass. I've been done out of one daughter's wedding as it is. I won't be cheated of another. Tell that Charlie Atherton to pull his socks up, eh?'

'Charlie's done his part – at least, he's got his CO's consent to marry. I need to do the same, then hopefully we can confirm it for the 2nd of May.'

'Well, don't be long about it. I'll sing hymns at Her Lady-ship's wedding gladly but it's for thee I'll be dancing a jig, Bobby. Nice to have one son-in-law I can shake by the hand without reservation.'

Bobby laughed. 'You didn't always talk about Charlie that way.'

'Aye, well. He's not Tony Scott, which goes a long way in his favour.'

'Dad...'

'I know, I know,' he said, picking up his cloth cap and jamming it on his head. 'I'll not make trouble. Don't mean I'm happy about it.'

'Tony's doing everything he ought to, isn't he? He's about to start a new job, he's made Lil and the baby respectable, and he's not going to drag them to any of the blitzed cities. Wait and see, that's all I ask. If he lets Lil down then I'll be first in the queue to give him a bloody nose, but he's earned himself the right to a chance.'

'We'll see how he goes on,' was her dad's non-committal answer. He scanned her customary weekend costume of jumper and trousers. 'Are you not going to work? I thought Reg was keeping you on while tomorrow.'

'He wants me to get him a walk for the next number, now the weather's warmer,' Bobby said, pulling on her walking boots. 'After breakfast I'm heading up Bowside by the drover's path, then I'll type it up tomorrow before the wedding.'

'All the way up there? Long way, that.'

'I suppose Reg is worried Tony won't be able to manage the walks page, with his asthma and weedy city legs,' she said, smiling. 'Either that or he's trying to do me a favour.'

'This is Reg's idea of a favour, is it?'

'He's noticed I'm struggling to focus, I suppose,' Bobby said with a shrug. 'A walk in the fresh air is just what I need to clear my head.'

–

Bobby didn't tell her dad what else was on her mind, although she was sure she must have flinched when he had talked about her wedding plans. The fact she would be leaving on Monday, to face an unknown life among strangers, wasn't the only reason she was struggling to concentrate at work.

There had been no letter from Charlie for a fortnight now. Normally she would get at least one letter a week from him – often more. She had kept an eye on the post to Moorside and knew that Mary, too, hadn't heard from him in the last two weeks, although as he wrote to his sister-in-law rather less frequently than his fiancée, there wasn't the same feeling of panic at the farmhouse as had taken root in her.

It felt like she was holding her breath constantly, feeling her innards plummet every time Gil or a boy from the village appeared outside Moorside with something to deliver. Always she feared that this time it would be the eternally dreaded telegram.

Of course it was possible that Charlie's letters had only been held up, but Bobby couldn't help fearing something far worse.

She knew her mind would remain unsettled until she had been reassured all was well.

She breathed deeply as she strode the lower flanks of Great Bowside, the peak that towered over Silverdale. It was still 'white ovver' in places higher up, with a cap of snow at the summit, although the early spring sunshine shone brightly. Here and there, little patches of purple butterwort and golden tormentil shone among the brown heather, like heralds of the new season. The walk up the mountain held so many memories for Bobby, and she couldn't blame the wind when sharp tears stung the corner of her eyes.

She had made the journey to the peak on several occasions, but there were three incidents that stood out in her mind. The first was when she and Charlie, in their early courting days, had walked to the shepherd's hut halfway up and rain had forced them to seek shelter. That was when she had first woken in Charlie's arms, and thought seriously about how it would feel to awake there every day. The second was the night of horror when a Wellington crewed by trainee airmen had crashed below the peak, and Bobby had led a rescue party to bring down the survivors. And the third, and sweetest, was the day Charlie had taken her to the summit and asked her to be his wife. Bobby rubbed her fingers over the engagement ring under her gloves, remembering how he had held her while they watched the sun set. She was glad she would get to see the view from the summit one last time before leaving Silverdale.

Charlie had looked at her with such admiration that night of the crash, when they had marched up here with only a dim torch and a bag filled with bandages and aspirin. And yet it had been Charlie who had shown a new side to himself at the top, when he had challenged a pair of village men who had mistaken the Free Polish survivors for German spies. Bobby realised now that she had been given a glimpse, that night, of the man war would cause Charlie to become. Or perhaps the man he'd always been, somewhere inside, just waiting for a crisis of life-or-death proportions to bring him to the fore.

That hadn't been the first time Bobby had come face to face with death, but it had been the first time she had witnessed the sort of death war could bring. When she had seen the smoking bodies in the plane, it had brought home exactly what she had to fear when the man she loved left her to join the RAF.

It took Bobby nearly two hours to arrive at the spot where the Wellington had crashed. There was little left, now, of the fuselage. Most of the pieces had been plundered by local lads, supposedly to donate for salvage. Bobby had her suspicions that they had more likely been sold to Pete Dixon, who had a thriving side trade in scrap metal. But there were still a few shards of jagged aluminium lying around.

Bobby went to rest her hand on one, closing her eyes as she said a silent prayer for the men who had died here that night. She would think of them tomorrow, as she watched their comrade Teddy Nowak – who had so nearly joined them in the next life – marry the woman he loved.

When she had finished paying her respects, she continued on to the summit.

Her mind drifted back to Topsy, sitting between Teddy's knees as she pretended to read his palm. She thought, too, of something Lil had said in one of her letters: about a girl in the Wrens who could tell the future by laying out cards. Such tricks were nonsense, Bobby supposed. Still, it would be a skill to have, wouldn't it? To see the future.

She felt like thoughts of the future occupied most of her waking hours these days, making it impossible to live her life fully in the present. Big thoughts that affected the whole world, such as who would win the war and what would happen after, and little thoughts – although not so little to her – about what would happen to her, and the people she loved. What would be waiting for her in her new life as a WAAF? How would Tony and Lil get along after the baby arrived? Would her father's mental state remain stable with his new living arrangement? Could Tony hang on to his job at *The Tyke*? How would Topsy and Teddy fare as man and wife, given the physical toll placed on them by his injuries? Would Bobby's hard-won career as a reporter still be open to her when she returned from the war? And above all, what would happen to her and Charlie in the face of all the changes happening both outside and within them?

Bobby had sometimes pondered why she didn't feel more excited about her forthcoming wedding. That was how brides were supposed to feel, wasn't it? She ought to be like Topsy, walking on air, hardly able to wait for the day she would be legally and spiritually joined with the man she loved. She had told herself it was because the date hadn't yet been confirmed, which meant it didn't quite feel real despite the ring on her finger. But it wasn't that.

There was just so much uncertainty. How could she think about a wedding when every time a message came, she dreaded hearing that the man she had pledged herself to had been injured – or killed? When it seemed like the war would go on and on forever? It was almost as if her mind, trying to protect her, had created a barrier beyond which she was not allowed to peep. It struck Bobby that despite thinking constantly about the future, she didn't entirely believe in it.

There was so much worry and fear that it felt hard to find the joy in anything. Even in moments of quiet content, when for a brief time she could forget the war and appreciate what was around her, a worried whisper soon dragged her back to the reality of what was happening out there in the world. Always she thought of Charlie, and where he might be, and if she would ever see him again.

At the summit of the fell, Bobby stood by the flat rock where she had sat with him the day she had accepted his proposal. She peeled back her glove to let her sapphire engagement ring catch the light of the sun.

Tears rose as she remembered his warm arms around her, and the soft chuckle of the grouse as they had looked down into the valley bathed in golden light. That peaceful moment, knowing

Charlie belonged to her and she to him, had seemed to promise a better future to come – a future with a world at peace. But would it ever arrive?

Something about looking down on the settlement below, the houses little more than specks and the people who inhabited them invisible, brought a dizzying sense of perspective. It ought to make you feel insignificant, a view like that, but it didn't – not for Bobby. It didn't matter how numerous human beings were, or how small in the general scheme of things: they mattered, every one. Like the nail for want of which the war was lost, every tiny person could be the one to shift the course of the conflict. Even her.

As she looked down into the valley, Bobby felt herself in the grip of something for the first time. It was exactly what Charlie had once tried to describe to her – a sort of nervous euphoria; an overwhelming feeling of something that wasn't joy but made her body feel as though it was. There was a dizzying, reeling recklessness to it. Could fear ever feel like joy? It was overwhelming, and intoxicating in a way she wasn't sure was good for her.

She understood, finally, what Charlie had meant when he had said he felt ready to go out there and save the world. She understood why it mattered so much to him to have the wedding as soon as they could. It was about seizing control – about making a future of their own despite the buffeting they were being given by fate. Like Charlie, she no longer felt that she could wait. The world could do as it would, but this future didn't belong to the world. It belonged to them.

But when she descended from the fells and returned home, there was still no letter waiting for her.

Chapter 25

Lilian and Tony arrived in the late afternoon. What with preparing for Topsy's wedding and her own imminent departure, it had been over a month since Bobby had last been to Bradford to see her sister. She stared as Lilian struggled to get her huge frame through the door.

'Oh my word! You're enormous, Lil.'

Lilian laughed. 'Thank you, darling sister.'

Tony followed her in with their suitcases.

'I'll put these in your room, shall I, Bob?' he said.

'It's your room now,' Bobby said, smiling rather wistfully. She turned her attention back to Lilian as he disappeared with the cases. 'I'm serious though. You must have at least four babies in there.' She frowned. 'It couldn't be twins, could it? They do say they run in families.'

'Oh, don't say that. Wouldn't it be just my luck?' Lilian said with a groan. 'The doctor seems to think it's just the one, at any rate. He's going to be a strapper.'

Bobby smiled. 'You look good though. Glowing and all that. How do you feel?'

Lilian winced as she put a hand in the small of her back. 'Sore. I'm glad we're here finally. The Wicked Mother-in-law's been looking daggers at me ever since I got too big to help much around the house.'

'Oi. That's my mam you're talking about,' Tony said as he came back in. He slipped an arm round his wife and gave her a kiss. 'It'll be nice to have you all to myself though.'

Bobby smiled. They seemed happy enough, in spite of a shaky start to married life. That was something.

'Did you see the cot?' she asked. 'A gift from Reg and Mary.'

'Aye, very smart,' Tony said.

'It belonged to their little girl. I was surprised they wanted to part with it, but Mary said she'd love to see it used for another little one.'

'That's kind of them,' Lilian said. 'We'll thank them later. Is Dad at work?'

'Yes, but he could be back any time now.' Bobby took a piece of paper and a key from her pocket. 'Now, I've written out my daily itinerary – everything I do in the morning before Dad gets up and in the evening before he gets home. I know you won't be able to manage much of it, but Mary's going to help, and I've arranged to pay Ida Wilcox a shilling a day to come and char for you. I've tried to repair as much of the roof as I can, but Tony, you and Dad will need to pitch in as well. And...' She held the key out. 'This is yours now.'

Lilian reached for it, but Bobby's hand instinctively closed around it.

Lilian frowned. 'Bobby?'

'Ugh. Sorry, I don't know why I did that.' She dropped the key into Lilian's palm. 'It just suddenly occurred to me that I was really going.' Bobby glanced around the cottage. 'I'll miss this place,' she said softly. 'I hadn't realised until now quite how much.'

–

That night, Bobby slept better than she had for some time. She was tired after her walk, and the smell of Charlie in the box room, which had caused her such mental turmoil the last time she had slept there, felt strangely comforting after so many days of not hearing from him. She enjoyed a dreamless, restful sleep, feeling as though he was there at her side – although there was an emptiness when she woke and found that he wasn't.

She awoke the next morning – the morning of Topsy's wedding – some time before her alarm clock, and after washing and dressing, went downstairs to the parlour to type up an account of her walk. Reg hobbled in on her an hour later.

'You again?' he said, taking a seat at his desk. 'I thought you'd resigned to go to war.'

'I wanted to get this walk typed,' Bobby murmured, not looking up.

'That'll keep while tomorrow. Go get your breakfast, lass. You work too hard.'

Bobby glanced up to smile. 'That's rich coming from you.'

'Aye, well, I'm an old man. Nowt else to do with missen at my age.' He nodded to her typewriter. 'Taking it with you when you go?'

Bobby looked at the old Remington as if seeing it for the first time. It had been a gift from her parents when she had graduated from Pitman's College many years ago, second-hand even then, but old though it was, it had served her well. For the past fifteen months it had sat here, on her desk in the Athertons' parlour. The idea of it not being here… for some reason, that felt even more final than when she had handed over the cow house key.

She was going. She wouldn't be here any more. Tony would sit at this desk, doing her job. It was Tony and Lil who would sleep in her bed at the cow house, and take care of her father. And Bobby would be… who knew what she would be doing?

'I don't know,' she said in a slightly choked voice. 'I suppose I'll leave it at the cow house. Tony's got his own machine and I won't need it where I'm going, will I? I'm sure the WAAF have got plenty of typewriters.'

'Nay, take it with thee. Never know when you might have a bit of time to do some writing. Don't want to let those skills stagnate, eh?'

'I suppose not,' Bobby said vaguely.

'Oh. While I've got you here.' Reg took a fat envelope from a drawer. He limped to her desk to hand it to her.

'What is it?' Bobby asked.

'Leaving present.'

Bobby slid her hand into the envelope and drew out a book. It was a hardback edition of the memoir of her hero, Dorothy Lawrence: a woman reporter who had disguised herself as a man in the last war and served at the front.

'For me?' she said, running her hand wonderingly over the dust jacket.

'Aye, so you won't forget what you're really good at.' He summoned a rare smile. 'Stand up, will you? I'd rather say my goodbyes now than in front of the rabble.'

She did so, and Reg reached over the desk to shake her hand.

'Good luck, Bobby. You've been a right decent worker. Doubt I'll ever find better.' He looked a little awkward. 'And... well, you're a good lass. Come back to us when it's done, won't you? You and that brother of mine. Like I said before, we'll always have a home for the pair of you here.'

Bobby smiled. This was the closest Reg had ever come to admitting he valued her not only as a reporter but as a member of his family. She knew he would be embarrassed beyond belief if she hugged him, however, and contented herself with shaking his hand heartily.

'I'll miss you too, Reg,' she said.

'Aye, well, no need to talk soft about it. Go get some breakfast, eh?'

Bobby started to go, but Reg put a hand on her shoulder.

'And don't forget what I said,' he told her. 'Keep that writing brain of yourn working hard, like your pal Miss Lawrence did.'

'Don Sykes said something very similar the last time I saw him.'

'Don always recognised summat in you it took me a long time to see. Too long a time.'

'What was that?'

Reg smiled. 'A newspaperman.'

Bobby met his eye. 'Is there any point keeping my skills honed though, Reg, if I've got no job to come back to?'

'I thought you might say that,' Reg said. 'Look, I can't promise I'll take you back – wish I could. I don't even know if we'll still be here. But if there's still a *Tyke* and there's still a Reg Atherton responsible for it... well, we'll see where we are, eh?'

–

Topsy's wedding was to take place at the Anglican church in the village, St Peter's, that afternoon. Bobby had offered to help her prepare, but Topsy had wanted no one with her on the morning of her wedding but Mrs Hobbes.

'Someone ought to tell that girl it's only the groom it's bad luck for her to see before the ceremony,' Mary observed as she, Lilian and the two Parry girls helped Bobby get ready.

Bobby's maid of honour dress was a smart floral one that Topsy had loaned her. The fact she had something new and pretty to wear rather than her best, but increasingly shabby, blue crepe was creating at least a little festive atmosphere in her heart. She was doing everything she could to banish preoccupation about her imminent departure so she could fully share in her friends' joy.

'I think Topsy wants to make a big entrance in her silk gown,' she said with a smile. 'It was her grandmother's apparently, although it's been refashioned into something a little less Victorian. Topsy's absolutely refused to let anyone but Mrs Hobbes see it before the wedding.'

'Are you and the other bridesmaids not to walk down the aisle with her?'

'There are no other bridesmaids. She only wanted me, and she didn't want to be attended down the aisle.'

Mary smiled. 'Topsy will do things her own way.'

'I'm not complaining,' Bobby said. 'I'd hate to have everyone looking at me. It's going to be bad enough on my own wedding day.'

'Bobby, may I brush your hair?' Jessie asked, giving the chestnut waves hanging loose over her shoulders an awed look. Lilian had lent her sister a little hair oil, and for once Bobby's tresses were smooth and manageable, free from their habitual frizz.

'No, Bobby said I could do it,' Florrie insisted.

Lilian smiled. 'How about if you brush Bobby's and Jess does mine? It isn't quite as long, I'm afraid, but it's just as thick.'

'Oh, yes please!' Jessie said, clapping her hands.

They were in Mary and Reg's bedroom, with Bobby sitting on the edge of the bed facing the mirror. Lilian sat down next to her. The two little girls clambered up behind them, brandishing a hairbrush each.

'Now, be gentle,' Mary warned them. 'You know how you both shout when I pull at your knots.'

'We will,' Jess said solemnly as she started brushing Lilian's shoulder-length hair.

Lilian laughed. 'I could get used to this. My own personal salon. Girls, I shall expect regular beauty treatments now I'm to live here, in all the most fashionable styles.'

'Oooh, yes,' Florrie breathed. 'I wish Bobby could stay too, then we could do her hair to match.'

'I'll be home on leave before you know it,' Bobby said. 'I'll tell you all about life in the Air Force and we can make up some games about it.'

'And will you let me wear your WAAF hat?' Jess asked eagerly.

Bobby smiled. 'All right. But you must be very careful with it, and you'll have to take turns with your sister.'

'Will Uncle Charlie come home to play too?' Florrie asked. 'Then I can wear his hat and Jess can wear yours.'

Bobby experienced a pang as she thought about Charlie. She had rushed over to the cow house when she had seen Gil deliver that morning's post, but once again there had been no letter.

'I sincerely hope so,' she said, forcing her voice to stay bright. She didn't want either the girls or Mary to pick up on her worry.

'I'm not sure how keen he'll be on a game of Beauty Salons though, Florrie.'

Jessie giggled. 'I bet he'd play if we asked. He'd look so funny wearing lipstick, wouldn't he, Florrie?'

'Which of our valiant forces friends are to be at the ceremony then?' Mary asked as she applied some rouge to Bobby's cheeks. 'Are those young Canadians joining us?'

'Chip and Sandy are. Ernie couldn't get leave from his instructor post.'

'You've heard from him?'

Bobby felt her colour rise, and wondered why that should be.

It was a fair question. She and Ernie were friends, after all. Mary knew she had other male friends as correspondents – Don for one and Piotr for another, although perhaps the fact they were both married added a degree of respectability. Even so, Bobby had wondered if a letter from Ernie might arrive at some point.

She hadn't heard a word, however, although he always asked to be remembered to her in the letters he wrote to Teddy and Topsy. He was down in the south-east somewhere now, Topsy informed her, a long way from Silverdale.

Bobby couldn't deny she missed his warm smile and teasing jokes, but after how they had parted, it was something of a relief that he hadn't tried to engage her in a private correspondence. Before, she would have welcomed it, even been the one to begin it, but it didn't feel quite proper now.

'No, but he writes to Teddy,' she said in answer to Mary's question, hoping her heightened colour had been sufficiently disguised by rouge. 'Topsy's hopping mad about him not getting leave. She wanted him and Piotr to be at the head of the guard of honour. I imagine her father's friend at the Air Ministry got an earful about it.'

'She thinks the world revolves around this wedding of hers,' Mary said, smiling. 'The fact the Air Force have got a war to fight probably hasn't even occurred to her.'

'Silk gowns and guards of honour,' Lilian said with a wistful sigh. 'That's exactly the sort of wedding I always pictured.'

'Oh, them's nobbut frills,' Mary said dismissively. 'It's not how you do it, it's the husband you find yourself lumbered with once it's done. Pout please, Bobby.'

Bobby puckered obediently so Mary could apply some lipstick: rose pink to match the flowers on her dress. It was rather nice to be dressed and brushed like a favourite doll.

Mary stood back to examine her handiwork. 'All done except for styling your hair. What a shame it isn't the fashion to wear it loose, as girls did at weddings when I was young. You look as blooming and bonny as any film star, young Bobby.'

Bobby blushed. 'Don't be daft.'

'Yes you do. It's just a shame our Charlie couldn't get leave to see you.' Mary smiled. 'Mind you, he'd not be satisfied until Topsy had agreed to make it a double wedding.'

'What will your wedding be like when you marry Uncle Charlie, Bobby?' Florrie asked as she ran the brush through Bobby's hair.

'I'd like to have the date confirmed before I start making plans,' Bobby said. 'It's probably dreadful bad luck.'

'Why are so many wedding things supposed to bring bad luck?'

Mary laughed. 'You'll find out when you've a husband of your own, Flor.'

'What will you do?' Lilian asked Bobby. 'I suppose you and Charlie have talked about it.'

'Charlie says he doesn't mind how we do it so long as it's done and legal. At any rate, it'll have to be a simple affair. We won't have long to organise everything.' Bobby was quiet for a moment. 'Mary is right though. As nice as it is to celebrate, it's only window dressing, isn't it? It's Charlie that's important – Charlie and me. As long as we can be together, I don't care a fig about the rest of it.'

Mary smiled. 'Well said, my love.'

'Oh, but we'll still be flower girls though, won't we?' Jessie asked anxiously. 'Uncle Charlie promised.'

Bobby laughed. 'No matter how we manage things, Jess, I promise the two of you will be there with baskets of petals over your arms.'

'I do hope you can do it in May, when there'll be plenty of flowers to be had.' Mary looked rather dreamy. 'A girl ought to be married in the spring, when the landscape is as blooming as she is. I can just see you, Bobby, ornamented by nature – always the best ornaments for a bride – and Charlie so handsome in his uniform. What a happy day that will be! There was a time I despaired of seeing that young rascal respectably wed.'

'Have you had a letter recently?' Bobby asked, as casually as she could. She had seen Gil drop something in, but someone had scooped it up before she could see the envelope.

'Aye, we had one this morning. Were there not one for you?'

Bobby felt as if she could breathe again. If Mary had had a letter, that meant Charlie must be safe.

But then why was there nothing for her?

'Not this week,' she said. 'It's been held up, I suppose.'

Mary nodded. 'You can't rely on post from military. I don't know what they do with it. I'm sure half of it must get tipped in with the salvage or used to light campfires.'

'Yes. I'm sure that's it.'

It was strange though. If a letter from Charlie had come through to Moorside, why should those he had written to her at the house across the way have disappeared into the ether? While Bobby was relieved he was safe, she couldn't help worrying that something else might be wrong – something that involved him and her.

Chapter 26

The sun shone as Athertons, Scotts and Parrys walked to the church to celebrate a coupling that, although it had been less than a year since the two people involved had first met, still felt too long in coming. Tony walked with Reg and Rob, seemingly anxious to make a good impression as he chatted and cracked jokes. Mary shepherded Florrie and Jessie, endeavouring to make sure they didn't soil their best clothes by indulging in their favourite pastime of jumping in puddles. Bobby, meanwhile, took the opportunity to have a little quiet conversation with her sister.

'It's strange, isn't it?' she said dreamily to Lilian.

'What?'

'Well, this. Ten months ago, I saw a plane crash into a mountain. When we found Teddy, he was so broken, his breathing so weak, I daren't let myself believe he'd survive the night. And now I'm to be maid of honour on his wedding day.'

'They've had quite the love story, those two, haven't they?' Lilian said with an appreciative sigh.

'And with the best of endings. It looked shaky for a while. Teddy was so determined Topsy could have a better life without him. It feels odd to think she could have been marrying Archie today.'

'Her cousin won't be coming, I suppose.'

Bobby laughed. 'What, didn't I tell you? Archie's to give her away.'

Lilian blinked. 'You're joking! After she ditched him?'

'It was a little more complicated than that. Archie played his part as much as any of us in bringing them together. Anyhow, he's thrilled for them.'

'A true happily ever after,' Lilian said, simpering. 'Let's hope you'll get yours soon too, Bobby. 1942 seems to be the year for weddings.'

Bobby nudged her, nodding in Tony's direction. 'Speaking of which, how's life for the newlyweds?'

Lilian smiled at her husband, who was now deep in conversation with Reg. He caught her eye and smiled a little bashfully back.

'He's really trying, bless him,' she said. 'I don't want to count any chickens. It is early days still. But now we're out of that awful suffocating house of his mother's, it finally feels like we've got the chance to be happy.' She coloured slightly. 'He said he loved me last night.'

'He's said it before, hasn't he?'

'Yes, but this felt different. Before, I felt like he said it because he knew he ought to. But this time, when he was holding me and looking into my eyes the way men do in films… it felt real, Bobby.'

'Did you say it back?'

'Not yet. I couldn't say it unless I was really sure I felt it. But if things keep on as they are… then soon, I hope.' She smiled softly. 'I never would have believed Tony Scott could be the one for me, but adversity makes for strange bedfellows, as they say – sometimes quite literally.'

'I suppose it does.'

Lilian squeezed her sister's arm. 'I know you're worrying about leaving, Bob, but you honestly don't need to. We're all in the best place for us.'

'You'll write, won't you?'

'Of course, every week.'

Bobby lowered her voice. 'How did Dad pass the night?'

'He asked for a drink after tea,' Lilian said quietly. 'I fetched it, obviously. I know it's always worse if we try to keep it from

206

him once he's asked for it. Anyway, it at least knocked him out. There was some whimpering in the early morning, but I soon got him quiet.'

'Did Tony hear?'

'No, he slept through. I've tried to prepare him. It can only be a matter of time until Dad has one of his fits.' Lilian sighed. 'Dad's still struggling with the pregnancy. He can hardly bear to look at me now I'm big.'

'He'll come around.'

'I hope it's soon, that's all.'

Daffodils lined the path to the church, its stained-glass windows sparkling like precious gemstones in the sun. Bobby could see the vicar at the door, greeting people as they arrived. There were to be a small number of guests: mostly friends from the village and the airmen's hospital at Sumner House. Topsy's grander acquaintances – friends of her father's, the young people she knew from schooldays and the fashionable men who always seemed to hang around her – had been told that there was little room in the church, but they would be welcome in the church hall afterwards.

This was an excuse, of course, in deference to Teddy's feelings. He had allowed his bride to do as she wished when it came to the reception, but had begged that the ceremony itself would be as intimate as possible.

'I suppose I'll be back here next month for your wedding,' Lilian observed. 'You might have to push the pews a little further apart for me by then.'

'Assuming the WAAF approve my leave.' Bobby sighed. 'Lil, I'm worried.'

'I told you, there's no need. We'll be all right.'

'Not about you. It's Charlie. I didn't want to say anything to Mary, but it isn't just this week I haven't had a letter. It's been over a fortnight. He never normally goes so long without writing.'

Lilian shrugged. 'They'll be caught in the post. How many times when I was in Greenwich have you had letters from weeks back arrive all at the same time?'

'Well, a few, but—'

'Letters from military do seem to get held up more frequently than civilian post. I'm sure it's nothing to worry about.'

'I hope not, but if Charlie's letters to me have gone missing, why should one have turned up at Moorside? Surely if one gets lost on the way, they all should.'

'Not necessarily.'

'Still, I can't help worrying. I wish I could speak to him. Perhaps it's nothing, but I'd like to hear him tell me everything's all right between us.'

Lilian raised an eyebrow. 'Any reason it shouldn't be?'

Bobby rubbed her cheek. 'Not that I can think of.'

'He hasn't cooled off?'

'Not at all. In fact he's been fonder than ever, although he can have some dark moods these days.' She paused. 'I did wonder though…'

'What?'

'Something happened, Lil. Well, technically nothing happened, but it's been on my mind. My conscience says I ought to tell Charlie, and yet it seems so unfair to give him another thing to worry about. I shouldn't confess things that'll upset him to ease my own selfish conscience, should I?'

'Bobby, what are you gibbering about?' Lilian asked. 'You want to tell Charlie about a thing that didn't happen?'

'It sort of happened. It felt like it happened, but then afterwards it seemed so foolish that I persuaded myself it was nothing.' Bobby took Lilian's elbow to hold her back, lowering her voice. 'There was something… something with Ernie King.'

'No! That good-looking Canadian?'

'Yes, him.'

'I told you he had his eye on you, didn't I?'

Bobby massaged her temples. 'He can't have. I mean, it's just so unlikely. He's got girls chasing him all over the place, and I was sure it was Topsy he wanted. Well, why wouldn't he?'

'What did he do? Get fresh? Did he kiss you?'

Bobby would have liked to have heard a little more sympathy in her sister's tone, rather than the obvious relish for gossip. Still, Lilian took her hand and gave it a squeeze.

'Nothing like that,' Bobby said. 'We slipped on the ice when we were walking home one night and I landed on top of him.'

'You didn't! Then what happened?'

'Like I said: nothing. He was a gentleman, as always. Didn't even touch me. But there was... a look.'

Lilian laughed. 'You're letting a guilty conscience eat you up over a look?'

'I know, it's silly. Still, it felt like it meant something at the time, and I was worried I might have encouraged him without realising it. I couldn't believe he'd ever see me that way so I never told him off when he flirted.'

'A little innocent flirting between friends is harmless,' Lilian said with a shrug. 'Good for the ego, when your young man isn't around to pay you compliments. It's hardly a torrid affair, Bobby.'

'But I never meant to flirt back! I mean, Ernie talks that way to everyone,' Bobby said, somewhat defensively. 'I didn't think it was *flirting* flirting. I thought he was just being courteous.'

'Where is he now?'

'Cambridge. They packed him off to be an instructor while he heals from an injury.'

'And has he written to you? Taken any steps towards actual, unambiguous courting?'

'No. Teddy's his correspondent. Ernie asks after me, but he does that for all his friends in Silverdale.'

'Then you've done everything right,' Lilian said. 'It sounds innocent enough, in spite of this so-called look. Nothing to get

Charlie upset. I don't think you ought to feel obliged to confess when there was no substance to it.'

'That was what I thought, but then his letters stopped out of the blue. I was worried someone might have been whispering gossip in his ear.'

'What gossip could there be? All right, so Ernie can be a flirt, but you said he does that with everyone.'

'Yes, but gossip has a way of making mountains from mole-hills. If I only had a letter so I knew everything was still right between us…'

They were right by the church now. Lil patted Bobby's arm.

'It'll be nothing,' she said. 'I'll keep an eye on your post and send any letters straight to you at Ryland Moor, all right? I bet there'll be three or four together next week.'

'I hope you're right.' Bobby smiled at her, feeling marginally better, although she knew she wouldn't feel fully reassured until she saw Charlie's writing telling her once again that he loved her. 'Thanks, Lil. I wish you were coming with me, so I'd have someone to talk me out of my barmy notions.'

The young vicar nodded as they reached the door of the church. 'Good afternoon, ladies. We're not having a bride and a groom's side today, since the groom's family are of course unable to attend, but the couple have asked that the two front left pews be kept empty. Otherwise, please sit wherever you wish.'

'Um, I'm the maid of honour,' Bobby said. 'I think I'm supposed to sit somewhere special, aren't I?'

'Ah, yes. In that case, take a seat at the front on the right.'

'Thank you.'

'Why are the front left pews to be kept empty?' Lilian whispered as they went in.

'One is as a mark of respect to Teddy's crew, who died on the mountain,' Bobby whispered back. 'And the other is for his family in Poland. It's where his parents and sisters would be seated if they were here.'

'It's so sad that they won't see him married. I don't suppose they know it's happening, do they?'

'No. The poor man doesn't know if they're still in Poland, or even if they're alive. I hope there can be a reunion one day.'

Lilian eased herself with difficulty into a pew beside Tony while Bobby took her place at the front next to the matron of honour, Mrs Hobbes.

'Afternoon.' She nodded to the goose on Mrs Hobbes's lap. 'And hello, Norman. You look dapper today.'

Norman was wearing a pale blue ribbon around his neck on which was threaded the wedding ring. He looked none too pleased about his role as page boy, but out of respect for the occasion he forewent his usual honk. His wife Jemima was unable to attend, as she kept watch over the couple's first clutch of eggs.

Not long afterwards the groom arrived, being wheeled down the aisle by Piotr, the best man. Teddy was in a black morning suit and top hat which Bobby assumed had been loaned from among Topsy's acquaintances, or possibly by Archie, the original groom. Piotr, of course, was in his RAF uniform. He winked at Bobby as he passed by, and she smiled back. It was nearly two months since she had last seen her friend, who had finished operational training and been placed on active service with an all-Polish bomber squadron. His wife Jolka was present too, sitting with their young son Tommy. The toddler looked to be in a petulant mood, and Jolka soothed and bounced him as she watched her husband proudly.

Bobby could see many of her friends in the congregation, now she took the time to look around: Anglicans, Catholics and Methodists alike coming together to celebrate the nuptials.

Chip and Sandy, Ernie's Canadian comrades, sat near the front with some airmen from the hospital who were mobile enough to attend. These were to make up the guard of honour, and the convalescents had been given special permission to cast off their hospital blues and don service dress for the occasion.

Little Gil Capstick was present too, blushing as he sat beside Mabs Jessop, who, according to popular rumour, he had long been sweet on. There was Louisa Clough, the postmistress, and her husband Wilfred. There was Stanley Henderson and Arthur Egerton, two men who had been part of the rescue party that had brought Teddy and Piotr down from Great Bowside. And—

Bobby squinted, then beamed with pleasure. Sitting near the back of the church were two people she hadn't expected to see – another love story she had played a key part in, and one of the first friends she had made in Silverdale. It was Andy Jessop and his wife Ginny, smiling placidly as they held hands. Andy was well into his eighties, nearly blind now, and lived high up in the fells in his ancient farmhouse at Newby Top. It would never have occurred to Bobby he would be able to make it down to the village for the wedding, but whether by motorcycle or mule, he had managed it. She waved energetically at the elderly couple, and Ginny waved back before whispering to Andy to tell him who was there.

Everyone, it seemed, was smiling – everyone except the groom. He looked rather solemn as he regarded the empty pews dedicated to his absent family and fallen comrades. His expression kindled, however, as the organist struck up the wedding march and he prepared to receive his bride.

From where Bobby was seated, she could see only the unmarked side of Teddy's face: not the one that had been so badly burned the night his plane had crashed. He looked very handsome, with his golden curls, delicate features and the sensitive, almost poetic expression in his dark eye – the other had been left without sight as a result of his injuries. She felt a touch of pride as she watched him preparing to marry the woman he loved. Bobby had been a part of that. She had helped to save his life, and overcome the depression of spirits that had nearly persuaded him to walk away from Topsy forever.

She had few positive feelings associated with that night on the mountain: only horror at the sight of the bodies in the plane, and guilt that she hadn't been able to save the men who had died up there. But now she would have this: the memory of Teddy's face, glowing with happiness as his story finally got its happy ending.

All eyes turned to the door as the bride entered on the arm of her cousin Archie. He smiled placidly on the assembled company, seemingly happy enough at the change in places between himself and Teddy. The sun shone through the stained-glass windows, creating a carpet of coloured light to guide them to the pulpit.

Bobby suspected that her sister, seated a few rows behind her, would shed an envious tear at the sight of Topsy's dress. It was a sumptuous dove-breasted cream silk, with a full skirt and a bodice panelled with lace – not at all old-fashioned thanks to Mrs Hobbes's skill with a needle. There was no train, but a fine lace veil trimmed with a coronet of white hothouse roses fluttered behind the bride. A bouquet of the same flowers was clutched in her hands. Bobby felt quite star-struck, watching this beautiful stranger who was one of her closest friends, and almost blushed when the bride threw a smile her way.

'Oh, isn't she lovely?' Bobby breathed to Mrs Hobbes. 'Look at Teddy. He's crying.'

Mrs Hobbes pursed her lips as she watched Topsy walk down the aisle, beaming and nodding at her guests on both sides. 'Now I knew she'd do this. Time and again she's been told to stay solemn and look straight ahead. And she would refuse to wear the veil down.'

'It's better like this. Look how happy everyone is.'

'Yes,' she said in a choked voice. 'You're right, Bobby. Let the young people do it their way. I'm sure it's all the same to God.'

Bobby shuffled to look at Mrs Hobbes, who was smiling now even while tears trickled down her cheeks. Topsy had no memory of her real mother, who had died when she was a baby, so the eccentric nanny was the only one she had ever known.

'How does it feel?' Bobby whispered.

Mrs Hobbes sighed. 'I do miss that little girl I raised, as mischievous and wayward as she could be. But I'm proud to know the woman she is. Never prouder than today.'

The music stopped when Archie and Topsy reached the pulpit. Archie kissed his cousin on the cheek and whispered a few words to her before taking his seat.

The vicar nodded to Bobby and Mrs Hobbes, who stood to flank Topsy while Piotr did the same at Teddy's side. Norman was led up too. He glared at the vicar, to whom he seemed to have taken a dislike. Perhaps he thought the capacious white surplice indicated that this was a type of large gander, here to challenge his masculine authority.

'Oh! Do wait,' Topsy said, as the vicar opened his mouth to begin. The next moment she was hoisting her beautiful dress up so she could kneel on the cold flags level with Teddy.

'That's better,' she said, beaming around the congregation. 'It wouldn't do to begin married life all unequal, would it? I want us to start as we mean to go on: facing life side by side.'

There was a ripple of laughter around the church, and a few dabbed eyes as well. Teddy looked moved, and reached out to press Topsy's hand.

Bobby found she had little to do as maid of honour but stand beside her friend, and occasionally give Norman a cautionary nudge with her toe when he looked tempted to nibble on the vicar's surplice. She was glad nothing more was demanded of her. Watching Teddy and Topsy say their vows, their faces filled with happiness and love, she found herself rather wobbly. For a worrying moment she even thought she might faint, but she managed to summon her strength. The emotion of the moment the lovers were joined very nearly overwhelmed her. She couldn't help picturing herself standing where Topsy knelt, Charlie beside her as they promised before God to love and cherish one another, always. But would that picture ever become a reality?

Chapter 27

After the ceremony, the men of the RAF and RCAF held their sabres in an arch above the church door, looking no less gallant for the fact that a number of the wounded men were forced to support themselves with sticks. Topsy wheeled Teddy through as the happy couple, laughing and blushing, were showered with rice and hot pennies by cheering villagers.

It felt like everyone who hadn't been at the ceremony had come out to cheer Mrs Tadeusz Nowak, formerly Lady Honoria Sumner-Walsh, into married life. Both bride and groom were well liked in the village. Silverdale took a lot of pride in 'Her Ladyship', as Bobby knew they would always refer to Topsy in spite of changes to her name and title, who was admired for her generosity, her willingness to muck in and her absence of condescending airs. Teddy, too, had been adopted by the village as one of their own since the night he had been carried down almost dead from Great Bowside. Bobby had never seen such a crowd, nor heard such a racket.

There were strangers in the crowd too, and Bobby noticed as she walked to the church hall that a number of rather grand motor cars were now dotted around the village. These, she presumed, belonged to Topsy's upper-crust friends. Certainly none of the local farmers could afford vehicles like that.

She wondered fleetingly where they were getting their petrol from. Reg had had to take his old Wolseley off the road months ago thanks to cuts in the fuel allowance, and it had recently been announced that from July, petrol coupons for civilians would be done away with altogether. Rationing was supposed to guarantee an equal share for all, but it did seem that when it came to the upper classes, different rules applied.

The reception was as typically Topsy as the wedding itself, in that it ignored every convention in favour of being exactly what the bride wanted.

When Bobby entered the church hall, she was expecting to find sedate rows of tables set for a meal, adorned with some of the gold-trimmed tablecloths she had spent so long stitching. There were certainly a number of tables draped in the cloths, but these had been pushed against the walls, where they almost buckled under the weight of floral arrangements and food.

Her newly married friend Bess Jenkins's eyes would bulge out of her head if she could see such a spread, after what she had told Bobby of her own modest wedding feast: spam sandwiches and jam tarts. A few tables had been laid out for sitting at, but most of the floor was clear, and a dance band were seated at the front of the room.

The happy couple arrived at that moment. Bobby watched as Piotr and Chip lifted Teddy's wheelchair inside, with Topsy hopping up the steps beside him. Topsy beamed as the band launched into a swing version of the wedding march. Bobby, who was nearest the door, claimed her friend for a hug while some of the men came over to shake Teddy by the hand.

'All the joy in the world, my love,' Bobby said, giving her friend a squeeze.

'Thank you, darling.'

'The spread looks incredible. Are people to just help themselves?'

'That's right. I didn't want some stuffy meal with speeches and all that rot. I wanted everyone up dancing. We had to have a few tables for the old folk, but I don't want to see a single person under seventy sitting down today.'

'This is more grub than these people will have seen in years,' Bobby said, running her wondering gaze over it all. 'All the village housewives will be running home for bigger handbags.'

She could see Jessie, Florrie and some of the other children staring pop-eyed at the sweet things, and knew they'd set upon them like locusts as soon as they were given permission to help themselves.

'As long as everyone enjoys themselves.' Topsy smiled at Teddy, who was being slapped on the back by Piotr. 'But I mustn't neglect my new husband.'

Teddy grinned when he caught her eye, and wheeled himself to her. He bowed and held out a hand. 'A dance, Mrs Nowak?'

'It would be my pleasure, Mr Nowak,' Topsy said, giggling as she dropped a curtsey. Piotr took charge of the wheelchair so Teddy could lead his new bride to the dance floor.

Bobby watched as Archie entered with another young man, who she recognised as one of Topsy's fashionable friends. She had seen him once before, at Topsy's Christmas party. He was blinking in puzzlement.

'I don't get it, Sumner,' she overheard him saying. 'What is this place?'

'It's a church hall, Dolly. Don't they have them where you are?'

'I wouldn't know, I've never looked.' The young man known as Dolly stared at the new husband and wife moving around the floor, Piotr pushing so that Teddy could lead his bride in a waltz. 'Why here? Why not the Dorch or somewhere, if she can't have it at her place?'

Archie shrugged. 'No use asking me. You might remember I resigned from the role of groom.'

'Who are all these people?'

'Farmers and their families mostly. They live in the village.'

'Farmers?' Dolly gazed blankly around the hall. 'I don't understand. Is it some sort of wheeze?'

'No, it's just Topsy,' Archie said with a laugh.

'What could she be thinking of, marrying a Pole? She could have had anyone. I mean, the man can't even walk.'

'I suppose she was thinking that she loved him,' Archie said as he reached over to help himself to an hors d'oeuvre.

Dolly curled his lip as he watched the odd dance: Topsy clasping Teddy's hand while he was wheeled in time to the music. 'Look at them. It's absurd.'

'Tops doesn't think so. I've never seen her look so proud.' Archie spotted Bobby and smiled. 'Excuse me, old man. There's a young lady here I simply must ask to dance.'

He left his friend to approach her.

'I'd love to, Arch,' Bobby said before he could ask.

Archie grinned and took her hand to pull her on to the dance floor, where a few other couples had joined the newlyweds. Chip had taken charge of Teddy's wheelchair so Piotr could enjoy some time in the arms of his wife. Their little son Tommy was now in the care of the Parry girls as they examined the tables of food, making a mental inventory so they could show off to any friends at school who hadn't been lucky enough to be present. Lilian had dragged Tony on to the floor as well. He struggled to hold her close with her swollen belly between them, but nevertheless wore an expression of pride in his pretty wife and the visible evidence of his virility.

'I was hoping I'd get the chance to give you a whirl,' Archie said to Bobby. 'Best part of the day. Mind you, I can't deny I had a tear in my eye when I handed the old girl over earlier. Appropriate, what? The old groom giving her up to the new.'

'Your friend Mr Dolly seems a little confused by it all,' Bobby observed.

'Topsy can have that effect on people. They're so used to one way of doing things, you know, and then along comes Tops with her mad ideas. But Dolly's not a bad sort, deep down. He's just got the hump because he thought he might have a chance with her himself.' Archie gestured to a handsome middle-aged woman looking down her nose at proceedings as she spoke with a high-ranking RAF officer. 'Did you notice that Mother was here?'

Bobby glanced at Topsy's Aunt Constance. 'I thought she'd sworn she wouldn't come.'

'She did, but then she heard Topsy's Uncle Geoffrey would be attending – that's Air Marshal Sir Geoffrey Badham to the rest of us oiks. I think Mother has rather set her cap at him. Having given up on marrying me off for money and status, she's determined to do it for herself.' He looked approvingly at Bobby's floral dress. 'I say, you do look smashing. Is your chap here?'

'No, he couldn't get leave.'

'And no Ernie King to share you with either. That means I can have every dance to myself.'

Bobby smiled. 'Aren't you worried Mother Dearest will cut you off if she sees you waltzing with the gamekeeper's daughter?'

He laughed, flushing a little. 'Ah, now you're going to force me to reveal my deep, dark secret. I was hoping to save it until at least one of us was squiffy. Things never sound quite so foolish after half a bottle of wine.'

'What is it?'

'A job.'

'You finally found something? What are you doing?'

He smiled. 'That's the embarrassing part. I suppose you thought I was joking, after our pantomime when I said I might audition for ENSA. Well, I thought, what the hell – why not give it a try? Playing the fool is really the only thing I was ever any good at. Anyhow, I suppose they must be desperate because they've assigned me to a troupe.'

Bobby blinked. 'You're joining an ENSA troupe?'

She knew Archie had been keen to find a job that would give him some degree of independence from his mother's tightly knotted purse strings since being invalided out of the RAF, but the idea of Bobby's upper-class friend joining the organisation that provided entertainment for the troops – Every Night Something Awful, as wags liked to joke the initials stood for – had never occurred to her.

'That's right,' Archie said. 'Chap there lost the other half of his double act in the Blitz so he needs a new stooge. The gag is that he's a cloth-cap-wearing salt-of-the-earth type and I'm to be the aristocratic idiot he outwits.' He grinned. 'Suits me perfectly, don't you think? I won't even need to rehearse.'

'You in ENSA! I didn't expect that, I must say.'

'I know, isn't it madness? We're being sent to Northumberland in a few weeks to entertain some soldiers. I hope the cook there has been saving up their egg rations. They'll need some rotten ones when I get on stage.'

'Oh, I think it's wonderful,' Bobby said, beaming at him. 'You were marvellous in our pantomime. Loads better than any ENSA comedian I've seen. I hope you're sent to entertain wherever I am.'

'Why, are you going somewhere?'

'To the RAF training school ten miles away. I got called up to the WAAF – I leave on Monday. I'm ever so nervous.'

'Then I ought to make the most of you, if you won't be here the next time I come.' The tune they had been dancing to ended and Archie took her hand to lead her to the tables of food. 'Let's get some tuck and have a little talk somewhere private, shall we?'

There wasn't really anywhere private indoors, so after helping herself to a small chicken leg, a boiled egg and a piece of bread and butter, Bobby followed Archie outside with her plate.

She picked up the chicken leg.

'Do you suppose this hen had stunted growth?' she asked. 'I've never seen such a tiny leg.'

'Probably pigeon,' Archie said. 'I imagine someone sent Tops a brace or two from their hunting bag as a wedding gift. You could have had another, you know. Looked like there was plenty there.'

'I've got so used to counting every mouthful, I can't bring myself to break the habit.' She frowned at the little leg. 'I wonder what Topsy's planning for the bones. You could get a lot of stock out of what's on that table.'

Archie laughed. 'You're talking like a housewife already, darling. Not married yet, are you?'

'No. Not yet,' Bobby said quietly. 'How about you? Have you managed to find yourself a suitable wife?'

'I don't need one now I've found a job,' Archie said airily. 'I mean, unless that's a proposal. I'll always make an exception for you, Cinders.'

'I think Charlie might object,' Bobby said, laughing. She lowered her voice. 'Any other romances on the cards, while it's just the two of us?'

Archie didn't answer. He avoided looking at her as he nibbled on his pigeon leg.

Bobby mentally kicked herself. Had that been the wrong question to ask? It wasn't like Archie to look so solemn. Perhaps it was too soon after losing Ned, the fighter pilot he had loved, for her friend to be considering a new lover.

'Sorry,' she said. 'You're thinking of Ned, I suppose. I shouldn't have been nosy.'

'It's not that.' She noticed that Archie was now smiling softly. 'I don't want to tempt fate, that's all.'

'There is someone?'

'Perhaps there is.' He looked up to grin at her. 'I'll tell you what. Next time we see one another, I'll tell you all about it. Wherever we are and whatever the circumstances, you can hold me to that. What do you say?'

She smiled. 'It's a deal.'

'So you're off to the WAAF, eh?' he said as they ate. 'Bumped into a WAAF pal of mine from RAF days recently. She was an erk when I met her, training as a plotter – you know, tracking enemy raids and all that. She's got a code and cipher commission now. It sounds like the RAF have moved her on to grand things since she and I were stationed together.'

Bobby swallowed down a mouthful of bread and butter. 'Oh?'

'Yes, I ran into her at a club in London on embarkation leave. Couldn't say where she was going, of course, but I suppose it will be Africa. She hinted she's doing terribly important work in intelligence. It sounded like something out of a spy novel.'

Bobby frowned. 'They're sending her overseas?'

'So I understand. She was bouncing with excitement about it.'

Bobby ate her egg in thoughtful silence, her mind wandering along a new avenue.

She had decided not to challenge her call-up because she had felt it was her duty to do her bit, but the prospect of joining the forces had given her little pleasure. She had a vague idea of spending her days typing stuffy military communications: nothing to tax her brain.

But now Archie had opened her mind to other prospects. Some of those in the women's services did go overseas, didn't they? There were WAAFs right in the thick of it, doing important work intercepting codes and ciphers, plotting courses for aircraft, interpreting aerial photographs and other activities vital to the course of the war.

All her life, Bobby had dreamed of doing something important. When she was young, she had harboured an ambition to earn a place on a daily newspaper, breaking stories of national significance – perhaps even climbing as high as editor. Then *The Tyke* had come into her life, and taught her that 'important' wasn't always the same as 'grand'. Working on the little magazine had been an education, teaching her that when it came to people – 'people before things,' as Reg constantly told her – there really was no such thing as 'trivial'.

But now her mind drifted back to those early ambitions. She thought of the book Reg had given her, the memoir of her hero Dorothy Lawrence, and how she had served on the front lines... and began to wonder. Could Bobby, too, be that woman?

She couldn't do what Charlie did. She couldn't fly. She couldn't fight. But she was intelligent, hard-working and as tenacious as any man, and she was sure she had a hell of a lot more to give to the war effort than bloody shorthand typing.

Chapter 28

Bobby's train of thought was interrupted by the arrival of Andy and Ginny Jessop, accompanied by Andy's granddaughter Mabs. Andy leaned on Mabs's shoulder while Ginny fussed around him, making sure he was fully covered by his muffler and coat.

'Stop thy fettling, lass,' he said with a hoarse laugh. 'I'll not drop dead o' cold afore we get there, I promise.'

'Hullo,' Archie said in a low voice to Bobby. 'Here's a fine local specimen. He looks like an old poacher.'

Bobby laughed. 'It's my friend Mr Jessop.' She waved to Ginny, who hailed her.

'It's Miss Bancroft, Andy,' she said to her husband, and he beamed.

'Do you mind if I leave you to have a little talk with them?' Bobby asked Archie. 'I feel like I'm on a sort of farewell tour today. This is probably the last time I'll see everyone from the village before I leave.'

'Oh, don't mind me,' Archie said cheerily. 'Just be sure to save me all your dances and I shan't be in the least jealous who you speak to.'

Bobby squeezed his shoulder, then went to join Andy and Ginny.

'Mabs, I can help your grandfather if you want to go in,' she said. 'Gil was looking for you before. I suppose he wanted to ask for a dance.'

Mabs tossed her head. 'Huh. He can *ask* all he wants.'

'Now don't be haughty, young miss,' Ginny told her sternly. 'Gil's paying you a compliment and the least you could do is be gracious. One day you'll learn to look past what's outside to what's in.'

'Listen to thy step-nana,' Andy said, nodding. 'Yon post office lad's worth ten of the ones tha meks a fool of thyself running after.'

Mabs ignored them.

'Is Ernie inside?' she asked Bobby.

'No, he couldn't get leave.'

'What about Sandy?'

'Yes, I think so.'

'I'll give him a dance if he asks then. Gil Capstick can go whistle.'

She left them to go in, head held high.

Ginny shook her head as Bobby took Mabs's place at Andy's side, threading her arm through his so he could lean against her. 'That lass gets more wayward every day.'

'Poor Gil,' Bobby said. 'It's hard for the local lads to compete with the Canadians. They must seem very exciting and exotic to someone Mabs's age.'

'Always it's uniforms and foreigners wi' that girl. I despair of her ever settling, I really do. Lord knows what the forces will make of her if she's called on to go.'

'Army could be t' mekkin on her,' Andy said. Bobby realised she was walking a little too quickly for him as he shuffled along, and slowed her steps to match.

'Or it could be t' ruining of her,' Ginny muttered. 'I'm sure my girls were never so wilful.'

Andy grinned at her. 'Nay, but tha was, eh, Gin? Don't think I'm too old to have forgotten.'

Ginny smiled and nudged him. 'Now you've no right to hold them days against me, Andy Jessop. I was nobbut a bairn then.'

'Well, no more is our Mabs. She's noan long turned nineteen. She'll be reet, lass, don't tha worry. Just has to learn her lessons her own way, same as we all did.'

'Be careful, Mr Jessop,' Bobby said. 'Here's a step.'

Between them, she and Ginny helped the old man inside and guided him to a seat at one of the tables. Ginny sat beside him, but Bobby remained standing. Andy smiled up at her, squinting to make her out with what was left of his sight.

'And how's our lass from t' paper?' he asked.

Bobby sighed. 'Soon to be the lass from somewhere else entirely. I feel like I'm here to say goodbye as much as to celebrate Topsy's wedding.'

'Is it soon tha goes to t' Air Force?'

'Yes, it's this Monday.'

'What'll they give thee to do there?'

'Administration, the lady who interviewed me said.'

'Administration?' Andy said, frowning. 'That typing and such, is it?'

'Yes, like a secretary does.'

He shook his head. 'Nay, that's not for thee. Waste o' that good brain of thine.'

'Well, perhaps not,' Bobby said, thinking about what Archie had said. 'There might be other work for me, if I impress them.'

Ginny smiled. 'Are you going to win the war for us then, Miss Bancroft?'

'I'll certainly do my best,' Bobby said, laughing.

'Just be sure to come back when tha's won it,' Andy said. 'It's here tha belongs. Remember that.'

'I won't forget.'

'We'll be flitting soon too,' Ginny said soberly.

Bobby frowned. 'You're not moving away from Silverdale?'

'In a manner o' speaking. Only as far as my daughter's in Smeltham, but we've to leave Newby Top. It's not healthy for Andy now, and I must admit it's getting into my old bones as well. We're not young, Miss Bancroft. Cold, rattling farmhouses up in t' fells are no place for folk our age.'

Andy sighed. 'Never thought I'd see t' day I'd leave the old place. I'd eight siblings born in front of that fireplace. Three bairns, five grandbabbies, four great-grandbabbies. I'll noan get to see another generation.'

'I am sorry,' Bobby said quietly. 'I know how attached you are to the place. But Mrs Jessop is right: you ought to think of your comfort.'

'Aye, it'll be summat to be warm and in walking distance o' t' pub,' Andy said with a grin, earning him a nudge from his wife. 'Sad to think my days of striding over them hills are done with, mind. Can't even enjoy 'em with my een now they've packed in.' He sighed. 'All I can do is wait for t' fell wind to blow my way so I can smell them.'

Bobby smiled. 'I know that smell well enough. Blooming heather, burning peat and muck-spreading.'

'Aye, that's it.' Andy put out his hand. 'Well then, tha'd better say goodbye, eh? Here's hoping it's not last one.'

Bobby shook his hand, and then his wife's.

'I'll write,' she said.

'Aye, be sure tha does, and Gin can read it me. I'll miss thy bits in our paper,' Andy said. 'Ta-ra, Miss Bancroft. Fare thee well, wherever life takes thee.'

Bobby left them and approached Mary, who was standing near one of the food tables with Teddy, holding a small piece of wedding cake as if it was the most delicate bone china.

'Bobby, will you please give your friend permission from both man and God to enjoy her cake?' Teddy said. 'I cannot persuade her to eat it.'

'Royal icing,' Mary breathed as she stared at the delicacy. 'And marzipan! Not crushed haricot beans and almond essence, or any of the ersatz stuff we've been making do with – the real thing! Wherever did it come from, Teddy?'

'It is our friend Flying Officer King we must thank,' Teddy told her. 'The Canadian rations are rather more generous than ours, it seems. Though he could not be with us, he kindly donated sugar, butter and fruit as his wedding gift so that Maimie might bake a fruitcake.'

Mary shook her head wonderingly. 'There must be a week's sugar ration just in this little piece. I know I'll never be able to sleep if I eat it.'

'Please, I insist. It is my wedding day, you know.'

Mary looked hesitant, but she broke off a little piece of icing and put it in her mouth. She closed her eyes as she sucked it.

'Oh, that's just wonderful,' she said with a deep sigh.

She frowned when she opened her eyes to look at Bobby, who was watching the dancers absently. There were now eight or nine couples, whirling around to 'Sweet Georgia Brown'. Topsy was dancing with Archie, laughing as he threw her about. The children present – left to grow wild in the absence of adult supervision – weaved between the dancers, giggling as they chased one another.

'Is everything all right?' Mary asked.

'Hmm?' Bobby roused herself. 'Oh. Yes. I was just talking with Andy Jessop.'

'How is he? In good health and spirits?'

'I think so,' Bobby said slowly. 'Except that he and Ginny are leaving Newby Top. They're moving in with her daughter in Smeltham.'

'That's for the best. I wonder they stood it as long as they did. My bones would be stiff as owt if I had to live in that old place, and I'm half Andy's age.'

'I know.' Bobby sighed. 'Everything seems to be changing though. I wish it wouldn't.'

'Things must change from time to time,' Teddy observed. 'They cannot remain as they are forever.'

'I just wish they didn't have to change now, when I'm about to say goodbye.'

Teddy nodded to the cake in Mary's hand. 'You do not finish your cake, Mrs Atherton.'

She looked at it longingly. 'Oh, I couldn't. It's too naughty. I think I'll take it home to make it last.'

'As you wish.'

Mary tutted when she spotted something at the other end of the hall. 'There's Jessie helping herself to more lemonade. She'll be sick if she has anything fizzy after all that running about. Excuse me.'

She half walked, half ran to prise the drink out of Jessie's hands.

Bobby crouched so she was level with Teddy.

'This is quite a party,' she said.

'I only see Topsy's smile,' he said, beaming in his wife's direction. 'The wedding ceremony was all for me, so I could call her my wife. This reception, it is all for her. I wonder, sometimes, how two such different beings could ever have come to fall in love. I like everything that is quiet and calm; she, everything that is noisy and gay. But while I have not her capacity for joy, I love to see it shining in her face.'

Bobby took his hand to press it. 'And you'll see it frequently over the years. Every happiness, Teddy.'

He turned to smile at her. 'It is all thanks to you. My saviour on the mountain, who brought me to my love.'

'Well, it really ought to be Charlie who's given that title. He was the one who treated you when you were so close to death and brought you to the hospital.'

'Ah, but it was you who made the men come for us. I will not forget it.' He turned back to look at Topsy. 'It is not many women who would have looked on me then and done anything but recoil as from a monster.'

'But Topsy didn't, not even for an instant. You were unconscious, but I saw it. The compassion she felt from that first moment, and love too, perhaps. I am glad you changed your mind about marriage, Teddy.'

He sighed. 'Sometimes I wonder if I was right. Still it haunts me, that I can never give her a child. But I loved her too much to see her married to a man I knew could never feel half of what I did.'

'You were right to do so. I believe that with all my heart.' Bobby smiled at Topsy and Archie, playing the fool on the dance

228

floor to make the children laugh. 'See how happy she is, because of you.'

But still Teddy looked wistful as he watched his new wife play with the children.

'Her own babies would have been so precious,' he murmured. 'Yes, and she would have loved them so. Sometimes I imagine their faces, and it brings tears into my eyes. I will do everything I can to make her happy, but this one thing, more important than all, my body is now too broken to do.' He looked at Bobby. 'And so you are to leave us for the war. To whom then will I tell my troubles?'

Bobby smiled. 'To your wife, of course. But I hope you'll write – you and Topsy. I feel like I'll go mad with homesickness if I'm not kept informed about everything going on here.'

'Certainly. We will not allow you to forget us.'

Topsy came hurrying over.

'Oh, Teddy,' she said breathlessly. 'Do come and dance again. Archie says he'll manage the wheelchair. It's "Boogie Woogie Bugle Boy" after this slow one and I know it will be an absolute scream watching Arch try to keep up with the steps while he pushes. Will you?'

Teddy smiled. 'I don't suppose I am allowed to refuse you anything today. If you wish it, my Topsy.'

'Sorry, Birdy, but he is my husband, you know,' Topsy said as she commandeered the wheelchair. 'Grab yourself a partner and come dance. Piotr and Jolka are on the floor, and your sister hasn't let that chap of hers sit down for one in spite of her swollen ankles. There's Chip standing about if you need a man.'

'Soon,' Bobby said. 'I'd just like to stand and be quiet for a moment.'

Topsy frowned. 'Are you all right?'

'I need a little time, that's all, then I'll join you.'

'Well, if you must.'

Bobby watched as Topsy wheeled her new husband to the dance floor. She let her gaze drift over the dancing couples:

sweethearts and spouses, holding each other close as their bodies drifted, oblivious to everything but one another. Most of the young men were in uniform, and some of the women too – mostly the khaki of the Army and slate blue of the Air Force, with one Wren present to add to the sober spectrum in her suit of navy blue.

Bobby closed her eyes and let the sounds of music and merriment wash over her. She tried to shut out the image of the uniforms, and any thought of the war.

If she listened carefully, she could pick out the voices of her friends and family. The Parry girls, giggling as they played with their friends. Reg and Mary, talking to her father. Lilian and Tony, Piotr and Jolka, Topsy and Teddy, Andy and Ginny. She tried to fix this moment in her memory – the people she loved best, safe, filled with joy, untouched by the conflict raging outside. Soon it would be the day after tomorrow, and a new life would be waiting for her. But at least she could take this one perfect moment with her.

Chapter 29

The day after the wedding – Bobby's last as a civilian – rushed by all too quickly in a flurry of packing and preparation. The morning soon dawned when she would have to leave Silverdale and go to her new life in the armed forces.

She tried not to linger over goodbyes. She knew that the longer she spent on them, the more painful it would be. Farewells were exchanged quietly in the kitchen at Moorside after a last family breakfast. One by one she took a sober leave of Tony, her father, Lilian and Mary, and finally the Parry girls, who wept copiously as they hugged her. Bobby tried to maintain a bright demeanour for their sake, but she couldn't help a few tears escaping.

It reminded her of the sunny day Charlie had left for the RAF, and how they had lined up to say goodbye in the garden. This wasn't the same – she wasn't going into danger the way he had been – but it felt just as heart-wrenching. Just as final.

'Oh, girls, I shall miss you,' Bobby whispered, bending to kiss first one little ginger head, then the other. 'Tell Mary all your news to send. Don't forget me.'

'We wouldn't. Not ever,' Florrie managed to say through her sobs. Jess was too overcome to speak.

'Now, childer, you must let Bobby go,' Mary said gently. 'She'll miss her train if she don't leave soon.'

Florrie reluctantly detached herself, still sobbing, but Jessie refused to let go. Mary, who had tears in her own eyes, had to carry the little girl away. Bobby swallowed hard as the two children were taken from the room.

'Please let me and Dad come with you to Skipton Station,' Lilian said, coming forward to embrace her. 'I hate the idea of you going off alone.'

'I'd rather you didn't.' Bobby took out a handkerchief to dry her eyes. 'It'll only set me off crying again. I don't want to arrive with swollen eyes. Besides, there's only room in the trap for me and Reg.'

But it proved no good trying to keep her eyes fresh. As soon as Reg and Boxer had dropped her off by the Black Bull to wait for the Skipton bus, Bobby felt tears pricking once more. She watched the little pony and trap as it plodded back to Silverdale, eventually becoming no more than a speck, and felt as if it were taking her life away with it. By the time she was on a train, she had already soaked one handkerchief and was forced to rummage through her suitcase for another.

It seemed strange that such a short journey could nevertheless feel like a complete separation from the world she knew. When Bobby got off at the small station that served the village of Beckfoot, nearest RAF Ryland Moor, she was still surrounded by the same rolling landscape and heath-covered fells as she had been an hour earlier on leaving Silverdale. And yet she felt like she had landed on another planet.

According to the letter she had been sent, she and the other recruits would be collected by lorry and taken to the camp. Bobby found a gaggle of women outside the station who she assumed must be her fellow WAAFs-in-waiting.

They seemed to have bonded already, chattering, smoking and laughing together. Bobby stood at the edge of the group, the last to arrive, feeling awkward.

One woman with a lilting Welsh accent – or rather girl, for she couldn't have been more than nineteen – turned to look Bobby up and down. Bobby attempted to smile, but it came out more of a grimace. The girl wrinkled her nose before turning back to her companion. Bobby saw her mouth the word 'prig'.

Bobby turned away and rummaged urgently for her handkerchief to mop up another tear. Already she was failing to make friends among this new group of people. If they marked her down as not only a prig but a cry-baby, she'd find herself a social pariah before the lorry had even turned up to collect them.

A wave of homesickness billowed through her as her eyes rose to the fells, dragging her mind back to Silverdale. She thought of Lilian, and wished her sister was here.

Bobby had always struggled to make friends in groups of her own sex. Boys had been easier – at least, once she had passed the age where the two sexes shunned each other as a matter of course. They often teased and joked, which she enjoyed, and as long as they didn't get fresh or go all soppy romantic then platonic friendships were easy enough to strike up. But with other girls, Bobby could often feel like an outsider.

Too frequently they seemed to see her as an oddity. She was largely indifferent to matters of dress or hair, she was too quiet to enjoy going out much and she had never had any interest in casual boyfriends: all things her peers would bond over. She knew she probably came across as cold on first acquaintance. It had been lively, likeable Lilian who had made friends easily when they had been at school, and helped her twin be accepted within the group. Left to herself, Bobby was sure she would have been a far lonelier child.

Pushing down the wave of homesickness, she turned back to the group of women, wondering what Lil would do. No one would ever look at her twin and declare her to be a prig. How would Lilian join the conversation? Some easy compliment about dress or hair? Something about the films she loved?

Bobby sidled up to a group and lurked by them, trying to smile a Lilian-esque smile as she waited for an opportunity to join in.

'It's a shame they didn't get whoever designed the Wren uniform to do the WAAF one as well,' a well-spoken woman with dyed blonde hair was saying. 'Obviously it's still ten times better than those frumpy ATS tents, but the belts make your arse look the size of a panzer tank.'

'You should see the undies they give you with your kit,' a woman with a Yorkshire accent piped up. Bobby looked at her, recognising the voice. 'My sister showed me hers when she come home on leave. The girls on her base call them blackouts and knockouts – their mufti ones are knockouts, I mean, and the kit ones are blackouts. Honestly, they look like Queen Vic's drawers. Knitted dark blue bloomers right down to your knees. Our Trish refused to wear hers. Said she'd rather do time in the glasshouse than spend all day with an itchy backside.' The woman caught sight of Bobby and grinned. 'Heyup. Didn't think I'd see you again.'

It was Carol Boyes, who Bobby had met the day of her medical. She smiled, pleased to see a familiar face.

At that moment, an RAF lorry pulled up and a tiny WAAF NCO who had been driving the hefty vehicle jumped out.

'All right, ladies, pile in,' the Motor Transport sergeant said. 'Don't get too comfy, it's not a long ride. Squadron Officer Mulligan, the WAAF commandant, is waiting to welcome you.'

Bobby frowned. 'Mulligan?'

'Ugh, not that old cow,' groaned Carol, who had appeared by her side. 'Didn't realise she was in charge here. She gave me a right hard time at my interview. Looked at me like dirt. Did you have her as well?'

'Yes,' Bobby said. 'She was tough on me too.'

Carol glanced at her as they clambered up the tailboard into the back of the lorry. 'I thought you were going to get out of it. Didn't you say you were needed to make tea for your dad or summat?'

'I decided against applying for postponement in the end.'

There were benches in the lorry and several of the women made themselves comfortable. It was rather crowded, however, and Bobby opted to remain standing. Carol stood by her.

'How come?' Carol asked, taking out a cigarette.

'I just felt it wouldn't be right. That I ought to do my duty for the war effort, the same as others are.'

Carol laughed. 'Do your duty? Blimey, get you.'

'Isn't that why you joined up?' Bobby asked.

'You must be joking. Show me the way to the officers, love. That's what I'm here for.'

'Oh, yes. I remember you said you hoped you might meet someone.'

'Well, eventually, but I'm not in any hurry. The WAAF sounds a right laugh, the way our Trish tells it. You can have a different boyfriend every night if you want.' Carol tapped her arm. 'Relax and enjoy yourself, Bobby. We'll have a great time.'

'Um, I'm engaged though.'

A woman nearby — the slightly older one with the dyed blonde hair who Bobby had heard comparing uniforms earlier — turned to join in.

'Oh, there's no need to worry about *that*,' she said. 'In the forces, is he, your chap?'

'Yes, the RAF. He did part of his training at Ryland Moor too.'

'Bus driver?'

Bobby blinked. Did they have buses in RAF Motor Transport?

'No, he's a pilot,' she said.

The woman let out a peal of laughter. 'Oh Lord, you are green. I mean, does he fly bombers? Bus drivers are what the fighter pilots call the bomber pilots.'

'Oh. Yes. He just started flying ops a few months ago.'

The woman turned to Carol. 'Here, can I scrounge one of your ciggies?'

'Sure, Mike. Here you go.' Carol handed one over. 'You want one, Bobby?'

'No, thanks.'

'Your man'll have a girl on the side wherever he is, so don't you feel guilty about enjoying yourself,' the woman called Mike told Bobby, cigarette wobbling in her mouth as she lit it. She examined the gold band on her wedding finger complacently.

'Everyone's got a girl within easy reach in the Air Force, David says.'

'That's what I heard too,' another woman chimed in. 'The last boy I walked out with was a soldier. He told me the lads in his barracks joked that RAF really stood for Running After Fluff. Randy buggers, these airmen, he said. Suppose the job does that to them, never knowing if they'll buy it next time out. Makes them want to live in the moment.'

'Huh. That or being men,' another girl said with a roll of her eyes. 'One thing on their minds, the lot of them.'

'My David's got two doe-eyed young WAAFs googly about him at his base, neither with any idea the other exists – or that I do, of course,' the woman called Mike said, drawing lazily on her cigarette as all eyes turned to her. She clocked Bobby's blank look. 'Oh, David's my husband. He's a pilot too – fighter squadron. We made an agreement for as long as there's a war on: he has his little dalliances, I have mine. It's the only way we can bear being so far apart.'

'You mean you have affairs with other men?' Bobby said, blinking.

She heard one of the women titter, and wondered if she really sounded so naive. Was this the way the world worked in wartime – this free and easy attitude to love?

'But of course I do,' Mike said. Bobby wondered fleetingly what the name might be short for. 'We adore one another, naturally, but we have to get through this damn war. Seems to me it would be the bloodiest thing in the world if we couldn't have a little fun while we can't be together.' She cast an unimpressed glance over Bobby, in her frumpy old coat with hair shoved into a bun. 'You think that's terribly wrong, I suppose.'

'Well, no,' Bobby said, determined not to cement her reputation as a confirmed prig by sounding shocked. 'That is to say, it isn't really any of my business.'

Carol burst out laughing. 'Bobby, you're a hoot.'

Bobby smiled uncertainly, unsure what exactly she had said that was such a hoot. Was she being made fun of? She never had

236

found it easy to tell. The lorry juddered over a dirt track, and she grabbed at the battered tarpaulin that covered the vehicle to steady herself.

'Believe me, every man serving away from his wife or sweetheart has got someone who's keeping him warm at night,' Mike said, blowing a stream of smoke from one corner of her mouth. 'So do the wives and sweethearts, if they've got any sense. At least David and I are honest with each other about it.'

Bobby felt dizzy from the shaking of the lorry and the frowst of cigarette smoke, and even more so from the shock of this strange new world she had landed in the middle of. She began to feel queasy, too, as the vehicle rocked along, and was glad when they stopped. The sergeant who had driven them dropped the tailboard and they all came piling out.

'Leave your luggage and gas masks and follow me,' the sergeant said, and they stumbled after her across a muddy field in their inadequate civilian shoes.

Bobby glanced around as they walked. She had often tried to picture the camp while reading Charlie's letters, but it wasn't quite as she had imagined.

RAF Ryland Moor was constructed over several fields, no doubt requisitioned from some unfortunate local farmer. Although she knew it was a small station, to her untutored civilian eyes it seemed huge: row upon row of curved Nissen huts – brick-fronted with corrugated metal roofs – interspersed with some sturdier-looking wooden constructions, and of course the aerodrome with its hangars and concrete runways. She assumed the Nissen huts they were headed towards were the WAAF accommodation, clustered around a concrete parade ground.

And Lord, it was bleak. It was just how Bobby imagined the German prisoner of war camps. Everything was grey: the huts, the parade ground, the glowering sky above them. It felt utterly desolate.

'Blimey, this is grim,' Carol muttered.

Mike laughed. 'What were you expecting, a Girl Guide camp?'

'Our Trish's billet is in a house with three others. She says it's cosy as anything. They've got a fire, wireless, gramophone. We'll freeze our bums off in them huts.'

'It's only for six weeks,' Mike said. 'I suppose they think it'll toughen us soft, flabby civvies up.'

Their destination was the parade ground. Once there, the women – some forty or so – were chivvied into a line by the NCO. There was a roll call as their names were checked off a list. Bobby noticed Mike grimace as she answered 'present' to what was evidently her full name: Violet Carmichael.

A short while after, the officer Bobby had met at her interview – Squadron Officer Mulligan – appeared. She was just as stern and unsmiling as Bobby remembered while she walked along the line of recruits.

'Welcome to Ryland Moor, ladies,' she said. 'Some of you will have had long journeys. You'll be taken to the Waafery cookhouse shortly, where you will be issued with the first of your kit – a knife, fork, spoon and mug, which you will guard with your lives – before being provided with tea, coffee and something to eat. After this you will be fitted for uniforms and given your service numbers. But before that, some rules.' Mulligan flashed them a dry half-smile. 'Firstly, men.'

Carol let out a snort that she quickly disguised as a cough when the officer's gaze swivelled towards her.

'In the first two weeks of your time here, there will be absolutely no fraternisation with the recruits in the airmen's quarters,' Mulligan told them, pacing up and down. 'After this, some fraternisation will be allowed, although you will of course be kept under strict discipline. You should speak to male instructors only as far as concerns the subject in which you are being instructed. You will receive no letters from home in this two-week period, nor will you send any beyond a single communication to notify your families you have arrived safely –

or you may use the phone in the Waafery recreation hut if your home has a telephone. After this, communication will cease until the two weeks have passed, although, in the event of an emergency, telegrams will of course be allowed.'

'Oh, I say,' Mike muttered disgustedly.

Mulligan turned a biting gaze on her. 'Did you have a question, Aircraftwoman?'

'Yes, I did actually, ma'am,' Mike said, thrusting out her chin. 'I wanted to ask why we're not allowed to write to our people or fraternise or all that.'

'The two-week embargo is designed to get you into the swing of military life. We have found complete immersion in our routines for that period is the surest way to make a WAAF out of a civilian. You did not join the RAF to go to dances, after all.'

'Didn't I though?' Carol muttered.

'The dormitories, you will find, are rather sparse in home comforts, but you should nevertheless have everything you need,' Mulligan went on. 'Sixteen women will be housed in each Nissen hut. Domestic nights will be Mondays, when an officer will thoroughly inspect your kit and dorms. The bugle will wake you every morning at six a.m. Those listed for fatigues should be given priority for use of the ablutions block, which is the concrete structure behind your huts, and all will be expected to be ready for breakfast at seven a.m. After this you will turn out for parade and drill practice, followed by lectures and specialised skills training according to your assigned trade. On Tuesday and Thursday afternoons and Saturday mornings there will be a route march, weather allowing, and on the other days you will have PT. Following this, those not on fatigues will have study and domestic time until your evening meal. You will in every way be treated as are the male recruits – with some allowances made for the differences in your biology, of course.'

This produced a muffled snigger from Carol, but it was soon replaced by a look of horror on hearing the next sentence.

'The bugle will sound lights-out at half past nine, which must be strictly observed,' Mulligan told them calmly, to hushed gasps from some of the night owls present.

'Of course, we do not expect you to live like nuns,' Mulligan went on, in a slightly warmer tone. 'The wearing of light powder and rouge is not forbidden – in fact, we encourage our WAAFs to ensure they are feminine at all times. There is a recreation hut where you can relax in your leisure time, with a wireless and so forth, and after the first two weeks you may go into the villages or towns on a pass when off-duty. There is a tea room in Beckfoot, as well as the all-important fish and chip shop, and a picture house, services club and other entertainment in Skipton. Dances will be held in the NAAFI canteen on Saturday nights, for both airmen and airwomen.' Her brow set into a stern frown. 'But we expect you to remember that you are here to work, and to learn. The WAAF is a proud institution with a reputation for turning out smart, industrious young women, and I will come down very hard on anyone who fails to uphold that reputation.'

Bobby saw Carol roll her eyes.

'There will be some people who will not like you,' Mulligan went on. 'Those who sneer at women in uniform – who believe your place is not in the theatre of combat but in the home. Those who make lewd and suggestive comments about your morality, because they fear female independence. Men who will patronise you, and refuse to afford you the respect your rank is due. Hold your heads high, ladies, and never let anyone tell you that your contribution to this war does not matter. Have no doubt that no matter what trade you find yourself in, the world would be damned without you. You are dismissed.'

After the welcome speech, the women were shown to the cookhouse for a meal of sausage rolls with mustard pickle, after which they were marched to one of the huts to be fitted for uniforms. This involved no actual measuring: just an RAF sergeant who looked them up and down and called out a number, following which a pile of clothing was thrust into their arms.

After this, they visited the medical officer. Here, Bobby was forced to go through the humiliating ordeal of having her hair checked for nits, as though she were a child at school, and then sit through a dental inspection. The women were then told to strip to the waist and parade in their bras past the medical officer to be inoculated in each arm against various diseases. The camp MO was a man, of course, and Bobby's cheeks were ripe with blushes as she hurried to cover herself up afterwards.

They then queued for their service numbers, which were given to them by a tough-looking RAF warrant officer with a Lancashire accent.

'Remember that from now on, names mean nowt except to your civilian chummies,' he told them. 'To the RAF, we're each of us no more than a number. You'll give this to eat, to go on leave, to be put on charge and to get paid. You'll put it on all your letters, and your civvy friends will put it on those they send back – no number, no letters.'

After being issued with their numbers, they were shown to a lecture room. In here they sat down to take the maths, aptitude and psychology tests that would decide on their suitability for different trades.

'I thought our trades were decided when they interviewed us,' Bobby whispered to Carol.

'That's more of a check, to see if we've got skills they need,' Carol whispered back. 'I hope I do all right. I was always a dunce about tests, and they'll lock me in the cookhouse for the duration if I don't turn in a decent score.'

Bobby turned the maths paper over with some trepidation, wondering if she would be expected to show knowledge of advanced calculus or something. She didn't fancy being assigned cooking duties for the duration either. The questions didn't pose too many problems, however, and she felt confident she had got a reasonably good score.

She hoped so. Ever since Topsy's wedding, she had been thinking about what Archie had said: about his WAAF friend who had been posted overseas to work in intelligence. It had made her realise that she could be so much more here than merely a uniformed secretary. The RAF seemed to have pigeon-holed her for admin work, but if she could prove she had brains as well as decent typing speeds, perhaps they would realise she would be better employed elsewhere.

The last question on their test papers asked what trade they would be most interested in. Bobby skimmed the list. Radio mechanic, photographer, balloon operator, fabric worker, cook, aircrafthand, batwoman, clerk: general duties, clerk: special duties…

She tried to find 'plotter' – the role Archie's friend had begun her RAF career with – but no such trade was listed.

'Excuse me,' she said quietly to the WAAF NCO supervising them. 'I can't see plotter listed here. You know, the WAAFs who track enemy raids and things.'

The woman frowned. 'Who told you about plotters?'

'Um, I've got a friend training to be one,' Bobby fibbed. The woman's expression seemed to suggest that the existence of plotters wasn't common knowledge, and she didn't want to get Archie into any trouble.

'Oh. Well, it comes under special duties.'

'Thank you.'

Bobby put a tick next to the role of 'clerk: special duties' and handed in her paper.

Chapter 30

'That sour-faced old hag!' Mike ranted later, standing in front of the mirror in the boned corset, coarse cotton bra and long wool knickers that had been issued during kitting out earlier. 'What's the idea, locking us up like convent girls? Just because she hasn't had a man since bustles were in fashion.'

The dormitories could accommodate sixteen women, each pair sharing a bunk bed: eight on one side of the hut, eight on the other, with a stove in the middle to keep them all warm – at least that was the idea, although the women of Hut 17 had quickly found they couldn't get the thing to light and were shivering in the cold waiting for an NCO to turn up. A noticeboard was mounted at the farthest end of the hut, to which various announcements and itineraries were pinned. Each pair of bunk beds had a chest of drawers between them, and a shelf above with hooks to hang up their uniforms.

Bobby had found herself sharing the bunk beds closest to the door with Mike, while Carol and the young Welsh girl, Dilys – the one who had called Bobby a prig – had the neighbouring pair. Bobby was sitting on her bottom bunk, writing a letter to Charlie and listening to the rain hammering on the tin roof while the other women ranted about their new commandant.

'That's not what I heard,' Carol told Mike, in a confidential tone. 'I was talking to Mavis, one of the NCOs, over our sausage and mash tonight. She told me on the quiet that Stewpot Mulligan was forced to transfer here from Harrogate after the RAF officer she was engaged to ditched her for someone else.'

Mike laughed. 'No wonder she hates men then. I don't blame him either, poor beggar.'

Dilys wrinkled her nose. 'Her engaged? She must be at least forty.'

Carol was shuffling into her new skirt. They'd been issued with a full service uniform each: shirt, tie, tunic, skirt and cap, although greatcoats and spare uniforms had yet to arrive. Everything here seemed to be in a state of half-readiness as the camp had hastily prepared to receive its new female recruits. Carol fastened on her jacket and tightened the belt, then went to stand by Mike so she could look in the mirror on their chest of drawers.

'What did they bother sizing us for if they were going to give us any old rags?' Carol grumbled. 'This skirt is at least two sizes too big. Ugh, and you're right, Mike: I've got a backside like the front of a bus.'

'Your sister wasn't wrong about these blackout knickers either,' Mike said. 'Talk about passion-killers. I'm not wearing them no matter how cold I get, otherwise I'll never get a man. I fully intend to start having some fun as soon as possible, in spite of old Stewpot's diktats.'

'How do you manage it?' Dilys asked, her voice tinged with admiration. 'It's all right for your husband. He isn't going to have any babies.'

'Oh, I know all the ways,' Mike said breezily. 'A couple of kids tugging at my skirts is the last thing either of us would want, whether they were David's or someone else's. We've got plans for after the war. We're going travelling, see the world.'

'What ways are there?'

'French letters, for one, of course, although some men can be funny about using them. But there are plenty of other tricks. Stick with me, girls, and I'll teach you all about it.'

'Richie would wallop me into next week if he thought I knew what French letters were,' Dilys observed. 'He's my lad back in Swansea. He thinks it's serious, but I don't. I joined up to find someone better.'

Carol picked up Bobby's photograph of Charlie in uniform, which she had placed on the chest of drawers to face her bunk. 'This your feller?'

'That's right,' Bobby said vaguely. She was trying to focus on her letter. Her arms were aching from the injections she had been given, and after already composing a brief letter to Lilian, every word she formed felt painful.

Carol let out a whistle. 'Nice. How did you manage that?'

'Oh, just by being my charming self,' Bobby said with a smile, forcing herself to sound jovial. She knew that when the bugle sounded lights out, the homesickness would really start to bite. For now, she was just trying not to cry, or to alienate the women she had found herself with any further by seeming standoffish.

She tried to shut out the buzz of conversation and concentrate on her letter.

> *You mustn't worry if you don't hear from me for a while. The strict WAAF commandant has imposed a sort of purdah, and after this letter I'm not to communicate with the outside world until a fortnight is up. I'll still be thinking about you, and writing down everything about my new life here to send when I'm allowed. Please write the same as always, so I'll have a nice pile of letters to open when I'm free again. In the meantime, I'll speak as soon as possible to Squadron Officer Mulligan – that's our WAAF senior officer – about permission to marry, and whether I can have home leave for the 2nd so we can set the date officially.*
>
> *There's a telephone in the recreation hut here, so we shall be able to talk sometimes too once the ban is up. It feels like so long since we last spoke. Even this morning feels like half a lifetime ago after all that's happened today.*
>
> *It's been some time since I had a letter from you, darling. Have you been writing as usual? I know they're*

probably only held up in the post, but I can't help worrying. Do write as soon as you can, or send a wire if you're worried it won't get through, and let me know everything is all right.

Bobby paused to dash away a tear. She couldn't stop herself from dwelling on what Mike had said earlier. She had often worried about her and Charlie drifting apart while they were far away from each other, but surely he couldn't stop loving her, just like that? He had been so affectionate in his last few letters, and eager for their wedding.

And yet flying ops must be such a frightening, isolating experience. The sort that caused you to crave warm arms to hold you, and make you feel safe and alive. Men in the full virility of youth naturally desired the company of women, and when they faced death on a daily basis, the urge to be with someone physically was probably stronger than ever. Charlie had the same urges and desires as any other man his age. He had never struggled to attract the attention of women even as a civilian, and such was the glamour surrounding pilots that he could no doubt take his choice when it came to female company. Could he... could he have met someone else?

As she fumbled once again for her hanky, Bobby became aware that the young Welsh girl, Dilys, had approached the bunk and was reading her letter over her shoulder. She grinned when Bobby looked up.

'Trouble in paradise?' she asked, arching an eyebrow.

'Just some missing letters,' Bobby murmured, looking away, but the girl had already spotted the tear on her cheek.

'You sure blub a lot,' she observed. 'You made it with this fiancé yet, or are you saving yourself? You look the type.'

Bobby blushed deeply. 'That's... none of your business.'

Dilys laughed, none too pleasantly. 'Oh my word, you *are*! No wonder he's stopped writing to you.'

Mike glanced over. 'Leave her alone, Dilys. Aren't you going to visit Aunty? It'll be lights out in half an hour and you haven't washed.'

Aunty, Bobby had learned, was the euphemistic name for the ablutions block, where the wash facilities and two latrines were located.

'I'm not going out in this rain,' Dilys said, throwing herself down on her bunk. 'What does it matter if I smell when we're to be deprived of masculine company? Bugger it, I say.'

Bobby stood up. 'I need to go. I haven't washed yet either.'

She threw on her coat and headed for the door, grateful for the opportunity to be by herself for a short time. At least in the rain, she could cry all she liked.

However, as soon as she got outside she felt a hand on her shoulder. Mike had put on her coat too and followed her out.

'Hey, are you all right?' Mike asked. 'You sounded choked up just now.'

Bobby forced back fresh tears. 'I suppose I'm just homesick. I know it's pathetic when I'm practically down the road from where I lived before, but I feel like I've gone a thousand miles.'

'I hope I didn't upset you before, when I said that everyone in the Air Force had someone on the side. I didn't realise you and your fiancé were having problems.'

'We're not having problems,' Bobby muttered. 'Some of his letters have gone astray, that's all. We're to be married on the 2nd of May, if we can both get leave.'

'I'm sure if you have faith in him, he must be one of the good ones,' Mike said kindly. 'Sorry for talking out of turn. I never do know when to keep quiet. We ought to be friends, now we're bunkies.'

Bobby summoned a smile. 'I'd like that.'

'And don't mind that kid Dilys. She's just showing off to prove she's one of the big girls. It can be dog eat dog in places like this.' She smiled wryly. 'Trust me, I went to boarding school.'

Bobby pushed damp hair out of her face. 'Have you been in the forces before? You seem to know a lot about it.'

'In a way. My father was an officer in the Army. I spent my early childhood being dragged from camp to camp. Don't worry, I'll look after you.'

'Thank you.'

Bobby had been unsure what to make of Mike, whose view of the world seemed so very different to her own, but she was craving a kind word more than anything right now. She hadn't realised how much she needed someone who would be a friend to her, however little they might have in common.

Mike shivered as she pulled her coat around her. 'Bloody freezing in this rain. You ought to hurry, if you don't want to start your first full day on charge. Not long until lights out.'

—

Bobby didn't sleep much. She lay awake on her hard, uncomfortable bed under hairy Air Force blankets, feeling unbearably wretched as she listened to the snores of her bunkmate and the heavy rain rattling the tin roof. Although she had been fighting back tears most of the day, now she was at liberty to indulge in the catharsis of a good cry, she found they wouldn't come. Her arms and shoulders ached like hell, she felt hot and then cold and then hot again, and she had a sick, empty feeling in her stomach. The arm ache and fever flushes she put down to her vaccinations, but the empty feeling was all her own.

Everything was so much harder than she had thought it would be. Yes, she had been worried about leaving, but she had, after all, left home once before. It wasn't so very long ago that she had uprooted herself from everything she knew to begin a new life in the Dales, and while that, too, had been daunting at the time, she had soon come to see the place as her home. Bobby had assumed she would adjust to this new military life as well as she had eventually done to the world of

Silverdale. Now she was here, however, she was beginning to doubt whether that could ever happen.

She had never been in this sort of environment before. It felt strange to be so very... so very *insignificant*, just one face among many, stripped of your name and labelled with a number. Everyone forced to eat the same, dress the same, even walk the same, as if they were a single person copied over and over. School had had its challenges but it hadn't been like this.

She could hear sniffs coming from other bunks, muffled by pillows. Bobby suspected these had more to do with homesickness than cold. Many of the girls here were young, probably experiencing their first time away from home. She was sure she even heard some sniffles from Dilys's bunk.

It reminded her that young men and women were being plunged into a life like this every day, with no choice but to cope. Lilian had done it, and Charlie, and her brothers. So why did it feel so difficult for her? Bobby had always believed she was a resilient person, yet now she wondered if she could even get through her six-week basic training without breaking down.

It wasn't that she disliked the people she had found herself among. As hedonistic and worldly as Mike seemed, she had been kind earlier when Bobby had needed kindness, and offered her friendship. For all her abruptness, Carol was bouncy and good-natured, and seemed to have acquired numerous friends already. Perhaps even Dilys would improve on acquaintance – as Mike had said, she wasn't much more than a kid. But it felt like the other women shared a camaraderie from which she was excluded, and she couldn't help feeling like an alien amongst them. She didn't want to be labelled a prig or a stick-in-the-mud, but nor did she want to be dragged into that heady world of dances, men, drinking and flirtations around which the lives of her new acquaintances seemed to revolve.

Bobby had found Mulligan cold and intimidating when she had met her at the recruiting centre, yet the final part of her welcome speech today had struck a chord. The officer's face

249

had been filled with a steely pride when she had talked about standing up to those people who sneered at women in uniform, and the men who would try to persuade them they were less than they were. Bobby had stood a little taller when Mulligan had talked about taking pride in their contribution to the war effort, although the others may have rolled their eyes, and she had determined she would wear her WAAF uniform with distinction.

But when she had tried on that uniform earlier and looked at herself in the mirror – this pale, frightened little thing blinking under her peaked cap, ill at ease in a set of clothes that seemed to have been made for someone else – Bobby wondered if she could ever feel like she belonged here.

Chapter 31

The next day, Bobby discovered that the first thing the WAAF expected its recruits to learn was how to queue.

They were awakened by the sound of an efficient bugle at six a.m. This was the same time as Bobby would have risen at home, giving her an hour to pump the water and do her chores before she needed to start getting ready for work, but after a night containing no more than two hours' sleep, she groaned just as much as the other women when she dragged herself out of bed.

As they queued outside the ablutions block, shivering and jiggling on the spot to get warm, Bobby felt how foolish she had been to believe that life in the cow house would have prepared her for the military. The outhouse they had shared with Moorside may have been cold, the water often frozen in the lavatory bowl in winter, but at least she had never had to wait long to use it. Now not only her arms but her whole body ached after a night struggling to get comfortable on the thin mattresses, and by the time her turn came to wash, her hands were almost too numb to turn on the tap.

They were given just an hour to wash, dress, use the latrines, tidy their bunks and make themselves presentable before marching to the cookhouse for breakfast. An NCO who had been placed in charge of their hut strode up and down barking instructions as, bleary-eyed, the new WAAFs prepared for their first day.

'Hair is not to touch collars at any time,' Corporal Bennett told them. 'Minimal rouge, please, ladies. A WAAF is feminine but never garish. Look sharp or we'll be late for breakfast.'

After everyone had dressed, the corporal gave them a lecture on the correct way to 'stack' their beds. In the RAF, Bobby learned, beds were stacked rather than made. The three mattresses, known as biscuits, had to be piled on top of each other with utmost precision, then the blankets and sheets arranged alternately with the third blanket folded lengthways and wrapped around. Untidy stacks, they were told, would be pulled apart and the culprit forced to remake them until the inspecting NCO was satisfied.

'Obviously it would be impossible to win a war with an untidy stack and hair touching our collars,' Mike whispered as they stood by their bunks watching this demonstration, and Bobby smothered a smile.

Once beds had been stacked and inspected, the women were made to package up their civilian clothes to be sent back to their families. Bobby stood in her new uniform, with its itchy lisle stockings and the long woollen 'blackout' underwear, and felt rather helpless as she watched the brown paper parcel containing her clothes be taken away. In parting with it, she felt as though she was saying goodbye to the last remnant of her life in Silverdale.

The next queue was for breakfast, the WAAFs lining up two by two for a plate of bacon and eggs. While the queueing was tedious, the portions were relatively unstinting, and Bobby cheered up slightly as she tucked in.

By the time the day was nearly over, she had spent almost all of it in some sort of queue. They had queued for photographs, queued for pay books, queued for button polish, queued for tape and marking ink to sew into their uniforms, and finally queued to find out if they had been accepted for their preferred trade.

'Rank and number?' an RAF flight sergeant demanded when she reached the front of this last queue.

'ACW/2, 2172954,' Bobby told him.

The new service number felt strange as it rolled off her tongue. She was no longer Bobby Bancroft but ACW/2, 2172954. The impersonal – inhuman – sound of it sent a shiver down her spine.

Her father still remembered his army service number from the last war. He never forgot that, although in the darkest times he might forget the names of his daughters, what day it was or even what year. Sometimes she heard him mumble it in his sleep. Bobby wondered if, when she was a wizened old woman, this new and unfamiliar identity label would feel as much a part of her as her own name.

'2172954,' the man said, looking at his list. 'You're to be trained as a clerk, general duties.' He handed her a pamphlet. 'Impressive test scores, I see. Well done.'

Bobby frowned. '*General* duties? You mean administration?'

'That's right.'

'But I ticked special duties on my test. Er, sir,' she added, grimacing at the oversight. 'Sorry, ought I to have saluted?'

The flight sergeant smiled kindly from under his handlebar moustache. 'No, I'm not an officer. NCOs aren't saluted, and you shouldn't call us sir. Better get that right from day one or you'll have someone barking at you.'

'Sorry. I thought since you outranked me...'

'It's the King's commission you're saluting. Strictly for officers only. Don't worry, love, you'll soon get the hang of it all.'

'Right,' Bobby said. 'Um, do you know why I wasn't accepted for the trade I ticked, si— Flight Sergeant? Weren't my test scores good enough?'

'I'd be surprised if they weren't. I suppose one of the big bugs must have decided you were better suited to general duties.'

'Oh. Thank you.'

Bobby left, her spirits sinking.

She wasn't sure why plotter had suddenly become her ambition. She had never heard of it until a few days ago, but the way

Archie had described it had made it sound sort of important. And if his friend was anything to go by, it could lead to bigger things – a commission, and perhaps even overseas posting.

But it wasn't to be. She was to be no more than a secretary in uniform after all, despite her apparently impressive test scores.

She trudged back to Hut 17 and threw herself down on her bunk. Everyone was now off duty, and Mike, Carol and Dilys were on their bunks awaiting the dinner hour. Mike was reading a magazine, Dilys was filing her nails and Carol was studying a leaflet.

'What's up with her?' Dilys asked Carol, jerking a thumb in Bobby's direction.

'What is up with you?' Carol asked.

'Nothing really,' Bobby said. 'I didn't get the trade I wanted, that's all. I was hoping for special duties clerk but I've been given general duties instead. I suppose I shouldn't be surprised. Stewpot did tell me the WAAF only wanted me for my short-hand typing.'

'That's not bad though,' Mike said, putting down her magazine. 'Better money than batwomen and cooks, once you've qualified. What is it, fifteen bob a week?'

Bobby glanced at the pamphlet she'd be given, which was headed *Notes for the Information of Candidates*. Clerk came under Group IV, which for an Aircraftwoman Second Class meant daily pay of two shillings tuppence plus fourpence a day war pay. She did a quick mental calculation.

'Seventeen and six,' she told Mike. 'I was on twenty as a civilian though.'

'Yes, but now you've no clothes or rations to pay for. Besides, a swotty sort like you will soon rise up the ranks. You'll be an NCO in no time, Bobsy.'

'It isn't really about the money,' Bobby said. 'I just thought there might be more important work for me to do in the WAAF than typing.'

'Well, you don't have to stick with it. You can apply for different training, once you've bedded in a bit.'

'Can I? I thought once they gave you something, you were lumbered with it.'

Mike shrugged. 'Only if you let yourself be lumbered with it.'

Bobby's gaze fell once again on the pamphlet, and its tables of trades and wages. She would be able to send very little of her wage home to help her family for as long as she remained a lowly erk, as the aircraftwomen were known. But if she acquitted herself well, perhaps Mike was right – maybe there could be the chevrons of a non-commissioned officer in her future. As a corporal, she would be earning twenty-eight shillings a week – eight bob more than Reg paid her. That would make a big difference to her family, especially after the baby arrived. Perhaps she might even gain a commission, if she worked hard.

The thought cheered her a little, and she glanced up to smile at the other women.

'Did you three get what you wanted?'

Bobby watched as Carol passed the leaflet she had been studying to Dilys in the bunk below, somewhat surreptitiously. Dilys looked at it and let out a little giggle.

Carol turned to grin at Bobby. 'Oh, I hit the jackpot. Waitress. I start tomorrow lunchtime in the officers' mess.'

'Is that the jackpot?' Bobby asked. Waitressing didn't sound like it would be one of the higher-paid trades.

'In the *RAF* officers' mess – you know, where the men eat. Must be because I told our beloved Stewpot I worked in a hotel before joining up. I'm happy enough with the lower wages if it'll get me close to the officers.'

'I'm to be trained as an aircrafthand,' Dilys said, wrinkling her nose. 'That means I'll be in trousers and shapeless battledress tunics all day long. I'll look an utter fright. We have to change into service dress for socials though.'

'What about you?' Bobby asked Mike.

'Wireless operator,' Mike said, sounding proud. 'It's what I wanted. I've been revising Morse for yonks so I'd be able to ace the tests. David will be thrilled.'

'Why did you want to do that?'

'The wireless operators transmit messages between planes and their base. They talk the aircraft down when they get into trouble. David told me an operator saved his life once. I knew then that when I joined up, that was what I wanted to do.'

Carol laughed. 'I never realised you were so noble, Mike. You sound like Bobsy.'

Mike shrugged. 'I can't have depths?'

'I'd have liked to do something like that,' Bobby said with a sigh. 'I just hope I don't spend the rest of the war filing.' She glanced over to the bunk opposite as Dilys once again sniggered at the leaflet Carol had given her. 'What's that thing you're passing around?'

'Take a look,' Carol said, grinning. 'Dilys, let her see.'

Dilys flashed Bobby a suspicious glance. 'Are you sure we can trust her? She might tell.'

'Don't be silly, Dil,' Mike said. 'Let her have a look.'

Dilys passed it over, somewhat resentfully. Bobby took it, intrigued as to what could be on this contraband piece of paper.

The illustration on the front showed a woman sitting on a bed half undressed, her breasts exposed while she rolled down her stockings. Nearby, a foreign serviceman – American, Bobby thought from the uniform – was smirking as he loosened his tie. Underneath, it bore the legend *While you are away...*

'It's a riot, isn't it?' Mike said. 'David would just scream if he could see it. It's completely illegal for us to have it, of course, so you mustn't say a word. Carol smuggled it back.'

'I borrowed it from Mavis, the NCO I've been getting friendly with,' Carol told Bobby, looking rather smug over this influential new pal. 'The sergeant pilot she's walking out with brought it back from North Africa.'

'But what is it?' Bobby asked, staring wonderingly at the lewd, highly detailed image. It looked like the cigarette cards of pin-up girls she sometimes used to find hidden while tidying her younger brothers' room.

'A Joe Goebbels special, in honour of the Yanks coming over,' Carol said. 'Propaganda leaflet Jerry's been dropping on our troops out in Africa. The idea is to damage morale by making them think their women are all having it away with foreign soldiers at home. Of course it backfires completely, Mavis says, because the men just roar their heads off, thank old Joe for the picture and tear out the part with the nudey lady to pin up in their bunks.'

'Don't you think it's funny, Bobsy?' Dilys demanded, watching her through narrowed eyes. 'Or will you go running to Stewpot and get us all put on a charge?'

'Of course I do. It's an absolute scream.' Bobby forced a laugh, handing the lurid propaganda leaflet back to Carol.

But she couldn't really find anything amusing in it. The sight of the half-dressed woman, preparing to go to bed with her foreign lover while her man was away, unsettled her. It made her think of Charlie, and her still-simmering guilt over Ernie King, and everything Mike had said about the assumption of infidelity during wartime.

Perhaps the women here were right. Perhaps she was too sensitive; too serious; too naive. She knew she was prone to thinking too much. Unfortunately it was the only way she knew how to be.

'I'd love to meet a real-life American,' Carol said dreamily, gazing at the male figure on the leaflet. 'I bet they're just like out of the pictures.'

'My David knows a couple. Eagle Squadron,' Mike told them. 'He says they're a pair of thugs. Anyway, Car, I'm sure you'll get your chance soon enough. The papers say there are GIs pouring in by the hundreds now.'

Dilys sat up. 'Come on, let's go to the rec hut and play records until dinner. Might as well, since that's the only fun we're allowed to have.'

Mike lowered her voice. 'Unless we sneak out after lights out. One of the girls in 19 told me there's a pub in the village. It's not a long walk.'

Carol snorted. 'Stewpot never mentioned a pub when she was telling us about tea rooms and chip shops, did she?'

'Some of the men are bound to hang around there. What do you think, girls?'

'We shouldn't,' Bobby said. 'What if we got caught?'

Dilys rolled her eyes. 'How did I know you were going to say that?'

'Come on, Bobsy.' Mike hung over the edge of her bunk to peer at her. 'Live a little, eh?'

'No, honestly, I couldn't. You all go if you want.'

'Not going to tell on us, are you?' Dilys demanded.

'Of course not,' Bobby said. 'I'll try to cover for you if anyone asks questions. Still, I wish you wouldn't. We only just got here.'

'She's right, you know.' Carol, to Bobby's surprise, came to her aid. 'I wouldn't half feel small if I got put on a fizzer my second day. Being absent without leave is a damn sight more serious than smuggling Jerry leaflets, and it'd go on our records too. Our dad'd wear me out if he heard about it.'

'And Stewpot might lock you in for even longer as punishment,' Bobby pointed out. 'She might even confine you to camp for the whole training period.'

Carol nodded. 'I bet she would an' all. Rubbing her hands with glee while she fastened on the manacles.'

'How can she rub her hands if she's fastening manacles?' Mike asked.

'All right, clever clogs. It's a figure of speech.'

'I suppose you're right,' Dilys muttered. 'The old cow looks like she'd be jankers-happy. Oh, but two weeks without a single dance or date! I swear I'll actually die of boredom.'

'It's all right for you, Carol,' Mike said, glaring at her. 'You'll be waiting on the officers, won't you? Have them all to yourself while we're locked up here in our sackcloth and chastity knickers.'

Carol grinned. 'Don't worry, girls, I'll be sure to save the best talent for us. I'll give you a full report tomorrow night and tell you which ones I've earmarked for each of you. As soon as we're free, we'll have dates ready and waiting while the other lasses are scrabbling for our leftovers.'

'Very kind, but I'll waive my share of the favour,' Bobby said, smiling as she waggled her engagement ring.

'Oh, come *on*,' Dilys said, rolling her eyes. 'You're not going to be a spoilsport about everything, are you? You're as bad as Stewpot, with her "great and glorious pride of the WAAF" crap.'

'I'm not going to be a spoilsport. I can't go on dates, that's all,' Bobby said, flushing as she remembered the picture on the leaflet. 'I know you see it differently than I do, but I won't judge you if you don't judge me.'

'That's fair enough,' Mike said to the other women. 'Still, Bobsy, I don't see why you shouldn't get yourself a little camp boyfriend to keep you company. You don't have to do anything, if you're absolutely convinced the fiancé's keeping himself pure for you. A dance and a flirt is the least a young woman deserves. It's necessary for our self-esteem – and our purses, come to that.'

'You said it,' Carol agreed. 'An innocent fling never hurt anyone. You need an officer to pay for stuff with a training wage of one and four a day.'

'And what if this officer expects payment in return?' Bobby asked, raising an eyebrow. 'You know what I mean.'

'Just make sure you've got your blackouts on,' Dilys said with a grin. 'They'll quench his ardour.'

'Ha bloody ha.'

Carol shrugged. 'You can tell him to sod off if he tries owt. He can't make you, can he? Well, he can, but he won't. Us three would look after you.'

Bobby smiled, touched. She knew she was the outlier in this new group she had somehow become a part of. She knew they had adopted her more for reasons of proximity than fellow-feeling. She knew that Dilys, at least, didn't like her, and tolerated her only because of her admiration for Mike. She half-suspected that the nickname they had given her, Bobsy, was at least as mocking as it was playful, especially given it was Dilys who had started it. It was nice to know that Carol, at least, saw her as one of the gang.

'I really don't want a date,' Bobby said. 'But I would like to have some fun when they let us out. I've got no intention of sitting by myself every night for the next six weeks, and I don't see why I need a man on my arm to enjoy myself.'

Mike grinned. 'That's the spirit.'

'I'm still going to pick you out an officer tomorrow though,' Carol said, flopping back on her bunk. 'Just in case you change your mind.'

Chapter 32

Bobby continued feeling wretched with homesickness over the next few days as she learnt the routine of her new way of life. The weather remained stormy and wild, which matched her mood, and route marches and outdoor drills were suspended in favour of indoor parades in the gym.

She began to get used to the sight of herself in her new military attire, and to hear herself addressed as 'airwoman'. She learned how to drill, march and parade; how to salute, and who and when to salute; how to take care of her kit; a great deal on the history of the Royal Air Force in the rather tedious lectures they were forced to sit through, and a huge amount of RAF slang.

Some she knew already thanks to Charlie – she was aware, for example, that square-bashing was parading, an erk was someone with the lowest rank of aircraftman or aircraftwoman, and to be put on a fizzer was to be placed on charge – but Bobby soon found there was a lot more to learn. Her cutlery items were known as irons, recruits were called sprogs, Mae Wests were the inflatable life vests worn by aircrew, muftis meant civilian clothing, the Waafery was the women's quarters, jankers meant being confined to camp, and there were many, many others. It was like learning a whole other language.

Bobby acquitted herself well in her new role – at least, she avoided getting a ticking off from any officers or NCOs. And yet she still had that lingering feeling of outsiderness. She felt like she was forever on the edges, not belonging: a civilian in WAAF's clothing. She hoped this feeling would disappear in time, but all the other women seemed to have found their places after a few days to settle in. Bobby couldn't understand why it wasn't happening for her.

She felt, too, like she was becoming a whole other person in this strange new world, short time though it had been. She had understood herself in Silverdale. There, Bobby Bancroft was 'the lass from t' paper' – someone people recognised and respected. She had had a job to do and she had taken pride in the fact she was good at it. Here, she was just another rank and number. It felt like all the confidence she had built while doing a man's job in a man's world disappeared overnight, leaving a nervous, trembling girl in its place.

Yet her place in Silverdale hadn't come naturally to her at first either. She had spent her first month on *The Tyke* trying and failing to win over the curmudgeonly locals who couldn't see her as anything but an interloper, homesick for her old life in Bradford. But she had stuck it out, given it her all, and eventually the village had come to feel like home. Why should this feel different?

After thinking it over, Bobby eventually worked out why. It was because in Silverdale, she had had a goal. Her job on *The Tyke* had been her chance to make it as a reporter, and she had wanted that enough to bear many trials. More importantly, she had had a choice. Here she was a mere pawn of the war, and the independent spirit within her couldn't help but rebel at being pushed around by fate. But what could she do? Bobby only hoped that when the war was done with her, she would still remember how to be the woman she had been before.

Basic training, she quickly discovered, mostly covered things such as drilling and parading, RAF protocol, keeping kit and quarters in good order, first aid, personal fitness and, for those not already familiar with them, such delightful domestic tasks as scrubbing latrines, washing dishes and peeling potatoes – the essentials of military life. Specialist training courses relating to their trades would follow once the RAF had turned them from civilians into airwomen. Nevertheless, a small portion of each day was spent developing trade-related skills, which was how Bobby found herself assigned to clerical duties for the WAAF commandant, Mulligan.

'How'd you get that job then?' Dilys demanded when Bobby told the other women.

Bobby blinked. 'How? I don't know. The adjutant just told me to report to Stewpot's office.'

'Stewpot made a pet of you, has she? I never heard of sprogs doing typing for the big nobs. They've got NCOs for that.'

'I don't think she's even noticed me,' Bobby said truthfully. 'I'm to share duties with another WAAF: two hours each per day. I imagine they needed a couple of recruits with typing experience and my name was pulled out of a hat.'

–

Bobby approached her first afternoon's work alongside 'Stewpot' with trepidation, wondering if the officer would remember her from the day of her interview. Unfortunately, she did.

'Bancroft,' Squadron Officer Mulligan said when Bobby reported for duty. 'I thought you weren't keen on joining us. Postponement refused, was it?'

'Um, no,' Bobby said. 'I mean, no, ma'am. I decided not to apply. Felt I ought to do my bit.'

'Glad to hear it.' She took a seat at her desk. 'But do stop that stuttering and mumbling, girl. We need no "ums" and "ers" in the WAAF. Speak out with confidence and you'll find people will instinctively respect you.'

'Yes, ma'am. Sorry.'

There was another desk at a right angle to Mulligan's bearing a typewriter and various papers, but as Bobby hadn't been given any order to claim it, she waited to be told to sit down.

'Be seated,' Mulligan said, rather impatiently. 'There are some letters to be typed, and in half an hour I have a meeting with Squadron Leader Gardiner, my RAF opposite number. You will type a transcription in shorthand, then transcribe into longhand for the records.'

'Yes, ma'am.'

'I must admit, you arrived at a rather opportune time. The corporal who acts as my secretary is on urgent compassionate leave, and WAAF HQ swore they couldn't spare me a replacement for at least four weeks.' Mulligan looked rather vague. 'Husband injured, I believe – or he may have been killed. I was glad to see we had a couple of recruits with shorthand skills who could take over Hudson's tasks until she was fit to return.'

So that explained Bobby's assignment. Not a privilege but a necessity. She was glad to be able to justify this apparent special treatment to Dilys – although an afternoon locked in with their stern commandant didn't seem much like special treatment to her. However, as she hadn't been asked a question, Bobby merely said again, 'Yes, ma'am.'

'Well, get to work then.'

Bobby picked up one of the letters she had been asked to type, pleased to see that Mulligan had a clean, neat hand – a hundred times easier to read than Reg's – then put it down again.

'Squadron Officer?'

'Yes, Bancroft?'

'Um, I was hoping to have an opportunity to talk to you.' Bobby flinched, remembering the instruction not to fumble her words. She tried to speak out more confidently. 'I'd like to request permission to get married, on the 2nd of May. My fiancé can only get leave then. He's a pilot on operational flying. What do I need to do, please?'

'You must put your request in writing to the CO, Squadron Leader Gardiner, along with a leave pass form,' Mulligan said vaguely. 'We do try to limit personal commitments during basic training, but if the boy is one of our own then I doubt it will be any trouble. You can hand them in to the station warrant officer.'

'Thank you.' Bobby paused. 'Sorry, but may I ask a question?'

Mulligan looked up. 'Why are you apologising? Do you want to ask a question or don't you?'

Bobby blinked. 'Well, yes, I do.'

'Would a man say sorry for wanting to ask a question? Or would he just ask permission?'

'I imagine he'd just ask permission.'

'Then you do the same. What is it?'

'I wanted to know...' Bobby hesitated. 'I suppose you saw how I did in my tests. And I suppose you know I wanted special duties. I was hoping I could train as a plotter. Why was I assigned to general duties instead?'

Mulligan frowned at her. Bobby felt her cheeks burning. She wondered if she had crossed a line and was about to be charged with insubordination. This was one thing she hated about the military. None of the normal rules of human engagement seemed to apply, and she had no intuitive understanding of what the new rules were.

'Your typing and shorthand speeds were impressive,' Mulligan said at last. 'We can use those skills in the WAAF. Good, fast, accurate typists are always valued.'

'Yes, but surely if I did well in the tests then there's more important work I could be doing?'

Mulligan fixed her in a steely gaze. 'Don't assume that because other work sounds more heroic or glamorous, the work you've been assigned isn't important. All our work is important. Without it, the RAF couldn't function, which means the war could not be won.'

'I know, I just... thought I could be more help in another area.'

'Answer me this, Bancroft. Why do you think the work of a plotter is more important than that done by our WAAF clerks, or cooks, or the girls getting blisters on their fingers sewing parachutes?'

'Well, because it's…'

'Men's work?' Mulligan asked, lifting an eyebrow.

'That isn't what I was going to say.'

'But it's what you were thinking. It's what everyone thinks, whether they know it or not. It's work that would, in other circumstances, be done by a man, and therefore intrinsically more valuable. Cooking, sewing, typing: they come under the umbrella of women's work, and like all work done by women, tend to remain invisible. But a man who isn't fed cannot fight, Bancroft. If parachutes aren't competently sewn, men will die. The work of a clerk keeps the wheels of the Air Force turning. Do you see that?'

Bobby pondered this. Was that what she had been thinking – that administrative work had less value because it was so often allotted to women? Perhaps she had.

'I thought I could help the war effort more by using my brain, that's all,' she mumbled.

'Let me teach you the hard truth of life in the forces, young lady. You do the job that's put in front of you, just as every soldier, sailor and airman fighting for this country is doing. No more, no less. Everyone here has come from a different background in civilian life, and they have each been assigned a job that we feel is the best fit for them. We won't be victorious if everyone spends their time looking for greener grass on the other side of the fence. Do the job that's in front of you.'

'Yes, but surely—'

'That will be all, Aircraftwoman,' the officer said sharply. 'I try to be lenient with new WAAFs in their first week, knowing they still have one foot in civilian life, but I would advise you not to test the limits of that privilege. Go to your work – that's an order.'

Bobby did as she was told, feeling as she so often had since arriving here – about as insignificant as a worm.

–

Four days later, there had been only slight improvement in the weather. It had dried up enough, however, for the women to be told that they would head out on their first route march the following day.

Bobby couldn't say she was looking forward to it. She had heard about route marches from her male RAF friends. In her mind was an unpleasant image of being made to march twenty miles over the fells in full kit, only to return, covered in mud and other unsavoury substances, to the prescribed ten-minute bath in five inches of lukewarm water. Even on the night she had climbed Great Bowside to help the injured airmen, she had at least been able to return home to a soak in a steaming mustard bath, a hot water bottle and a comfortable bed.

After she was off duty, Bobby returned to her dorm. Most of the other women had finished work and would now be in the recreation hut, listening to the wireless and playing cards, but Bobby wanted to see if tomorrow's fatigue duties had been pinned to the noticeboard yet.

They hadn't, but she noticed that one of the women had added another strike to the tally counting the days until their two weeks of isolation were up.

To her new friends, the tally meant just one thing: men. They had little interest in the lowly male recruits, but the officer instructors were another matter. The women spoke of these knights of the air as if they were demi-gods, and longed for the day they could see them up close.

The tally meant only one thing to Bobby too. Letters. She was longing for news from home, but even more than that, she was desperate to see if her last letter to Charlie had produced a response. If she could only know that everything between them was as it ought to be, she could relax a little. As it was, the constant worry that something might be wrong kept her on the very edge of her nerves. Without post she had no way of knowing if he had written back, or if a backlog of letters from the past four weeks might have caught up with her. She hadn't received any urgent telegrams, thank God, so she at least knew he was safe. It was his heart she now feared for.

'Just seven more days,' she murmured to herself as she walked to her bunk. 'Good God, but there must be *something.*'

She found Dilys and Carol on their beds. Dilys was lazing around in her illegally retained civilian knickers and rather grubby bra while laying out cards for a game of Patience. Carol was lying on the bunk above, gazing dreamily at the corrugated ceiling while she smoked a cigarette.

'Afternoon,' Bobby said, summoning the mask of joviality she always wore around the others. She had been hoping to have a few minutes to herself before dinner, but no such luck. 'I thought everyone would be in the rec hut.'

'I needed to get out of that smothering uniform and let my skin breathe.' Dilys glanced up from her cards. 'How's Stewpot's pet then?'

'I'm really not. I don't even think she likes me. Just my typing speed.' Bobby waved a hand in front of the dreamy Carol. 'What's up with you?'

Carol gave a deep sigh. 'I've met him, Bobs.'

'Who have you met?'

'The one. Honestly, I'm ruined for other men now.'

Dilys rolled her eyes. 'What she's trying to tell you is that she's besotted with some officer she served lunch to today.'

Bobby sat on her bunk and started rolling down her itchy lisle stockings. 'Who is he, Car?'

Carol put out her cigarette and pushed herself up, her eyes sparkling. 'You'll never guess. He's a Yank! My first one.'

Bobby frowned. 'What would a Yank be doing here?'

'He was in an RAF uniform. Guess he must be a whatchamacallit – you know, the ones that joined our Air Force right at the start. Eagle Squadron.' Carol sighed again. 'And Bobs, he looks so like Robert Taylor it's untrue.'

'Doesn't exist,' Dilys muttered as she went back to laying out her cards. 'You shouldn't read so many film magazines, Car. They're giving you hallucinations.'

'Honestly, he's solid – dead solid,' Carol said with a grin. 'Those shoulders! I didn't get his name but I guess he's a new instructor. Never served him before so he must be just arrived, which means hopefully no one's got their claws into him yet.'

'Why would they send a Yank here as an instructor?' Bobby asked. 'The Eagles are fighter squadrons. Ryland Moor trains bomber crew.'

'Maybe they sent him especially for me,' Carol said, smirking.

'So much for finding men for us all,' Dilys grumbled. 'Should've known you'd bag the best one for yourself.'

'There's plenty to go around,' Carol said airily. 'I've got my eye on some for you three, don't worry.'

'I told you—' Bobby began.

'Yes, we know, you're far too deeply in love to ever betray the wonderful Charles,' Carol said, clutching her heart. 'Like I said, this is in case you change your mind. Just remember though, ladies: the American flying officer's mine, all right?'

Chapter 33

Bobby didn't have long to wait to set eyes on the new love of Carol's life: this handsome American officer. In fact, she saw him the next day, when the women arrived at the hut where they were forced to sit through long, dull lectures on the history of the service.

'Surely we must know everything there is to know about the history of the RAF by now,' Mike muttered as they went in.

'It's not history today,' said one of the WAAFs filing in alongside them. 'I heard it was going to be first aid.'

'No, that's not right,' another said. 'We've got a first aid demonstration after lunch, before the route march.'

'Well, what is it then?'

'International relations or something,' another woman said, stifling a yawn. 'Some officer is going to talk about cooperating with foreign Allied services and all that rot. Here, let's grab a desk at the back and see if we can have a crafty kip while they're droning on.'

'Oh blimey.' Carol grabbed Bobby's arm. 'I bet it's him!'

'What, your divine Yank?'

'Who else could it be? There aren't any other foreign officers in the mess.'

'But you said he was RAF,' Bobby pointed out. 'Why would they get an RAF officer to talk to us about working with foreign services? If he's one of ours he won't have any special knowledge, even if he is American.'

'I don't know, do I? I'm sure it has to be him though. Come on, before the good desks are taken.'

Carol dragged her three friends to the front. Since most recruits preferred to sit as far back as they could, out of sight of the lecturer, they were able to claim a place right in the centre.

'You'd better be right about this, Car,' Dilys whispered. 'Otherwise we've got an hour of having to sit up prim and proper for some ugly old officer while everyone at the back is playing Noughts and Crosses.'

A man appeared and mounted the lecturer's podium – a short, squat RAF NCO. Carol looked devastated, until she realised this wasn't the lecturer but someone to introduce him.

'Settle down, ladies, settle down,' the man said pompously. 'This morning's lecture will be on the subject of "Our Commonwealth Allies, and How We're Stronger Together". In a moment it will be my privilege to introduce Flying Officer Ernest King of the Royal Canadian Air Force, who has recently joined us at Ryland Moor.'

Bobby blinked. 'No!'

'Shush, Bobs,' Mike murmured, ventriloquist-style. The NCO glared in their direction, but didn't reprimand them for talking out of turn.

'Flying Officer King is taking a temporary hiatus from operational flying while he heals from an injury sustained in the course of his duties,' the man went on. 'I hope you will remember to treat him with the respect he deserves. Now, notebooks at the ready.'

The NCO went to fetch Ernie, and Bobby took advantage of the hubbub that arose while the WAAFs hunted for writing materials to whisper to Carol.

'I thought you said he was a Yank,' she hissed.

Carol shrugged. 'Well, he sounds like a Yank. Anyway, he's still bagged.'

'What's up, Bobs?' Mike asked.

Bobby tucked an escaped tendril of hair under her cap, feeling flustered. 'Nothing.'

'It doesn't look like nothing,' Dilys observed. 'You're red as anything, you are. What's the secret?'

Bobby was spared the necessity of answering by the arrival of the NCO, showing in their speaker. As soon as Ernie entered, twenty-odd heads swivelled in his direction.

Behind her, Bobby heard a WAAF whisper to her friend, 'Bloody hell! How many coupons do you need for something as sweet as that?' Her pal guffawed appreciatively.

Bobby couldn't avoid him noticing her. Thanks to Carol, they were directly in front of the speaker's podium. Sure enough, she saw Ernie blink when he spotted her, and then the twitch of a smile. She didn't smile back but looked straight ahead, summoning all the military professionalism she could muster.

Ernie King, here! Topsy had told her he was down in Cambridge.

Various emotions flooded her. Pleasure at seeing her friend looking so well after his recent injury, with his arm now out of its sling. Guilt, still, over that night on the ice. Confusion about what the look he had given her might have meant. Worry about Charlie, and how he would feel if he knew Ernie was here with her while he was far away. Fear about whether he would still care, or if he had really forgotten her. But more than all that, Bobby felt an overwhelming sensation of comfort at seeing a face that belonged to home. Ernie King, something familiar amongst all this strangeness, felt like a panacea for the gnawing homesickness she was unable to shake off.

He had mounted the podium now, and was endeavouring to catch her eye. Bobby allowed him to do so, flashing a small smile. He smiled warmly back before turning his attention to the recruits waiting for him to speak.

Bobby didn't hear much of the talk on Commonwealth relations. She was too bowled over by Ernie's unexpected appearance. What she did hear didn't sound particularly enthralling, although you might have thought Ernie was another Svengali, the way he seemed to hold his audience rapt. It was clear Carol was going to have some competition for his favours.

Would he speak to her, afterwards? Bobby half hoped he wouldn't. Her friends were already suspicious about her pink cheeks. She could dissemble her way out of that, perhaps, but if Ernie acknowledged their prior relationship, she would be bombarded with questions about him.

After the lecture, the pompous NCO engaged Ernie in conversation. For a moment, Bobby thought she might be able to slip out unseen in spite of the crowd of women pressing through the door so they could be first in the queue for lunch. The NCO disappeared as she was preparing to fight her way out, however, and Ernie hailed her at once.

'Hey. Slacks.'

Her friends hadn't hurried to leave, lingering to enjoy a last gaze at the object of Carol's affections. They stared at Bobby on hearing her thus acknowledged, and she cursed her stupid flushed cheeks.

'Ernie,' she said, smiling warmly. Despite the muddle of emotions, she was genuinely pleased to see him. 'I mean, sorry.' She whipped off a salute. 'Flying Officer King.'

He laughed. 'At ease, Aircraftwoman Slacks. It is Aircraftwoman, I assume?'

Bobby laughed too, relaxing a little. 'Yes, ACW/2, the very lowliest of erks. May I shine your boots, sir?'

He stepped towards her, and for a moment she thought he might take her hands, but he didn't, thank God.

'No, but you can have a drink with me in the NAAFI tomorrow night.' He nodded politely to the other three, who were goggling at him wonderingly. 'And your friends, of course. It's good to see a familiar face.'

Carol came forward to slip her arm through Bobby's. 'We'd like that, wouldn't we, Bobs?' She beamed at Ernie. 'I'm her best friend.'

Ernie laughed. 'A new best friend already? You've barely been here a week, Slacks. Have you forgotten Her Ladyship so soon?'

Mike frowned. 'Ladyship? What ladyship? Bobsy, do you know a ladyship?'

Bobby cursed Ernie silently. What did he have to go and say that for? She was struggling enough to shake off a reputation for holier-than-thou primness without it getting out that she knocked around with the landed gentry.

'Oh, it's just a nickname for a mutual friend,' she told Mike airily, casting Ernie a keep-quiet look. 'Mrs Nowak. I was maid of honour at her wedding recently.'

'A wedding that the RAF decreed I had to miss,' Ernie said. 'How about tomorrow night then, girls? Bobby, you can tell me all about the nuptials over a drink.'

'I'm afraid we're not allowed,' Bobby said, ignoring a glare from Dilys. 'We're not even supposed to be talking to you. Fraternisation with your kind is strictly forbidden until we've been here a fortnight.'

'Didn't you listen to my talk? I thought we were fostering Commonwealth relations.'

Bobby smiled. '"Your kind" meaning men, not Canadians. Sorry, but you'd have to take it up with our WAAF commandant.'

'I might do that.' He gave her another warm smile. 'I'm glad you're here, kid.'

He strode off towards the door, but Bobby called to him.

'Ernie, wait! Have you had any news from Teddy?' she asked. 'We're not allowed to receive letters for a fortnight either. I'm dying to know how everyone is at home.'

'I had a letter from the new Mr and Mrs Nowak just before I left Cambridge,' he called over his shoulder. 'Happy to report that all's joyous with the honeymooners. I'm told the old lady's just become a proud gran of nine feathery grandchildren.'

'Oh! You mean Norman and Jemima's goslings have hatched?'

Ernie laughed. 'Sorry, I have to go. I have to be on the airfield in ten minutes to take a sprog up. Meet me in the NAAFI tomorrow and I'll let you read it for yourself, OK?'

'You know I can't. Mulligan would have my head.'

'We'll see about that,' he said, grinning, and left the hut.

'Bloody hell!' Carol stared at Bobby like some wondrous thing. Mike had fixed her in an awestruck gaze as well, and even Dilys looked reluctantly impressed. 'All right, tell us *everything*.'

Bobby shrugged. 'He's a friend from home, that's all. I didn't know he was being moved here. Last I heard he was in Cambridge.'

'What kind of a friend?' Dilys asked, narrowing one eye.

'What kinds are there?'

'Men and women can't really be friends,' Mike said. 'Sooner or later he goes gooey on her or she does on him, or something happens between them when they're tight, and it all ends up one big mess.'

Carol frowned at Bobby. 'Is that it, Bobs?'

'Don't be daft,' Bobby said, fighting a blush. 'It isn't always like that. Ernie was billeted in my village and we got to know each other performing in a Christmas pantomime.' She glanced at Mike, who was smirking. 'Honestly, that was all there was to it. He helped me with my Lambeth Walk.'

Mike snorted. 'I'll bet he did.'

Dilys gave Bobby an impressed nod. 'Maybe you're not so clueless after all, Bobsy. Sounded like he was keen to make a date with you.'

'It wouldn't be a date. It's comforting to see a familiar face in a new place, that's all – for both of us.'

'He invited us to the NAAFI tomorrow,' Mike said reverently. 'I mean, we obviously have to go. He's an officer, isn't he? He could put us on a fizzer for disobeying orders.'

'I doubt Stewpot's going to see it that way,' Bobby said, laughing. 'Come on, let's bimble over to the cookhouse. We'll be at the back of the lunch queue as it is.'

'This is wonderful though, Bobs.' Carol claimed her arm and gave it a gleeful squeeze as they headed to the cookhouse, Dilys and Mike walking off ahead deep in gossipy conference.

'Now you can tell me all about him, and if he can get us special permission from Stewpot so we can meet in the NAAFI, I can get my hands on him before any of the others. Quick, tell me everything you know.'

Bobby blinked. What did she know about Ernie, really? Not that much, now she came to think about it.

'He's from Alberta,' she said. 'His parents have a farm there.'

Carol's eyes gleamed. 'A farm like... a plantation? Like Ashley Wilkes in *Gone with the Wind*?'

'I shouldn't think so. That's at the bottom of America, isn't it? Ernie's from near the Rocky Mountains.'

'So he's rich?'

Bobby laughed. 'I have absolutely no idea, Car, I've never asked.'

'What about brothers and sisters?'

'I really couldn't say. We only met last autumn, when we started rehearsing the pantomime. We haven't talked much about anything personal.'

'Oh.' Carol sounded disappointed. 'Well, you must at least know if he's got a sweetheart at home. Or a wife, God forbid.'

Bobby frowned. 'I don't know actually. I presume not.'

'Why?'

'I'd have expected him to mention it. Besides, he was courting a mutual friend of ours before she married – the one we were just talking about, Topsy Nowak. Well, not courting exactly, but he definitely had his cap set at her.'

They had reached the cookhouse now, and joined the back of the queue.

'If she's just got wed then it's the perfect time for me to sweep in and fill her place,' Carol said, cheering up again. 'You'll help, won't you? Put in a good word and all that?'

'I doubt my good words will carry much weight, but I'll do what I can,' Bobby said, smiling. 'Don't be disappointed if he's not interested though, Car. Ernie's sort of... old-fashioned. A bit stuffy about certain things.'

'What's he old-fashioned about? He can't be more than twenty-six.'

'He's got very definite ideas about men and women, and the roles they ought to play in life,' Bobby told her. 'He says the war's making women less feminine. Encouraging them into immoral behaviour, like drinking too much and picking up men. We used to clash about it all the time – in a friendly sort of way, I mean.'

'Oh, he sounds just whizzo,' Carol said dreamily.

Bobby glanced at her. 'Really? I thought you joined the WAAF especially to have some of that sort of fun.'

'Even so, I don't want a husband who approves of all that, do I? All it means is that he'll be out drinking and picking up women while I'm stuck at home with a bunch of screaming brats. Some lads are all right to have fun with, but when it comes to husbands, I want an old-fashioned gent who'll look after me.' Her brow lowered. 'Someone who's the exact opposite of my dad.'

'I thought you wanted to enjoy yourself before settling.'

'That was before I saw Ernie King,' Carol said with another smitten sigh. 'You won't tell him, will you? What I said about wanting lots of boyfriends and all that? You can't now we're best friends.'

Bobby smiled. 'I won't breathe a word.'

Chapter 34

'There's something for you on your desk, Bancroft,' Squadron Officer Mulligan told Bobby when she reported for duty the next day.

'What is it, ma'am?'

Bobby was finding it hard to get used to being called by her surname, which felt sort of manly, and to addressing the WAAF officers as 'ma'am'. It sounded so formal and old-fashioned, as if she were a servant in a country house.

Mulligan didn't look up from what she was writing. If possible, she looked even sterner than usual.

'Take a look,' she said.

Bobby approached her desk. On it she found a letter of just a few short sentences. It was addressed to her and signed 'Sqn Ldr Wm. Gardiner'. That was the RAF commanding officer – the big boss of the camp.

'It's your official permission to marry,' Mulligan said, looking up. 'And your marriage leave's been approved as well. You'll find a signed pass chit underneath.'

Bobby blinked at the letter. 'Oh.'

'I'm happy for you to send wires to your family and fiancé, in spite of the ban, so you can inform them. I imagine you'll have a lot to arrange.'

'Thank you.'

Bobby felt a little dazed. She had spent so much time thinking about Charlie, worrying about him, both longing for and fearing the day she would discover whether or not any letter had come from him, that she had entirely forgotten seeking permission to wed.

It was decided, then. A firm date could be set – Saturday the 2nd of May. The church could be confirmed, friends could be invited, a small reception arranged, and in a mere fortnight she would find herself a married woman.

But there remained that treacherous whisper: *If he still wants me…*

'Is everything all right?' Mulligan asked.

'Hmm?' Bobby pulled herself together. 'Sorry, Squadron Officer. I hadn't expected it today, that's all.'

Mulligan sighed. 'Come here a moment, Bancroft.'

Bobby hesitated, then went to sit in the chair on the other side of the officer's desk.

'Did I do something wrong, ma'am?' she asked.

Mulligan fixed her in a stern, but not unkind, gaze. 'That was what I wanted to ask you.'

'I'm sorry?'

'Well, never mind. Is he steady, this young man you're marrying?'

Bobby thought about this. It wasn't a word that would have been used to describe the Charlie Atherton she had met eighteen months ago, but he had changed a lot since then.

'I believe he is, now he's in the RAF,' she said.

'And you love him?'

Bobby was rather taken aback by this question. Had Mulligan called her over to give her a talk on the facts of life? She felt the colour rising to her cheeks at the thought.

'Very much,' she said quietly.

'Good. Good.'

Mulligan fell silent, seemingly lost in thought. Bobby remembered what Carol had said, about the RAF officer Mulligan had been involved with who had ditched her for someone else. It was hard to imagine their stern, pinched-faced commandant in love.

'Am I to go back to work, ma'am?' Bobby asked when Mulligan had been quiet some time.

Mulligan roused herself. 'Not yet. I need to speak to you about something.'

'What is it?'

The officer met her gaze. 'Bancroft, I received a request this morning from a young man regarding you and your friends, although I got the sense it was you he was mainly concerned with. The sort of young man it can be hard to say no to – at least, he seemed to think so,' she said with a tight smile. 'I did say no to him, however. I've been alive too long to fall for the charms of overgrown schoolboys who think they can twist any woman they meet around their little finger. Do you understand?'

'I'm... not sure.' Bobby assumed the overgrown schoolboy in question must be Ernie King, although she couldn't guess where the conversation might be going.

Mulligan shuffled some papers. 'You're a steady girl, Bancroft. I've been keeping my eye on you. You didn't want to join the WAAF and you didn't want to spend your time typing letters and orders, but you've tried hard to do the job that's in front of you, just as I asked. I can see this way of life comes harder to you than to the others, yet you've given it your utmost. You aren't one of those giggling idiots who join up just to chase men.'

'That's a little unfair,' Bobby heard herself saying. That was almost certainly overstepping the bounds between officers and other ranks, but she couldn't help feeling defensive of the other women.

'Oh, I don't only mean your friends,' Mulligan said, waving a dismissive hand. 'They're all like that when they get here, particularly the younger ones. For many, it's the first taste of freedom they've had in their lives. They soon settle down. Some of the best WAAFs I know spent their training period acting like it was the last days of Rome. But I can tell you're not one of those, Bancroft. You're intelligent, you work hard and you've got your head screwed on.' She met Bobby's eyes. 'So I'd hate to see you fall under the spell of some handsome peacock with a glamorous accent practically on the eve of your wedding.'

Bobby laughed. 'Oh. I know what you... no, it isn't like that between Ernie and me. I suppose it is Flying Officer King you mean. We were friends, before. In my civilian life, I mean.'

Mulligan frowned. 'Friends?'

'Yes. Just friends, nothing more. He was billeted in my village and we worked together to produce a pantomime for the children. I saw him in our lecture yesterday and he wanted me to meet him in the NAAFI to swap news of mutual friends, but I told him it wouldn't be allowed.'

'This is the true state of affairs? He hasn't made any... propositions? I know he's become a favourite among the other girls.'

'That's truly all. I know the other WAAFs think I'm greener than grass, but I grew up with two brothers and worked in an all-male office for years. Believe me, I'm savvy enough not to fall prey to some wolf.'

For perhaps the first time since she had known her, Bobby saw the commandant smile.

'I'm glad to hear it,' she said. 'My decision still stands, of course. I can't make exceptions for individual women. But I'm pleased to hear your relations with Flying Officer King are no more than they ought to be. I must admit, I was concerned for you.'

Bobby smiled warmly back, thinking how easy it could be to misjudge someone.

She had respected Mulligan from the moment she had heard her speech, urging her WAAFs to stand tall against those who might undermine them, but even so, she hadn't liked her much. The officer had seemed so cold, so lacking in compassion and kindness, that it had been hard to warm to her on any personal level. Bobby had been convinced that Mulligan hadn't liked her much either – ever since her interview, when the officer had seemed to mark her down as a shirker. But now, Bobby found she had come to rather like 'old Stewpot' after all. There was a human heart beneath the stern crust, if you took the trouble to go hunting for it.

'That's good of you, ma'am,' she said. 'But honestly, there's no need to worry. Flying Officer King is a friend, and I can assure you that's all he ever will be. May I return to work?'

'There was one more thing,' Mulligan said. 'You have family nearby, I think?'

'Yes, in Silverdale. Why do you ask?'

'I wanted to enquire how you'd feel about staying on here, after your basic training is complete. I've been impressed with the work you've done for me, and HQ tell me it will be at least a month until they can send a replacement for Corporal Hudson.'

'She isn't coming back?'

'No. I understand her husband's injury means he now requires constant care. She's to be discharged on compassionate grounds.' Mulligan leaned towards her. 'I know this isn't what you wanted to be doing, and I won't press if you'd prefer to move on with the other girls after passing out. But it would allow you to spend a little more time near your family, and... well, if you still had your heart set on being a plotter, I could help you get a place on a suitable training course. You've a good brain in that head, Bancroft. Whatever your trade, I can see a bright future for you in the WAAF.'

Bobby considered this. That word, 'future', jarred her rather. It still felt like such a hazy, will-o'-the-wisp idea. No sooner had it started to take on a form then a gust of wind came and turned it back into mist.

Don had been right: Bobby was bored in her new work, however necessary it might be for the smooth running of the RAF. There was so little to occupy her brain in the daily mind-less transcription of militaryese, learning how to operate the camp teleprinter, sorting post, filing records in the orderly room and other admin tasks that were the lot of the WAAF general clerk. The thought of doing it for several hours every day felt mind-numbing. Nevertheless, the option to remain close to her family for a little longer was appealing. And Mulligan was offering her the chance to do something truly important when her time here was up — something that could save lives, and perhaps even help turn the tide of the war.

'Thank you,' she said at last. 'I'd like that very much.'

—

Three days passed, each one seeing another mark added to the tally in Hut 17. Eventually, on Saturday morning, there were thirteen marks on the board — the penultimate day of their isolation.

Bobby could feel her body vibrating with nervous tension. Of course she was desperate to know how Lil, Tony and her father were getting along at the cow house. She was keen to learn from Mary how preparations were going for the arrival of Captain Parry, and she hoped there might be a letter from Topsy. But it was Charlie, and the prospect of one or more letters from him, that kept her heart perpetually in her mouth.

He must still love her. Perhaps love could peter out if it was neglected, but it didn't stop all of a sudden, and Charlie had seemed to love her so much. Whatever Mike's husband David did while his wife was far away, whatever other men did, Bobby felt certain Charlie would be true to her.

She could still remember the way he had held her the last time they had seen one another: the tender, hungry lips he had pressed to hers, and his eagerness — almost his desperation — for their wedding day. It was inconceivable that his feelings could have changed so suddenly and drastically, or that he would ever stray.

That was what Bobby tried to tell herself. But there was another voice: one that whispered cruel, painful, pitiless things to her when she lay on her hard bunk at night.

Hadn't he been a flirt when she first met him? Didn't he have every girl in the village in love with him, once upon a time? Isn't he a man, with desires and urges like the rest?

But what worried Bobby most wasn't that Charlie was a man like any other. It was the thought that he was afraid, far from home, dealing with the daily risk to his own life as well as the constant grief of men he had bonded with being killed in action. If Bobby was lonely and frightened here in the WAAF, how much worse must it be for Charlie?

It wrung her heart to think of it. He must need love so much, now. She could imagine how he must long for warm arms around him, and the hushed whisper of a tender voice that comforted and reassured. How she wished she could give him those things! But the war had decreed they had to part, and she couldn't in all honesty say she would blame Charlie if, in his need for comfort, he had found another love. It would break her heart, but she couldn't blame him.

She wondered if she should have done what Mike had, and given her blessing for Charlie to seek comfort of the purely physical variety with other women. War was such a unique situation, where none of the usual rules of romantic relationships seemed to apply. At least then, she would know his feelings were with her even if his lips were with someone else. But she couldn't. The idea of Charlie holding someone the way he held her, all those sensations she had been proud to feel belonged to her alone being stirred by another... no. She couldn't bear to think of it, and she was sure Charlie would feel the same about the idea of her with someone else.

Or he would have, when he still cared...

Bobby tried to smother the treacherous thought. There was no point giving in to such whispers; not until she knew for sure. She had sent the wire sanctioned by Mulligan to let Charlie know their marriage had been approved and they could officially set the date for the 2nd of May, but had opted not to notify the folk at Moorside until she heard back from her fiancé.

She was sure there would be something from him tomorrow, even if it was a letter breaking things off. He couldn't ignore her and hope she disappeared, surely. That just wasn't Charlie.

Saturdays were half-days, with parade and a route march in the morning but the afternoons free to do as they wished. After they had completed square-bashing around the parade ground, the WAAFs lined up in front of Mulligan.

'Good morning, ladies,' the squadron officer greeted them. 'You will be pleased to hear I have good news for you this glorious sunny Saturday.'

Mulligan didn't beam – Bobby wasn't sure she was capable of such a thing – but she did regard them more complacently than she was wont to do.

'What's she got planned then?' Mike murmured.

'You have now been here nearly two weeks, and have conducted yourselves, I must say, admirably,' the squadron officer told them. 'Not a single one of you has been on charge, and you are routinely smart, polite and conscientious, although I know what a shock it can be to leave civilian life and enter a military environment. I am exceptionally proud of you all. I have spoken with Squadron Leader Gardiner and he shares my opinion that you have proven yourselves a credit to the service. Thus we have decided that with today being Saturday, following your route march, we will end the embargo period early. You will all be issued with your post, be free to write to or telephone your families, and this evening the RAF officers have kindly offered to host a dance for all ranks in the NAAFI canteen.'

There was a buzz of excited conversation among the women, and Carol grabbed at Bobby's arm. No doubt she was thinking of Ernie King, who she hadn't spoken to since the day of his lecture, although she had apparently spent a lot of time trying to catch his eye in the officers' mess.

'Tell you what, she's not such a bad old stick, is she?' she whispered to Bobby.

Bobby shrugged, feeling it better to remain non-committal. There was a definite 'us and them' between the officers and other ranks, and she didn't want to cement the view that she had become Mulligan's pet erk.

'She has her moments,' she whispered back.

'Now, now, ladies, settle down,' Mulligan said, actually smiling for once. 'Return to your quarters, please, and prepare for today's march. Then you will have the remainder of the day to catch up with news from home.'

Chapter 35

Bobby had dreaded the route marches before she had experienced one, and it was certainly true that there was little worse than a wet, windy, muddy tramp over the hills with no home comforts to come back to. But when the weather cooperated, they were her favourite part of her new life.

On the fells, she didn't feel homesick. She could shut out the sound of chatter and pretend she was striding up Great Bowside with Charlie by her side, or imagine she was hiking to see her friend Andy Jessop in his farmhouse at Newby Top. From a certain vantage point she even thought she could make out the tiny dot of Silverdale in the far distance, and smiled as she thought of her friends and family there, going about their day.

Bobby found it hard to enjoy today's hike though, in spite of the sunshine, the birdsong and the spring flowers bursting out all over. Her head was too full of thoughts of Charlie, and what might be waiting for her when the women were finally allowed their post. All the fells did was remind her of him.

The WAAFs weren't sent on long-distance marches – at least, not compared to the RAF recruits, who might go as far as twenty miles in a day. Today's hike was to be a mere six miles. Still, that was more than enough for Bobby's less countrified companions.

'Ugh,' Carol said, wrinkling her nose as she wiped something off her shoe. 'Cow muck. Hope I don't stink of it for the dance tonight. How does a ruddy cow get up here?'

'That's sheep muck,' Bobby told her. 'Dales sheep are like mountain goats. They can get everywhere.'

'Since when did you become an expert in the difference between cow and sheep muck?' Dilys demanded.

Bobby shrugged. 'I like walking. You quickly learn that sort of thing here.'

'Never catch me traipsing through fields of muck, ruining my stockings,' Dilys muttered.

Bobby smiled. 'Is this not what your people do? I thought Wales was all running through the valleys in those funny hats on the trail of feral herds of male voice choirs.'

Dilys gave her a dirty look before marching off. She had tried to hide it, but Bobby saw her face crumple as she walked away, almost as if she was going to cry.

'What did I say?' Bobby asked, turning to the others. 'I didn't mean to be nasty. I was trying to make her laugh, that's all. I keep trying to make friends, but she just looks daggers at me.'

Carol shrugged. 'I guess Welsh people get a bit sick of the English taking the mickey. There's no need for her to be that sensitive about it though. She's said a lot worse to you.'

'I don't think it's that,' Mike said quietly. 'She's got something on her mind. I wouldn't take it personally, Bobby.'

Bobby watched Dilys striding off. 'What is it?'

'It isn't for me to say.' Mike sighed. 'Poor kid.'

They walked on, Bobby wondering what it could all be about.

She had learnt a little about her companions over the past two weeks, and had soon found there was more to them than she had assumed. All were volunteers rather than conscripts – in the WAAF by choice, unlike her.

Violet Carmichael, known as Mike, was twenty-seven years old, curvy, platinum blonde, fun-loving and glamorous. On first meeting her, Bobby had marked her down as a good-time girl with a somewhat cynical outlook on life and love. She had been surprised to learn, however, that despite her aversion to having children, Mike had a strong motherly streak. It was she who had taken the other three under her wing, and helped them find their feet in this strange new life. Bobby had also discovered that in spite of the unconventional arrangement at the heart of her marriage, Mike had a deep love for her husband David.

Carol, too, had her secrets. She had told Bobby at her medical that she had followed her sister Trish to the Air Force in search of a husband, but Bobby had seen the bruises on her friend's skin when they had been changing. Dark references to wanting to escape a stern father had quickly pointed Bobby to the real reason the Boyes sisters had been keen to leave home and find men who could protect them.

Dilys Baines's boyfriend Richie sounded just such another. At only eighteen, Dilys had joined up to escape his jealous rages and his fists, hoping to meet someone better.

Dilys continued walking apart. Even when they stopped on a stretch of limestone pavement for a cup of tea from their Thermos flasks, she sat a little distance away.

'She's still cross with me for teasing her,' Bobby said to Mike and Carol. 'I ought to go make it right.'

'Be careful,' Mike said as Bobby stood up. 'She's liable to bite someone's head off today. Possibly literally.'

Bobby headed to where Dilys was sitting. She wasn't drinking tea but writing in a notebook.

'Hello,' Bobby said, taking a seat by her.

Dilys ignored her. However, Bobby wasn't going to be put off. She was determined to make a friend of this girl, one way or another.

'Look, I'm sorry about before,' she said. 'I was trying to make a joke, but I guess it came out wrong. That's the story of my life really. I'm not good at making friends – never have been. If I offended you then I apologise.'

Again Dilys remained silent, but she deigned to shrug, which Bobby thought might be a good sign.

'What are you writing?' she asked, squinting at the note-book. She couldn't understand a word of what was written there. To her eyes, it seemed a mere jumble of letters.

'Letter home,' Dilys mumbled.

'What code is that?'

Dilys's mouth twitched. 'It's Welsh, Dumbo the elephant.'

Bobby smiled. 'I thought you must be spying for the Jerries. Who's it to?'

'Richie. He'll have a fit if I don't write soon as I'm allowed.'

'Didn't you say you were going to ditch him?'

'I can't.' Dilys hunched over her notebook. 'Not yet.'

'Why not?'

'Because… what if I can't get anyone better?' She shuddered. 'End up an old maid like Mulligan?'

'Better that than with a man like him,' Bobby muttered darkly. 'Besides, you've got plenty of time to meet someone. A good man, who values and deserves you.'

Dilys turned to look at her, scowling. 'Why're you being nice to me?'

'Because I want us to be friends.'

'No you don't,' Dilys said, still scowling. 'I've seen how you look at me.'

'How?'

'You know full well. Like I'm not worth a damn. Like you think you're better than me.'

Bobby frowned. 'Now why on earth would you think that?'

Dilys shrugged again, and went back to her letter.

Bobby thought back to the day they'd met, when she had heard Dilys condemn her as a prig. She tried to recall all their interactions since then. She knew she could be stiff and awkward with new people, but did Dilys really believe Bobby despised her?

Or was this not really about her at all?

'Does he make you feel like that?' she asked quietly.

'Who?'

'Richie. Does he make you feel like you're worthless?'

Dilys looked up sharply. 'Who said that? Was it Mike?'

'No one said it. I'm saying it,' Bobby said. 'He does, doesn't he?'

Dilys bit her lip, fighting back tears. Sensing she was embarrassed, Bobby looked away.

Colourful spring flowers had popped out across the peaty fells after so many weeks of rain: golden saxifrage, purple dog-violet. Bobby took a deep breath, listening to the harsh whistle of a curlew and thinking of home. When she turned back, she found Dilys watching her curiously.

'What?' Bobby said.

'What are you looking at? Your eyes have gone funny.'

'Just... this place, I suppose. Don't you think it's beautiful?'

Dilys turned an unimpressed gaze on the rolling country around them. 'This? It's just fields. Bright lights, busy theatres, Piccadilly Circus at Christmastime – that's what I call beautiful. That's where I'd have wanted to be when they turn the lights back on.'

'Well, and who says you won't?'

'Richie wouldn't ever take me to London. He's never even left Swansea. He just wants to stay there the rest of his life and play darts in the pub every night.'

Bobby shrugged. 'Then go without him. Go with someone else, or by yourself if you like, and tell Richie he can jolly well go hang.'

A reluctant smile appeared on Dilys's face. 'You'd do that, I bet.'

'If that was where I wanted to be.' Bobby drew in another deep breath. 'Nothing beats this for me though. The freedom of it. Now, my twin sister Lilian, she'd be off with you to the bright lights. Lil's all about the good times. You'd never have called her a prig.'

'I'm sorry I called you that,' Dilys murmured. 'You're not a prig. I thought you were dead stuck-up, but you're not really, are you?'

'No. Just a bit odd and shy,' Bobby said, smiling. 'I'm sorry if you thought I didn't like you. I mean I didn't much, but only because you were mean to me, not because I think I'm better than you or any of that. I'd much rather be friends.'

'Does she have a lot of boyfriends, your sister?'

'Not any more,' Bobby said quietly. 'She... she found out she was going to have a baby. Now she's married to the father.'

Dilys lowered her head. 'Me too,' she whispered.

Bobby stared at her. 'Oh, Dilys, no.'

'I think so. I haven't seen the quack, but I should've got my curse a week ago. That's what the letter I'm writing's about. I have to tell Richie, don't I? I mean, it's his. I've never been with any other lad, though he must've accused me of it a hundred times when he was tight.'

'Oh, sweetheart.' Bobby put an arm round her and gave her a squeeze.

'You won't tell anyone, will you? I told Mike about it, and I don't mind Carol knowing, but I don't want it to get around camp. I'll see the MO if it doesn't come this week, but I want to keep it quiet as long as I can.'

'Of course not.' Bobby leaned round to look at her. 'But please... if this Richie is violent with you, I wish you'd think again about going back to him. You don't have to, even with a baby coming.'

'How can I not, when he's the dad? At least Rich doesn't hit as hard as some of them. He's never broken anything. Always keeps it where no one'll see.'

Bobby swore under her breath.

'He's a brute,' she muttered. 'Please, Dilys. For your sake and the baby's, run away from him. He won't stop, whatever he might promise.'

'What, and be an unmarried mother?'

'Better that than a battered wife.'

'Who'd look after us then?' Dilys swallowed. 'My mam's strict Chapel. She won't let me in the house if I go back with a baby and no husband.'

Bobby sighed. 'I wish I knew the answer to that. You really shouldn't have to make that choice.'

Dilys looked up at her. 'What's your man like? He ever raise his hand to you?'

'If he did, I can promise he wouldn't be my man for long.' Bobby smiled. 'He's sweet. Funny. Brave. Good with children and animals. He respects me, and the things I want to do with my life. He's... apart from my sister, I suppose he's my best friend.' She sighed. 'At least, he was.'

'Because he's not been writing, you mean?'

'Yes. He's always written regularly, then suddenly, nothing for weeks. It's possible they've been held up, but if there's nothing again this afternoon... that'll be five weeks without a word, although I know he's been writing to his brother and sister-in-law as usual.'

'You think he's found someone else? Mike says all the airmen have got a girl on the side.'

'They can't have. Not all of them. Not Charlie.' Bobby's gaze drifted to her engagement ring. 'But it's so hard to know. He has changed, since he joined the RAF. He has these unpredictable dark moods, and he has to live with so much death and fear. I'm worried the war's changed him so completely, it's driven him away from me.' She glanced at Dilys. 'Sorry, I shouldn't be burdening you with this. You've got your own worries.'

'No, it's nice. I mean, it's not nice what's happening to you, but I like you telling me things.' Dilys looked different without her customary expression of hostility: younger, sweeter, more like a girl than a woman. 'And I won't pass it around, I swear.'

'Thank you.'

'You shouldn't give up hope though. It probably is just missing post. There might be a pile when we get back.'

'Oh, I do hope so,' Bobby whispered.

–

When they returned to camp, they found their letters had been distributed and left on the bunks. Bobby felt a smidgeon of relief when she saw that there was indeed a sizeable pile waiting for her, but she didn't dare look at the envelopes. Instead she snatched them up, mumbled an excuse and ran to the ablutions block, where she could shut herself in the latrine and open her post without being observed.

There was one letter from Mary, two from Lilian, one from Topsy and Teddy, one from Piotr and one from Jolka.

But still nothing from Charlie.

Chapter 36

Bobby sat frozen, staring at the letters spread across her knees. For a moment she thought she might be going to vomit, and swept the letters to the ground to hold her head over the privy. Nothing came up but a lump in her throat, however, and the sting of tears.

But she couldn't give in to them. Paramount in her mind was Charlie's safety. If anything had happened to him, it was his next of kin who would have been notified. She knew Mary would have wired right away if there had been any bad news, but there was a chance even with a telegram that it might have gone astray somewhere between Silverdale and here. As soon as she had suppressed the queasy feeling, Bobby snatched up the letter from Mary, which was postmarked two days ago, and quickly skimmed what it had to say.

And… there was nothing. Mary wrote happily about the innocuous goings-on at Moorside: stories of the scrapes the two evacuees had been getting themselves into, and her difficulties finding suitable furnishings for the cottage they would soon be moving into with their father. There was only a single mention of Charlie, in a postscript where Mary enquired whether their wedding had been approved and if Bobby could let her know whether it would be the 2nd of May as planned so she could confirm with the vicar. Charlie, apparently, had said nothing about it in his most recent letter home.

Bobby pressed her eyes closed, trying hard to hold back tears. The duty NCO would hear if she gave in to sobs, and demand to know what she was doing in there. Her head throbbed, and her hands shook so much that she could barely keep hold of Mary's letter. Any relief she might have felt about the fact Charlie was safe was entirely squashed by the horror of the realisation that he hadn't written. No delays in the postal service could account for five weeks of missing letters. And Mary, it seemed, had been hearing from him just as usual. He hadn't mentioned a word to his family about their wedding date, although he had surely received her telegram about it. All his eagerness for that event seemed to have evaporated, just like his love for her.

Despair gripped her, but she didn't entirely give up hope. Lilian had sent two letters, and one envelope looked rather fat. It was possible Bobby's missing letters had gone to the cow house, and her sister had forwarded them on.

But again, Bobby was disappointed. The fat envelope didn't contain letters but the latest number of *The Tyke*, which carried Tony's first byline piece.

Bobby opened Lil's other letter to see if there was any mention of Charlie, but once more there was nothing. Lilian wrote with news of their father, who, she said, was adjusting as well as could be expected to their new living arrangements, and rather proudly boasted about how well Tony was settling down to his new job. But again, the only reference to Charlie was tucked into a postscript – merely to say that no letters had arrived for Bobby, so Lilian hoped they had found her at her new address.

Then the tears came. She couldn't hold them back. They fell silently, her body juddering, blotting the ink on the letters that had fallen at her feet.

It was over. He'd forgotten her. It was the only explanation that made sense. If he was writing to his family as usual with no mention of her… he must have found someone else. At any rate, he obviously no longer wanted her.

She took out her handkerchief to mop up her tears. It was one Charlie had given her, with his monogram and an embroidered horseshoe. Bobby struggled to keep her tears inaudible when she remembered the day he had given it to her, 'for luck', he had said – the day they met.

She wasn't sure how long she sat on the floor of the latrine, hugging her knees and sobbing into the itchy lisle stockings of her uniform, but after a time a soft knock sounded at the door.

'S-sorry,' she managed to stammer, assuming it was the duty NCO. 'I'm... not feeling well.'

'Bobsy, it's me,' Mike's voice said. 'What's wrong? You've been gone ages.'

Bobby hesitated, then opened the door.

'Oh, honey lamb,' Mike said when she saw the tear tracks down her friend's face. 'Nothing from the fiancé?'

'I don't think I've got a fiancé,' Bobby whispered. 'Not any more.'

'Come here.' Mike wrapped her in a hug, and Bobby squeezed a few more tears out on the shoulder of her friend's WAAF tunic.

'I know it feels like your heart's breaking,' Mike said quietly. 'But this too will pass. One day, when you've found someone better, you'll realise he never deserved you.'

'He did,' Bobby whispered. 'I'm sure he did. I can't understand how his feelings could have changed, just like that.'

'He's a man, my love. You can't rely on even the best of them. We all have to learn that the hard way.' Mike let her go. 'Come back to the dorm. Everyone else is in the rec hut, passing round a bottle of gin someone smuggled in before the dance. You take as long as you need to have a good old weep and I'll ward off anyone who comes over to pry, all right?'

'Thank you,' Bobby murmured, glad to have someone to tell her what to do while she felt so helpless.

'Don't forget your letters,' Mike said, scooping them up from the latrine floor.

Bobby eyed them listlessly. 'I'm not sure I want them. They only remind me of him.'

'You won't say that tomorrow.' Mike tucked the letters into her pocket and took Bobby's arm.

Mike was right: Hut 17 was indeed deserted. Bobby sat on her bunk, feeling numb now her tears were spent. It didn't feel real. And yet it had to be, didn't it?

It was over. Charlie Atherton, the man she loved, the first and only real romance of her life, was no longer hers. And perhaps soon she would receive a letter from Mary to say someone else was going to be his wife, and she would have to go to the wedding in the little chapel in Silverdale, hear them say their vows and smile as if she didn't care...

It was the sheer *cowardice* of it that she couldn't understand. The silent treatment, when he knew she would hear from Mary that he was still in touch with the folk at Moorside. Why would he do that? Whatever else she had thought Charlie was capable of, she would have believed that to be beneath him. If he had met someone else, she'd have thought his honour would prick him to confess it to her frankly, like a man. Just a few short weeks ago she would have sworn it wasn't in his nature to be so underhanded, or so unkind. It felt like such a whimpering, pathetic way for their love story to end.

Mike placed Bobby's post on her bunk.

'You'll want these later, I'm sure.' She picked up the copy of *The Tyke* Lilian had sent. 'What's this?'

'It's the magazine I used to work for,' Bobby mumbled. 'I was a journalist as a civilian.'

'Were you? You never told us that.'

'I thought you might tease me.'

Mike flicked through the magazine, smiling. 'It's rather a sweet little thing. Did you get any good news from home to cheer you up?'

Bobby appreciated her friend's attempts to take her out of herself, but she wished Mike would go drink gin with the others in the recreation hut. She didn't have any energy for small talk.

'Not enough,' she said quietly.

'Read your letters again. Perhaps there's more in them than you noticed the first time.'

Bobby ignored her. She just sat staring at Charlie's photo on the chest of drawers, and tried to understand how that familiar, handsome face – those lips that had told her so many times between kisses that they loved her entirely and devotedly – could have caused her such deep, deep pain.

After a while the numbness started to fade, however, and her gaze drifted to the pile of letters. She picked up Mary's and read it through, trying to banish thoughts of Charlie so she could appreciate what her friend had to tell her.

Soon, a very small smile appeared on her face. Mary wrote about Jessie's fears for her hens when she moved out of the farmhouse, and how she had created little box-nests for each of them so they could stay sometimes at the Parrys' new cottage 'for holidays', as the little girl said. Bobby could just picture it.

'That's better,' Mike said when she saw her smile. 'Read the others.'

Obediently, Bobby took up Lilian's letter.

That was all good news too, now she read it with fresh eyes. Tony seemed to be behaving himself, both as a husband and employee, and the truce with their father held strong. There had been no increase in their dad's drinking. It was hard to tell from a letter, but Lilian sounded happy, and spoke of the preparations she had been making for the arrival of the baby.

'I wonder if I might be able to get a pass out next Saturday,' Bobby said to Mike. 'I'd like to see my family, even if it's only for a few hours.'

'I don't see why not. Get a form from Bennett, then you can ask Stewpot to sign it at dinner.'

Bobby read her letters from Piotr and Jolka, then finally the one from Topsy – it was signed by both Topsy and Teddy, but she could tell from the exuberant style which Nowak had been responsible for its composition. It was full of the lovely things they had seen on their honeymoon in North Wales and

Norman and Jemima's babies, all of which Topsy had named after famous film stars.

And you absolutely must come to visit very soon, Birdy, the letter ended.

> *There's something I'm dying to show you, up at the airmen's hospital. I'm still going to be nursing there, even though I am a married woman, and I know you'd be so interested. Next time you have some leave, come straight to us. Don't bother answering this letter — we'd much rather have your own self than words on a page.*
>
> *Yours, Topsy and Teddy*

Bobby wondered why Topsy should be so keen to show her something at the hospital. That was Topsy's domain, not hers.

'You see, I told you they'd make you feel better,' Mike said. 'Now wipe your tears away and I'll help you do your make-up for the dance. You look a fright, Bobs.'

'I'm not going,' Bobby said, blowing her nose on Charlie's hanky. 'I'm really not in the mood for a party.'

'Nonsense,' Mike said stoutly. 'Best thing for you. Take your mind off he-who-shall-not-be-named and remind you how many more fish there are in the sea. Better fish, who know how to treat a girl properly.'

'Honestly, I can't. I just know if anyone asks me to dance, I'll blub all over him. I'll bring everyone down with my miserable face.'

'You're coming and I won't take no for an answer. Have a few drinks with the girls and toast to the demise of every swine who thinks he can treat us like dirt. Better than lying here sobbing on your own.' Mike picked up the photo of Charlie, waved a two-finger salute at it and shoved it in Bobby's drawer. 'There. A clean slate.'

Bobby gave a damp laugh. 'I'll go for a little while, but only if you promise to protect me. I swear I never want to see a man again. Don't let Carol matchmake for me, and if you see any airman heading in my direction with longing in his eyes, just punch him right in the nose.'

Mike grinned. 'It would be my pleasure. Come on, let's get that face of yours washed up.'

'All right.'

Bobby stood to follow her out. Then she paused, looking down at her left hand. After a moment, she slid her engagement ring off and put it in the drawer with Charlie's photo. She shoved a pile of kit on top so they were hidden from view before following Mike to the ablutions block.

Chapter 37

The dance in the NAAFI canteen was to begin at seven p.m. It was the last thing Bobby was in the mood for, but since she could tell Mike wasn't going to let her get out of it, she made herself presentable in best blues and a pair of contraband silk stockings. Mike had assured her a blind eye was always turned to a few luxuries that would allow them to feel more feminine at social events. Bobby was hoping that after half an hour, her friends would be so caught up in the party that she could slip out and retire to bed to cry in peace.

By the time she, Carol, Dilys and Mike arrived, the party was in full swing. WAAF recruits were taking full advantage of their new freedom, hurling themselves around with the airmen while a gramophone blared out 'Deep in the Heart of Texas'.

Everyone seemed to have a bottle of beer, and the air was heavy with smoke. As they entered, winks and wolf whistles greeted them from a gaggle of men still without partners. Since these were mere recruits, however, Mike silenced them with a withering look of contempt.

'I told you we should've got here early, Mike,' Carol muttered, glaring at the WAAFs already dancing. 'Now this lot have had first choice of the men.'

'They're only dancing with erks,' Mike said dismissively. She nodded to a table where three male officers were seated. 'There's your man, look. And he's generously brought friends for us.'

Bobby hung back when she saw Ernie.

'Can't we find a table just for us?' she asked. 'You know Mulligan doesn't approve of other ranks getting chummy with officers.'

'Are you joking?' Carol turned disbelieving eyes on her. 'We need to get in there, before someone else snatches them.'

'You go. I'll get us drinks or something.'

'No you won't, they'll get us drinks. That's the whole point.' Carol took her arm. 'Besides, we need you. You're the one who knows him. If we stand about nonchalantly, he might ask us to join them.'

In fact they didn't need to stand around. Ernie had spotted them and stood to wave them over.

'Slacks. Hey,' he called. 'Free at last, huh? Why don't you and your pals sit with us?'

'Thank you, that's very kind,' Carol said, trying and failing to sound aloof. 'We were just going to buy drinks.'

'Nonsense,' said one of the other men: a startlingly blond pilot officer with a clipped moustache who wore the half-brevet of an observer. 'Won't hear of it. Carter, go get these young ladies some drinks. Everyone shuffle up and make room.'

Carter, the youngest of the three and clearly used to this sort of treatment, rolled his eyes as he stood to obey.

'What are you ladies having?' he asked. 'There's beer or… well, more beer. That's rather it, I'm afraid.'

Mike smiled. 'We're all happy with beer. Thank you.'

He looked at the men. 'I don't suppose one of you lazy blighters is going to help me carry them?'

'Oh, there's no need for anyone else to get up,' Dilys said, blushing a little. 'I can help.'

'Righty-ho,' Carter said jovially. 'Back soon, chaps.'

Bobby hung back, waiting for Mike and Carol to draw over some chairs so Carol could claim the spot next to Ernie. He had already stood up to let the women sit down, however, and when they were seated he pulled up a chair beside Bobby. He looked at her curiously.

'What?' she said. She wondered if her eyes were still red. She had bathed them in cold water for ages to hide the signs of her crying fit earlier, and Mike had employed all of her skill with make-up, but Ernie King seemed to have a knack for spotting when things weren't right with her.

'I'm not sure,' he said quietly. He raised his voice. 'Well, boys, shall I make the introductions? This is Aircraftwoman Bobby Bancroft, an old friend of mine.' He paused. 'And in fact, I don't know the names of these other ladies. Sorry. I'm not really sure why I offered to make the introductions.'

The blond officer laughed. 'Honestly, Canada, you're hope-less. Alfie Stone. Pleased to meet you, ladies.' He took Mike's hand, who was nearest him, and pressed it to his lips.

'Carol Boyes,' Carol said eagerly, thrusting her hand in Ernie's direction. She looked hopeful he might kiss it, but Ernie just gave it a polite shake.

'I'm Mike,' Mike said. 'And our friend is Dilys.'

'Mike,' said the blond pilot officer, Alfie. 'Doesn't suit you a bit. What's it short for?'

Mike smiled. 'Ask me to dance and I might whisper it to you.'

'I will too, by Jove,' Alfie said, grinning. 'Come on then.'

He jumped up to lead her to the dance floor, leaving the others blinking after them.

'Your friend's a fast mover,' Ernie observed.

'She says that in war, there's no time to waste,' Bobby said. 'We all have to cram months into minutes.'

Now it was only the three of them, Carol's eyebrows seemed to have taken on a life of their own. They danced up and down in Bobby's direction, with the clear message that three was a crowd.

'Um, I have to go,' Bobby said, starting to rise. 'I just spotted a friend on the other side of the hut. I should say hello.'

'Oh, no. Not when I've finally got a hold of you.' Ernie put a hand on her shoulder. 'At least stay and have one drink. Never mind friends over there. You've got a friend here you're long overdue a conversation with.'

'Well... all right,' she said, sinking back into her seat.

Carol glared at her, but Bobby wasn't sure what other excuse she could conjure that wouldn't sound terrifically rude.

Dilys and the young officer, Carter, arrived with a tray of bottled beers.

'Now here's someone who can claim a mutual acquaintance with you,' Ernie said to Bobby. 'Young Carter's been on this base ever since he was pulled from active service. He's taught a lot of recruits how to fly, haven't you, Carter?'

'I've taught my share,' Carter said, with pardonable pride. 'King tells me you're engaged to Charlie Atherton. Top man, that. Pleased to hear he's doing well.'

Bobby felt tears rise at the mention of the name, and she looked away. Carter frowned; Ernie blinked. Dilys had noticed something was wrong too. She stared at Bobby, and, with studied casualness, knocked over her drink.

Carter jumped up as beer dripped from the table, and Bobby shot her friend a look of gratitude.

'Oh my, I am *so* clumsy,' Dilys said, with a good impression of horror. She set the bottle upright and took out a handkerchief to dab at the puddle. 'Did any get on your uniform, Danny?'

'No, you missed me,' Carter said with a smile. 'But now you haven't got a drink. You must let me get you another.'

'That's all right, I only spilt a little.' Dilys glanced at Mike and Alfie dancing. 'Besides, I'd rather dance than drink.' She flushed. 'I mean, if you wanted to dance.'

'Best offer I'll get all night,' Carter said, laughing, and they, too, disappeared.

Bobby had her tears under control now, but it was too late. Ernie had seen, and was once again regarding her curiously.

'Any news from home?' he asked her.

'Yes, I had a few letters today,' Bobby said. 'One from the Nowaks. Topsy was telling me all about the new arrivals – the goslings, I mean.'

Carol blinked. 'You mean, like, baby geese?'

'Yes. Her...' Bobby paused, wondering how best to describe Mrs Hobbes. 'Her foster mother has a pet goose. Norman. He's a cantankerous old thing, but he finally found a lady goose who'd have him. He was page boy at Topsy's wedding recently.'

'Your friend had a *goose* for a page boy?'

Bobby laughed. 'If you knew Topsy, I promise that would make perfect sense.'

Ernie smiled, his eyes cloudy with nostalgia. 'They were happy times, weren't they? Working on the pantomime with her and you and the old lady, watching Archie and Sandy play the fool while that feathery horror Norman glared at us. Sure took the edge off flying ops.'

Bobby sighed. 'We talked about doing *Dick Whittington* this Christmas, didn't we? But the war seems to have other plans for us.'

'You know, there was a time I thought I'd never be happy on this wretched, soggy little island,' Ernie said. 'All I wanted was to go home and shake the dirt of it off my heels for good. But it creeps up on you, this place. The Dales, I mean. One day you wake up and realise that in spite of the rain and the grumpy natives and all the dashed sheep, it's become a part of you.'

'I don't see what's so special about the Dales,' Carol said, sounding sulky about this conversation she couldn't play a full part in. 'I bet Canada's a thousand times more beautiful.'

'Yeah, it's a hell of a country,' Ernie said. 'But a piece of me will always be here, I think, wherever I drag my tired old bones to after the war – if I get to the end of it.'

There was a moment's silence after this sober reflection, Ernie and Bobby alone with their thoughts and Carol looking increasingly annoyed at being left out. She was waggling her eyebrows again, but Bobby paid no attention.

'You going to go home then, now you're allowed out?' Ernie asked Bobby.

Bobby nodded. 'Next Saturday. Mulligan said she'd sign a pass for me.'

'I'm going back too, the day after tomorrow. I've a few days of leave due and I'd like to deliver my congratulations to the new Mr and Mrs Topsy personally.'

Bobby smiled. 'You're right, that is what they ought to be called.'

Ernie took out a cigarette and lit it. 'So how are you finding the Air Force, girls?'

'I think it's whizzo,' Carol said, eagerly seizing on a subject she knew about. 'The best service by a mile. Although I do think the Canadian uniforms are so much nicer than the RAF ones.'

'They're practically identical.'

'Yes, but they look better, somehow.'

'How about you, Slacks?' Ernie asked.

'What is this "Slacks" all about?' Carol demanded, peevish at once again having failed to secure his undivided attention.

Ernie laughed. 'When I met your friend, I don't think I saw her in anything but pants for months. I was starting to wonder if she had legs at all.'

'You're so right. Women ought to be feminine,' Carol said, nodding sagely, but Ernie had once again turned his attention to Bobby.

'So?' he said. 'Think you'll stick with us for the duration, Aircraftwoman Slacks?'

'I don't suppose I have a choice,' Bobby said. 'I can't help feeling sort of... wrong about it though. Like I'm lacking a sense of purpose here. But I am trying to find my place.'

'It's a man's domain, war. We can dress you dolls up like airmen, but it is just that, at the end of the day: dressing up. Trying to make a place for you where none ought to be.'

'But it isn't the other dolls – I mean, women,' Bobby said. 'It's just me. I don't fit, somehow.'

'You're not enjoying military life then?'

'Well, some of it. I like the people I've met,' she said, with a smile for Carol that did little to appease her friend's bad mood.

'And the route marches. Even when they're wet, they're my favourite part of the day.'

Ernie laughed. 'Seriously? I've never met an airman who wouldn't give his right arm to fling those accursed route marches into the sea.'

Carol nodded. 'That's what I think. Rotten, damp, dirty things.'

'They make me feel like I'm at home,' Bobby said dreamily. 'You can see right over the fells – almost as far as Silverdale.'

'You should see it from the air,' Ernie said. 'Now that's something. I do it every day, teaching the sprog pilots how to handle their bombers, but it still blows me away.'

'Oh, I wish I could!' she said, turning wide eyes on him. 'That must be heavenly.'

He narrowed one eye. 'Hey, that's not a bad idea. How'd you like to come up with me for a joyride sometime?'

'No, thanks all the same,' Carol said, although the invitation hadn't really been addressed to her. 'I get sick from heights.'

'Would that be allowed?' Bobby asked Ernie.

'Well, not exactly, but brass turn a blind eye to the occasional flip as long as there's an officer to take responsibility. I know Gardiner secretly thinks it does you girls good to see what it's all about up there. Seems only right we baptise you properly if you're to carry the name of airwoman.'

'You really think it would be all right?'

'Sure. I'm doing a training flight tomorrow. Why don't you come along?'

'I'd love to, if it's not going to get us into trouble.'

A young RAF recruit approached them, looking sheepish.

'Sorry, but would one of you girls like to dance?' he asked. 'All my mates have got a partner and I feel daft on my own.'

Carol glanced at Ernie, hesitated, then shrugged.

'I will. Might as well.' She drained her beer and stood up. 'Come on then, sonny.'

Chapter 38

Ernie laughed as Carol and the recruit walked off. 'We seem to have driven your pal away. Are we that dull, do you think?'

'I think we might be,' Bobby said, smiling.

He shuffled round to look at her. 'And now she's gone, you can tell me what's the matter.'

She flushed. 'What makes you think anything is?'

'Come on, Slacks. I saw your face when Carter mentioned your guy. And don't think I haven't noticed that white mark around your finger and the ring that's conspicuous by its absence.'

'Please, Ernie, don't. I just… I can't.'

He blinked as a tear she couldn't keep in escaped.

'Sure,' he said gently. 'If you don't want to talk about it, that's your prerogative. Just thought you might welcome a listening ear.'

'Not from you.'

'Why not? Your new girlfriends seem nice and all, but you've known me longer.'

'I…' She swallowed hard, endeavouring to push back the threatening tears. 'Because I'll weep all over you, that's why. Talk about anything else. Silverdale, Canada, anything. I don't want to think about it until… until it's bedtime and I have to.'

'If that's what you want.' Ernie was still watching her with a worried expression. 'I hate to see you like this, Slacks.'

'Yes, well, I hate being like this.' She closed her eyes. 'But I don't want to go to bed,' she said quietly. 'I thought I did, but there won't be any sleep waiting for me. Just thoughts, and pain. If you really want to be a friend tonight, talk to me. Make me think about anything else, please.'

Ernie watched her for a moment, then took something from the breast pocket of his tunic and put it down in front of her.

'Take a look at this. It arrived today from my mom.'

It was a photograph: a man and woman in middle age, arms around each other, both grinning very Ernie-like grins. The woman had her dress rolled to the elbows and looked merry, rosy-cheeked and like she wouldn't brook any nonsense. The man was the image of Ernie with a couple of decades added, handsome and grizzle-haired, with a full beard that gave him the look of a seasoned outdoorsman. Beside them were a couple of equally merry-looking kids. Behind was a large wooden farmhouse that looked to be straight out of *Tom Sawyer*, with a porch and a white picket fence. Snow-capped mountains that would dwarf Great Bowside rose up in the distance.

'It's beautiful,' Bobby whispered. 'This is your family?'

'Yeah. Mom, Dad, kid brother and sister.' Ernie smiled a little wistfully at the picture. 'When I left, young Joey there was still in braces. In another year, he'll be old enough to go to war. I guess Maggie will have grown up too before her big brother gets back again.' He glanced at her. 'I wish you could meet them. They'd love you.'

'I'm sure I'd love them.' Bobby looked again at the photograph. 'They seem so happy.'

'That's the life out there. Mountain air, wholesome food and hard work. Man, my mom can cook! I can't deny I've gotten fond of this place, but in the words of Dorothy Gale, there's no place like home, right?'

'You must miss it.'

'Yeah,' he said with a sigh. 'I wonder, sometimes, if I'll ever go back. I'd like to see the old place again.'

For a moment, Bobby thought he was talking about settling in England permanently after the war. Then she realised what he meant.

'You will,' she said, giving his hand a brief squeeze. 'I'm sure of it.'

'Seems arrogant to think I'll be lucky when so many aren't. Nice to know I'm in your prayers though.' He looked up from the photograph to smile at her. 'Now there's a life that'd suit you, Slacks. If you think the piffling little hills you call mountains around these parts are beautiful, you ought to see the Rockies. Nothing to do but milk the cows, care for the little ones and fix your eyes on the sunset. Not a worry in the world apart from raccoons getting in the trash and the occasional straying bear.'

'That sounds wonderful,' Bobby said with a sigh. She blinked. 'Sorry, did you say bear?'

He laughed. 'Yeah, it's grizzly country out there. Mostly they're more scared of us than we are of them.'

'I promise I am definitely more scared of them.'

'Well, you look like a lady who could handle a shotgun. I'm sure you'd be striding the mountains like a true woodsman in no time, gun over your shoulder and a bearskin shawl on your back.'

They were interrupted by Mike, who ran over hand in hand with the officer she had been dancing with, Alfie. She took a long drink from her beer bottle.

'Oh Lord, this is a party,' she said breathlessly to Bobby. 'Carol's as tight as an owl, God bless her little spectacles. There's gin being passed around if you want any, Bobs.'

'Thanks, but I'm fine with beer,' Bobby said, toasting Mike with her bottle.

'Not asking this young lady to dance, Canada, you pig?' Alfie said, grinning at his fellow officer.

Ernie glanced at Bobby. 'Sorry, I guess that was rude. Would you like to?' He smiled as the music for 'The Lambeth Walk' came on the gramophone. 'They are playing our song.'

'Oh, no,' she said, laughing. 'You know what a mess I always make of it.'

'Suit yourselves.' Mike dragged Alfie back to the floor.

Bobby followed them with her eyes. Dilys had hitched her skirt up past her suspenders while she did the Lambeth Walk, displaying knickers that were quite definitely knockouts and not blackouts. Carol was tripping over her feet and giggling as she attempted the steps, having sought solace for Ernie's neglect in gin, while her equally drunk partner took advantage of the situation to let his hands wander where they shouldn't. Mike was whispering something to Alfie – of what nature Bobby could only guess, but Alfie flashed his partner a very suggestive smirk in response.

Bobby glanced at Ernie. He was watching too, scowling.

'What did I tell you?' he muttered. 'You put women in uniform, let them loose in a camp and pretty soon they've turned into a bunch of drunken pick-up girls. These your new friends, are they, Slacks?'

'That isn't fair,' Bobby said. 'OK, so Mike and the rest like to have a good time. I don't see what's so wrong with that. They'll only be young once.'

'The dame with the glasses can barely stand up. If a WAAF officer sees the Welsh one flashing her panties in uniform, she'll find herself on a charge before she can blink. And I don't suppose Alfie's noticed the mark on that phoney blonde job's wedding finger where she's taken her ring off – not that he's the type to care.' He looked at Bobby. 'What is it? Fiancé?'

'Husband,' she said, flushing. 'But it's more complicated than that. They've got an understanding.'

His gaze flickered to her own wedding finger, and the mark left by her engagement ring. 'I don't suppose...'

Bobby scowled. 'Really? That's what you think of me?'

'No.' He rubbed his head. 'Sorry. That was a low thing to say. I guess I just don't want to see you end up that way.'

'What way is that?'

'That way,' he said, nodding to the women. 'Exposing your-self to a roomful of strangers, too drunk to stand, getting cheap kicks with guys you just met.' He curled his lip at Carol. 'There's nothing uglier than a drunken woman.'

'While you boys go back to your dorms for prayers and Bible study of an evening, I suppose,' Bobby said, glaring at him.

'It's different for men.'

'Why? Because you have to fight?'

He shrugged. 'Partly.'

Bobby shook her head. 'You think you're so bloody *noble*, don't you? Dealing with this great weighty conflict while we're typing and swooning over you, to be patted on the head like good little girls or sneered at like tarts, depending on whether we meet your approval. Just playing at war, aren't we? Secretaries and cooks and surrogate mothers, and surrogate wives when that's what you need, sanctioned in best blues.'

Ernie blinked at her. 'That was a hell of a speech.'

'I just don't see what right men have to look down on us because we can't fly. Could you win this without us? Could you?'

'I never said what you girls were doing didn't matter, did I?'

'Then why so holier-than-thou about how we choose to let off steam when we're off duty?'

'This is why disease is rife in the services. Women who were probably nice girls in civilian life, acting fast just because they can. Men taking God knows what back home to infect their poor wives with. It's disgusting.'

'It takes two people to do that, doesn't it?' Bobby countered. 'I know what men get up to when they're away from home, and airmen the worst of the lot. "Running After Fluff", right? Isn't that the joke? Is it so surprising that women want to live in the moment just as men do, when times are so uncertain?'

'Well, perhaps not, but—'

'Or do you think that because you're risking your lives, you're entitled to treat us as a perk of the job?' she went on. 'I've heard the crude things people call us in the WAAF. Airmen's comforts. Pilots' cockpits. Men who think airwomen and their bodies are no more than playthings to amuse them between ops. I thought you, at least, might have the gallantry to show us a little respect.'

His scowl lifted, and he smiled at her. 'You know, I've missed you telling me off.'

Bobby folded her arms. 'I never met anyone who deserved it as much as you do.'

'It's only for being friends with you that I've come to realise what a massive hypocrite I am.' He nudged her. 'Truce? Come on, we were having a nice time before.'

Still Bobby frowned, however.

'If you knew the first damn thing about those women's lives, you'd have more respect for them,' she said. 'All you know is that they're enjoying themselves at a party after two weeks of being locked in, and you condemn them for it. Why should it be for you to judge? Oh, sorry. Why should it be for you to judge, *sir*?'

'It shouldn't,' he said quietly. 'You're right and I'm wrong. I was boorish and rude and I consider myself duly chastened. Forgive me and let's go dance.'

Bobby shook her head. 'Not tonight. I'm not in a dancing mood.'

'But you do forgive me?'

She sighed, her anger disappearing as quickly as it had arisen. 'There's nothing to forgive, I suppose. I know you and I will never agree about these things.'

'And you'll dance with me to prove we're still friends?'

'I'd rather not, Ernie.' She pressed her fingers to her temples. 'I'm getting a headache. I ought to go to bed.'

'Come on. Just one, to prove I'm really forgiven, then I'll walk you back to your hut.'

'Well… all right. But only this one.'

She stood up and let him lead her to the dance floor.

Bobby had danced with Ernie King many times, but there was something about this dance that made her uncomfortable.

She wasn't sure why. She had always felt a little guilty about being in Ernie's arms even though it had felt impolite to refuse, knowing Charlie might be jealous, but as the aching in her chest and the lightness of her wedding finger reminded her, there was no longer any reason to feel guilt. And there had been no reappearance of what she now thought of as 'the look'. Bobby was almost convinced she had imagined the whole occurrence. Ernie had been kind to her tonight when he'd seen she was upset, and eager to have her company so they could talk over old times, but there had been nothing lover-like in his behaviour.

So why did she feel unsettled? As he wrapped one arm around her waist, took her hand and drew her closer while the sweet, husky notes of Marlene Dietrich singing 'Falling in Love Again' played over the gramophone, she felt her body stiffen.

Of course, Ernie noticed this immediately. He was a devil for noticing things, that man.

'Something wrong, Slacks?'

'No.' She summoned a smile. 'It feels like a long time since I danced with anyone, that's all.'

'We've done this plenty, haven't we?'

'We have.'

'And I've always kept my hands to myself?'

'Always.'

'Then relax.'

He was looking into her eyes while he swayed her, smiling, but it wasn't 'the look'. Ernie's eyes sparkled in a way that made her think of the merry, handsome family in the photograph. There was nothing romantic in the way he was regarding her now. Still, Bobby closed her eyes to shut out his face.

She had to ask, no matter how humiliating it felt to do so. If she was going to be stuck on this base with him for another two months, she had to know once and for all what his feelings were.

'Ernie?' she whispered.

'Hmm?'

'That night, when you fell on the ice…'

He laughed. 'Oh yeah, you jumped on top of me. You might at least have bought me dinner first.'

Bobby flushed. 'What I mean is, when I was struggling to get up, and you said… I don't remember what exactly, but it did feel…' She drew a deep breath. 'What I'm trying to ask is, do you… you know, like me?'

Ernie looked puzzled. 'Sure I do. You're a swell kid, even if you are a little too fond of telling me off. Why do you have to ask?'

'I don't mean…' Bobby bit her lip, wishing she hadn't started this conversation. 'I meant, do you *like* me? Do you like me… the way you used to like Topsy?'

'What way was that?'

'All right, now you're being deliberately obtuse.' She glanced at Mike, dancing with her officer conquest nearby. 'Mike says… she says men and women can't ever really just be friends. That feelings always show up to complicate matters.'

'Ah. I get you.' Ernie smiled, and gave her waist a squeeze. 'Like I said, you're a swell kid. I've missed you since I left Silverdale. There are some nights, like tonight, when I'd even go as far as to say you look kinda cute. But as I told you once before, Slacks: romantically speaking, you're really not my type.'

Bobby exhaled with relief. 'That's what I thought.'

'I suppose the gentlemanly thing would be to declare I was passionately in love with you,' he said, grinning. 'But then the ladylike thing would have been for you to look at least a little disappointed when I said I wasn't, and not so darned relieved.'

Bobby flashed him a full smile, letting herself relax. 'Come on. You're not going to cry over one lost admirer among so many, are you?'

He glanced at her left hand, resting on his shoulder as they danced. 'Does that make a difference? Will you tell me what happened, now you know my intentions are pure?'

She allowed her body to rest against his, enjoying the feeling of safety that came from being held by a strong pair of arms when you knew those arms had no ulterior motive.

'Nothing happened,' she whispered. 'That's just it. I haven't had a letter for five weeks, though I know Charlie's been writing to his family. I think…' She swallowed. 'I think he must have found someone else. I don't understand how he could have seemed to love me so much and then just stopped, as if those feelings never existed.'

'I guessed it must be something like that,' Ernie said. 'I'm sorry, kid. You deserve better. I hope you find it.' He tilted her chin up. 'Come up with me tomorrow, OK? It's my last flight before I go on leave. Let me show you this country you love as it looks from the heavens.'

She smiled. 'I'd like that very much.'

Chapter 39

The next day was Sunday, when the WAAFs were expected to attend a service at the camp chapel straight after breakfast. In deference to the fact there had been a dance the evening before, however, both breakfast and church were scheduled for half an hour later than usual. Nevertheless, there were many groans that spoke of sore heads when the bugle blared to wake them up.

Bobby had already visited the ablutions block, and she was dressed and ready by the time her friends showed a leg.

The party had done her one favour. It had tired her out, which meant she had managed to get some sleep in spite of how miserable she was feeling. She had left the NAAFI after her dance with Ernie to nurse a head throbbing from too many tears, and must have been fast asleep by the time her friends had rolled in. But when she had woken around four a.m., she had found herself unable to drift off again.

'Morning, traitor,' Carol said, glaring at her. 'Have fun last night, did you? You certainly got over that Charlie lad quickly.'

Bobby flinched at the mention of his name. 'It wasn't like that. Ernie and I are friends, that's all.'

Carol rolled her eyes, then winced as the action hurt her aching head. 'Oh, right, sure you are.'

'Honestly, you should have heard him on the subject,' Bobby said, summoning a smile. 'He thinks I'm "a swell kid", as he puts it, but about as sexually appetising as overboiled cabbage.'

Carol blinked. 'Did he really say that? He only seemed to want to talk to you all night.'

'Yes, about old times. We were swapping stories of mutual friends and talking about home. I mean, you heard us. I can promise the conversation didn't take any passionate turn after you went to dance.'

Carol seemed to perk up at this, although she groaned as she sat up straight. 'So I've still got a chance?'

Bobby grimaced. 'Honestly? I'm not sure you have. Like I said, Ernie can be terribly stuffy about certain things. He has strong views about drunken women, for one.'

'Oh Lord. Why did I touch that gin?' Carol moaned, burying her head in her hands. 'If it wasn't for Mike saving my bacon, that airman would've had it all his own way with me. Greasy little oik he was. My arse is black and blue from being pinched.'

'I liked my one,' Mike said. 'Alfie and I made a date to go to the pictures tonight, if I can get a late leave pass.' She grinned. 'You know, where it's good and dark.'

'Does he know about David?' Dilys asked.

'Oh, yes. I'm always honest. He doesn't mind a jot, as long as David doesn't. Most men don't.'

'I've got good news too,' Dilys said, flushing a little. 'I got up in the night to visit Aunty, and what do you think had decided to put in an appearance? I actually cried with relief.'

'Oh, darling.' Mike beamed at her. 'That's wonderful news. Now, you and I will have a little talk later and make sure you're ready for the next time, all right?'

'I'm not going to hurry into any "next time". I've learnt my lesson.' She smiled shyly. 'But I wouldn't mind seeing some more of that Danny Carter.'

'I'm so glad for you, Dil.' Bobby stretched across the gap between their bunks to press her friend's hand. 'Did you send that letter to Richie?'

'No, thank God, but you can bet I'll be sending him one today. A letter to break it off.'

'Good for you, lass.' Carol crawled painfully down the ladder from her bunk. 'We ought to get ready for breakfast, although

I'm sure I'll throw up if I try to eat anything. Mike, Dil, are you coming?'

'I am.' Mike climbed down too, and they headed for the door.

'Dil, wait.' Bobby stood up as Dilys prepared to follow. 'I wanted to say thanks. Last night, when you spilled your beer to stop the men noticing I was upset. You were a real brick.'

'Well, that's what friends are for.' She narrowed one eye. 'Is that true, what you said to Carol about the Yank she fancies? He certainly looked like he was after you.'

'Canadian,' Bobby said, smiling. 'Yes, it's true. He was waxing very eloquent about how much he doesn't and wouldn't ever see me in any romantic light. I suppose my pride ought to be hurt by that, but to be honest I was just relieved. I hate it when romance gets in the way of a perfectly good platonic friendship.'

Dilys smiled. 'You do talk strangely.'

'Do I?'

'I don't know many girls who'd get told they were ugly by a good-looking man and say they were happy about it. Every WAAF in the camp's dying to get their hands on that Ernie King, you know.'

Bobby laughed. 'Well, he didn't actually say I was ugly, although I'm sure it was only his natural gallantry that restrained him. But yes, I'm glad to know we're just friends and nothing more.'

'I suppose you must really love this Charlie, if even someone as good-looking as Ernie King can't tempt you,' Dilys said with a sad smile.

'Yes.' Bobby bit her lip. 'I wish I didn't,' she said in a quavering voice. 'I wish I could make the feelings stop just as quickly as Charlie was able to, and then the pain would go away. But I can't. I don't know if I ever will be able to.'

'Do you think he ever loved you, really? Plenty of them say it, if they think it'll get them into your knickers.'

'Charlie never tried anything like that,' Bobby whispered. 'And… honestly, I don't know. Sometimes I think he couldn't have, really, because how could that just stop? But then I remember how he used to hold me like he couldn't bear to let me go, and his voice whispering that he loved me with so much tender earnestness…' She swallowed a sob. 'That had to be real. It had to be. I couldn't have just imagined it.'

'Perhaps you shouldn't give up on him,' Dilys said softly.

'How can I not, when there's been no word for so long?'

'I just feel like if it was me… I've never had a love like that. You know, one that felt real and forever and all that. When I was with Rich, I stopped believing such a thing could even exist. But you've had that, so it must be able to, mustn't it? And if I had it, I feel like I wouldn't ever give up on it.'

—

Later that day, Bobby went to meet Ernie in one of the hangars. She had no worries, now, that he might intend more than she was comfortable with. She only felt grateful to have a pleasant experience to look forward to, and a friend who cared enough to want to take her mind off things.

There were assorted aircraft in the hangar: a number of smaller planes, and three large bombers Bobby recognised as Vickers Wellingtons. Ernie was standing beside one of them with a young erk, the white flash on his cap indicating he was aircrew in training. Both wore battledress and leather flying jackets. Ground crew milled around behind them.

'Slacks. Hey.' Ernie greeted her as usual, with a nickname and a grin.

'Sir,' she said, saluting. Since there were others present, she thought she ought to keep things formal.

'Put these on.' Ernie handed her a helmet and flying jacket. Bobby did so, leaving her cap on a table full of flying kit. The two men strapped on helmets too.

'You won't be able to wear a parachute over your skirt, but it doesn't matter, we won't be flying high enough today for you to use one,' Ernie said.

'All right.'

'This young man is Aircraftman Alistair Harper,' he told her, nodding to the recruit, who grinned chummily. 'He doesn't need the additional flying hours, to be honest. He's doing me a favour because I wanted to get one last flight in before I went on leave. Funny how you miss it. Harper, have you got the book?'

'Right you are, sir,' Harper said jovially. He produced a book and pencil and handed them to Bobby.

'What is it?' she asked.

'We call it the Blood Book,' Ernie told her. 'Everyone has to sign it before they go up. It's just to say that you absolve the RAF of responsibility in the event of your death.'

She blinked at it. 'Oh.'

'Is that OK?'

'Of course. Do I have to sign it in actual blood?'

Ernie laughed. 'No, pencil will do fine.'

She opened the book and, after hesitating a moment, signed her name.

Ernie climbed the stepladder and opened the cockpit door. 'Shall we?'

'After you,' the young erk said politely to Bobby, but her gaze had been arrested by the enormous bulk of the Wellington. She had seen so many silhouetted against the sky, and never thought about what monsters they must be close up. It was incredible they could stay in the air. This was probably the closest she had ever been to one – apart from one other occasion.

'The last time I saw one of these up close, it was on fire,' she murmured.

Harper frowned. 'Sorry, miss?'

'That's Aircraftwoman, not miss,' Ernie reminded him. 'You need to stop thinking like a civilian, Harper.' He came back down the ladder. 'Get in and take the controls.'

Harper saluted. 'Yessir.'

'Sorry,' Ernie said in a low voice to Bobby. 'It hadn't occurred to me, when I asked you to come up... I'd forgotten about the crash. Are you going to be OK?'

'Yes.' She summoned a smile. 'I couldn't help thinking of it, that's all. Let's go.'

'It's going to be rather snug, I'm afraid,' Ernie said as he mounted the ladder behind her. 'These cockpits weren't designed for three.'

Once inside, Ernie gave her a quick tour while a ground crew WAAF took the ladder away. It was indeed very small, and Bobby had to bend her knees to fit in. Ernie, who was over six feet tall, was bent almost double beside her.

'Ryland Moor mostly uses Ansons and Oxfords for flight training, but since the occasional OTU is posted here, it's lucky enough to have three Mark IC Wellingtons at its disposal as well,' he told her. 'Pilot sits here, of course.'

He nodded to Harper at the control wheel. Numerous dials indicating goodness knew what were before him on the dashboard. Bobby couldn't help thinking of Charlie, sitting in that very spot in his own cockpit.

'These older kites would have a co-pilot too, but heavy bombers like the Avro Lancasters they're bringing in now have phased them out in favour of a flight engineer,' Ernie went on. 'Navigator and wireless operator would be in the belly behind, nose gunner up front and of course rear gunner in the tail turret.'

Bobby gave an involuntary shiver.

'Something wrong?' Ernie asked.

'I was just thinking of Piotr. He was in the tail – the rear gunner. That was why he...' She flinched. 'Never mind.'

'Strap yourself into the co-pilot's seat and I'll squeeze between you.' Ernie watched as she did so, then crouched beside her. 'All right, Harper, you know what you're doing. Take us up.'

The plane juddered as it taxied down the runway like a huge, bumpy bus, then Bobby felt a sensation like her stomach dropping out of her body when it started to lift from the ground. The noise was tremendous as they became airborne. She grabbed Ernie's arm and gripped it tightly.

'Still all right?' he asked quietly.

'I just hope I don't throw up. Some airwoman I am.'

'Don't worry. We're all the same our first time out.' He nodded to the pilot. 'Nice and smooth for the lady, Harper. We want to keep pretty low today. Level her out at angels four. That ought to keep us clear of the peaks.'

'Right-oh, sir.'

Bobby continued to feel queasy as the plane climbed. Her head was tight and painful, and there was a ringing sound like a telephone in her ears. Ernie was speaking, but she could no longer hear him.

'What?' she shouted.

'I said, hold your nose and blow!' he called out. 'It'll relieve the pressure.'

Bobby did as he said, feeling utterly ridiculous. There was a popping sound, and suddenly she could hear the rushing of air and the deep-throated roar of the twin engines. Soon, Harper started to level the plane out and before long they were flying smoothly in a cloudless sky. She relaxed a little, and loosened her grip on Ernie's arm.

'I think you left a bruise,' he said, laughing.

'Sorry.'

'Don't worry, I can take it.'

'It feels so gentle now we're level.'

'We're travelling at a hundred and eighty miles per hour.'

'Are we?' Bobby blinked. 'Gosh.'

He nodded to the window. 'This is what I really wanted you to see.'

She followed his gaze, and what she saw took her breath away.

Spread out like a map was a glorious patchwork of fields in green, yellow, brown and red, dotted with barns and farm-houses and dappled with gold where they were touched by the sun. Sparkling rivulets and chalky-looking drystone walls divided up the landscape. And rising above the valleys in which little settlements nestled were the fells, painted in every shade of green, looking on like strong protectors of the landscape.

'Oh, Ernie,' Bobby whispered.

'That's what I hoped you'd say.'

And then she saw it. So fleeting she might have missed it, if she hadn't turned her head at just that moment. The look – the same one he had given her that night on the ice, clear and unmistakeable. A yearning, tender, hungry look. But almost as soon as it appeared, it had gone.

'What?' Ernie said, noticing her staring.

'I…' She glanced at Harper. 'Nothing.'

'So, was this worth signing your life away in the Blood Book?'

'Yes,' she whispered, her gaze once more drifting to the view through the cockpit canopy. 'I think I'll remember it as long as I live.'

They flew for a while in silence, Bobby mesmerised by the sight of the sun-bathed countryside spread out below her.

'We ought to take her back,' Ernie said to Harper after a little time had passed. 'Turn her around, Aircraftman. Bobby, would you like to take the controls for a minute?'

Her eyes widened. 'Me? Oh, no, I couldn't.'

'Of course you could.'

'Honestly, I can barely manage to keep my bike from wobbling, let alone a plane. I'm sure to crash it or something.'

Ernie smiled. 'We won't let you crash it. Harper, let the lady take the wheel.'

Bobby regarded the controls with horror as Harper let go. She lunged for the unmanned wheel. It was a real struggle to hold it steady.

'Ouch,' she said, grimacing as she wrestled with the thing. It seemed to have a will of its own. 'You pilots must really be strong.'

The plane listed a little to one side. Ernie leaned over her and put his hands on hers.

Bobby stiffened. His arms were around her, in a way that somehow felt far more intimate than dancing. She could feel his hot breath on her ear, and smell the shaving soap he used.

'Some turbulence to fight against there,' he murmured close to her ear. 'A little more to the left and we'll have it beat.'

'Can I stop now, please? I know something will go horribly wrong if I do this too long.'

'All right.' Ernie moved back, much to her relief. 'Harper, you're back on.'

Bobby shifted gratefully aside to let the airman take the wheel again.

'Well, I think you can now say you've earned the name of airwoman,' Ernie told her with a grin.

He kept talking as Harper brought them down, explaining what each dial measured and what everything in the cockpit did, but Bobby was only half listening.

The look she had seen him give her had been unmistakeable, this time. She had been loved before – she knew that had been real, whatever might have happened since – and she had seen that same look so many times in another man's eyes. And yet Ernie had sounded completely genuine, last night when he had promised his feelings for her were strictly friendly...

After they landed, one of the ground crew brought the stepladder over so they could climb out. Bobby felt rather wobbly back on land, and gripped each step tightly while she climbed down.

'How do you feel?' Ernie asked.

'A little dizzy.'

She pulled her helmet off, removed the flight jacket and reclaimed her WAAF cap.

'I was wobbly after my first time too,' he said, smiling. 'Here, take my arm.'

'It's all right. I can walk.'

Her next steps gave the lie to this claim, however. She reeled violently, forcing Ernie to catch her.

'Whoa. Come on, grab hold and I'll walk you back to the henhouse.'

'Henhouse?'

He laughed. 'Sorry. That's what us fellers call the Waafery.'

'Oh.'

Reluctantly she took the proffered arm, and they left the hangar.

'Where are we going?' Bobby asked as he led her towards some scrubland on the edge of their camp. 'The Waafery's the other way.'

'Scenic route. Best thing for post-flight wobbles is to walk them off.' He glanced at her arm, threaded loosely through his. 'Don't be shy about grabbing on. You weren't when I was taking you up.'

'Sorry. I didn't mean to hold on so tight. I was frightened.'

He smiled. 'Worth it though, wasn't it? I'll never forget that look in your eyes. That's where beauty comes from in a woman, not paint and curled hair. That expression of innocent joy.'

And there it was again. The look. Bobby pulled her arm away and turned to glare at him, clutching at a bush to steady herself.

'All right, Ernie King, what the hell is going on?' she demanded.

He frowned. 'What do you mean?'

'You. You with your eyes, and your… your compliments, and all your things. Holding me like that in the plane.'

'I was helping you steer.'

'You were not. You were getting fresh, that's what you were doing, under cover of instructing.'

'Fresh? I barely touched you!'

'You breathed on me.'

He laughed. 'All right, I'm sorry I breathed on you. It's a little hard not to when we're packed in like sardines. Harper wasn't complaining.'

'Not only that. You… looked at me.'

'Am I supposed to avert my eyes unless you're veiled? I'm not that old-fashioned.'

She wanted to believe him. He certainly sounded jocular enough. But this time, Bobby knew what she had seen.

'You bastard,' she whispered, feeling the sting of tears. 'You lied, didn't you? You said… but it was nonsense. It was all nonsense.'

'Honestly, Slacks, I don't know what you're talking about. If you're still feeling guilty over this dream boy of yours—'

'Charlie!' Bobby yelled, with a vehemence that surprised her as well as Ernie. She swallowed hard. 'Call him by his name, damn you,' she whispered. 'I know you know it.'

'OK,' Ernie said, looking alarmed. 'Charlie then. You don't need to feel guilty any more, Bobby.'

'Please, just tell me the truth.'

'The truth?'

'Yes. Not that line you shot me last night while we were dancing. Tell me what's real, Ernie.'

Ernie laughed. He turned away. Then he turned back, striding towards her with a look in his eyes that scared her. A second later, he'd grabbed her roughly by the shoulders and his lips were on hers.

Bobby's eyes widened in shock. He pulled away almost immediately, looking as surprised as she felt.

'Sorry.' He rubbed his neck. 'I don't know why I did that.'

'What…'

He started pacing, laughing softly even while he scowled. Bobby had never seen him lose his composure so utterly.

'Ernie?' she whispered.

'OK, so I lied,' he said. 'Lied through my teeth, just so's you wouldn't run away from me screaming. And if that makes me a heel then I guess I'm a heel.' He turned to face her, frowning. 'Just what is it about you, anyhow?'

'What?'

'You.' He gestured vaguely in her direction. 'God knows I did my best. I'm not someone who makes a habit of going after other men's girls. Persuaded myself there was nothing in it – you and me. But the truth is, I mean, if you want the honest-to-goodness, straight-up truth, I…' He laughed again, turning away from her. 'I'm goddamn crazy about you.'

'What?' Bobby held on to the bush for support. 'No. That was Topsy.'

'Oh, Topsy, Topsy. Topsy's a cute kid, yeah, but there was never any Topsy – not for me. Maybe I wanted you to think there was, but…' He shook his head, as if to rid it of something, and Bobby saw that he was trembling. 'What I don't get is why *you*. You snuck up on me, somehow, and by the time I realised I was bewitched it was too late to damn well fix it.'

'Ernie, calm down. You're frightening me.'

'Yeah, I guess I would be.' He closed his eyes as he struggled to regain his composure; then, when he was calmer, he approached to take her hands.

'Sorry,' he said, his voice soft now. 'Didn't mean to sound angry – not with you. I hurt you when I grabbed you before?'

'Um, no,' Bobby said dazedly.

'Look, I don't expect you to do anything about it. I know you're still head over heels for the other guy, even if he is a son of a bitch who doesn't deserve you.' He brushed her chin with his thumb tip. 'But if you thought there was a chance, one day, then I'd wait for you. As long as it took.'

'But… we're so different,' Bobby whispered. She couldn't help but be filled with pity for this man: pain in his eyes and his strong, powerful frame trembling. She had just had her own heart broken, and it filled her with grief to be the cause of those same gut-wrenching feelings in anyone else.

'Are we?' He brought one palm up to cradle her cheek. 'I could give you a life, Bobby – fresh and pure, the sort a girl like you ought to have. A home, kids, the wide-open spaces, and so much love. My family have got money, and the farm will come to me someday. You'd never want for anything.' He glanced down at her naked wedding finger. 'I'd be honoured if it was my ring you were wearing.'

'That life does sound wonderful.' She met his eyes. 'But it isn't me.'

'It could be. I saw your face on the plane. If you think this place is beautiful, you'd weep over Canada.' He held her gaze. 'Come back with me.'

'I need more than open spaces and a farmhouse to make me happy, Ernie,' Bobby said quietly. 'We're not alike, you and I – not the way a husband and wife ought to be. I need work – work for my brain. You want a woman you can dress in ribbons and lace, who'll be satisfied with cooking and keeping house. I'm sure there are dozens of marvellous girls who'd be thrilled to fill that place. But it isn't me.'

'It's the other guy, isn't it?' he said, with a sad smile. 'I'd be a fool to think you could put him out of your heart just like that. Some girls, maybe, but not you.'

She closed her eyes. 'It isn't only Charlie. I'm just not convinced we could make each other happy.'

'I can wait. As long as you need to put the old love behind you.' He pressed her hand to his breast. 'At least give me the chance to show you how happy I could make you. You make me better, Bobby. You open my eyes to a way of looking at things I've never considered.'

'You don't need me for that. Just your own good sense, and a little compassion.'

'Will you at least let me see you while you're here? Just friends, if that's what you want, and we can get to know each other better.' He stroked her cheek. 'And if I can't make you love me the way I do you, then we'll call it quits. But since we're stuck in this place, both of us unattached, what have you got to lose by giving me the chance?'

'I…' She looked down at the ground. 'I… don't know.'

Sensing victory on the horizon, Ernie took her in his arms. Bobby didn't embrace him back, but nor did she repel him. A deep sigh escaped her.

It felt good to be held again by strong arms that loved her and wanted to keep her safe. To feel she was no longer alone. She just wished she could forget they weren't Charlie's.

Charlie had forgotten fast enough though, hadn't he? He had been able to lose himself in the comfort of someone else's arms, with no sickening sense of guilt to hold him back. How could his love have died so quickly and thoroughly, while hers felt like it was eating her up from the inside?

'Well?' Ernie whispered.

'Can I have time to think about it?' Bobby whispered. 'It's so sudden. So strange.'

'Sure. Sure.' He held her back to beam at her. 'Whatever you need, kid. I'm going tomorrow, staying with Topsy and Teddy for a few days. I'll meet you in the NAAFI on Thursday at nineteen hundred hours, OK?'

'Thank you.'

Before she could object, he bent to plant a single soft kiss on her lips.

'I know I'm not the guy you'd choose,' he whispered. 'But if you just gave me the chance, Bobby, I'd spend every minute proving to you I was worth the choosing.'

Chapter 40

Bobby did think about Ernie's proposition, or she tried to. But her mind was so clouded with thoughts of Charlie, she couldn't make any sense of what he was asking from her.

It was bewildering. Ernie King! And he was really in love with her. This man, who could take his choice when it came to women. Handsome, exciting, and wealthy too apparently, with a life to offer that would exceed the wildest dreams of any other WAAF on the camp. Yet he had chosen her – the one woman of his acquaintance who couldn't return his affections. It was certainly flattering, but that didn't help her decide what answer she ought to give. She wasn't going to let a massaged ego make her choice for her.

Could she have feelings for him, once she got over her love for Charlie? Would she ever get over it? It didn't feel possible, but she couldn't go on feeling this way the rest of her life, surely. The pain would be unbearable.

Yet whenever Bobby thought about Ernie, and tried to picture him taking Charlie's place in her heart, Dilys's words forced their way into her brain. *If I had a love like that, I wouldn't ever give up on it…*

But what choice did she have? She couldn't make Charlie love her, if his affections had been engaged elsewhere. She refused to be one of those pathetic creatures who cried their life away for the love of a man who was indifferent to them. And here was another man, kind and brave, offering her his heart. When she thought of Ernie standing before her, his large frame shaking while he confessed his feelings, she felt such overwhelming pity.

She was fond of him. He made her laugh, and she enjoyed his company. She even enjoyed their occasional battles. That wasn't love, but perhaps Ernie was right. Love might grow as they found out more about one another.

So why did her heart whisper that she was doing something wrong, whenever she had almost made up her mind to say yes?

Bobby felt like an automaton over the days that followed, going through the motions of her life in camp while her brain wrestled perpetually with thoughts of Ernie and of Charlie.

She didn't feel like she could talk to her friends about what had happened. Carol had still only half forgiven her for monopolising Ernie the night of the NAAFI dance. Strangely, when she did eventually confide in someone it wasn't any of her peers. It was Mulligan.

She was typing in the commandant's office on Thursday afternoon, the day Ernie was expected to return from leave, when Mulligan slapped a letter Bobby had typed down on her desk.

'Bancroft, you'll type this again,' she ordered. 'It's riddled with errors.'

'Literals,' Bobby murmured.

'I'm sorry?'

'Hmm?' Bobby roused herself. 'Oh. Sorry, ma'am. When I worked in newspapers, typing errors were called literals.'

'Well whatever you want to call them, you've been making far too many the last few days.'

'I'm sorry. I'll do it again.'

'See that you do.' Mulligan's glance drifted to Bobby's wedding finger, and her voice softened. 'Look, I can't pretend not to know there's something going on. It's up to you if you choose to talk to me about it, but as your senior officer, part of my responsibility is for your welfare. If you need anything, my door will always be open.'

Bobby couldn't help it. She burst into tears.

'Th-thank you,' she whispered through the sobs. 'You've been... so kind.'

Mulligan sighed. 'Come and sit at my desk, Bancroft.'

Bobby did so, mopping her eyes with her handkerchief.

'I'm sorry,' she whispered. 'I know my mind hasn't been on my work. I will get better.'

'Your wedding's off, I suppose.'

'Yes. My fiancé... ex-fiancé. He stopped writing to me. You might as well cancel that leave I booked for early May.'

'Do you know why he stopped writing?'

'I suppose there must be another woman.' Bobby laughed through the tears. 'And as if my love life wasn't complicated enough, three days ago Ernie King asked for permission to court me. He'll be in the NAAFI this evening, expecting an answer.'

Mulligan blinked. 'Ernie King wants to court you?'

'He wants me to marry him and move to Canada. He says he'll wait for as long as it takes to make me fall in love with him.' Bobby blew her nose. 'Sorry. I don't know why I'm telling you this. There's no one I can talk to. My friends here wouldn't understand.'

'He'll wait as long as it takes, will he?' Mulligan said with a dry smile. 'How like a man. They always seem to think that if they want something badly enough, they'll get their way in the end. Even something as elusive and delicate as a woman's heart.'

'What answer do you think I ought to give him? I'd value your opinion.'

'What answer do you want to give him?'

'I don't know,' Bobby mumbled. 'When I think about how he looked when he asked me – how much pain he was in – I feel like I owe it to him to say yes. But my heart keeps whispering that if I do, I'm betraying Charlie. I know that's foolish, after he threw me over, but I can't just change my feelings.'

'I do know how you feel,' Mulligan said quietly. 'I had someone I cared deeply for, once. Even now, I think that if

334

someone else were to show any inclination… but never mind me. Just know that you don't owe Ernie King anything. Think of what you owe yourself, and choose the path most likely to bring you happiness when you reach the end.'

'I want to. It's so hard to see clearly through the fog.'

'I know.' Mulligan reached out to give her hand an awkward pat. 'This isn't the advice you'll probably get from anyone else, especially not your friends. Young women do tend to have stars in their eyes about romance, no matter how cynical they profess to be. But my advice is to ignore your heart, and follow your head. I know it's got a good brain inside it. Choose wisely, Bancroft, but most importantly, choose for yourself.'

—

That evening, Bobby stole out of the recreation hut, where her friends were laughing as they read out their stars and listened to Gert and Daisy on the wireless. She knew if she told them she had a date to meet Ernie in the NAAFI, many awkward questions would be asked. Certainly she would never be allowed to go unaccompanied.

She had made a decision. She wasn't sure it was the right one, but it was the one her head told her she ought to make, regardless of the guilty prodding of her heart.

Sure enough, Ernie was waiting for her. A cigarette was resting in the ashtray, lit, but he seemed to have forgotten to smoke it. He just sat alone with his chin on his hand, staring into space.

Bobby slid into the chair next to him. He glanced up, and took off his cap.

'Slacks.' He summoned a smile. 'Hey. Missed you, kid.'

'Are you all right? You look preoccupied.'

'Just having a row with my conscience. Don't worry about it. You want a drink?'

'Um, no, thank you,' Bobby said, puzzled by his odd behaviour. 'How are Topsy and Teddy?'

'Thriving. Funny how they get along so well together, isn't it? They're not at all alike.'

'I know.'

'A bit like us, huh?'

'Perhaps.'

'Listen, Slacks—'

'Please. Let me go first.' Bobby took a deep breath. 'Look, Ernie. I've been thinking, and… I can't promise anything. My feelings for Charlie… you're right, they aren't a tap I can just turn off. Believe me, I wish I could. But I'm fond of you, and I do appreciate how you feel. I mean, I'm honoured, really, that someone I respect as much as you should feel anything of that nature for me. I am sorry to have caused you pain. And… well, to cut to the chase, the answer's yes. I don't know if I'll ever be able to feel what you want me to feel, but I think I owe it to myself, and to you, to at least see what's at the end of the path. So… yes. The answer to your question is yes.'

Ernie made a noise in his throat and closed his eyes tightly.

Bobby frowned. 'Ernie?'

'It's a yes?' he said quietly. 'You'll be my girl?'

'I will. Or at least, I'll be your friend to begin with and we can see what the future brings.'

'Oh… God.' He laughed bitterly, pushing his fingers into his hair.

'Is something wrong?'

'You don't know how much I've dreaded hearing you say that.'

Bobby blinked. 'This was what you wanted, wasn't it? I'm sorry I can't offer more – not yet – but we can see where things go.'

Ernie just sighed, the muscles in his face working feverishly. He looked like a man with a battle raging inside him.

'Slacks… look, you know how I feel about you,' he said in a choked voice. 'I really don't want to do this. But if I don't, I'll despise myself for as long as the Almighty decrees I'm going to live.'

'Do what?' Nothing he was saying seemed to make any sense.

'I... I have to withdraw the offer, all right?'

'Withdraw the offer?' Bobby stared at him. 'I don't understand.'

'I can't do it. I'm sorry.' He laughed again. 'You remember once asking me if I'd ever stand aside for the love of a woman as Teddy did, and I said she'd have to be one hell of a girl?'

'I remember,' Bobby said, feeling more confused by the minute.

'Good. Hold on to that thought.' He opened his eyes again, and turned to grasp her hands. 'You've arranged some leave this weekend, right?'

'Yes, on Saturday afternoon. Not that they know it at home. I'm planning to surprise them.'

'Do me a favour while you're there, will you? Go see Topsy.'

'I won't have time to see everyone. I've only got a few hours, and I really want to visit my family.'

'You have to see Topsy. She's got something to show you.'

Bobby frowned. 'Something to show me?'

'Yeah. At the hospital.'

'Oh yes, she said something about that. It can't be that important though, surely.'

Ernie laughed his bitter laugh again. 'Trust me, you'll want to see this.'

Bobby looked down at her hands in his. 'Ernie, I'm confused. What's going on?'

'Just do as I ask. Please, as a favour to a friend.' He leant forward to plant a kiss on her forehead, then stood up. 'Go see Topsy. If the answer's still yes after, come find me. But I know you, Bobby, and I'd bet everything I have that it won't be.'

Bobby stared after him as he strode out, his face twitching with strong emotion. What the hell was going on?

337

Chapter 41

The strange scene with Ernie was still playing in Bobby's head two days later, as she boarded the bus to Silverdale.

She was starting to wonder if she had some sort of man-curse on her. It seemed she had no trouble getting men to fall in love with her, but they had a frustrating habit of running away in horror shortly after. Ernie had seemed so fervent in his declaration of love. How could that have changed just three short days later?

In the pocket of her uniform was the engagement ring Charlie had given her. It had belonged to his grandmother, and Bobby felt that by rights it ought to be returned to his family. She wasn't looking forward to the conversation with Reg and Mary explaining how things currently stood, but they needed to know.

Bobby had left her photograph of Charlie back in Hut 17, however, buried under a pile of undergarments in her drawer. She couldn't quite bring herself to part with that – not yet.

It was with depressed spirits that she travelled the old familiar route towards Silverdale. She knew she ought to be excited to see her family after what felt like years away. She had a lot to tell them, and no doubt Lilian had plenty to share too. Her father would be pleased to see her, Mary would hug her in her motherly way, and the Parry girls would knock her off her feet as soon as they saw her. But everything was coloured by the knowledge that she had the news of her broken engagement to share. She hated to go home only to shed tears, but it couldn't be avoided.

Her spirits did rise a little, however, as the familiar fields of home drifted past. Nothing could be more beautiful than the Dales in spring, she was sure – not even the Canadian Rockies. Dazzling carpets of wild flowers in every conceivable colour were spread across each field not occupied by livestock.

It took her back to the previous year – the cuckoo time, before Charlie had gone to war when they'd been newly courting. Nights in the dance hall in Settle, holding each other with hardly an ear for the music, they were so caught up in one another. Fish and chips under the arches, and passionate embraces under cover of the blackout...

Bobby felt tears start to rise, and had a stern word with herself.

It was on this bus, too, that she had last seen Ernie King before her call-up. She remembered how relieved she had been to find out he had survived his crash; how she had thrown herself at him for a hug, never suspecting... oh, what a mess it all was! She let out a deep sigh.

Thinking of Ernie reminded her of his final words. He had been very keen for her to visit Topsy. What mystery was awaiting her at Sumner House? It was all rather strange.

It was soon time to get off at the stop opposite the Black Bull. Bobby stood for a moment to breathe in the air of her home. Strange how it seemed to smell differently to the camp at Ryland Moor, although there were so few miles between them.

She set off walking towards Silverdale, admiring the blue-bells, buttercups and daffodils that lined the road and breathing in lungfuls of fresh, heady Dales springtime. She stopped, however, when she reached a crossroads.

One road would take her to Silverdale, and home to the folk at Moorside. The other led to Sumner House, where she would find Topsy, Teddy and Mrs Hobbes.

She had to return to camp by seven. There wasn't long, and she had come especially to see her family. Without her bike, the walk to Sumner House was time she could ill afford to spare. But Ernie had been so adamant about a visit to Topsy...

After hesitating a moment, she set off down the track to the stately home. There would still be time to have a decent visit with her family if she didn't stay too long, and she had to admit she was keen to find out what the mystery was.

Topsy answered the cottage door in her nurse's uniform. Bobby was greeted effusively as ever by her friend.

'Oh, Birdy, we've missed you to pieces,' Topsy said, embracing her tightly. 'Come inside and tell us all the news. You do look smart in your uniform.'

'I can't stay long,' Bobby said as she followed her in. 'I haven't been home yet.'

'That's all right, I have to go back to the hospital soon. I just came home to serve Teddy a late lunch. Oh, but you must see the babies before you go. They're in here by the fire.'

Bobby smiled as she was shown into the parlour, where Jemima sat with a gaggle of fluffy grey goslings. She welcomed Bobby with a hiss, as if to remind her that these precious ones were not to be touched. Norman, on the other hand, sat aloof in his basket, supremely uninterested in his little family. Mrs Hobbes was knitting in her rocking chair and Teddy was sipping a bowl of soup from a tray. The feeling of having been gone for at least a century started to subside, seeing her friends just as they had been when Bobby had left.

'Bobby,' Teddy said with a smile. 'So you have come home to us.'

'Only for a few hours, I'm afraid. I couldn't resist calling in to meet the new arrivals.'

Topsy had fallen on her knees by the goslings, and started introducing them to her one by one.

'This is Lana, and here's Clark,' she said. 'Oh, and Errol – but don't speak to him. He's very much his father's son, the grumpy little fowl. And Ingrid and Humphrey and Bob and Bing—'

Mrs Hobbes laughed. 'Well, Bobby, you can see nothing much has changed. Becoming a married woman hasn't taught our Topsy better manners. Luckily she still has this old lady around to offer guests a cup of tea.'

'Thank you, but I really don't have time,' Bobby said. 'It's a flying visit, that's all. I don't have long to see everyone.'

Topsy looked up. 'How is Charlie? Have you heard from him lately?'

Bobby flushed, glad she was wearing gloves so the absence of her engagement ring wouldn't be noticed. She really didn't want to have this conversation – not now.

'I don't have any news to share, I'm afraid,' she answered truthfully.

'Well, did you see Ernie? I'm so glad the two of you are on the same base. It must be a comfort to have a friend there.'

'I did,' Bobby said, trying to keep her voice even. 'That's really why I came here first. He was very keen for me to pay you a visit. Something about the hospital.'

'Oh yes, you must come up and see!' Topsy said gleefully. 'I can't help being proud about it. I'm so glad you're in uniform, so the matron won't be cross about me bringing in civilians.'

'But what is it I'm to see?'

'The new ward. Teddy and I donated the money for all the beds and equipment – to mark our wedding, you know, after the staff there took such good care of him. It's to be for those rehabilitating after amputations. There's a little plaque with our name on and everything.'

'That's wonderful, Topsy, but I honestly don't have time. Can it wait for another day?'

'Please, it won't take any time at all. I've been so excited to show you.'

Bobby couldn't help relenting when she saw the eagerness in her friend's eyes.

'Well, all right,' she said. 'But I can't stay long.'

'Hurrah!' Topsy jumped up and grabbed her hand. 'We'll go now. The men who are mobile will be taking their exercise hour, so it will be quiet.'

'Um, goodbye, everyone,' Bobby said as Topsy dragged her from the room. 'Teddy. Mrs Hobbes. Geese.'

'Never mind them,' Topsy said impatiently. 'There's no time to lose.'

Bobby felt rather dazed as Topsy led her with great haste up the path to the stately home. She couldn't understand why her friend – or Ernie King, for that matter – would be so keen for her to see this new ward.

As Topsy had predicted, the matron didn't resist when she saw Bobby's WAAF uniform. Topsy dragged her to the new ward and pointed proudly to the door, which bore a brass plaque with the inscription *The Nowak Ward*.

'It's marvellous, isn't it?' she said. 'Of course I know it's only for the war and then it will go back to being the plain old drawing room, but it was ripping of them to do it. I said we didn't expect any recognition.'

'Um, yes,' Bobby said, trying to summon a little enthusiasm for her friend's sake. 'I can see why you're proud, Topsy.'

'It's really for Teddy's sake. He was very keen to help other wounded airmen. Now he's married to me, we can do ever so much good between us.' Topsy turned to her. 'But you want to see your family, and here I am rabbiting on.'

'No, I'm glad you brought me,' Bobby said. 'It was a lovely, kind thing for the two of you to do. But I do need to go home now. Sorry.'

'I'll show you out. I just want to pop my head into the common room and make sure the men have gone out for their exercise hour. Those with leg injuries need exercise to help them heal, but they can be lazy so-and-sos. Without we nurses to bully them, I'm sure they'd do nothing but sit and smoke.'

Bobby followed Topsy to the old library that now served as a common room for the convalescent airmen.

'And this one is the worst of them all,' Topsy said, nodding to a man staring gloomily into the fire while he smoked a cigarette.

'I can't do a thing with him. Perhaps you might have better luck, Birdy.'

Bobby stared. She grabbed at her friend's arm for support. It was Charlie.

Chapter 42

And yet it wasn't Charlie – not as she remembered him. As he pushed himself to his feet with the aid of a stick and limped towards them, Bobby saw that he was gaunt and pale. One eye was closed, and there was a burn scar that ran over it from his forehead to his cheek. He wasn't in his service uniform, but in the hospital blues that marked him as a wounded man.

'Charlie,' she whispered.

In that instant, she forgot everything that had happened between them. The lack of letters, and the pain she'd experienced when she had believed he must have found someone else. All she knew was that he was hurt, and she wanted to hold him so, so badly. She stepped towards him, but he turned away from her, scowling.

'What's she doing here?' he demanded of Topsy.

'I brought her.'

'I told you I didn't want her.'

'I'm sorry,' Topsy whispered. 'I know I promised, Charlie, but I couldn't let you. It isn't fair. Besides, I didn't really break my word. I never told her you were here.'

Bobby reached out to touch him, afraid he might be a dream, but he was solid. 'Charlie, how did you... what's happening?'

'I can't do this.' Charlie turned back to them, his features hard. 'You had no right, Topsy. No right at all.'

'No, you had no right,' Topsy said staunchly. 'Do you know how it hurt, when Teddy left me? How much worse it was than anything else he could have done? I won't watch you destroy yourself. I'm your friend, and I won't.'

'I don't understand.' Bobby felt light-headed, and sank into a chair. 'You're not here. You're in Binbrook. Mary would have said...'

'Mary doesn't know,' Charlie said quietly. He turned to her, and there was so much pain in his open eye that it made Bobby wince. 'You have to go, Bobby. I can't see you.'

She felt so helpless and confused. She wanted to hold him. She wanted to slap him. She didn't know what she wanted, except to feel him against her and know he had always been hers.

'You don't think you owe it to me to tell me what's happening?' she demanded, getting to her feet again. 'Why did you stop writing to me, Charlie?'

He laughed bitterly. 'Ask my nurse.'

Topsy shook her head. 'It has to be you. Why don't the two of you take a walk? Charlie, you know the doctor said you have to keep that leg moving.'

'I can't,' he whispered, closing his eye. 'I told you. I can't do this.'

Bobby felt a wave of pity and love for him. She took his arm.

'Come on,' she said softly. 'I'll talk for both of us, until you feel you can.'

He didn't resist but meekly allowed himself to be led outside, leaning heavily on his stick. For a little time they walked in silence, out to the lake in front of the house.

'I missed you,' Bobby whispered after a while.

Charlie laughed softly. 'Oh God.'

'What?'

'Nothing. I just... I hear your voice a lot. When I'm sleeping, and sometimes when I'm awake.'

'I thought you didn't care to hear it any more. When you stopped writing, I thought...' She swallowed. 'That there must be someone else.'

'Never,' he said quietly.

She turned to face him, her voice trembling. 'What happened, Charlie?'

His face twitched, and he didn't seem able to meet her eyes. Bobby longed to hold him, but she didn't dare. Not until she could understand. Everything seemed to say that here was a man in deep pain, of the emotional as well as the physical kind.

'One of our engines was damaged,' he said. 'Butcher Bird. Our rear gunner took the bastard down but it was too late, he'd got us. We made it back to Blighty but I had to crash land. We lost two.' He pressed his eyes closed. 'Stevens, the navigator. And... and Bram.'

'Oh, Charlie, no.' Bobby thought back to her one meeting with the shy lad Charlie had taken under his wing during training, when their bigoted former CO had targeted the boy for his faith. 'I'm so sorry.'

'It was my fault,' Charlie said in a choked voice. 'I ought to have ordered the crew to bale out. I thought I could get us all back safely. I was a fool.'

'You made the choice you had to make in the heat of the moment. If you'd baled out, you might all have died.'

'You think that helps?'

'No,' Bobby said, lowering her gaze. 'I know it doesn't. It should, but it doesn't.' She glanced at his wounded leg, and the burn over his eye. 'Why didn't you tell anyone you were here?'

'I couldn't bear to have anyone see me like this. Mary and Reggie think I'm still in Binbrook. I've been writing to them as if I was.'

'They're your family. They love you. Why on earth wouldn't you want them?'

'You don't understand, Bobby.' He spun away from her. 'I couldn't bear to have them know... to have anyone know. I knew I had to give you up, and it broke me. I didn't want anyone. I wanted to have died in the crash, with Bram and Stevens. At least then you'd remember me as a man. A hero, even. Now what will you remember me as?'

She frowned. 'What do you mean?'

'The injuries. It isn't just my leg. I can't... the quacks say I might not ever be able to...' He laughed – an unfamiliar, un-Charlie-like laugh, mirthless and flat. 'For so long, I dreamed about what it would be like when we were married. Our life together. Our family. It felt like that was what it was for, all the horror – to earn that future. Then to have it snatched away, and know I had to let you go... I couldn't bear to write. It would only have made it real.'

'So you hid from it,' Bobby said softly.

'Yes,' he whispered. 'Perhaps that makes me a coward, but everything had been taken away from me, Bobby. Everything.' He closed his eye. 'The shrapnel didn't just get my leg. The injury goes all the way up my thigh and... do you understand? I couldn't be a husband to you. I couldn't be a father. The quacks sat me down, and they told me I was half a man. I died another kind of death, that night we crashed.'

Bobby stared at him for a long time. He stood leaning on his stick, humiliated, defeated, refusing to meet her eye.

'Look at me,' she said softly.

'Please, Bobby. Just go.'

'Charlie, for God's sake, look at me!'

He forced himself to meet her gaze. Still his agitated features worked with strong emotion.

Bobby stepped towards him. She took off her glove and caressed the burn scar around his eye.

'You've been in so much pain,' she whispered. 'My poor boy.'

He glanced at the hand on his cheek. 'You stopped wearing your ring.'

'I thought I wasn't welcome to.' Her fingers ran over the angry red scar tissue. 'I'd very much like to hold you. If that would be all right.'

'You ought to go,' he said again, but without real conviction this time. He didn't object when she wrapped her arms around him. He just sagged there, and sighed against her.

347

'I'm sorry,' he whispered.

'What are you sorry for?'

'For all the things I promised that I can't give you. For failing you just as I did the men in the plane. For everything.'

'The only thing you ever promised me that I gave a single damn about was yourself, Charlie.'

'The Charlie I promised you then doesn't exist any more.' He swallowed a sob, and buried his face in her shoulder. 'There's just this left,' he murmured brokenly.

'What's left is you.'

He held her back and looked into her face. 'I can't make love to you, Bobby. I can't give you children. You can't in all honesty tell me those things don't matter to you – those things another man could give you and I can't. Because they bloody have to, don't they?'

Bobby was silent for a moment.

'It won't ever heal?' she asked quietly.

'Not completely, the quacks say. Things might never be… like they were before.'

Again, she was silent.

'It's all right,' Charlie said in a hushed, flat tone. 'There's nothing to berate yourself for. It's only what anyone would do.'

Bobby took off her WAAF greatcoat and spread it on the grass.

'Isn't it a glorious day?' she said, sitting down and lifting her face to the sun. 'Sit by me, Charlie.'

Charlie hesitated, and for a moment she worried he was going to leave, but eventually he lowered himself to the ground.

'This reminds me of the spring before you went to the RAF,' she said dreamily. 'Picnics here, watching the geese swimming about. We always ended up taking half the food back with us. There was too much kissing to be done to spare our lips for eating.'

'It seems a lifetime ago.'

'How do you like my uniform?'

He smiled, and looked a little like himself for the first time. 'Very much. The Air Force suits you.'

'I'm glad you think so. Ernie King doesn't approve at all. He thinks women in uniform are an abomination.'

Charlie frowned. 'King?'

'Yes, he's one of the instructors now at Ryland Moor.'

He sat in silence, glaring into the distance.

'You've... been seeing a lot of him?' he asked after a bit.

Bobby picked a few daisies and started idly threading a chain. 'A little. He took me for a flip in one of the Wellingtons a few days ago.'

'He took you up there?' Charlie scowled. 'Damn fool! What could he have been thinking, putting you in danger?'

Bobby laughed. 'He didn't fly me to Germany or anything. He wanted to show me the Dales from the air. It was beautiful – just like the view from the top of Great Bowside.'

Charlie sighed softly, and she knew he was thinking of the day he'd proposed to her, on top of the mountain as the sun set.

'Did he try anything with you?' he asked.

'Well, he kissed me a couple of times. Oh, and he asked me to marry him.'

Charlie spluttered. 'He did what?'

Bobby's lip twitched to see him react. The jealousy seemed to do him good, overcoming for the moment that weary resignation it was so pitiful to see.

'He wants me to move to Canada after the war,' she said. 'Raise a brood of ruddy, healthy mountain children, living the life of gentlemen farmers. It sounds a wonderful life, in spite of the bears.'

Charlie turned away, scowling. 'Are you not going to leave? I've told you enough times that I don't want you here.'

Bobby rested against him. 'Must I? I'm quite happy where I am.'

'You shouldn't sit so close. Your fiancé might object.'

'I don't think he would at all,' Bobby said softly. She drew the sapphire ring from her breast pocket and slid it back on to her finger.

Charlie stared at it, then blinked up at her.

'What does it mean?' he whispered.

'It means I don't love Ernie King. I love you, Charlie Atherton, stubborn, foolish and pig-headed as you are. Whoever you've been, whoever you are, whoever you're going to be, there's only room in my heart for one man and it's you. Ernie knows that. It's why he and Topsy conspired to get me here today. I love you, I've always loved you and I bloody well want to marry you.'

'But I can't—'

She leaned forward to stop his lips with a kiss.

'I don't care,' she whispered. 'I won't walk away from you. I couldn't, as long as I know you love me still. You do, don't you?'

'Of course I do,' he whispered. 'But you must care, Bob. How could you not?'

She placed the daisy chain she had been making over his head, and his mouth flickered with a smile.

'Do you know what Teddy told me the day of his wedding?' she said. 'Why he went back to Topsy after having made up his mind she'd be better off without him? It was because he knew that even though he couldn't give her a child, no other man would be able to love her as much as he did.'

'Even so, you can't pretend this doesn't matter. That it doesn't make a difference.'

'I admit it isn't how I saw our married life together,' she said quietly. 'I do want to be with you, body as well as soul. But if I can't have the first part then I'm grateful to still have the second, and be able to say we belong to each other.'

'Ernie King could give you so much more than I ever could.'

'But he can't change the fact I'm in love with you.'

'Not... you wouldn't take me just for pity?'

'Charlie.' She pressed his hand to her lips. 'Don't you know me better than that?'

He laughed then – a true Charlie laugh – and embraced her fiercely.

'I thought this was the end,' he whispered. 'I thought life had nothing for me any more. And now there's you.'

She peppered his neck with kisses, and watered it with a few tears too. 'I've missed you so much.'

'At least go away and think about it though, darling. It's such a big change in our plans. You shouldn't make a decision in haste.'

'If I do, will that make you feel better?'

'Yes, I think it will. I need to know you truly want this new future. That you're going into it with eyes open.' He stroked her cheek. 'And if you decide it isn't what you want after all, I'll never resent you for it. I want you to be happy.'

She sighed. 'It hurt me a lot when I thought you didn't care, Charlie.'

'I'm sorry. I was so deep in the hole, I couldn't think of any pain but mine. That was wrong. But if you knew, Bobby, how empty everything felt to me after the crash...' His face crumpled with pain. 'How I felt I'd rather be dead than have you know what had happened to me...'

'I do understand,' she said, taking his hand. 'I do. But please, don't ever shut me out like that.'

'You forgive me?'

'I suppose I have to, don't I? If I'm going to be your wife.'

He smiled and kissed her forehead. 'Like I said, there's no need to make a rushed decision about it. Take as much time as you need, OK? When you've made your choice, I'll be right here.'

Chapter 43

The matron was waiting for them back at the hospital, looking stern. She proceeded to give both Topsy and Charlie a dressing down on the subject of smuggling in lovers on the pretence of showing them door plaques. Charlie flashed Bobby something like his old schoolboy grin while he was being told off, and she smiled back.

For the first time since leaving for the WAAF, she felt a lightness of heart. Charlie was here, and he loved her, still. Yes, there was pain alongside the joy. He was injured in a way that was going to affect both their lives, in his mind as well as his body. Bobby could sense the mental anguish that came from feeling as though everything that made him a man had been stripped from him. No doubt many challenges lay ahead that were undreamed of in the days before the war had touched their lives. Still, he was hers. They would make it all right, somehow, the two of them.

Topsy escorted her from the hospital and walked with her as far as the path.

'Did he tell you about his injuries?' she asked.

Bobby nodded. 'He was embarrassed to give details, but I gathered he'd been hurt in the groin. That he won't be able to… that married life might look a little different than we'd expected.'

'And you're going ahead, still?'

'He wanted me to take time to think about it, but I don't need to. I love him, Topsy. Of course I'm going ahead.'

Topsy beamed at her. 'Oh, you are the most heavenly creature. I knew you would. I felt guilty going behind his back, but I couldn't let that foolish boy grieve his life away knowing you hadn't the faintest idea he was here and wounded. It reminded me of how close Teddy and I came to losing each other, all for his silly man's stubbornness.'

'Has Charlie been dreadfully depressed?' Bobby asked quietly.

Topsy bowed her head. 'Very much so. He refused to let me speak with his family, even though the RAF sent him here to convalesce so he could be close to them. I felt entirely helpless trying to cope with his moods. Honestly, I'd started to be really afraid for him, he seemed so low. That was why I confided in Ernie. I knew he could get you here, and you'd be able to help Charlie better than anyone else.'

Bobby smiled at her. 'You're an angel to help.'

'You did the same for me, once,' Topsy said shyly. 'I had better go back to work. You'll want to see your family. Perhaps you oughtn't to say anything to the Athertons about Charlie though. I think he'll want to write to Reg and Mary himself, now he's seen you.'

'Yes, you're right. But it doesn't matter, I'm not going home. I'm going straight back to Ryland Moor.'

Topsy frowned. 'I thought you were going to visit your father and sister.'

'Not today.' Bobby took her arm. 'Topsy, I need your help. If I write some notes and leave them at the cottage, can you make sure they're delivered to the people they're addressed to just as soon as everyone at Moorside knows what the state of affairs is here?'

Topsy blinked. 'Well, yes, of course. What are they for?'

'There'll be one for you too. Everything will be explained.'

'Any message for Charlie?'

'No, but there is one thing you can do for me at the hospital.'

'What is it?'

'Just tell me this – is there an RAF chaplain on site?'

–

Bobby bumped into Carol back at camp, walking between the Waafery recreation hut and the ablutions block.

'Bobsy,' she said in surprise. 'I thought you weren't coming back until this evening.'

'There's been a change of plans.' Bobby grabbed the other woman's hands and spun her around. 'I'm getting married, Car.'

Carol blinked. 'You what?'

'You heard me. I'm getting married.'

'Hey, where are you going?' Carol called after Bobby as she hurried away.

'To see Stewpot,' Bobby called back. 'I need to arrange some urgent leave.'

'Why urgent?'

'I'll explain later. Tell the others, will you? I'm really getting married!'

Mulligan listened with a rather shell-shocked expression as Bobby explained everything that had happened – that her fiancé had been injured, was now in an RAF hospital not ten miles away and that she would like to take the marriage leave she had requested for the 2nd and 3rd of May after all. The commandant granted her request without objection, however. The following Saturday, Bobby Bancroft was walking once again down the track to Sumner House – this time with no intention of ever going back up it under that name.

–

Mary was the first to greet her when she knocked on the door of Topsy's cottage. She looked tired, but beamed when she saw Bobby.

'Oh, you're a sight for sore eyes,' Mary said as she threw her arms around her.

'Topsy gave you my note?' Bobby asked.

'Yes. Reg is up at the house now, making his brother presentable. Topsy and everyone else are inside.'

'And Charlie doesn't know?'

'Hasn't a clue. Now come inside and let me dress you. The girls are desperate to help turn you into a bride.'

'Wait.' Bobby put a hand on her friend's shoulder and lowered her voice. 'Before we see everyone. How is he, Mary? How are you?'

Mary sighed. 'It was a shock, I must admit. As far as we knew, he was in Binbrook, thriving and healthy. I'd never dreamed he was so close to home, and in such a state. He's lost so much weight.'

'I know. It shocked me too.'

'The sooner they let me take him home and tend to him as only someone who's loved him as a mother can, the better it will be.' She smiled. 'But he full grinned when I mentioned you. I knew when I saw that smile that he was still our Charlie, just as long as he had you to lead him out of the dark.'

Bobby smiled even as she let slip a tear.

'Thank you,' she whispered.

'Now, come inside. We've got the whole family here, all dying to see you.'

Mary led her in, and Bobby beamed to see her little family crowded into Topsy's parlour. Her dad was in his best Sunday suit, his remaining hair combed and slicked. Tony and Lilian, her sister now roughly the size of a house, stood beside him. Jessie and Florrie were in their best dresses, petal-filled baskets over their arms and bouncing with excitement. Teddy, Topsy and Mrs Hobbes smiled at her. Even Norman seemed to smile as he sat with his goose family.

'Oh, I am glad to see you all.' Bobby embraced each of them in turn. 'Even you, Tony.'

'Huh,' her brother-in-law grunted. 'Ta very much.'

'You're sure you're ready to do this, lass?' her dad asked quietly when she hugged him.

'I am if you are. You'll give me away?'

'With a song in my heart, if it's to a man who'll make you happy.'

'It is.' She kissed his cheek. 'Thanks, Dad. I love you.'

'Aye, well. Same to you, eh?' he said, rubbing his cheek.

'There'll be time for hugging and kissing after,' Mary said in businesslike fashion. 'Bobby, come into Topsy's room. Lilian, Jess, Florrie, you can help. And mind, girls, when you see your Uncle Charlie remember you're not to jump all over him. Don't forget he's hurt his leg. It'll likely be a while before he can laik as he used to.'

'Yes, Mary,' the pair chanted dutifully.

'Do Reg and Mary know?' Bobby murmured to Topsy as she followed her into the bedroom. 'The extent of his injuries?'

'No,' Topsy whispered back. 'He only told them he'd been wounded in the leg. I don't suppose he'd want them to know.'

When they entered Topsy's room, Mary took a dress from the cupboard. 'Here we are.'

Bobby smiled. 'My Cinderella ballgown.'

'I always had intended it for a bride. I've trimmed it up with new lace, and the girls have picked fresh flowers to ornament it.'

'I thought you'd rather have some of our hothouse roses, but Mary was sure you'd prefer wild flowers from the hedgerow,' Topsy said.

'Mary was right,' Bobby said, smiling at her friend.

'Now, get into your dress and we'll set this pair of trouble-makers on your hair,' Mary said. 'How will you wear it, Bobby?'

'Loose, I think,' Bobby said, rather dreamily. 'I know it isn't the fashion, but it feels right. Just brushed over my shoulders, with a garland of flowers. And no rouge, please. Only a little powder.'

Mary smiled. 'Aye, he'll like that. All right, ladies, let's go to work. We don't have long.'

'Let me take down your hair,' Lilian said, leading Bobby to the chair at Topsy's dressing table. She took off her sister's WAAF cap and began removing hairpins.

'A wedding day at last,' she said softly. 'I don't suppose this is how you pictured it.'

'It's exactly how I pictured it, Lil. I never did picture a wedding the way you always could. I only saw Charlie.'

'Yes, I suppose you did. Well, perhaps you had it right after all.'

'This is the third wedding in our little circle this year, and every one different from the others,' Bobby said. 'You and Tony. Topsy and Teddy. And now Charlie and me.'

'They say things are lucky that come in threes,' Lilian said. 'I hope for all our sakes that they're right.'

Once Bobby was dressed, she went to present herself to the folk in the parlour. Her dad actually had a tear in his eye as he took in her loose, flowing hair and the simple but elegant white dress Mary had fashioned from odds and ends of material.

'By, but you look like your mam,' he said quietly.

'Bobby, you are quite beautiful,' Teddy said.

Mrs Hobbes nodded. 'And so say all of us.'

'Even I have to admit you don't scrub up too bad,' Tony said, and Bobby laughed.

'Well, come on then,' her dad said. 'If I'm to give a daughter away today, I want to get it over with.'

Bobby smiled and took the arm he offered.

'Matron's been recruited into our cabal, along with the chaplain, of course,' Topsy told them as they set off for Sumner House. 'She's going to unlock the back door to the orangery – that's what we use as the chapel – and we can wait at the pulpit for Reg to lure Charlie to us.'

'It's going to be a strange sort of wedding, with the groom walking down the aisle instead of the bride,' Lilian said with a laugh.

'And him not having a clue about it.' Topsy's eyes sparkled. 'A surprise wedding. It's the most romantic thing I ever heard of. I can't wait to see Charlie's face when he sees how beautiful you look, Birdy.'

Bobby was starting to feel nervous now. She had been so sure this was a good idea. It seemed symbolic, in a way. So many times when Charlie had been eager for their wedding, she had tried to persuade him to wait until things were more settled. She felt differently now. She needed to be with him, having come so close to losing him. Needed to prove once and for all that it was him she wanted, no matter what.

And yet… would he be angry that she hadn't told him what she was planning? Suppose he said no – just walked away? She had spent the past week imagining the look of joy on his tired, haggard face when he saw her, waiting to promise herself to him at last. It hadn't occurred to her, until now when she was on the brink of meeting him at the altar, that she might see a different emotion written there.

The chaplain and matron were waiting for them when they reached the orangery. The matron was so stern usually that it felt strange to see her wearing an unaccustomed expression of benevolence.

'Oh, you look just lovely,' she said to Bobby, and rather surprised her by kissing her on both cheeks. 'Now, the chaplain will tell you where you all ought to stand. I'll go prod the groom in this direction. He was rather sullen this morning at not having heard from you, although he'll be smiling soon enough, of course.'

She bustled off, leaving the chaplain to take charge.

'Who is the maid of honour?' he asked.

'Oh! I hadn't thought.' Bobby looked from Lilian to Topsy. 'May I have two? I don't want to choose.'

'Neither of us are maids any more, Bob,' Lilian said with a laugh. 'All we have here are a superfluity of matrons.'

'Well, it isn't a requirement,' the chaplain said, smiling. 'Perhaps if you all take a seat, and the bride and her father may stand. We're making up the rules as we go today, it seems. That does seem to be par for the course when it comes to wartime weddings.'

'All right, girls, prepare to do your job,' Mary said to the children. 'When Reg and Uncle Charlie come down the aisle, you must follow and throw your petals. Elegantly, mind, not like you're bowling a cricket match.'

The girls didn't need telling twice, and skipped to the door that connected the house with the orangery to wait for the oblivious groom.

Charlie's voice was audible outside now.

'Honestly, Reggie, I appreciate you visiting but I'd like to be left alone now,' he was saying. 'I'm exhausted.'

'You're not exhausted, you're sulking, you mardy little bugger,' they heard Reg say. 'You heard what the doctor said. You need exercise for that leg or it'll seize up. Believe me, this is summat I do know about.'

'You've been walking me around on it for an hour. Never mind seizing up, it'll drop off if you make me go much further.'

'Aye, all right, I suppose you've done enough. We'll go to the end of this glass bit down here, then I'll leave you alone.'

'Can we not go back now?'

'A bit more won't kill you. Stop bloody complaining.'

Topsy gripped Bobby's arm. 'This is it,' she whispered. 'All the happiness in the world, Birdy.'

She gave her friend's arm a squeeze and sat down. A moment later, the doors opened and Charlie came in, limping on his stick with Reg behind.

'Well, here he is,' Reg said. 'And a devil of a time I had getting him here as well, the lazy little—' He caught sight of the chaplain. 'Ahem. Excuse me, Father.'

Charlie was blinking at the scene in front of him. 'What's going on?'

Bobby felt suddenly shy. She could feel herself blushing.

'Um,' she said. 'Hello.'

'Oh! We don't have music,' Topsy said. 'All right, come along, everyone.'

She started humming the wedding march. The others joined in, which Jess and Florrie took as the cue to start tossing petals about with gay abandon. Charlie started to laugh, although he still looked dazed.

'Come on then,' Reg said, half escorting and half poking him down the aisle. 'That lass there isn't getting any younger. Lord knows we've all waited long enough for this.'

It was a strange little wedding scene: the groom being escorted down the aisle of a hospital chapel by his brother while the guests hummed the wedding march; the bride waiting for him in a pantomime dress and a garland of hedgerow flowers. And yet it felt right.

'Bobby.' Charlie took her hand when he reached her, then glanced at her father in his best suit, and at the chaplain. 'What is it?'

'Haven't you guessed? It's our wedding day, daft lad.'

'You did all this?'

She stood on tiptoes to kiss him. She didn't know if that was proper etiquette for a wedding – probably they were supposed to wait until after they were married. But it felt like the natural thing to do, so she did it.

'I want to marry you, Charlie,' she whispered. 'I didn't need any time to think about it. I always knew. Will you?'

'I… yes.' He laughed. 'Too bloody right I will. Sorry, your honour.'

The chaplain smiled. 'Plain Reverend is just fine. Still, if we could keep the colourful language to a minimum.'

Charlie's dazed expression had lifted at last. His eyes kindled as he drank in his bride. His hand found its way to her hair, and he ran a lock through his fingers.

'You are simply the most beautiful thing I've ever seen,' he said softly. 'Do I really get to keep you?'

'Always, after today.'

'Are you quite certain, darling? There's no way back.'

'Good, because I don't want to go back.'

Bobby's dad clapped Charlie on the shoulder.

'Well, lad, take care of her,' he said. 'You've got a treasure there.'

'I know it,' Charlie said, smiling at him.

'Welcome to the family, eh?' Rob left them and sat down.

Charlie gripped Bobby's hand tightly as they turned to the chaplain.

Bobby wasn't sure what answers she gave during the ceremony. There had been no time to rehearse responses. The chaplain didn't correct her, however, so she presumed it was all OK. There was no ring, but Topsy darted forward to loan hers until one could be got. Bobby felt a little dizzy as words ricocheted around her brain. *To love and to cherish… in sickness and in health… till death us do part.* For something so momentous, it seemed to go by in a rush.

And always, she kept her eyes fixed on Charlie. She didn't see, now, his unshaven chin, hollow cheeks, the burns around his eye or the drawn, haggard appearance that spoke of too many weeks trapped in pain and grief. She only saw the expression of love in his open eye – that expression she feared had been an illusion.

But it hadn't. He loved her. He had never stopped loving her, and now he was hers. Whatever challenges the future brought, they would face them together.

'I think I probably ought to kiss you,' Charlie whispered.

'What?'

'He just declared us man and wife, Bob.'

Bobby blinked. 'Did he?'

Charlie smiled. 'Come here then.'

He pulled her on to his lips, and the tiny congregation let out a cheer.

'It's done,' Bobby whispered when he drew back. 'Has it really happened, Charlie?'

'It's really happened. How does it feel, Mrs Atherton?'

She brought one hand up to caress his burnt face. 'Say that again.'

'I said, how does it feel, Mrs Atherton?'

She smiled. 'It feels just wonderful.'

A letter from Betty

Hello, and thank you for choosing to read *A Wartime Wedding in the Dales*. I do hope you enjoyed the latest book in the series, which is number four of six.

In this latest visit to Silverdale, the war finally comes to call for Bobby. She wrestles with a difficult decision when she is forced to choose between her duty to her family and her duty to her country, and considers her place as a woman in the society of the 1940s. Eventually she leaves her home for a new life in the Women's Auxiliary Air Force, where the loneliness she experiences is compounded by the silence of her airman fiancé Charlie. Although Bobby and Charlie finally find their happy ending, Charlie's injury and their respective wartime roles mean there will be many challenges to face in their married life.

I'd absolutely love to hear your thoughts on this book in a review. These are invaluable not only for letting authors know how their story affected you, but also for helping other readers to choose their next read and discover new writers. Just a few words can make a big difference.

If you would like to find out more about me and my books you can do so via my website or social media pages, which can be found under my other pen name of Mary Jayne Baker:

Facebook: /MaryJayneWrites
Bluesky: @maryjaynebaker.bsky.social
Instagram and Threads: @MaryJayneBaker
Web: www.maryjaynebaker.co.uk

Please do stay tuned for announcements about further titles in this series. Thank you again for choosing *A Wartime Wedding in the Dales.*

Best wishes,
Betty

Acknowledgments

I'd like to thank my amazing editor at Hera, Keshini Naidoo, to whom this book is dedicated, and the rest of the team at Hera and Canelo for all the work they have put in on this book. I'd also like to thank the talented authors of the RNA Saga Chapter on Facebook, especially Suzanne Hull and Vicky Beeby for their invaluable help pointing me towards some of the more obscure historical documents used in researching this story.